DEA
IN THE
LAKES

DEATH IN THE LAKES

GRAHAM SMITH

bookouture

Published by Bookouture in 2018

An imprint of StoryFire Ltd.

Carmelite House
50 Victoria Embankment
London EC4Y 0DZ

www.bookouture.com

ISBN: 978-1-78681-626-9
eBook ISBN: 978-1-78681-625-2

Previously published as *The Silent Dead*

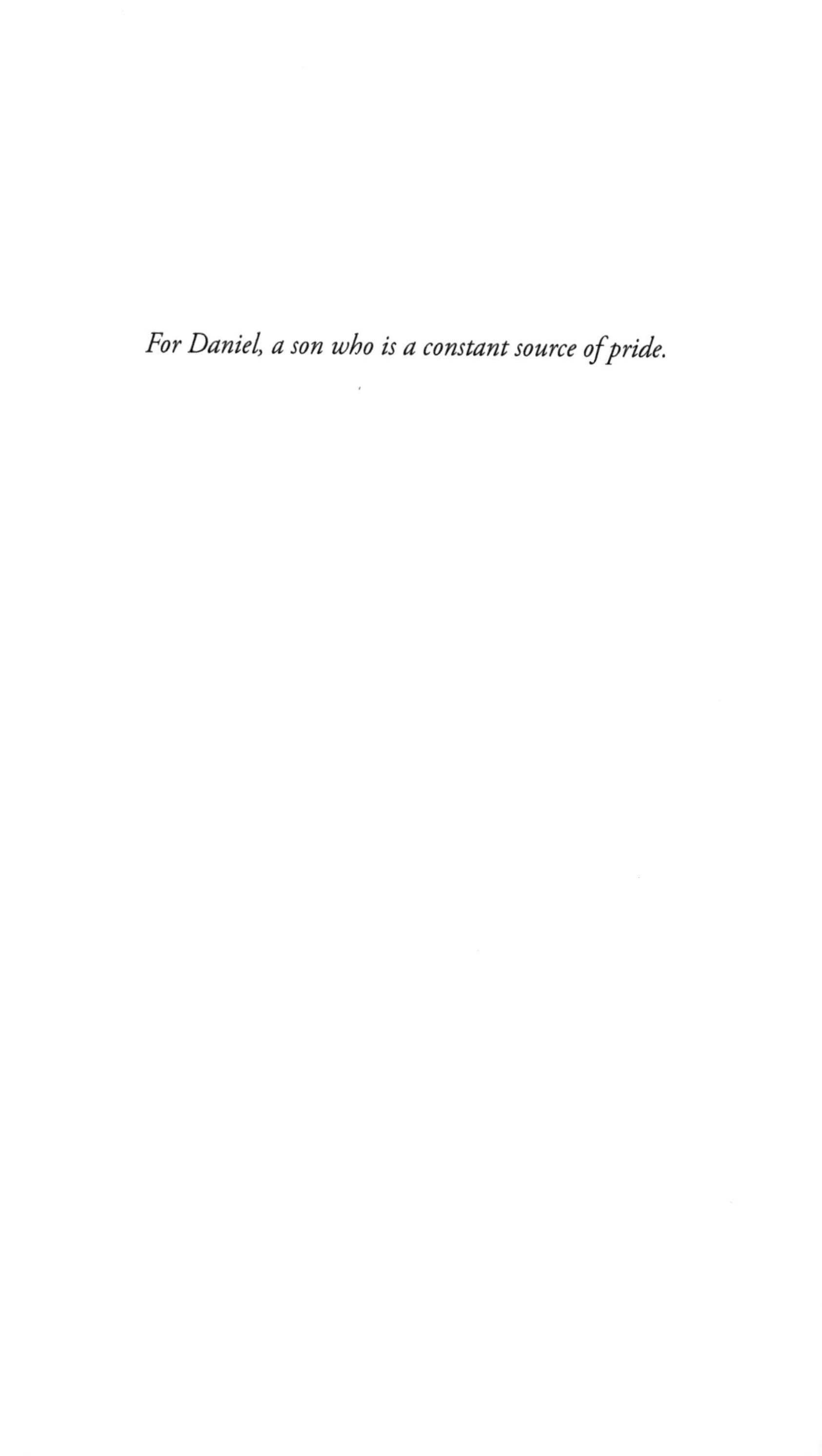

For Daniel, a son who is a constant source of pride.

CHAPTER ONE

The bride screamed. Not a scream of delight, but of utter terror.

Her big day had been going so well. The wedding ceremony at Arthuret Hall, five miles from Longtown, near the border with Scotland, was everything she'd ever dreamed it would be. Yes, the building may be little more than external walls now, but she'd always been fascinated by her grandad's tales of the days when the country house had been a casino, an officer's mess and a hotel after starting life as a country manor house. The surrounding area was rich and fertile farmland with gentle rolling hills and the occasional wood.

Now it was hauntingly sinister; there was a brooding romance in the remains of its former grandeur highlighted by the elaborate dormer windows that still stood jagged against the sky.

She felt her groom tug at her arm with a tenderness that showed his wonderful heart. Jason Welton was a good man. Not the best-looking man she'd ever dated, but certainly the kindest. At forty-nine, he was fifteen years her senior, yet age was just a number so far as Emily was concerned. What mattered more to her was that he loved and understood her, that he was a provider and would take care of her.

Emily let Jason and her maid of honour pull her away from the window, their concern at her distress showing on their faces. As neither was as tall as Emily in her wedding heels, they couldn't look in through the window let alone see down to the ground, to where she could see the corpse in the remnants of the house's cellar below.

Heavy footsteps accompanied the guests who'd come running to see what the commotion was about. She turned away from everybody and looked down at the stream, whose melodic tinkling now seemed disrespectful to the dead man, and gathered her emotions into a single focus. Today was the culmination of her dreams; a fairy-tale wedding to a rich man with a kind heart. She wasn't going to let it be spoiled by an uninvited guest, even if he was dead.

Her cousin was a copper. He'd be the one to keep people away and make sure the police were summoned.

Concerned faces gathered round her, but she painted her smile back into place and dismissed her scream as the result of a practical joke made in poor taste.

It was a lie though; she knew the body was real. Knew that she'd seen a decomposing corpse on her wedding day.

Emily sought out her cousin's face in the crowd and called him forward. He'd know what to do. She leaned into her cousin and told him what she had seen. He gave a terse nod and pulled his mobile from his pocket, as he moved over to the window. After a quick look he marched off. Whether he was going to try and get to the man to check for signs of life or not, Emily had no idea. There would be a protocol for such things, but she didn't know what it was.

No matter how she tried to remove the image from her thoughts, the corpse was etched onto her mind's eye. It was lifeless, still, with discoloured limbs that had been feasted on by the local wildlife. The head bald and immobile. The face looking down.

More than anything else, the body's limp, hanging position was the most disturbing feature. It was secured to a post and the arms were supported outwards by a cross member which ended at the elbows leaving the forearms to point at the ground. There was no doubt in Emily's mind that she'd found a murder victim. The man hadn't died by his own hand or misadventure, he'd been killed.

She pulled her mouth back into a smile though and walked after the photographer. Her cousin could deal with the body. This was her big day, and it wasn't as if getting upset could bring back the dead man. And besides, while she was the centre of attention, she wanted everyone's eyes on her. Though once the photographer had done his bit, she knew she'd need to have a much-needed cigarette before heading to the reception venue.

CHAPTER TWO

Beth tried not to let her irritation show at DS Thompson's attempts to belittle her. The man appeared to be under the mistaken impression he was God's gift, not just to women, but the world. If he thought putting her surname first and calling her Young Beth, instead of Beth or DC Young, would endear her to him, he couldn't have been more wrong.

She may well be the youngest in the FMIT team, by age, and length of service, as she'd only joined them at the start of the week, but that didn't give him carte blanche to rip the mickey. She'd met his type too many times before to be bothered by his offhand ways.

Their first meeting had given her the measure of him. He'd looked her up and down and let his eyes wallow on the front of her blouse for that second too long. But it was when he'd seen her face that she'd really met the man she'd be working with. She'd watched the pupils of his eyes contract, and the visible effort he made in not reacting.

Those were normal responses she encountered when meeting new people.

Since that initial meeting, she'd worked hard to make her integration into the Force Major Investigation Team as seamless as possible. She'd known it wouldn't be easy to join a tight-knit group and that she'd have to prove herself to each member of the team.

DS Thompson was her immediate boss and he'd been in FMIT for several years. He was pernickety and had a way about him that made it hard for Beth to like or respect him. The head of the team was Zoe O'Dowd, an experienced DI with decades of policing behind her and a no-nonsense manner. Beth had already been on the receiving end of her ire and it was not a pleasant experience.

Beth's transfer to FMIT from a regular CID team had become possible because she'd developed a knack for seeing beyond the obvious. She knew that she didn't always think in the same ways other people did. It was her greatest asset and also one of her biggest flaws. In her early police career, there were a few times her lateral thinking had brought her to the wrong conclusion as she overestimated a criminal's intelligence. It was a trait she'd learned to manage and since she'd wrestled control of her wilder ideas, or at least built a solid case to support her theories before sharing them, she'd earned herself a move to CID and then to FMIT.

For Beth, FMIT was the holy grail of police work as the team were handed all the best cases. A stabbing or a straightforward clubbed-to-death-with-an-iron would go to CID. Weird cases like this one were the realm of FMIT along with serious fraud, malicious murder, kidnapping and a whole host of other major crimes. The people they were apprehending weren't the impulse killers lashing out in anger, they were the career criminals who planned their crimes in detail. They were forensically aware and knew about investigative techniques. They knew to establish alibis, leave no trace and, most of all, they knew how the game was played. They'd clam up in the interview room or spout ready-made answers.

This meant the police had to be smarter than the criminals, had to be one step ahead and to always back up their theories with the kind of damning evidence that couldn't be refuted by even the slipperiest of lawyers.

Beth couldn't explain it if she was asked, but her mind didn't run on straight lines, it sought out the oddball explanations and the weird connections that evidence could sometimes present but not always reveal. It was a trait that she knew made her a better copper, and she thought laterally whenever possible. She even went so far as to challenge her mind on her time off with puzzle books, working out logic problems, solving riddles and other brain teasers where the answers were not straightforward.

From time to time, she'd get strange looks from colleagues or members of the public for blurting out her thoughts as random words without organising them into a coherent sentence. Whenever she did this, she'd hurry to present her thoughts in a more rational way.

FMIT had always been her goal; it got the most interesting cases with the toughest puzzles. Now she was on the team, she was determined to succeed, to earn the respect of her colleagues and to solve the crimes.

'Listen up, folks.' Beth and Thompson both turned to face DI O'Dowd as she addressed the room. 'DCI Phinn has given us a case and, from what I've heard so far, it's going to be an interesting one. There's a body been found up at Arthuret Hall, near Longtown, and it's quite clear the dead man was murdered.'

'Is that because of the injuries, ma'am?'

Beth cast a quick glance at DC Paul Unthank. Of the two men in FMIT she liked him best, not just because he was possessed with a rakish handsomeness, but because he was madly in love with his fiancée and didn't care who knew it. In a world full of guys either being metrosexual or overly macho, it was refreshing to find someone who trod the middle ground. Unthank was a decent, sensitive person who could still stand up for himself when the need arose. He was also intense about his privacy; other than knowing he had a girlfriend he loved, she knew nothing about his life outside of work.

'You could say that.' O'Dowd pursed her lips. 'Normally, I'd be telling you all about the injuries and giving you tasks. However...' she paused momentarily, 'this time I'd rather gauge your reactions when you see the body. I'll be honest with you, I've been investigating murders for more than twenty years and I've never seen or heard of anything quite like this before.'

'In what way, boss?'

'Forget it, Frank.' O'Dowd wagged a finger at Thompson. 'We're going there now and I will take each of you to see the body in turn. I'm looking for your first thoughts, your instinctive ideas and your feel for not just the crime that has been committed but the location where our killer has chosen to display his victim. Whether he was killed there as well is yet to be ascertained. For the moment we'll work on the theory he was, but that theory needs to be proven.'

As she filed after the others along the corridors of Carleton Hall, Penrith, where the Cumbria FMIT were based, Beth couldn't help but fixate upon the critical word in O'Dowd's briefing: 'Display': it could have meant a lot of things, but when a killer displayed a body, the number of possible meanings narrowed.

The vast majority of murders in the UK were committed by people known to the victim. They took place in heated arguments, fights that got out of hand, and the odd time a beaten spouse would strike back at their tormentor. Then there were gang-related murders. Not to mention the times robbery would go wrong. But on the whole, murderers did everything they could to make sure their crime was kept secret. When a victim was displayed in a particular way or posed in a certain position, then the killer had more on their mind than covering their tracks. Beth could feel her pulse race as she contemplated the fact that her first murder case in FMIT could, just maybe, see her part of a team pursuing a deranged killer.

By the time she climbed into the back of one of the pool cars and arranged her long legs so they weren't pressed into the back of the seat in front, she'd calmed herself down and was trying to remember all her training with regards to visiting a crime scene. The last thing she wanted to do on her first real case with FMIT was to contaminate a crime scene or destroy evidence with a careless act. On the other hand, she also wanted to impress her new

DI. Zoe O'Dowd had to be one of the most respected officers in the north-west as she'd been chosen above others to head up the FMIT. And that selection could have only come through earning a reputation for diligence, professionalism and an eye for detail.

Another worry for Beth was that she'd be betrayed by her own body. She knew only too well that while blood and gore didn't affect her, noxious smells would always cause her to gag. Top of the list was decomposing bodies, and there was no way she wanted to vomit in front of her new boss, let alone empty her belly all over a crime scene. As a native of Penrith, which stood on the north-eastern edge of the Lake District, she'd grown up with the smell of rotten flesh blowing across the town from the protein factory, but that didn't mean she was immune to the stench of decomposition.

Most of all though, she didn't want to give the odious DS Thompson an excuse to make her life miserable. Beth couldn't pinpoint why she believed Thompson had it in for her. She just felt as if he was watching and waiting for her to make a mistake. One slip, and he would attack.

Her thoughts rumbled back and forth during the half hour drive until they pulled off the road.

Arthuret Hall stood in the countryside between Longtown and Brampton. The area was lowland, with gentle rolling hills surrounded by the Southern Uplands to the north, the Lakeland Fells to the east and the Northern Pennines forming the southern edge. All of these higher areas were several miles away, but they could each be seen under the sun's fierce glare.

The lush landscape supported many farms, and the fields were a verdant kaleidoscope of colour as farmers grew oilseed rape and maize as well as more traditional crops such as silage and barley. Cows and sheep populated grassy meadows as well as fields that were so regimented they appeared to have been marked out by a cubist. Beth knew that Longtown's cattle and sheep market was used by the farmers drawn from many miles around.

Despite the proliferation of police and crime scene vehicles, Beth couldn't help but feel a chill enter her body as she looked at the hall's towering gables, the exposed stone surrounds of the dormer windows standing above the wallheads, and the multiple empty spaces that timber and glass had once filled. Along the top of the walls, grass, weeds and small shrubs provided a green fringe that framed the dormer windows' eyes with botanical eyebrows.

She'd grown up in a semi-detached house on a former council estate. There had always been people around: neighbours, family members and childhood friends. Yet this overblown house had been built to be a home to a single family.

Derelict now, it was missing the sense of life that inhabited any family home. It had been abandoned, though a new owner might one day try to breathe life into its soul. But the killer had chosen Arthuret Hall to display and possibly murder the victim, and that told her that someone had a connection to the old building.

CHAPTER THREE

Beth made sure that she breathed through her mouth when DI O'Dowd lifted the crime scene tape and waved her over.

Off to her right a couple of constables were talking to a woman who kept dabbing at her eyes. Beth ducked under the tape and took care to step on the footpads laid out by the CSI team. The protective oversuit she'd donned rustled as she moved, and the sun was still so high that it brought a sheen of perspiration to her brow.

Once inside the building, Beth could see rows of chairs and various areas decorated with garlands of fresh flowers. The front of the house overlooked a manicured lawn bordered by colourful flowerbeds. As picturesque as the gardens may be, Beth couldn't imagine why anyone would choose a dilapidated country house as a wedding venue. All of the walls may be more or less intact, but the building was nothing more than a hollow shell.

O'Dowd led her to a painted wooden partition, which Beth assumed had been constructed by the new owners. A panel had been removed, and they stepped from the paved area into a space yet to have even the scant renovations the section set out for the wedding had received. This part of the house was dilapidated and there was a bush growing in the corner, but none of this captured Beth's attention. In a lower area, that Beth judged from the row of joist holes at ground level in the walls was once a cellar, a man's body was suspended on a post.

In other parts of the area piles of rubble were overgrown with grass and weeds. Someone, Beth guessed a member of the CSI team, had propped an aluminium ladder against the wall at the side to provide access to the lower level.

Beth reached the bottom of the ladder and stood in front of the corpse. As she examined the dead man she could feel Zoe O'Dowd's eyes on her. As much as she was trying to impress, she knew she was being monitored. What Beth did and said now would be forever recalled by the DI.

The body's arms were held outright to the elbow by thick, black cable ties attached to a horizontal timber. Each arm had a tie at the top and bottom of the bicep to secure the body to the timber.

The body didn't look as though it was newly dead, which made Beth glad she was breathing through her mouth. So far as she could see, it was discoloured. Parts of the body's fleshier areas looked to have been scavenged on by wildlife, and these showed greater signs of decay. To Beth's mind the body had been here a number of days. The recent spell of warm weather the county had enjoyed would have hastened the rotting process.

Beth lifted her head and looked at the man's face. The eye sockets were empty and there were blisters around the mouth. Birds could be responsible for the missing eyes, but there was no way she wanted to jump to conclusions without some evidence to back up any ideas she put forward.

On closer inspection, she noticed the lips appeared to have been scorched. Beth's first thought was a blowtorch, but she knew the scorching could have been done with anything from a blowtorch to a cigarette lighter.

At the body's feet, three of the numbered plastic CSI markers drew her attention to areas where the weeds showed signs of fire damage. Coupled with the damage to the victim's mouth, they pointed to this being the place where the victim was killed.

The noisy clearing of O'Dowd's throat caught Beth's attention. Following the circling movements of the DI's outstretched finger, she padded round to the back of the body. The uneven ground made it awkward to keep her balance on the footpads, but Beth made it to the final one without incident.

She hadn't meant to gasp when she looked at the victim's back, but it was an involuntary reaction with a nasty side effect. As she exhaled, instinct and habit made her breathe in through her nose.

At once her stomach heaved and filled her mouth with bile. Beth pursed her lips together and swallowed down. Once, twice and then a third time until she felt it was safe to open her mouth and take a breath.

This was an action she'd had to do many times during her childhood in Penrith when a gust of wind had sent the stench of rotting flesh from the protein plant cascading through the streets and housing estates.

'Good girl.'

Beth's cheeks burned at O'Dowd's patronising comment, but she still gave her boss a nod of thanks.

Her eyes returned to the body. Seen from the rear, it took on a whole different perspective, which made sense of O'Dowd's cryptic briefing.

Beth leaned forward as far as she dared before she risked toppling forward, and examined the corpse with a greater level of care.

The folded black wings were where her eyes went first, but the point she ultimately focussed on was where they were attached to the man's back.

A matchbox-sized area of skin had been removed from each shoulder blade, and the thin bones, which usually attached the wings to the body of a bird, appeared to have been fused to them.

The idea that Beth couldn't shake from her mind was that whoever brought this man here, and left him in such a fashion, was only starting whatever project he planned. The whole tableau the killer had created was disturbing and horrific.

The mind which had dreamed up such a kill had to be warped. Whatever demons were haunting this killer needed to be contained, preferably by a lengthy confinement at Her Majesty's pleasure.

'Your thoughts please, Beth.' O'Dowd's voice was soft, as though she was being respectful to the dead man hanging between them. 'I know you're new to FMIT and haven't seen anything like this before, but then neither have I.'

'Bizarre. Twisted. Sick.'

O'Dowd gave her a stern look. 'Care to elaborate?'

'Sorry, ma'am. I don't know, this is so far off the wall I'm not sure what to think. Ritualistic is a word that springs to mind, but I'm not sure if it's the right word. I hate to tempt fate, but this is just so twisted in every sense of the word, and I can't help but worry it won't end here. I may be wrong, and this may turn out to be a one off with just the intention of killing this man, but I have a feeling that this is only the beginning of something bigger.'

Beth pulled her eyes off the wings and looked to O'Dowd to see how her words had been received.

She got a sharp nod of affirmation for her trouble.

O'Dowd's agreement gave Beth a confidence boost, so she dared to ask a question. 'I know there will have to be a post-mortem and I'm sure the CSI will have taken the victim's prints, but what happens next? While I was waiting for you to bring me here, I looked at the house, took a quick look at the surrounding buildings. There's nowhere here for anyone to live and I haven't seen any security cameras. The gate we came through after pulling off the road has a heavy chain round the gatepost and an open padlock hanging from it. I can't see us getting any witnesses or CCTV footage. The best hope we've got is that someone saw a vehicle parked in that lay-by outside the gate. I had a quick word with the woman who was looking after the wedding, but all she did was put out the chairs and show the guests where to go when they arrived. Evidently they have only just started hosting wedding ceremonies here, and there's little more than a bower for the celebrant to stand under and a few dozen chairs for the guests. One day they want to be able to offer it as a full venue, where you can have the party afterwards too, but they're not quite up to that yet.'

Beth saw O'Dowd's eyes narrow in assessment of her and wondered what her new boss would make of her observations.

'Who instructed you to go wandering around, asking these things?'

'Nobody, ma'am, it just seemed like a better use of my time than standing around waiting for you or DC Thompson to come back and give me some orders.'

'You're right, it was.' O'Dowd raised a finger in admonishment. 'Just be careful; you're quite obviously a smart person, but while you're of no worry to me, others – especially some male others, if you know what I'm saying – won't necessarily always see your initiative as a positive thing. They'll see it as a threat. Make sure you have your back covered and don't let your inquisitive streak lead you into trouble.'

As Beth climbed the ladder, she wondered if the warning was in regard to Thompson, or whether there were others she also needed to be wary of.

CHAPTER FOUR

He perched on a bar stool and ordered a glass of tonic water. Early on a Saturday evening was always a good time to visit the Hare and Hounds. It was one of the nights Tamara worked and she was such a pleasant girl. Not to mention attractive.

The bar was starting to fill up with diners as he knew it would. Tamara didn't just do the bar, she waited tables, which meant she'd be striding back and forth all night, her long legs probably encased in her usual skinny jeans.

If she was looking as good as she usually did, he'd dine here. Not only was the food good, and there was an early-bird menu, Tamara's presence in the room meant the scenery would also be excellent.

His breath caught when Tamara emerged from the kitchen with a piled plate in each hand. She wasn't wearing her skinny jeans today, instead she wore a skirt.

The skirt wasn't as short as he'd have liked, as it finished just above her knees, but it still gave him a good view of her legs and it was tight enough to let him see the curve of her bottom.

As always, she gave him a polite smile when she looked his way, but like the professional she was, her focus was on the customers awaiting the plates she carried.

He would eat here; savour the home-made steak pie, or better yet, a salad of some description. If he had the salad, he could also find room for a starter and dessert. That would give him a nice excuse to spend at least an hour and a half appreciating Tamara's beautiful figure.

The ring on her finger meant she could never be his, as did the thirty-plus years between them. Tamara had the vibrancy and beauty of youth, whereas he possessed the sluggishness and decrepitude of age. In terms of looks and appeal, he wasn't even playing the same sport as Tamara, let alone in the same league. All he had to offer her was appreciation, but even that wasn't something he could say out loud. It wasn't that he was nervous about telling her how beautiful and sexy he thought she was, he just didn't expect that she'd take his compliments the way they were intended.

He'd recently told two young women how attractive he found them. The first time had seen him berated and labelled a pervert. That had been humiliating enough, but the second time had been even worse. After returning to his car with a crimson handprint on his face, he'd vowed that never again would he verbalise his appreciation of the female form.

He took a seat at a table that allowed him to watch Tamara wherever she was and lifted a menu. This was a good night. Three slowly eaten courses admiring Tamara and then on to the Coach House. Wendy the barmaid was neither pretty nor young, but she had a generous cleavage and was always chatty with him. His evening would end with a few slow drives around the Crescent and along Lowther Street. Carlisle had a vibrant nightlife and both the Crescent and Lowther Street played host to bars and restaurants where he'd identified many of his angels.

The Crescent surrounded the former south, or Botcher Gate, of the old city known as The Citadel; while the gate had made way for a three-lane road, the circular guard towers with crenelated tops and pink sandstone walls still stood as a reminder of the city's warring past.

The area, now known as Botchergate, was the northern end of London Road and home to Carlisle's most hedonistic bars. On weekend nights, it was closed off to traffic due to the drunk people filling the street as they passed from one bar to another. Come the morning, the pavement was littered with the detritus of fast-food wrappers, dropped food and puddles of vomit.

He'd tried visiting the pubs and bars on Botchergate a few times, but in these places a man his age standing by himself attracted the wrong kind of attention. Too often they had looked right through him at the younger, hunkier guys they were trying to attract. Or worse, he'd been pointed at and sniggered over by the pretty girls he was there to admire.

Now he trawled the streets in his car, just looking for the girls who could star in his fantasies. It was a lower risk, isolated from the humiliation of being rejected.

In Tamara he'd found one angel for his dreams.

Next he had to find a companion for her. One angel at a time was never enough for him. He needed as many as he could possibly get.

CHAPTER FIVE

Beth filed along the receiving line for the evening guests behind DS Thompson, wishing she could be anywhere other than where she was. It was bad enough they'd been sent to interview the bride on her wedding day, but to make things even worse, Thompson hadn't listened when she'd tried to suggest they did everything they could to lessen the impact on the poor woman's celebration.

The reception venue was a place she'd never been to before, but she knew of Farlam Hall's reputation. It was the kind of high-end hotel which was out of her price range for all bar the most special of occasions. Picturesque and exclusive, it was an ideal place for a wedding reception provided your budget ran to tens of thousands. The marquee which dominated the garden would have cost six months of her salary and that was before you counted all the staff passing out champagne like it was water.

Beth saw the bride frown when she didn't recognise them, witnessed the way she looked to her new husband and saw her blank look reflected on his face. True to form, Thompson didn't allow the poor woman time to ask who they were before flashing his warrant card under her nose and introducing himself.

With the bride looking nonplussed by their presence, Beth hoped the insensitive Thompson would let her lead the questioning. It was bad enough that the bride had found a dead body at her wedding venue, to now have her reception interrupted by an oaf with all the sensitivity of a raging wasp would further ruin what was meant to be the happiest day of her life.

'We're terribly sorry to have to trouble you, today of all days, but I'm afraid the first few hours of a murder investigation are critical.'

'Can't this wait? I mean, we're meeting our guests for goodness' sake.'

The bride laid a calming hand on her husband's arm. 'It's okay, Jason. The police have to do their jobs, and if that really was a dead body… I need to tell them what I saw.' She looked to Beth and Thompson and pointed over her shoulder at the main hotel. 'There's a room in there where we can talk, it'll be more private than out here.'

As they followed the bride into a small library, a guest wearing a suit that matched the groom's lurched towards them, his foot a mere three inches from the train of the bride's gown, and stopped in front of Beth.

'Hey gorgeous, what you doing later?'

'Oh, let me check my diary. Ah yes, sorry, I'm rather busy avoiding men with alcohol on their breath and wedding rings on their finger.' Beth kept her tone light, though she suspected the man might have made a different comment if he'd approached her from the left instead of the right and seen her scarred face.

She brushed past him and then closed the door as soon as Thompson had stepped through it.

'As I said outside, we're very sorry to have to trouble you.'

'Don't worry, I know you have jobs to do.' The bride looked at her wrist even though there was no watch there. Just the faint outline of where one had been worn while she had sunned herself. 'Just be as quick as you can, please.'

'Of course we will.'

Beth surmised Thompson must have realised the disruption they were causing, and the bad press they could generate, as his tone was soft when he asked the bride a series of questions.

Rather than interrupt Thompson, she let him carry on until he'd exhausted his questions, then added a couple of her own.

*

When they'd finished interviewing the new Mrs Welton, and Thompson was driving them back to Arthuret Hall, Beth decided to share her thoughts on the witness. 'Call me cynical, but I'm not sure I believed everything she said to us.'

'Really, *Constable*.' The way Thompson said her rank made Beth lose the few shreds of respect she had for him. 'Were you not paying attention? That poor lass was fighting to hold it together. She's seen a dead body on her wedding day and here you are, questioning her character as soon as we're out of earshot. Let me tell you, Young Beth, if you want to succeed in FMIT, you're going to have to become a much better judge of character in a very short space of time.'

'With respect, sir, I was paying attention. I just think she wasn't as distressed by the experience as she should have been. I mean, you saw the body. Saw how gross it was.'

'I get it, you're jealous that she's tougher than you are. You need to drop it before you become tiresome.'

Beth fumed in her seat. It may have been self-preservation, a respect for Thompson's rank and experience, if not the man himself, or some other factor she hadn't yet worked out, but she didn't respond. She knew her cheeks were glowing crimson and that just added to her humiliation. She wanted to protest further, to argue with the arrogant DS, but something made her keep silent.

Thompson drummed his fingers on the wheel and clicked his tongue as he drove. The few days she'd worked in FMIT were long enough for her to know it was his thinking tic. Her problem was, she didn't know what he was thinking.

On the one hand, he could be reassessing what she'd said about the new Mrs Welton and realising he may be wrong.

Fat chance of that. A junior female officer would never be right in his eyes.

On the other, he may be preparing to tell O'Dowd she was useless, and that she had also been rude to one of the Weltons' wedding guests, after being paid a compliment by them.

Another option was that he'd said his piece and would allow her to move forward with her career and learn from him and O'Dowd.

She felt that idea was even more ridiculous than expecting him to say she was right.

CHAPTER SIX

Upon returning to Arthuret Hall, Beth and Thompson joined a serious O'Dowd and Unthank. The chastened look on Unthank's face warned Beth to choose her words with care when speaking to the DI.

Now darkness was imminent, the house's initial eeriness had increased as the gables and dormer surrounds were backlit by the setting sun. There were no sounds from wildlife or even farm animals. All she could hear was the puttering of the portable generator which powered the lights being used by the CSI team.

O'Dowd strode off towards a deserted area of the car park. 'Come over here.'

When the FMIT team arrived at the fence at the far end of the grassy car park, O'Dowd rounded on them. 'Some bugger has already leaked this to the press. I'm sure I don't need to explain how badly you'll need a proctologist if I find out it was any of you.' O'Dowd ran a hand over her face and pushed back the strands of dark hair that had fallen onto her forehead; she used the other hand to point at the house. 'Because if the press get wind of exactly what happened to that poor sod in there, we're going to face media pressure like you've never imagined. Not, of course, that media pressure should matter to any of you; the person, or indeed persons, who killed that poor man and left him here like that has to be caught. Preferably before he decides to put wings onto anyone else's back.'

O'Dowd gave each of them a stern look to emphasise her points.

'We spoke to the new Mrs Welton like you asked, boss.'

To Beth, it was inevitable that Thompson would be the one to break the uneasy silence. Typical that it would be a brown-nosed comment as he played the good little minion.

'And?'

'She was pretty shook up. When I questioned her she seemed to have thought it was a sick joke someone had played on her. She didn't realise it was real until we showed up. At least, that's what she said.'

'You're implying there are things you picked up that she didn't say.'

Beth was about to speak, but Thompson beat her to it.

'I think she was lying through her teeth.' Thompson pulled a face. 'She grasped the seriousness of why we were there as soon as she saw my warrant card. Never once did she break down, although there were a few times when I could tell she was acting. She looks to be about half the age of her new husband and, unless I'm mistaken, he's got a good few quid behind him. There was a marquee the size of an aircraft hangar for her reception at Farlam Hall. There must have been well over a hundred guests and Farlam Hall isn't the kind of place you or I could afford if we had to feed and water a hundred people. The cheapest car I saw there was a top of the range Jag, and there were still people arriving. If you ask me, and you just have, she knew all along that she'd found a murder victim and invented the practical joke story as a way of not letting it interrupt her wedding day.'

Beth struggled to keep her mouth shut as Thompson took her initial idea about Emily Welton being a liar and ran with it; but there was also a warning in his eyes that kept her lips sealed. There was nothing she could do about the scar on her cheek though. It always pulsed when she was annoyed as her half-ruined blood vessels felt pressured to work again.

'That's quite a leap. Especially considering she got her cousin to call it in.'

'That kind of proves my point, doesn't it?'

O'Dowd scratched her chin and adopted a pensive look that made Beth wonder if she'd been very wrong, and that Thompson was about to catch merry hell for her mistake. That would be the most poetic of all the justices. The idea thief berated for a bad idea.

'Not really. You might not get it, but no woman wants their wedding day spoiled. She found a body and did the responsible thing by getting a copper to deal with it. The poor woman will probably have nightmares after seeing what she saw. Do you think she should have put her wedding on hold?'

'Not exactly, boss.' Thompson's voice held conviction. 'But you should have seen the way she looked at her husband. Her eyes were filled with greed, not love.'

'So what? So she's married an older man with a few quid in his bank account. Unless she kills him for some reason, their relationship is none of our business. And another thing, have you any idea what a chauvinist prick you sound with theories like that?'

A coughing fit enveloped Beth as she fought not to laugh at Thompson getting a roasting for the theories he'd put forward. She'd noticed a lot of the same things herself, but had drawn different, less judgemental conclusions from them. Like O'Dowd, she'd taken the bride's side and empathised with what it must have been like to discover a dead body on her wedding day.

She now understood the warning the DI had given her earlier and cursed herself for her naivety in sharing a theory with Thompson. This wasn't the first time a male superior had stolen her ideas with the aim of taking credit for them, but she was determined it would be the last.

'She still shouldn't have disappeared off. She should have waited around to speak to us.'

'You make a good point, Sergeant. What did you do about it?'

A worried look touched Thompson's craggy face. 'Boss?'

'You thought she was withholding something and therefore interfering with an ongoing murder investigation. Surely you arrested her?'

The worried look wasn't so much touching Thompson's face now, as inviting it in for coffee and sliding its arm across unsuspecting shoulders.

'Erm… er, in the circumstances, ma'am, I thought it best to not attract any bad publicity. Would you like me to go back and arrest her?'

Beth hated him for it, but she couldn't help admiring the way Thompson had lifted the burden of decision from his shoulders and placed it squarely on O'Dowd's.

'First off, what would you arrest her for? And second, what would that achieve now? I'll tell you, it would make it look like you didn't know what you were doing the first time. Imagine the kind of publicity that would generate.'

'As you say, boss.'

She would never admit it to O'Dowd, but Beth caught a glimpse of mischief in her boss's eye as she toyed with Thompson.

Rather than waste any more time on a closed subject, Beth asked what news O'Dowd and Unthank had.

'We've got the square root of bugger all, and the only good thing we can say about that, is that it's confirmed as an accurate calculation.'

'I don't follow, ma'am.'

'You were right about there being no security cameras, about nobody living here and about the gate being locked at night.' A hand was raised in the halt gesture. 'And before you ask, the only key holders are the owner, the gardener and the woman who mans the wee shop cum reception place. None of them have admitted to leaving the gate open any time recently, or to having found it that way because of someone else's carelessness. The woman who looks after the shop was the one who put out the chairs and acted as the wedding planner because the place was closed to the public due to the wedding.'

'Do you believe them, ma'am?'

'Actually I do. All three of them are middle-aged which means they're all a long way from being either in their dotage, or immature idiots who'd forget how to breathe if their bodies didn't do it for them. The three of them seem trustworthy to me, and, while I know we'll have to consider them as suspects, I can't for one second see any of them being our killer.'

Despite O'Dowd's withering assessment of young and old, Beth couldn't find fault with her logic.

'Did you ask them why the body was found by a visitor and not staff?'

An eyebrow leapt upwards onto O'Dowd's forehead, and enough steel to construct a battleship filled her tone. 'Of course I did. I do know how to run an investigation.'

Beth dropped her eyes to the threadbare grass of the car park. 'Sorry, ma'am.'

'For your information, the owner has been away all week on business and only returned home this morning. As for the other two, before I tell you about them, describe the bride's physical appearance for me, please.'

Beth flashed her mind back to following Emily Welton towards the room where they'd interviewed her.

'She was tall, thin and had strawberry blonde hair. At least a couple of inches taller than me and I'm almost six foot.'

'The groundsman and the shop lady aren't tall; in fact, both are smaller than me. But when I tried to peer through the window that overlooks the cellar, as the bride did, I couldn't see the body. I had to stand on tiptoes to achieve it, and even then, I could only see the top of his head.'

'Sorry again, ma'am.'

'Well, at least you're asking the right questions, even if you're asking them of the wrong person.' O'Dowd stomped her feet and tossed a few scowls around as she fished a packet of cigarettes from her pocket.

As O'Dowd drew smoke into her lungs, a compact man wearing an oversuit stepped from the house and walked towards a small green car.

'Beth, do me a favour, and go see what Dr Hewson has for us.'

CHAPTER SEVEN

As she walked across to speak to Dr Hewson, Beth was working out the questions she would need to ask and preparing them into the right order. She knew the scarring on her face would draw his eye and then there would probably be the mini-stare followed by an embarrassed look away.

At first, such encounters had bothered her, and made her want to run away to a safe place, such as the sanctity of her bedroom, or maybe a shack on a deserted beach where the nearest she was to danger was reading one of her books on serial killers, but as the years had passed, she'd grown accustomed to the ritual. Now she used people's reactions to her scar as a way to judge their character. She lived with the scar and she'd come to terms with it; how others dealt with it spoke more about them than anything else.

Dr Hewson looked out from the boot of his car when she spoke his name. He straightened to his full height and looked up at her. 'Let me guess, Dowdy O'Dowd has sent you over to ask me about time of death, cause of death and a dozen other stupid questions that can't be answered until I have done a post-mortem.'

While Beth didn't care for the way that Hewson had given her DI a moniker that was overtly sexist, she didn't want to get on the wrong side of the pathologist at their first meeting.

'Actually *DI O'Dowd* asked me to find out if you had any preliminary thoughts. She never mentioned time or cause of death.' Her words were something of a lie as she knew that's exactly what O'Dowd had wanted to know, but to Beth it wasn't so much about being truthful, as salvaging an already bad situation. 'She spoke highly of you and said you're the best pathologist in Cumbria.'

Hewson raised a bushy grey eyebrow. 'Nice try, lass, but your flannel isn't going to wash with me. Thanks to cutbacks, there are only three pathologists for the whole of Cumbria.' A finger jabbed at his chest. 'One doddery old fool whose hands shake like buggery, a raw recruit who's so wet behind the ears it's a wonder she doesn't have gills… and me. And I've had so many run-ins with Dowdy over the years, I reckon I'd still make third place on her list despite the lack of credible competition.'

Beth licked her lips and kept her face neutral. It was obvious that the DI and Hewson had some sort of running feud, but while she didn't want to be drawn into the no man's land between them, she still needed to come away with some information from the pathologist.

Some officers might use charm and try to flirt in this situation, but that wasn't her way. To Beth, her mind was a far better weapon than her femininity. Instead she tried a different tack. 'Right. You don't like her and she doesn't like you. So I guess she's thrown me to the wolves by asking me to see what you know. I suppose you have two choices then: you can return her compliment to me, by telling me nothing and sending me back there to get a roasting from her, or, you can give me what you know at the moment, taking the higher moral ground and putting the case first.'

Beth let her gaze wander across the wallheads where the skeleton of the house was now backed by a deep royal blue as the sky darkened. For the first time that day, she noticed the strong earthy smell of the countryside. Somewhere in the trees an owl hooted loud enough to be heard over the generators powering the CSI team's lights.

The sound ought to have been reassuring, a return to normalcy. It wasn't though; instead it added a layer of spookiness to the atmosphere. Beth stuffed a hand into her jacket and wound her fingers around the handcuffs, collapsible baton and pepper spray she always carried. The action worked; it gave her the calmness she needed and pulled her away from macabre thoughts. The case was bad enough to deal with, without her adding unnecessary layers of horror.

Hewson took a puff on his e-cigarette and released a sizeable cloud of fumes that drifted past Beth. She caught a fleeting whiff of raspberry until the smoke dissipated on the wind. To her, raspberry was all wrong for a man of Hewson's intensity. It reminded her of the fruity lip balms she had grown out of using more than a decade ago.

She pushed his idiosyncrasies from her mind and fixed him with what she hoped was a patient but enquiring look. 'So what's it going to be? Which is most important, helping me catch whoever left that poor man in there?' Beth pointed to the area of the house where the victim was being examined by members of the CSI team. 'Or you scoring a couple of points against O'Dowd?'

The beginnings of a grin were twisted away from Hewson's lips as he opened his mouth to speak. 'You're good, lass. I'll give you that. There's not a lot I can give you until I get that poor bugger back to the lab though. He's mid-forties; in good physical shape for his age; there's significant burning around the mouth, which is interesting; and of course the wings attached to his shoulder blades.' He raised a hand to forestall Beth's comment. 'But you'll have seen all that for yourself. My early impression is that the wings were attached pre-mortem.'

Beth had guessed as much about the wings herself. Each shoulder blade had a rivulet or two of dried blood running downwards across the exposed bone.

'What else did you discover? Or rather, what preliminary assumptions can be made?'

'Good question.' Hewson tilted his head as he looked at her. 'Before I answer you, I'd like to know what you thought of the injuries to the lower part of our victim's body?'

Beth closed her eyes and pictured the man in his final stance as she spoke. 'The man's genitalia were missing, but they didn't look to have been cut off. Could it be that a fox, or some other animal, had stood on its hind legs to get an easy meal, as there were scratches on the man's legs, and what appeared to be bite marks and tearing on the remains of his scrotum?'

'Very possibly. What else?'

'His hands also looked to have been chewed on as each was missing fingers and had stumps, but again,' Beth winced at the memory, 'there were no clean cuts.'

'At least you're not blind.' Another cloud of raspberry vapour enveloped Beth as Hewson pushed the boot lid down with a metallic thud and leaned against it. 'I found a number of larvae nestling in the exposed eye sockets, and while there was some discolouration of the flesh, that's more to do with exposure to the elements than any rough treatment.'

'So you're saying that, apart from what happened to him here, he wasn't mistreated?'

'I am indeed. He wasn't beaten or tortured in any other way.'

'The eyes: were they removed by the killer or eaten by an animal?'

'Pecked out by a bird most likely. Soon after death would be my guess. The animal world doesn't show any manners when it comes to a free meal.'

The larvae were a clue to the length of time the body had been a corpse. Once a person died, insects, maggots and other creatures were drawn to it for a free meal. Some would lay eggs in the body as soon as they happened upon it. By studying the stages of development of larvae and pupae, pathologists could make informed guesses as to how long a corpse had been in situ.

'You mentioned larvae, what are they telling you – from what you've seen of them?'

This time Hewson's grin was allowed to blossom. 'You are good, DC…?'

'Young.' Beth held out a hand. 'Beth, if you prefer.'

'So, Beth, you're young by name and nature, yet you're not youthful. You're a serious beggar, aren't you? Driven. Probably something to do with that scar on your face.' Hewson tilted his head back and appraised the scar in a way that only a doctor could. 'I'd say that you picked that up about four years ago. Would I be right?'

Beth nodded rather than risk speaking and having her voice betray her amazement at Hewson's perception.

They may come less often now, but she still had occasional flashbacks and nightmares about the night her life had suffered irrevocable changes.

A night out with friends had been going well when a fight erupted. Beth and a friend had been trapped against a wall as two men traded punches.

A beer bottle had been smashed and thrust forward. Its intended target had swung an arm to deflect the blow. The attacker had put such force into his swing, the arm holding the bottle continued its arc until the jagged edges of the bottle made contact with Beth's cheek.

The plastic surgeon who'd tried to repair her face was competent, but nothing more.

She'd had no justice for her injury or disfigurement. As soon as they'd seen the blood gushing from her face, both fighters had charged from the bar and legged it down the road. Neither had been identified, let alone arrested or charged.

She didn't blame the intended target as much as the man who'd held the bottle. He'd been the one who had tried to wound and injure. In her more reflective moments, she recognised that any person would have done what the intended target did and deflected that bottle away from their face, and that it was nothing more than bad luck that had caused the broken bottle to connect with her cheek. But then, she reasoned, it had also been the intended target who'd thrown the first punch. And, as the person who started the fight, there was no way he was entirely blameless.

It didn't matter how much she reflected or used objective analysis on the moment her looks were stolen from her, justice was still awaiting an introduction to the man who'd held the bottle.

Even now, years later, she found herself scanning crowds looking for the one clue she had as to the identity of the men who were fighting. The man who'd deflected the arm holding the bottle had two lipstick kisses tattooed onto the left side of his neck. One was scarlet and the other pink. Part of her didn't expect to ever see him again, but that didn't mean she wouldn't keep looking.

Beth looked at Hewson, returned the frank appraisal he'd given her. 'The larvae. I'm not going to hold you to what you tell me without a full examination of them, but can you give me a ballpark number based on your best guess?'

'Judging from their development, they've been on the body four, maybe five days, so you're looking at the body being placed in situ between four and six days ago.' His eyes gave a mischievous flash. 'If Dowdy had asked me that question, I'd have told her between a day and a month.'

'I'm sure you would. Just as I'm sure she would have questioned your parentage if you had.' Beth gave a tiny smile to show that, while there was no malice to her words, she was just as serious as the doctor. 'Anyway, what about where the victim's arms were cable-tied to the horizontal bar? Were there any wounds caused by him fighting to free himself?'

Hewson cast his eyes to the sky. 'Yes actually, there were. Not significant though, more like he was uncomfortable and was trying to wriggle into a less painful position. They certainly didn't tie in with him exerting all of his strength into the action.'

'And finally, his fingers, was there enough of one to get a print?'

'I assume so; one of the CSI team dealt with that. Otherwise we have teeth.' The doctor pulled open the driver's door. 'Good luck with your investigation. I'd say I'm looking forward to working with you again, but that would mean some other poor bugger would probably have to die a horrible death, and perhaps it's tempting fate to wish for that. But I dare say I'll see you at the post-mortem anyway.'

Beth watched him pull away with her mind tumbling. The pathologist was a shrewd operator, and he'd not only passed his judgement on her – with the way his eyes had twinkled from time to time, she was sure he'd been on the point of flirting with her. Not in any kind of serious way that suggested he wanted to sleep with her, just enough to let her know that he'd enjoyed her company.

She pushed those thoughts away and focussed on the information he'd given her. The wings had been attached while the victim was still alive. He'd also been alive when fixed to the post.

A question leapt into Beth's mind and she turned on her heel and strode back towards the house instead of returning to O'Dowd and the rest of the FMIT team.

She used her torch to illuminate the timber hoardings that screened off the un-refurbished part of the house where the body had been left.

The hoardings had been painted a pastel green, and one sheet had been removed to allow the various police teams to access the area where the victim was found. Beth scanned the others until she found what she was looking for. The screws holding the plywood sheets in place had all been painted over. Except on the sheet nearest the cellar. The screw heads on that sheet had traces of paint on them, but they showed signs of scuffing that told Beth they'd been unscrewed after they'd been painted.

It was how the killer had got his victim into the cellar.

Armed with this knowledge she trudged off to speak to O'Dowd. The CSI team would have to claim the sheet of plywood in case there were fingerprints on it, and they'd have to check with whoever installed it and the house's owner in case it was one of them who'd removed the panel rather than the killer.

After everything she'd just learned or surmised, there was a lot for her to think about and there would be a mountain of paperwork to complete once they all got back to Carleton Hall. At least she hadn't made any plans for this evening.

With no boyfriend on the scene, there wasn't anyone who'd be aggrieved at her working into the night. The only person it would affect was Beth, and so far as she was concerned, losing a few hours of sleep was a tiny price to pay for bringing a killer to justice.

CHAPTER EIGHT

Once a grand manor house that dated back to the eighteenth century, with its high ceilings and thick walls, Carleton Hall was a substantial building whose air was more imposing than impressive. To Beth the building represented strength, order and power. It wasn't a showy house with painted ceilings, it was designed as a home for the wealthy people who paid fealty to the county's elite.

While such a building as their HQ may, in the past, have added a certain amount of gravitas to the police force, the reality was that it wasn't hugely practical and a lot of the rooms were too small for the number of people trying to work in them. Unlike the newer, purpose-built Durranhill Station at Carlisle, Carleton Hall was a make-do-and-mend solution. Every room had thick plastic trunking supplying additional power sources along with Ethernet and telephone connections to the various workstations that filled every available space.

The higher ranks occupied the upstairs rooms, with the chief super and the chief constable occupying the two large semi-octagonal rooms, which were the house's best, as they afforded their residents the most entrancing view of the local countryside.

One factor in Carleton Hall's favour was its location. While Kendal and Workington were larger towns than Penrith, and Carlisle was an historic city, none were central to the county.

Carleton Hall was sited a mile from the M6, and adjacent to the A66, which gave officers a good starting point to get to wherever they needed to be. Cumbria and the Lake District covered a huge area and its only motorway bisected the county on a north-south axis. From Penrith with a shift on, the FMIT team could be at Kendal in half an hour, Carlisle in fifteen minutes and Workington in forty.

These times were allowing for a fair wind; Cumbria was often beset with tourists and a lot of the main arteries around the county were twisty A roads. The tourists created a lot of congestion through their numbers and their slow pace as they took in the majesty of the Lakeland Fells and the tranquil lakes which drew them to the area.

Add to this mix a surplus of traffic and farm vehicles, and it was not uncommon for journey times around the county to be doubled. On more than one occasion, emergency service response times had suffered due to the presence of a caravan being towed along a country road and there not being a safe place where the driver could allow them to pass.

With long snaking lines of traffic a common sight on the A66 and the A595, and a constant in the tourist areas from Easter to November, a smart criminal could easily lose themselves in the crowd long before the police were anywhere near.

CHAPTER NINE

The early morning air was cool, but not so cool as to chill her exposed flesh. A quick glance at her watch as she turned onto Fell Lane told her that she was five seconds ahead of her usual time.

As part of her morning routine, Beth ran a course around the former market town of Penrith. The route was challenging, over hills of varying gradients. Regardless of the weather or the time of her shift, Beth went for a run at the start of the day.

Not just part of a fitness regime, she used the exercise to invigorate her mind as much as strengthen her body. The sights of early morning Penrith never changed much, but Beth had grown accustomed to their rhythms and had learned what should and shouldn't be in certain places at certain times. Like the girl in the skinny jeans and chiffon blouse who shouldn't be walking the streets at that time, but was. Beth saw the girl's expression and felt the tiniest pinprick of jealousy. While the girl looked tired, she also wore a satisfied look that made light of the fact she was on her way home after a wild night out.

Penrith was Beth's home town and while her love for it ran deep, she could be objective about it and its residents. She knew there was a housing estate where the inhabitants were three parts feral, and that although the protein factory had been forced to undertake new practices to eradicate the smell of rotting animals, the very fabric of Penrith retained hidden whiffs of the once all-pervading smell ready to engulf the unsuspecting.

She returned to the police house she rented and checked her watch as she reached the door.

'Yes!'

A pumped fist accompanied her triumphant hiss. Ten seconds had been shaved off her personal best.

Beth left the house some twenty-five minutes later, showered and dressed in a charcoal suit. Her hair was still wet from the shower, but her suit was dark enough that her ponytail wouldn't leave a noticeable damp patch. The drive to Carleton Hall was a short one but, as always, she used the few minutes to finish powering up her mind in preparation for the day ahead. It promised to be another long one. It was gone midnight when O'Dowd had called a halt and instructed them all to be back at their desks by seven.

As she parked, Beth spotted O'Dowd chewing on a cigarette with all the enthusiasm for life as the person who cleans the toilets at the diarrhoea clinic.

Beth walked towards the entrance and nodded at O'Dowd. 'Boss.'

The last thing Beth wanted to do was to get into anything with the DI out here. Since Thompson's irritating stealing of her theories yesterday, she'd toyed with the idea of making a formal complaint before deciding to learn from the experience.

As the new girl, she didn't want to go to the DI complaining so soon after joining the team. Rather than give Thompson the chance to repeat yesterday's behaviour, she'd decided she'd speak up for herself and make sure O'Dowd knew which ideas she'd put forward and what Thompson had contributed.

'You need to learn when to listen, when to speak and, most important of all, when to share your ideas.'

'Ma'am?'

This was not the start to the day Beth wanted.

'That report Thompson gave when you came back from seeing the bride who found the body, it was you who thought she was being cagey about something, not him.' The non-cigarette holding hand was raised to stop her interrupting. 'Don't try to deny it. I know him, have known him for years. For all he acts like he works on hunches and intuition, his next original thought will be his first. Plus, when you get angry, the colour of your scar changes by at least two shades. When he was spouting your ideas, it was glowing like a flare.'

'Sorry, ma'am.'

'Don't be sorry, Beth. Be smarter. I warned you and yet you still went running into the very thing I warned you about. You let someone else pass off your ideas as their own. You're a bright lass, and if you use half your brains in the right way, you'll go a long way in the force. However, if you don't have the capacity to listen and learn, you're no use to me and I'll have to admit I made a mistake when choosing you over the other candidates to join my team. Either wise up or admit you're not good enough to be on FMIT and go back to CID.' The cigarette arced from O'Dowd's fingers and landed at least six feet from the bucket of sand by the back door. 'It's your choice. Just do me a favour, make the one that's right for you and act upon it immediately. Because we have a murderer to catch.'

Beth again cursed her naivety of the previous day. Here she was in her first week on the highest-rated investigation team in the county and less than twenty-four hours into a major case being effectively told to shape up or ship out.

As she trudged after O'Dowd she was vowing to herself that she wouldn't make the same mistakes again.

CHAPTER TEN

Beth nodded a greeting to Unthank and took a seat at her desk. At the other side of the room, Thompson aimed scowls at the kettle as if his displeasure at the early hour was enough to make it boil itself.

'Right.' O'Dowd strode in brandishing a sheet of paper. 'Fingerprint results are in. We have a name for our victim. More than that, we have his address and just about everything we could want to know about him, with the obvious exception of who killed him. He is Angus Keane, a forty-two-year-old self-employed builder. Got himself arrested a couple of years ago for affray when he had a punch-up. According to the census report, he's survived by his wife and two daughters. His wife reported him missing several days ago.'

Beth sat back in her seat and allowed the hush of the office to wash over her. She may be new to FMIT, but she'd soon learned O'Dowd's penchant for the dramatic. Pauses like this one were the DI's way of emphasising points, and of making sure her team had the necessary time and motivation to digest the finer nuances of situations.

'Has someone done the knock?'

Beth shot a grateful look at Unthank, glad he'd been the one to ask the question they all wanted to know the answer to. Her previous DI had been a cruel man and had deferred the unpleasant duty onto the person who asked the question.

'No, Paul, no one's done the knock.' Beth saw the pen pointed her way and tried not to let her face show the sinking of her heart. 'Beth and I will go and inform the wife. You two can start identifying his family and workmates. We're going to need to speak to them.'

Beth raised a tentative hand. 'How much are you planning to tell the family, ma'am?'

'We have to tell them everything; the press has already got hold of this one, so anything we don't tell them will be found out anyway. We have to have full transparency, regardless of how much it may upset the family. And put your hand down, you're not at bloody school.'

To save herself further embarrassment, Beth changed the subject. 'Any word on the post-mortem, ma'am?'

'Tomorrow morning at half seven.'

'Tomorrow? Why not today? Why are they waiting until tomorrow?' The questions were out before Beth could stop them. The first forty-eight hours of any investigation were critical, to lose twenty-four of them waiting on a post-mortem was beyond ridiculous.

'Because the chief super is a man whose main aim in life is to have a balanced spreadsheet; because our budget is thinner than a prison roll-up, and because while there are three pathologists in Cumbria, annoyingly there's only one worth listening to, and like the pain in the arse he is, he point-blank refuses to work a Sunday.'

'Why?'

'Believe it or not, Dr Hewson is an ardent churchgoer, and for the last fifteen years he's been the organist at his church. He'll work twenty hours a day Monday to Saturday, but he won't do a thing on a Sunday. This plays right into the hands of the bean-counting chief super, so he's never pushed the issue.'

Beth was incredulous at the calm acceptance in O'Dowd's voice. While she knew she wouldn't dare, she wanted to go and bang on the chief super's door, demand the resources necessary to have the post-mortem done today, and then force Dr Hewson to pick up his scalpel. It was a moot point. Chief supers weren't at their desks on a Sunday morning unless there was a major flap on. As brutal and horrific as Angus Keane's murder was, one death, however grisly, wouldn't be reason enough to make the chief super attend.

As she looked at Unthank for support she could feel her clenched fists scrubbing at the desk.

The support didn't come. But neither did any censure.

O'Dowd and Unthank were looking at her with curious expressions while Thompson still hadn't looked her way.

Beth couldn't contain her frustration any longer. 'How are we meant to do our jobs with one hand tied behind our backs, ma'am?'

'One handed.' O'Dowd gave Beth a glare and then pointed her pen at Unthank and Thompson; she passed a sheet of paper to Thompson. 'Off you go, boys. Once you're in the vicinity, wait until I tell you I'm going in. We need to get the timelines right. Beth and I *must* be first.'

Beth knew what O'Dowd meant about timings. With social media such a powerful force, there had to be coordination between the teams to make sure family members found out the news in the correct order. They also had to ensure that until they'd spoken to key family members, the news was kept off sites like Facebook and Twitter.

Beth was about to rise from her chair when O'Dowd perched a buttock on the corner of her desk and motioned for her to remain seated.

'You ever played cards?'

The question seemed odd to Beth, but she answered it with honesty, certain O'Dowd's reason for asking would become clear. 'I suppose, I used to play gin rummy with my gran.'

'What did you do when you got a bad hand?'

'I don't know. I guess I played it as carefully as possible and looked for a way to turn it into a winning hand?'

'Good answer. Police work is the same as cards. You rarely get the hand you want, and if you do, it's usually because of dumb luck or someone else's stupidity. We have to play the hands we get dealt.'

'Sorry, ma'am. It just frustrates me that we can't get the full resources the case deserves.' Beth took a leap of faith, brushed the hair back from her face and looked into O'Dowd's eyes. 'How do you cope with the frustration?'

'I choose to use it as a propellant rather than kryptonite. Let your frustrations overwhelm you or dominate your thinking and you'll be an alcoholic in two years. Let them drive you and you'll be in my job in six.' O'Dowd flapped a hand at the seats vacated by Thompson and Unthank. 'Those two get it. They understand the way the game is played, and while they don't like the rules, they know how to play the game. What Thompson did to you yesterday, don't let it get to you. He's got external pressures, and between you and me, it's only his dedication to duty that's stopping him from getting signed off with stress.'

'I don't want to sound like I'm brown-nosing, ma'am, but thanks.' Beth knew O'Dowd was astute enough to understand what she meant.

'Think nothing of it.' O'Dowd stood and pulled a resigned grimace. 'C'mon, we've got three lives we have to shatter and, as rough as it's going to be, the sooner we've done it, the sooner we can ask Mrs Keane who she thinks might have killed her husband.'

CHAPTER ELEVEN

Sunday morning is a special time in most households. It's the time for a relaxing roll-together without the furtive weekday looks at the alarm clock, or the pressing knowledge of Saturday chores. It's the day of the week when a full fried breakfast happens at a leisurely pace rather than a bowl of cereal being gulped down or a slice of toast being carried out the front door between hastily brushed teeth. Sundays are about relaxation, kicking back and enjoying the company and full attention of loved ones.

Sunday mornings used to be sacrosanct to Beth. From her childhood memories, through her teens and right up until she'd joined the police, those first hours of the Sabbath were about recharging her batteries and preparing for a day spent with family or friends.

Yet here she was, metaphorical sledgehammer in hand, ready to smash and destroy that time for an entire family. O'Dowd would be taking the lead and would be the one to give voice to the unthinkable words, but Beth felt as if she was complicit just by her presence.

When time healed the raw wounds of loss, there would be a recollection of there being two coppers who tore apart the life of a mother and her children. The short, officious boss and the tall sidekick with the scars.

O'Dowd's knock on the door of the farm cottage was firm but respectful. Through a window, Beth could see two pyjama-clad children sitting on a couch eating toast.

The door eased open with the merest hint of a squeak from the hinges and a tousled head appeared.

'Hello.'

'Mrs Keane?' O'Dowd lifted her warrant card. 'We're here about your husband, Angus.'

'About bloody time. He buggered off last Saturday and it's taken you days to get here.'

Mrs Keane's words piqued Beth's interest and she caught the stiffening of O'Dowd's shoulders.

O'Dowd gestured at the open door. 'May we come in?'

It took a moment for her request to register, but Mrs Keane stepped to one side and waved them into the house. The place was a mess without being dirty. Rather it was the type of mess a parent had to deal with ten times a day when there were young children in the house.

As she stepped between the small wellies and dropped crayons, Beth saw a domesticity that was missing from the police house she called home. She could easily have stayed with her parents, as they still lived in the family home on the other side of Penrith, but she'd wanted to have her independence. Plus, by leaving home, she didn't have to put on a brave face to her parents every time she had a bad day. Her mother was a worrier, and she knew her father had had his reservations about her joining the police. Nor had she wanted to share a house with any of her friends. As much as she enjoyed their company, she needed her own space.

Mrs Keane tried to lead them into the lounge, but when O'Dowd saw the children she gave her head a tiny shake and let herself be directed into the kitchen.

'Mrs Keane. May I call you Suzy?'

'Yes.' Suzy caught something in either O'Dowd's face or her tone as she pulled her dressing gown tighter over the cerise pyjama top. To Beth the gesture was a defensive one, a mental putting on of armour. 'You're not here about him buggering off, are you?'

'Not exactly. I'm sorry, Mrs Keane – Suzy. But there was a body found yesterday; we ran its fingerprints and found them to match those we had on record from the time your husband was arrested for affray.'

'Body? You mean he's dead?'

'I'm afraid so.'

Suzy's back collided with the wall and she used it to keep her more or less upright as her legs folded. Her mouth was stretched wide as grief took hold of her.

O'Dowd bent to comfort Suzy. With nothing more useful to do, Beth put the kettle on. It was hardly in the manual of things to do at a time like this, but it gave her something to do and there was a restorative familiarity to a cuppa.

Suzy's wails pierced the air and prompted the thudding of tiny feet on laminate as two pre-school girls came running into the kitchen.

With two bundles of blonde curls wrapped around her, Suzy's inner strength returned and she parked her sorrow until she'd told her daughters that she was okay, and that she was only crying because she'd stubbed her toe.

The smaller of the children bent over and kissed each of Suzy's toes with a lip-smacking sound accompanying the movements of her head.

So far as Beth could tell, the girls knew they were being lied to as the looks they gave Suzy were dubious, whereas the ones she and O'Dowd got were downright suspicious. She didn't know whether to offer a smile or pull a funny face, which is what she normally did to amuse or entertain young children.

Both seemed inappropriate when those two innocent little girls had had their world destroyed; she didn't want them to have memories of a copper who'd smiled and joked with them before swinging the axe of destruction.

The taller of the two girls took her sister's hand and led her back towards the sounds of a cartoon.

'How?'

Beth looked to O'Dowd who pulled an empathetic face behind Suzy's back.

'How what, Suzy?'

'How did he die? How am I going to tell my girls their daddy's dead? How will we keep up the mortgage without Angus's wage? How has it taken you so long to find him? How am I going to tell the girls? Why him? Where was he found?'

Neither Beth nor O'Dowd tried to answer any of the questions. Instead they did what was so obviously needed and comforted Suzy. O'Dowd helped her onto a chair at the table, and Beth put a mug of hot sweet tea in front of her.

After a few minutes of contemplative silence, O'Dowd removed her arm from Suzy's shoulders and took a seat opposite her.

'You are bound to have a lot of questions, Suzy, and while I'll try and answer them honestly, some of the ones you've asked are beyond my scope as a human being, let alone a police officer. However, I have requested that a Family Liaison Officer join you this morning. They are experts at helping people in your terrible situation. They have subtlety and tact, whereas I'm more of a blunt instrument. My talents, and the talents of my team lie in another direction. Basically, we're the ones who get all the tough cases.'

Suzy knuckled her eyes and looked at O'Dowd with a shrewd expression. 'You say you get all the tough cases. Does that mean Angus was murdered?'

'I'm afraid it does.'

Beth saw a different side to the new widow once Suzy had digested the news her husband had been murdered, rather than an accident or suicide. It was there in the setting of the jaw, the pushing back of the shoulders and the minute lifting of her chin. Beth knew that Suzy Keane had realised that she'd never see her husband again. He might have walked out a few days ago, but whether he'd planned to return or not, there was no longer a chance of that happening. True to form, like all those who have been wronged, bewilderment was soon replaced by anger.

For the first time since they'd entered her home, Suzy looked into O'Dowd's eyes.

'Who killed him? Have you caught the bastard? Why was he killed?'

'I'm afraid we don't know who killed him yet.' Beth gave an apologetic shrug. 'We'll need to ask you a few questions shortly. Hopefully the answers you give us will help us identify his killer.'

'Promise me that you'll catch him, that you'll get the fucker who killed my Angus and nail his bollocks to the nearest wall.' Her arm pointed towards the lounge. 'My girls are in there; very soon I'm going to have to tell them their daddy's dead. If not for me or him, please, I beg you, catch the person who killed their daddy.'

As she listened to Suzy's plea, Beth felt her own conscience answering the call to arms. Those little girls would have a tough enough life growing up without a father. The only support she could offer them was the knowledge that the bad man who'd taken away their father had been caught and punished.

Regardless of the long hours or frustrations the case would put upon her; the two girls and their mother, as much as Angus himself, would be the ones she'd be fighting for.

Beth couldn't begin to comprehend the horror of losing a parent, let alone at such a young age. Her parents were still alive and she expected to have them in her life for at least another twenty or thirty years. For those little girls there would always be an empty seat at the table, no father to walk them down the aisle and a fight to understand why the killer chose to murder their daddy.

CHAPTER TWELVE

The showroom he entered was full of gleaming cars. Each polished to within an inch of its life. To one side a family were ooing and ahhing at the salesman's patter as he showed off a car to them.

None of this mattered to him. He wasn't there to look at cars; he was there for another reason.

He was hunting. Searching for angels.

Off to another side he saw a middle-aged woman looking with doe-eyes at a smooth-looking salesman half her age. That was a sale which was sure to be made. He judged the salesman only wanted to put his hand in her purse, while the woman might let him put his hands wherever he wanted.

Towards the back of the showroom were a number of desks, two had customers busy signing their lives away for a prestigious badge, and over the partition of a third, he could see a young woman talking into a telephone.

He watched as she hung up and turned to scan the showroom. When her face came into full view he gasped with pleasure. She was beyond gorgeous. As he looked at her he knew she was an automatic candidate to become one of his angels.

The smile she gave him showed immaculate teeth, a pair of cavernous dimples and a beautiful face that was framed by auburn hair that tumbled onto her shoulders.

She stood and walked towards him.

When she rounded the desk he saw her figure, took in the lithe frame enclosed in a calf-length grey dress with white flecks.

It clung to every part of her body and showed her supple flesh as she strode towards him, heels clacking as she proffered a hand.

Her perfume was delicate, with hints of a citrus fruit.

'Hello there. Are you looking for anything in particular? We have a lovely 5 Series that's very popular.'

'Do you?' He was relieved he didn't stammer. The girl's beauty had thrown him so far off kilter he didn't trust himself to say a full sentence without sounding like an imbecile. Or worse, a pervert.

The girl smiled and pointed to a shiny red car. 'This model is one of our bestsellers; would you like to take a look at it?'

'Please.' He tried a smile and hoped it didn't come across as a leer.

'Cool. May I ask what your budget is?'

At a loss as to what to answer, he looked at the car for a moment and spied the price on the stand beside the vehicle.

'Thirty-five thousand.'

'That's good. Do you have a car to trade in?'

He couldn't tell her about the old van he drove. 'No, it would be a straight sale.'

'Excellent. Well, the price on the stand there is for the base model rather than this one.' She gestured to the driver's side. 'Why don't you climb in, see what it feels like to sit in the seat of such a lovely car?'

He did as she suggested. When she climbed in beside him he pictured himself driving away with her. As mental images went, it was a work of art that could only be described as priceless.

A small part of his brain functioned enough to nod and coo when she pointed out the car's many features. It wasn't just her beauty that captivated him, it was the melodic tone to her voice. She had a cut-glass accent that made it sound like the bluest of blood flowed through her veins, and when he compared it to the harsher more guttural tones common to East Cumbrians, it gave him a glow warmer than the finest cognac ever had.

Meeting her was the highlight of his year. She would be one of his prize angels, if not the greatest prize of all.

He'd met her today through pure chance. He'd been on his way to Windermere, to a restaurant where the waitresses all wore flouncy skirts, when on an impulse, he'd parked up and then walked back a hundred yards to the dealership on one of the streets that wound their way into Kendal.

He always did his best to avoid the centre of Kendal; the one-way system baffled him, and he couldn't recall a time when he'd visited the town and managed to leave by the same road as he'd arrived.

For the man, car showrooms were always fertile hunting ground for angels. Dress codes were imposed in many of them, and there was always a level of flirtiness that accompanied the saleswomen's spiel. He would tour the ones round Carlisle and Penrith on infrequent occasions; too often and his prey would be scared off, yet for some reason, he'd never thought to explore the ones in Kendal.

It was all he could do not to agree to buy the car just to please her. Somehow he managed to resist the instant purchase, although he did agree to a test drive in the future. The allure of exclusive time in her company was too much to bear.

He said his goodbyes and took the card she handed him.

Sarah Hardy was her name and he had the sense not to make any jokes about resting on laurels or fine messes. Stan Laurel was a Cumbrian and had been born in Ulverston, a scant twenty miles from where he stood.

He'd only spent maybe ten or fifteen minutes with her, but she was already too important, too special, for him to mock, or even tease.

When he returned to his van he sniffed the business card, hoping to catch a hint of her perfume before he kissed it and placed it into his breast pocket. Next to his heart.

The test drive he'd let her arrange was a deception, but it would mean he could see her again.

CHAPTER THIRTEEN

Beth made yet another pot of tea and placed it on the table in front of Suzy's brother and sister. They'd come over after a frantic call from Suzy. Both were ashen-faced and the brother stank of stale alcohol. He'd driven here, but Beth had chosen to overlook that fact: cautioning him for drink-driving wouldn't help anyone. Most people had no idea of just how long it took for the body to break down alcohol. She'd been amazed when during her training she'd learned that the human body takes ten hours to fully rid itself of the alcohol in a bottle of wine.

Tears had been shed and fierce, supportive hugs exchanged with Suzy. The sister was an older, plumper version of Suzy, whereas the brother was a slight man with a stooped posture and lank hair.

Beth had been given no more than passing glances while she waited for the FLO to arrive. O'Dowd had scarpered at the first opportunity after questioning Suzy about her husband's possible enemies. At least the DI had promised to send Unthank over to collect her once the FLO was in situ.

Despite feeling as useful as a cardboard cut-out, Beth knew she had a job to do.

'I know this is a terrible time for you all, but I am afraid I do have a few questions.'

The sister buried her head in her arms and let out sobs of grief that heaved at her rounded shoulders. It was obvious the grief wasn't just for herself but also for her sister and her nieces, as Suzy had gone to tell her daughters the terrible news.

A nod from the brother gave Beth permission to start. He was doing his best at being manful and strong, but whether it was last night's alcohol, or his natural empathy, he was struggling to maintain his composure and provide support for his sisters.

'Angus wasn't reported missing until two days ago, yet Suzy mentioned he left home on Saturday. Do you know why your sister didn't contact us sooner?'

The brother gave a sigh, looked at the kitchen units and the floor before speaking. 'They have a tempestuous relationship. They'll be fine for a year or so and then there will be a big fall out and Angus will… *would* go back to his mother's for a week or two before they patched things up.' A shrug. 'That was their norm and it's the way they've always been. The only reason she wouldn't have reported him missing sooner would have been her anger at him. It was when he hadn't called to speak to the girls that Suzy started worrying. Whatever happened between the two of them, he always called his girls.'

Beth wondered if the fact that Angus had left before would help or hurt his children. The last time they'd seen their father would have been a heated situation where harsh words were spoken. Would that be his daughters' last memories of him, shouting and swearing as he left with a suitcase? And there were Suzy's feelings to consider; whether she'd been the aggressor or victim in their latest argument would be immaterial. She'd appoint the blame squarely on her own shoulders for him not being safe at home with her and the kids. Every word from her mouth would be analysed and criticised as she wondered if she'd been too brutal in throwing him out, or too accepting of his decision to leave.

Yet, the tumultuous relationship was a red flag to a police officer, and Beth had a duty to pursue this line of enquiry. Official statistics proved that most people who were killed died at the hands of someone they knew, and in a lot of those cases, the murders were committed by the victim's nearest and dearest. As horrific as it was to think of a wife killing her husband in the way Angus had been found, the investigation's first focus would have to be on eliminating the victim's family members and closest friends as suspects.

'Do you know why they split this time?'

As soon as the brother's scornful gaze landed on her, Beth realised she should have picked her words with more care.

An exasperated hand pointed towards the lounge. 'What does it matter what they fell out over this time? My sister is in there telling two precious little girls why their daddy isn't ever coming home.'

Beth held her tongue as it began to dawn on the brother why she was asking.

His top lip curled into a snarl. 'You think she did it? Are you crazy? My sister wouldn't harm a fly. She's terrified of spiders, but she still made us remove them from her bedroom on a sheet of toilet paper and release them outside. Whatever you're thinking is wrong, very wrong.'

'Please hear me out.' Beth returned his stare until he looked away. 'It's just hours into the investigation, we can't say anything for certain yet. We're still gathering facts and looking for clues.'

The brother's bottom jaw stuck out. 'Then think harder and look better. My sister isn't a killer and you're barking up the wrong tree if you think she had anything to do with his death.'

A hand snaked out from the older sister who lifted her head off her arms and grabbed her brother's hand. 'Peter.' A swallow as she fought for composure. 'The lass is just doing her job. Stop picking a fight with her and answer her questions. You're not helping anyone.'

Peter scowled at his sister, then turned his head to Beth and lifted an eyebrow. 'C'mon then, Miss Marple. Let's hear your questions.'

Beth ignored the insult. 'You said earlier that Angus had gone to stay at his mother's. Where does she live?'

'Longtown. Don't know the address.'

The address didn't matter. The question wasn't one Beth needed the answer to. It was just a soft question she'd asked to start the conversation – a minor detail. Each of the questions she planned to ask would increase in importance, but it was necessary to foster a willingness to answer in what had become a hostile witness.

'If he was staying with his mother, don't you think it was odd that the mother didn't report him missing?'

A confused expression covered Peter's gaunt face and he looked to his sister for help. She wiped a tear from each eye before answering. 'Maybe she is in Spain. She has a villa out there and I know Angus said she sometimes goes for a couple of months at a time.'

That was the kind of answer Beth had been hoping not to get.

'What about his work? Wouldn't his workmates have called him to find out where he was?'

'He's a self-employed builder. I dare say some of his customers would have called wanting to know where he was, but I guess he wouldn't have been able to answer his phone.'

A knock at the door made them turn their heads.

Beth gave an inward curse at the interruption to her questioning, but there was nothing she could do about it.

Peter went to answer it and came back trailing Unthank and a young blonde who was introduced as 'Kerrie the FLO'.

The FLO and Unthank crowded into the kitchen and shared polite nods with the sister.

'So, Peter.' Beth had to try again. 'Angus was a self-employed builder. Do you know if he ever had any problems with customers? You know, unpaid bills or complaints about shoddy workmanship?'

'No!' If the one-word answer wasn't emphatic enough, Peter's head gave a violent shake.

'What about the reason for his leaving Suzy, do you know anything about that? Did she kick him out or did he leave of his own accord?'

The head shake was less certain this time. 'I kept out of it. They'd always be back together in a fortnight anyway, so I never got involved.' He nudged his sister's arm. 'D'you know?'

Once again, tears had to be wiped away before an answer could be given. 'He accused her of cheating on him.' A sob. 'She denied it, of course, but apparently he'd stormed out saying he was sick of being taken for a fool.'

'He what? The hypocritical bastard had no right to accuse her of anything after what he did!'

Beth couldn't let Peter's comment pass. 'What did he do?'

'She caught him swapping gobs with some tart outside the pub.'

As much as she disliked Peter's crude and derogatory terminology, Beth kept her face neutral. 'When did this happen?'

'A couple of years ago.' Peter's face twisted into a feral expression. 'If that's what he's accused our Suze of, the bastard got everything he deserved.'

Peter may have felt that Angus kissing someone when his children were young was inexcusable, but it was not that unusual. The pressures of parenthood, not being the centre of attention in his wife's world any more – it was a cliché but it happened more than people ever realised.

At once Beth saw a whole tangled web that would have to be unravelled. Was Peter imbued with a sense of anger that went beyond a brother's concern for a bereaved sister? And if there was the possibility that Angus's claims had any foundation, could that put Suzy's alleged lover in the frame for his murder?

She realised what she needed to do was to get the sister alone to find out if there was any truth to the allegations of Suzy's infidelity.

That said, while there was no doubt Angus had been killed, having seen his corpse, Beth couldn't help but doubt it was a crime of passion. Too much thought and planning had gone into it. If her limited experience had taught her anything, it was that women who killed their spouses most often did so in a fit of temper fuelled by rage or self-defence. Angus's body had shown no signs of impact wounds from either a blunt object or a weapon such as a knife. Though they hadn't had a toxicology report yet, so perhaps it was too soon to make any assumptions. Women who carried out planned kills often used poison.

What troubled Beth most was the way Angus had been found. It just didn't fit with a domestic killing and spoke of a deeper issue. On the other hand, it could be he was staged that way to throw all suspicion away from family members.

At this early point, Peter was her prime suspect. He seemed very angry and too quick to speak his mind for her liking. Grief can do strange things to people, but she had the feeling he'd been angry with Angus long before he was killed.

She heard the squeak of a door opening. 'Peter, Harriet, can you come through, please?'

Both of her siblings stood to answer Suzy's call.

Once they'd left the room, Beth requested Kerrie keep her eye on Peter, and also try to find out from the sister any details she could about Suzy's alleged affair.

A huge part of the role of a Family Liaison Officer was to watch the family and listen for any slip-ups. Kerrie's monitoring of the family would be invaluable and, once she'd established their trust, she'd get far more from them than Beth or even O'Dowd could hope to get in an interview room.

As Beth walked out to the car, she vowed to herself that she would be careful about which of her suspicions she shared with Unthank lest he pull the same stunt Thompson had. She didn't think for a second that he would, but once bitten…

CHAPTER FOURTEEN

Sarah Hardy finished with the family who'd been looking at an X5 and turned to find herself faced with a timid-looking man. He wore good clothes and his watch looked to be worth several thousand pounds. The man was attractive without being handsome. Unlike the creep who'd been in earlier, she didn't mind the way this guy's eyes flickered over her.

She held out a hand. 'Hi, I'm Sarah, how may I help you?'

'I'm er, erm, looking for a new car. Something fast, but not too big.'

'How about an M3 or an M4?'

'That's what I was thinking.'

The smile that covered Sarah's face was genuine. The sale of either car would get her a decent commission. Plus there was a chance she'd be able to ingratiate herself with this guy. A quick glance at his left hand had informed her of his marital status, or lack thereof.

Sarah arranged to have an M4 available for him to test drive on Wednesday. By the time he was leaving with her card in his pocket, she was giving her wardrobe a mental stocktake, trying to decide which outfit would impress him the most.

With a rare lull taking place, she made herself a coffee and grabbed Veronica, the only other female saleswoman, for a quick gossip.

'You see that guy who I was just talking to?'

'I did, you lucky cow. He looks minted. That's got to be a sure-fire sale.'

'I hope so.' Sarah giggled in spite of herself. 'I also thought he was well fit, but Christ on a bike, he was hard work to talk to. He was so shy. Like, I had to take the lead and basically start every part of the conversation.'

'So he's the silent type.' It was Veronica's turn to giggle. 'Sounds like the perfect man; rich, fit and quiet.'

'You're not wrong there. Mind, you should have seen the one who was in before, dirty old sod hardly looked at the car, or my face.'

'You should wear a loose-fitting trouser suit, that'd put men like him off.'

'Yeah right.'

Sarah didn't need to say anything else. While their boss imposed no official dress code, beyond being smart, both she and Veronica always wore a skirt or dress rather than trousers. Sex sells and when your pay is heavily reliant on commission, you sometimes have to make sacrifices and be prepared to flirt a little.

Besides, she'd never had a bad experience at work until this morning, and in the greater scheme of things, a guy admiring her when she'd dressed to show off her figure was a compliment. That he'd fixated on it was more his problem than hers. Anyway, other than a shaking of hands, there was no way she'd be touching him, or allowing him to put his hands on any part of her body.

She didn't give it a moment's thought, and instead focussed on thinking about what she might wear for her more attractive customer's test drive on Wednesday.

CHAPTER FIFTEEN

Beth fired up her computer and grabbed a notebook. O'Dowd had listened to her findings and theories, given a curt nod of appreciation and then issued a set of orders about what she wanted them to do.

Across the room, Unthank kept his head down and carried on with his work. O'Dowd had laid into him for something minor, and it was clear he was smarting from the insults she'd hurled his way.

Once she'd logged onto the computer, Beth went online and started the task O'Dowd had given her – which was to research Arthuret Hall. It wasn't what she wanted to investigate, but she knew she had to follow orders.

It only took her a few minutes to learn the history of the grand house. Built in the seventeenth century by the Appleby family, it had been in the ownership of the Dacre-Applebys for almost two hundred years. The next owner had taken Arthuret for a surname and, the estate remained in the family's hands until the 1940s when the building was requisitioned by the RAF as an officer's mess, and during the later war years, it was home to evacuees from Rossall School in Lancashire. After the war, it was converted into flats for servicemen working at the MOD depot at Longtown.

Its next reincarnation was as a casino; The Borders Country Club was run by a man who was alleged to have gangland connections. When the licensing laws changed, the hall was abandoned to the whims of weather and vandals. By the early seventies it was a roofless, ruined shell. Only since early the previous year had it come back into use, as a bohemian venue for weddings, its still-beautiful and incredibly grand entrance hall an ideal place for a civil ceremony with enough room to accommodate up to a hundred guests.

The history of Arthuret Hall was fascinating and the more Beth read, the more she wondered if it had been chosen as the deposit site for a significant reason, or selected at random by someone who knew nothing of its history.

She wondered if Angus had a connection. Maybe he was descended from an evacuee, or an airman who'd lived there. Or maybe it was the killer whose ancestors had once inhabited the house. Or perhaps he'd been executed for non-payment of gambling debts, and his body had been dumped in the way it had in a former casino as a warning to others with outstanding debts.

It crossed Beth's mind that the killing could be connected in some way to the weddings that took place at the venue, but she couldn't figure out how beyond Angus Keane knowing someone who'd married there. According to O'Dowd's notes, Suzy hadn't known of a connection between her husband and Arthuret Hall, but that didn't mean there wasn't one.

Whichever way she looked at it, there was a shedload of possibilities to consider and she was grateful the burden of decision about which avenues they explored would fall on O'Dowd's shoulders rather than her own. Not only were there so many strands to investigate, each one was fraught with difficulties. It would be straightforward enough to find out if Angus was a gambler, but locating the records that listed the evacuees and the RAF men who lived there could prove to be a nightmare. Plus there were all the men who'd lived there when working at the MOD depot to consider.

There would be dozens if not hundreds of people to identify. Some of the house's occupants may still be alive, though even the youngest of the evacuees would be pushing seventy-five at best. To add to all that, there was the former owner who'd turned the house into a casino, with his shady past. Was it possible that a criminal empire had been passed down and Angus had been murdered by the owner's sons' or grandsons' henchmen?

Regardless of all these possibilities, there was every chance the house's history had no bearing on the case, and Beth was convinced their best chance of getting a result was to identify the reason Angus was killed.

She got Unthank's attention. 'Paul, have you got a minute?'

'Yeah, what is it?'

Beth outlined her findings and the various ideas she'd had to Unthank.

'Sounds like a right nightmare. It'll take us weeks to work our way through that many folk.'

'Any ideas on ways to hurry the process up?'

Unthank wagged a finger in front of his shaking head.

Beth got his meaning at once. Some things couldn't be hurried up and there were no shortcuts in a murder investigation. She was glad she hadn't voiced the same sentiment in front of Thompson or O'Dowd.

To change the subject, Beth asked Unthank how he'd got on with his own tasks.

'I've got the request in for Angus Keane's phone records and I have also asked for its geopositioning for the last week. I'm now on with running both his and his wife's family through the system to see what pops up.'

'Found anything?'

'Suzy's brother Peter has a couple of arrests for assault in his past and he was bound over for ABH about five years ago.'

'Sounds like he has a big temper for a little man. Do you think O'Dowd will pull him in?'

'Damn right she will.'

Beth's head snapped round at the DI's voice. She hadn't heard O'Dowd enter the room and she was glad she'd used the right terminology and hadn't prefixed the name with the insulting nickname that she was increasingly aware others used.

CHAPTER SIXTEEN

The name he answered to wasn't the one he'd been christened with. It was a name he'd adopted to protect himself. An insurance policy against being identified for the person he really was.

He tossed a casual smile to the waitress who brought over his lunch and picked up his knife and fork. This morning had gone so much better than he'd hoped.

Sarah Hardy had been such a godsend, an angel dropped from the heavens into his lap. Her presence was an unexpected bonus, like finding a winning lottery ticket, or receiving an inheritance from a long-forgotten great aunt.

The chance encounter had given him a target. He didn't need to hit that target just yet. Other pieces had to be brought into play first, but now he had time to cultivate Sarah, before he added her to his collection. She would be the finest piece he'd collected to date. Beautiful and graceful, she'd be a decorative thing to have around.

As he fed a forkful of salad into his mouth he felt his excitement grow. She would give him such a special thrill, pleasing him in every way that mattered. Her very presence in his life would lift him, give his creations meaning, and burn in the eyes of those who'd cast him down, belittled him and sought to destroy his very being.

For too long he had been the victim, the one to cower, and the person who never fought, or even answered back. Now he was the one with the power. He saw this every day, from the way people looked at him, to the way they reacted to his presence. He liked that people noticed him; it gave him the feeling of worthiness that had been absent from his childhood.

He'd sensed Sarah's attraction; it was easy to create: dressing in expensive clothes, using good manners and pretending to be shy worked every time for him. Even now, sitting in a country pub with a chilli-infused vinaigrette tingling his lips, he could see two young women giving him sidelong glances and checking out his watch.

Despite being left-handed, he wore his watch on his dominant arm so the women who recognised its worth didn't have to shift their eyes too far to see the bare ring finger.

He knew he was a manipulator, knew it wasn't a pleasant trait to have, but he didn't care. He'd been trained in the art of manipulation by the best. The teachings were now ingrained in him and he found himself getting everything he wanted, exactly when and how he wanted it.

He exchanged a smile with one of the young women.

Maybe he'd get lucky and she would be called Claire, or Carole. Her name could be something ridiculous like Candii and she'd still be of worth.

Regardless of the woman's name, he wasn't ready to add Sarah to his collection just yet. Still, there was nothing to prevent him grooming her for as long as it took him to add the two pieces which had to come before her.

CHAPTER SEVENTEEN

Beth listened as O'Dowd outlined her strategy for the interview with Suzy Keane's brother, Peter. Beth was to take the lead and O'Dowd would butt in from time to time. Her role wasn't quite that of 'good cop' to O'Dowd's 'bad cop', but there was no doubt that Beth was there to be the gentle balance to O'Dowd's stronger line of questioning. She was also aware it was another of O'Dowd's tests; that her boss would be monitoring her as closely as she watched Peter.

They were to start off speaking to him as a witness, but should he prove obstinate, or worse, mute, then they'd arrest him and apply some real pressure.

With O'Dowd seated opposite them across Suzy's kitchen table, Beth looked for a way to instigate the interview that wouldn't be antagonistic.

'Thanks for agreeing to speak to us again. We know this is a very traumatic time for you.'

'I'll do whatever I can to make sure justice is delivered.'

The statement from Peter was an ambiguous one. There were many examples of when criminals got cocky and talked themselves into trouble by thinking they were far cleverer than they were.

'For Angus's sake?'

'Justice won't help him now. It might give my sister some closure though. And my nieces when they are old enough to understand.'

'So you believe in justice then?' As the words came from her mouth Beth wondered if she'd made a mistake.

'Of course I do. Whoever killed Angus should be punished.' He gave a sly smile. 'I'm not talking about an eye for an eye or anything biblical. I'm talking about someone paying for their actions. About the police sending a killer to jail. About the rule of law standing firm in the face of adversity. Wasn't it Einstein who said that for every action there is a reaction? That's what I mean by justice.'

O'Dowd cleared her throat with a noise similar to that of a pump running dry. 'Actually it was Sir Isaac Newton, and the quote is, "to every action there is always opposed an equal reaction".'

'Same thing, isn't it?' Peter gave a nonchalant shrug. 'Still means we both want Angus's killer locked up, don't it?'

'We certainly do.' Beth felt it was time to apply a little pressure as Peter was way too cocksure. 'Though, we're not sure you have the same thing in mind.'

'What do you mean?'

Behind the belligerence of his tone, Beth detected a hint of fear. Perfect, she had planted doubts in his mind, now it was time to water them. There was already enough organic fertiliser in his head to make them grow.

'We've taken a look at your record, haven't we, DI O'Dowd?'

'Indeed we have. Made for very interesting reading. At the risk of boring you with statistics, the national average of male murder victims who knew their killer is 52 per cent. I'll admit that at 68 per cent, it's higher for women than men, but it's still a large enough number to make us consider the family as suspects. Now, those are national figures, so what they don't take into account are regional variations and individual victim demographics. However, I've been a copper in Cumbria for the best part of thirty years, the last twenty as a detective, and I have to tell you, we don't have the same gang-related violence that other parts of the country have to deal with. You're a Cumbrian yourself, so I need hardly tell you that we don't suffer any terrorist attacks. These things affect the national figures, but not the Cumbrian ones. So I'd say our realistic percentage is somewhere north of 65. So, bearing all that in mind, can you imagine my response when I found out the victim's brother-in-law has twice been arrested for fighting, and received a suspended sentence for ABH over a third incident? Not only that, but one of my team informed me that this suspect was also furious with the victim for an alleged act of infidelity. Let me tell you, Peter, with all the evidence that's pointing at you right now, I expect to be home in time for *Antiques Roadshow*.'

Cockiness returned, not just to Peter's face, but also his posture. 'Sorry to disappoint you. But I didn't kill him. And those fights you mentioned, and the ABH? They happened a long time ago. I've grown up, matured. Mind, I'm not quite mature enough to watch *Antiques Roadshow*.'

Beth winced at his implied put-down of O'Dowd. Yet the explosion she was expecting from her boss never materialised. Instead there was a calm indifference. It took Beth a moment or two to realise there was no way O'Dowd would let herself rise to the bait, and that whatever insults came her way would have to be met with the same lack of anger.

'Leopards. Revenge. Jealous.' When Beth saw two pairs of eyes looking her way she ordered her thoughts into proper sentences. 'Leopards don't change their spots; you were a fighter then and we think you're a fighter now. We think you killed Angus as an act of revenge for what he did with the other woman. We think you were jealous of him. He was taller than you, better looking, more successful.'

'Shall I save us all a lot of time?' Peter laid his mobile on the table. 'If you really thought I killed him, you'd have arrested me by now. We'd be having this conversation in a formal interview room with a tape recorder. We're not. Therefore you're on a fishing expedition and you haven't baited your hook.' He pointed at his mobile, which lay on the table beside a packet of cigarettes. 'If you check my emails, you'll see I was staying at the Rose Villa in Cornwall for the last week. Call them and verify it. I think the receptionist was called Joan or June, something like that. I spoke to her every morning and night. You might also want to check the GPS positioning of my phone. It will also show you I was in Cornwall. As a final piece of proof, call the number for James Haskett. He's the man I was working for. As a shopfitter. Working nights. For ten days solid.'

Peter sat back in his chair and folded his arms. The smug expression on his face was unnecessary, but he let it sit there anyway.

Beth didn't want to give him the satisfaction of her looking to O'Dowd for advice, so she reached for his phone.

O'Dowd got there first. She thumbed the device and checked the emails. Next she got Haskett's number from the phone and wrote it down. 'What's your number?'

With his number jotted under Haskett's on her notepad O'Dowd slid the phone back to Peter.

'I can see why you suspected me. But I have outgrown all that nonsense. I didn't kill Angus. I'll admit I thought he was a waste of space, but to kill him?' Peter shook his head and gestured towards the living room. 'No way. I didn't like him, but my sister and her daughters loved him. Killing Angus would hurt them far more than him.'

'We'll see.'

O'Dowd stood and stomped her way out of the room leaving Beth to trail after her.

CHAPTER EIGHTEEN

The interview with Peter hadn't given them anything new to go on and, as a result of this, O'Dowd's fractious temper had snapped and crackled all afternoon.

The timber panel had been dusted for prints and the report had identified seventeen different fingerprints on the front and none on the back. All seventeen had been run through the IDENT1 database but none had been recognised. More tellingly, the post and its crossed member had also been checked but had been found to be devoid of any fingerprints. This suggested to Beth that the killer had worn gloves. She hadn't expected to get a result so simply, as the murder had obviously been carried out with fore-planning, but every possible lead had to be followed up.

What Beth wanted most of all was to deliver justice to victims and their families. To do that, she needed to learn from the best minds, osmose their investigative techniques and understand their thinking.

She'd done well to get into FMIT, and while the greater wages and influence which came with promotion were attractive, the last thing she wanted to do was climb the career ladder to the point where she became a desk-bound administrator.

For Beth, the thrill of police work lay in catching out suspects in the interview room, chasing down leads and evidence to build a case that was sure to lead to a guilty verdict and, most of all, the puzzle. All her life she'd enjoyed challenging her brain and as a copper she got paid to solve puzzles. The big difference now was that the ones she solved would do a lot more than just give her a sense of satisfaction, they'd bring justice.

Beth was so driven that she'd signed up for the police on the morning of her eighteenth birthday. Her boyfriend at the time hadn't agreed with her decision and had sulked at the thought of her not being at his beck and call due to shift work and time spent away on training courses. The relationship was only a few months old, and when Beth had told him it was over, he'd accepted her decision with grace. It wasn't that she didn't care about him, she just knew that she could never love someone who didn't support her chosen career and understand her need to become a police officer. For her it was all about righting wrongs and delivering the closure only justice can bring.

He'd tried pushing her towards the modelling work she'd been offered. None of it had been too glamorous, but until she'd turned eighteen, she'd supported her waitressing income by modelling clothes for budget clothing stores and she had been offered the chance of turning it into a professional career. Looking back with hindsight, she realised that he'd wanted a model girlfriend he could brag about, rather than a police-officer girlfriend he could be proud of.

As much as it had flattered Beth to have been considered pretty, model material, the downside of that life was that she'd had to watch every bite, that as she turned eighteen the offers of work had taken on a different, more seedy nature and that in her experience the modelling world was largely populated by people Beth found shallow and bitchy. With only a couple of exceptions, every person she'd met on a modelling shoot was looking to advance their career; if others got trampled, then so be it.

Leaving that world behind was a decision Beth had never regretted.

That her looks had been taken from her when she became a victim of violent crime during her training was an irony she'd never shake off.

She had made sure the glassing had the minimum impact on her training. After she'd been discharged from the hospital, she'd had a week cloistered in her bedroom until the isolation bored her rigid. She went back to training the moment the doctors said she was fit to return and had spent her nights catching up on the work she'd missed.

It had been a distraction; a way of focussing her mind on something other than the pain and the fact that she would carry scars on her face until the day she died.

CHAPTER NINETEEN

Beth and Unthank exchanged a surprised glance when O'Dowd suggested they head off to their respective homes at just nine o'clock. Beth was prepared to work long into the night, but she wasn't going to disobey her DI in her first week in FMIT.

She'd called her mother to warn her that she wouldn't be round for her tea. Her mother always did a Sunday roast, and her chicken dinners had been the thing Beth had missed the most since leaving home. Whenever her shift pattern allowed, she made sure she was sitting in her usual seat at the kitchen table by five to five at the latest.

'Are you sure, ma'am?' Beth noted that even as she was speaking, Unthank was up on his feet shrugging his jacket on. As always, he just wanted to be with his girlfriend.

'You might as well get an early night tonight. Before you go though, Paul, I want you to get onto the RAF and the MOD tomorrow. I want the names of everyone who stayed there. Don't take no for an answer, regardless of what they say.'

'Ma'am.'

Beth only just stopped herself from raising a hand. 'What do you want me to do, boss?'

'You were keen to get the post-mortem results. I want you to be at Cumberland Infirmary for half seven to attend. Once that's done, come back here with DS Thompson and start getting me the names of the kids who were evacuated to Arthuret Hall.'

'Of course.' Beth tilted her head to one side. 'Ma'am?'

'What is it?'

'DS Thompson, ma'am.' Beth was careful to show the appropriate respect and choose her words with care. 'Where was he this afternoon? I thought it would have been all hands to the pumps.'

O'Dowd gave Beth an enigmatic look and then pushed the office door closed so they could speak privately. Beth was afraid she'd overstepped the mark and was about to get one of O'Dowd's infamous swearings.

'He went to see his wife.' A hand lifted to forestall comments. 'He was never supposed to be on shift today, so he took his daughters to see their mother. She has what they call early-onset Alzheimer's and is living in a care home. The last time he took the girls to see her, she didn't recognise them. So, as well as losing his wife, he's nursing a pair of teenagers through their grief at losing their mother. She's there in body, but her spirit has been stolen. He's agreed with the girls that this is the last time he'll take them to see her, unless they want to return of course. All three of them are having their hearts broken and he's got to be strong and look after his girls.' O'Dowd's sigh was filled with pity and frustration. 'Only Paul and I know about it at the station, and I'm only telling you because you're part of the team. Keep it to yourself, ignore his jibes and don't give him reason to vent at you, because if you do, he's likely to go too far because of the pressure he's under. And before you ask, yes, I have suggested he takes some time off or that he applies for a less stressful position. He thanked me for my concern and told me not to worry about him. Bloody men, eh?'

O'Dowd left the room.

Rather than going home, Beth gave her limbs a stretch then sat back into her usual seat. She lifted first one leg then the other and put her crossed feet on the desk.

With her chair tilted back she stared upwards. After a moment or two, her thoughts extended away from the watermarks on the ceiling and onto Thompson. When O'Dowd had spoken about him, she'd got the feeling the DI was unburdening herself as well as covering for Thompson.

Beth could understand that, the human psyche has its limits. Every person in the world had a different snapping point; some would fly into a rage at the slightest thing while others would bottle emotions until hate had festered to the point their mind was overloaded. When that point was reached, an explosion of volcanic proportions may ensue. Rhetoric every bit as corrosive as lava would erupt from the person as they vented their anger and frustration.

Some people didn't have the luxury of venting, either in daily rages or through the weight of multiple months and years of accumulation. These people were the truly strong ones. They kept things to themselves long after they should have raged, internalised their problems long after they should have been shared.

Nobody knew these peoples' secrets, for they did not share them. Instead they hid them behind a smile as false as the *Mona Lisa*'s, as they absorbed the stresses of others. They accepted the burdens weighing down on the shoulders of friends and family members, their strength admired, remarked upon, but also taken for granted, until one day, it's no longer there. The day the strength goes is the day the person breaks under the weight of all the pressures.

Now, thinking about Thompson and his ways, she could imagine the turmoil of his mind, understand his world and appreciate his sacrifice. He wasn't the kind of man she thought would be comfortable talking about his feelings. She guessed that he was more likely to bottle things up than overshare. For him, release would come in the form of eight pints and a curry with mates, or an hour and a half spent cheering for eleven millionaires while simultaneously insulting eleven others. Perhaps she was wrong and he painted or wrote poetry in his spare time, but there would be precious little of that anyway. He was filling the role of mother and father for his daughters as well as holding down a stressful job. Coupled with the grief he was bound to be feeling at losing his wife, to what was, at best, limbo, the pressure must be tearing at the fabric of his soul.

That he was still doing his job told Beth that behind his bluster and general obnoxiousness, Thompson was a good man, that he was someone who cared about putting criminals behind bars. You didn't apply to join FMIT if you weren't driven by something more than a pay cheque. Whether it was justice, the righting of wrongs or empathy for the victims that drove him, it didn't matter. So long as he was in his current post, he was part of a team that made a difference.

O'Dowd had said that she'd offered him a transfer. Yet, despite everything that was happening at home, he'd turned her down and stayed in FMIT. To Beth, the man's professional dedication said as much about him as the way he was looking after his wife and daughters.

Beth took her feet back down from the table and walked round to Thompson's side. On the left-hand side was a picture of a woman and two girls. All three were smiling, sticking out their tongues as they dafted about for the picture. It was a typical family portrait, clearly taken on a day filled with laughter. It spoke of happier times.

Beth wondered whether its presence would end up comforting or mocking Thompson, as she made sure she put it back in the exact spot where she'd found it.

CHAPTER TWENTY

As she parked outside Cumberland Infirmary, Beth took a moment to compose herself. The growling of her stomach had little to do with the breakfast she'd foregone. She was dreading the forthcoming experience; sleep hadn't come until the early hours as her mind had thrown her mental images of Angus Keane being dissected by Dr Hewson.

Sited where it was, off Newtown Road, in Carlisle, the hospital was well above the areas of the border city which had been affected by the floods of 2005 and 2015. It was a modern building and the main atrium always reminded Beth of an airport more than a hospital.

Rather than the front entrance, today she'd be entering the back way and would remain in the bowels of the building where the mortuary, laboratory and pathology rooms were.

The hospital backed onto farmland that fell away down to the River Eden, but Beth couldn't distract herself from dark thoughts by admiring the view due to the raised embankments which ringed the rear of the building.

Beth left two breakfast bars on the passenger seat of her car in the hope she'd still have an appetite after the post-mortem, and got out of the car. As she walked towards the entrance, Thompson's car pulled into a parking space nearby. When he climbed out, he didn't look as though he'd had any sleep at all.

As a professional courtesy and, if she was honest with herself, as a way to delay entering the hospital, she waited for him by the door as the beginnings of a rain shower pattered onto her head and shoulders. Thompson appeared and gave her a nod of greeting, and they went in together. His stride was a little slower than usual, which made Beth wonder if it was fatigue or reluctance that was impeding his progress.

'Here.' Thompson handed over a packet of mints and a small pot of VapoRub.

Beth knew what they were for at once. 'Thanks.' She popped a couple of mints into her mouth and used a finger to run a thin smear of the VapoRub over her top lip.

That Thompson had finally shown her a small act of kindness made her realise that he wasn't all bad. Despite the burden he was carrying, he'd still looked out for her.

'You ready for this?'

Beth hissed a breath out. 'Not really, but it has to be done.'

When they entered the mortuary, Dr Hewson was wearing a faded set of hospital scrubs, complete with mask and a surgical hat.

'Morning both.' His tone was bright and cheerful.

Beth supposed this was a good day for him. Rather than the humdrum, he had a genuine mystery laid out on the table in front of him. He'd been granted an atypical victim to pique his interest and stretch his professional muscles.

Hewson led them into the mortuary proper. Angus Keane lay face down on a stainless-steel table which had a second deck below that Beth deduced was to catch any liquids that leaked from the corpses Hewson worked on.

Against the stark white of the room's walls and flooring, the wings affixed to Angus's back appeared even blacker than they had at Arthuret Hall. The harsh lighting didn't help, and there was a chill draft as a ventilation fan sucked air out of the room with a mechanical fervency.

So far the only smells Beth had experienced were of unscented antiseptic and VapoRub. She hoped it would remain that way and the fan would remove all the puke-inducing odours. To be on the safe side, the position of a solid metal waste bin was duly noted.

Beyond the table bearing Angus Keane, there was another that held an array of surgical tools.

'Right, let's begin.'

Hewson switched on a Dictaphone and began to gently probe at the wings while giving a commentary of his actions. The outer parts flexed a little, but when his probe touched the stem which was attached to Angus's shoulder blades, there was no hint of movement. Beth heard him say the wings were attached with a glue of some kind.

Hewson swapped the probe for a scalpel and used the blade to slice a circle round the glue. It took him a few minutes but he managed to free the wing from Angus's right shoulder. He placed the wing's stem against a clear portion of the table and scraped a few slivers of the adhesive into a test tube.

'Here.' He passed the test tube across to his assistant. 'Test these for me, will you? I'm thinking either superglue or surgical adhesive.' The scalpel was pointed at Thompson and Beth. 'I don't care which it is, but our friends over there will.'

The second wing took longer to remove. Once separated from Angus, Hewson laid it with the other, then started to examine the edges of the areas where the skin had been removed.

A gloved hand waved them forward. As she inched towards the body, Beth made sure breaths were only taken through her mouth. It would be bad enough puking in here; to do it so close to the body would be unacceptable.

When they got to the side of the table, Hewson again used his scalpel to point. 'See this square, do you see how perfect it is? This isn't some rough gouge to remove the skin, it has been done with precision. Whoever did this had a steady hand, and I'd hazard that this wasn't the first time they'd done this.'

'You're right. It looks to be a perfect square.'

'There's one way to find out.' Hewson replaced his scalpel with a metal ruler and measured all four sides of the square. 'It's 62 millimetres on each side. Let's see just how good a surgeon our killer was.'

The ruler was placed diagonally corner to corner on the wound, then Hewson repeated the six measurements on the left shoulder blade.

Hewson's low whistle sounded odd in the sterile environment. 'This guy is good. Both areas are exactly the same size and one is a perfect square while the other is only a millimetre out.' He looked up from the body. 'I'll be honest with you, I wouldn't fancy my chances of replicating those cuts on a living person with the same level of accuracy.'

All of this information swirled in Beth's head as she watched Hewson work. As much as she wanted to focus on each point, she knew she had to file everything away for a more thorough inspection later.

Right now, she had to pay attention to what Hewson was saying and doing. Questions could be asked when he was finished.

After taking a series of photos, Hewson called his assistant over and together they rolled Angus onto his back.

He looked at Thompson. 'I presume you'd rather I concentrate on cause of death than the wounds which appear to be post-mortem animal bites.'

'Of course.'

Beth detected a hint of impatience in Thompson's voice, but Hewson had either missed the inflection or had chosen not to rise to it.

'Before I open the chest, or the head, I have to first do a few preliminary checks.'

Without waiting for Thompson's approval, Dr Hewson picked up his probe and bent over Angus's head.

First he peered at the empty eye sockets. A pencil torch was used to illuminate the pair of empty caverns.

Beth listened as he confirmed his earlier theory that Angus's eyes had been pecked out by birds.

Using both hands, Hewson squeezed at Angus's head then intoned into his Dictaphone that there were no obvious blunt trauma wounds that may have caused death. His probe touched Angus's lips and a little charred flesh rolled down the corpse's chin and onto the table. Gloved fingers took hold of Angus's chin and the probe was used to tease the lips apart.

Beth couldn't help taking a little step forward when Hewson gasped. Anything that provoked such a reaction from a seasoned pathologist was of interest to her, regardless of how gruesome it may be.

'What is it?'

Hewson picked up his pencil torch again and shone it into Angus's mouth. 'The inside of the mouth is every bit as scorched as his lips.'

With the pen between his teeth, the pathologist used his left hand to hold the mouth open and fed his probe inside.

A grunt and a nod were used to suggest Beth and Thompson took a look for themselves. Beth watched as her DS went first.

When he recoiled back, she took a deep breath and bent over to look inside Angus's mouth. Every part of the inside was blackened and scorched. His tongue was covered in broken lesions. When she looked to the back of Angus's mouth, she saw tonsils that resembled a pair of black cherries.

She took a step back and looked to Hewson. 'His mouth has been completely burned, hasn't it?'

'Definitely. I should imagine his windpipe blistered and blocked his airways. That's what I suspect was his ultimate cause of death.' He picked up a scalpel and pointed behind her. 'I need to check his trachea to confirm the theory. You may want to take a step back. This could be rather smelly.'

Beth added another smear of VapoRub and stood her ground. She didn't fail to notice Thompson had retreated to the back of the room. That could be a sign of either a weak stomach or hard-learned experience. Whichever it was, she'd made her stand and to move back now would indicate a weakening of resolve. Much as she may pity Thompson's domestic strife, there was no way she was giving him an excuse to take his inevitable frustrations out on her.

Hewson lifted Angus's head and placed a padded bolster under his neck. Now the head was tilted back exposing the throat.

The first incision he made was a delicate one which he used to expose one of the rubbery-looking pipes in Angus's throat. With a quick glance at Beth first, he pressed his scalpel against it until the point sunk in. With a deft movement he drew it along until he'd cut enough for it to gape open.

Again the torch went into his mouth as he used both hands to direct probes. With the tube teased open, Beth could see raw inflamed flesh which had pockets of loose skin everywhere.

When he removed the torch from his mouth, Beth listened to Hewson's technical description of what he'd found and waited for him to stop talking before she spoke.

'Am I right in saying that he must have breathed the fire down into his lungs?'

'You would. This bears further investigation which will happen when we look at his lungs later.' Hewson lifted his scalpel again. 'But having seen the state of the trachea, I want a look at his oesophagus.'

A half-remembered biology lesson informed Beth the official name for the windpipe was trachea, and that the oesophagus was the connection between mouth and stomach. Beth prepared herself for a noxious smell as Hewson cut into Angus's oesophagus. She watched as he opened it for inspection. It too was marked with crimson wounds and had sagging areas where blisters had deflated.

'Jeez. What does that mean?'

He looked up at her with confusion on the parts of his face she could see. 'I don't know. At least, I don't know yet. I will find out when I get a look inside him though.'

'Isn't it odd though? Him having burns in his windpipe is one thing if he'd breathed in the fire, but in his oesophagus, that doesn't make any sense at all to me.'

'Nor me. But I do know one thing, only fools and foremen comment on an unfinished job.' His eyes twinkled. 'You're not a foreman, so don't be a fool.'

'Sorry.'

'Don't be sorry. Be wise. I have at least a half hour's work to do before I open up his chest and get you the answers you want. Bugger off and have a smoke or a cuppa, or text your boyfriend, then come back in half an hour or so.'

Beth glanced at her watch. Being a single, non-smoker, all she could do was grab a cuppa. If the colour of Thompson's face was anything to go by, he needed the cuppa more than she did.

*

When they got back Dr Hewson was making the first incision into Angus's chest. Beth and Thompson both returned to their previous stations and stood without speaking.

As a precaution against any nasty smells Beth had smeared a fresh line of VapoRub onto her top lip. Thompson had done the same but his was twice the size of hers. The DS hadn't spoken to her while they'd had a cuppa. Instead he'd sipped at his tea and nipped outside and come back with the smell of cigarette smoke hanging from him.

Such was Hewson's focus, he didn't speak or look up to acknowledge their return.

Beth watched as the pathologist opened the chest and picked up an oscillating bone saw. Its whine as it cut through the ribcage was akin to fingernails being dragged across a chalkboard.

When the ribs were freed, Hewson levered them back until he could access Angus's internal organs.

'In light of what I've already found, I think that I should examine the lungs and stomach first. Any objections?'

The question was asked more out of politeness than being a serious query, as Beth knew that, in here, Hewson was in charge. All the same, she turned and looked at Thompson. He gave her a tight-lipped shake of the head.

'None.'

Hewson picked up his scalpel and, with deft movements, made the necessary cuts to allow him to remove the lungs and heart.

With the lungs, stomach and heart on a separate table, Hewson used his scalpel to slice along the length of the trachea, right to the point where it connected to the lungs. He teased the windpipe open and bent over it.

'Interesting.' He lifted his head and looked to Beth and Thompson. 'Do you see this?'

Beth stepped forward and leaned in for a better view. She expected Thompson to elbow her out of the way, but instead felt no sign of his presence.

When she looked at where Hewson was pointing she couldn't make any obvious deductions. 'See what?'

'The top of the trachea shows far more signs of scorching than the lower areas.'

'Is that synonymous with breathing fire into the lungs.'

'Correct.'

Beth couldn't see Hewson's face, but she heard the smile in his voice. It gave her a little flush of pleasure, and inappropriate though it was in the circumstances, she could feel her lips pulling themselves into a satisfied grin.

Hewson lifted his face from the organ mass. 'You better stand back. This isn't going to be terribly fragrant.'

The doctor was kind enough to wait until Beth did as she was told and had joined Thompson at the back wall.

This time his scalpel sliced open the oesophagus and carried right on until the stomach could also be peeled flat. The stomach was empty but that wasn't what almost floored Beth. A stench that she couldn't believe came from a human being fought at her nostrils, but she denied it entry and concentrated on breathing through her mouth while trying not to disbelieve what her eyes were showing her. The worst thing about the smell was the fact it also carried a weirdly familiar chemical tinge that she couldn't place.

Every part of Angus's stomach and oesophagus were laid flat before Dr Hewson. The upper areas of the oesophagus displayed blisters, charred parts and raw areas of flesh where skin had been sloughed off when the blisters had burst.

Whatever fire had burned Angus hadn't made its way right down to his stomach, but that wouldn't have made his death any less painful.

As Beth's mind reeled at the agony Angus must have endured in his final moments, it kept circling back to one point. The killer had to be found. She was on the investigating team and therefore it was her job to find him. More than her job, it was her duty.

Behind her she heard the rustle of clothes and the shuffling of unsteady feet. She turned and saw Thompson heading for the door. He trailed a hand along a wall as if needing its strength to support him.

'Well, as you're now the senior officer in attendance, what do you make of this?'

Beth looked up at Hewson's question. 'I don't know. Was some kind of burning liquid poured down his throat to kill him?'

'It's possible.' Hewson used a pair of tweezers to lift a small flap of charred skin. 'This is the epiglottis, it operates as a valve between the oesophagus and trachea to stop food and drinks going into our lungs. It's a fraction of the size it should be. I can't tell if he had burning liquid poured into him, or whether the liquid was put in first and then ignited. At least, not yet. From the smell of his stomach contents though, my guess would be the liquid was poured in first then lit.'

It took Beth a moment to get her head around what Hewson was saying, or not saying, as the case may be.

It was bad enough that there were wings attached to his back, but the fact he'd had his innards scorched took this to a whole new level.

'Say the liquid was poured in first and then lit. What exactly would have happened?'

Beth could see Dr Hewson's face was scrunching behind his surgical mask as he thought about her question.

'If that happened, the fumes in his mouth would have combusted at once and caused the burns we've seen.'

'Would the fire be drawn into his body? Would the petrol or whatever in his stomach catch fire?'

'I'd say not. Fire needs oxygen and provided the epiglottis stayed closed, the petrol in his stomach wouldn't ignite.'

'So it would just stay in his mouth and throat?'

'To a point. If the flames were still burning, he'd have drawn some of them into his lungs when he breathed in. I expect to find that his trachea and the upper areas of his lungs have blisters from burns on them.'

'Would these wounds have killed him?'

'It's possible, but not likely, the blisters blocked his airways. If it was petrol that was poured into his stomach, the fumes he'd breathe into his lungs from the residue in his mouth would attack the lung tissue.' A grave sadness overtook the doctor's eyes. 'The lungs would suffer chemical aspiration which would be hideously painful.'

'What if he'd kept his mouth closed so the killer couldn't light the petrol inside him?'

'Nothing would happen, but that's easily solved. A solid punch to the solar plexus would have him gasping for air. There's no sign of a bruise on his stomach though, so I'd say maybe the killer just pinched the victim's nose shut until he opened his mouth to breathe. Or even stuck a nose clip on him. You know, like swimmers wear?'

'Urgh. That's awful. You make it sound like the killer planned every detail.'

Hewson shrugged. 'I'm just looking at the evidence. I'd suggest you do the same.'

'Okay then. Was there any sign of a nose clip being used? Indentations on the nose, little bits of rubber scorched onto his skin?'

'None that I noticed, but it's possible the killer removed the nose clip once the petrol was poured in. The victim would have been coughing and choking on it, so his mouth would have been open.'

Beth did as Hewson had suggested and looked at the other evidence they'd collected, but she didn't feel any better for it. The surgical precision with which the skin had been removed from Angus's shoulder blades spoke of practice. If Hewson was right and a nose clip had been applied, it suggested the killer was either familiar with what he was doing, or knew a lot more than she did about the human respiratory system.

Her thoughts began to run along the lines that the killer was a doctor, or had had medical training, but with the internet, anyone could find out that information. You could learn pretty much anything with a few searches and a little patience. So far as the removed skin was concerned, a butcher or a chef would also have the knife skills needed to have done that.

Hewson laid down his scalpel and lifted Angus's lungs from his chest. A moment later he'd split the trachea open and laid it out flat. His next cut continued on from the trachea and showed that the blistering continued into the top of the lungs.

'Hmmm. This doesn't look good. These burns are probably the worst I've ever seen on lungs and I don't say that lightly.' Hewson looked Beth in the eye. 'I've had people who've died in fires show less flame damage to their lungs.'

'What does that mean?'

'It means you can get yourself off, lass. I don't think there are any other key details to come without hours of tests. Plus, I need to consult a few textbooks on this one.'

'Are you sure?' Beth was glad when he nodded. The sooner she could get out of here, the better. 'I know you can't be specific yet, but DI O'Dowd is sure to ask, do you have the official cause of death yet, and how soon can you get your report to us?'

'Don't quote me as I haven't finished yet, but in my professional opinion, the answer is almost certainly going to be fire-related. I'll send you my report as soon as I'm finished and have all the test results.'

CHAPTER TWENTY-ONE

O'Dowd strode into the office flanked by DCI Phinn. Never the sunniest of people, the DCI looked as though he'd been given a week to live and told he must spend six of the seven days juggling rattlesnakes.

His presence was an indicator of the severity of the case. He wasn't the hands-on type of manager unless there was something in it for him. That he'd shown up so early in their investigation told her that he was taking a personal interest.

While she wanted to be the one to solve the puzzle and identify the killer, Beth was glad he was there to help them earn justice for Angus and his family. Who reached the solution was nowhere near as important as catching the killer.

'Right you lot.' O'Dowd's expression was serious as she addressed them. 'Here're your tasks: DC Young, I want you on with finding out the names of the children who were evacuated to Arthuret Hall and the people who were tasked with looking after them; DC Unthank, you're to do the same for the RAF and MOD men.' A sheet of paper was pointed at Thompson. 'I want you to chase down these names and find out everything about them. They are the folk our victim may have had even the slightest of problems with.'

As O'Dowd had used formal titles in the presence of DCI Phinn, Beth made sure she did the same. 'Ma'am?'

'Yes?'

The word was snapped, but that didn't worry Beth. With the implications uncovered during the post-mortem sinking in, it was little wonder O'Dowd's temper was starting to fray. There had been a horrific murder and there were a multitude of leads involving what may potentially be hundreds of suspects.

'Are you bringing in a criminal psychologist?'

Phinn raised an eyebrow as O'Dowd bristled at Beth. 'Why do you ask that?'

'This murder is seriously messed up, ma'am. We've got a body with wings attached to its back and the post-mortem suggests that the victim had some kind of accelerant poured into his mouth and then lit.'

'I do know that, DC Young. I've plenty of experience investigating murders and they're all messed up.'

'I'm sorry, if I offended you. I'm certainly not questioning your judgement.' Beth tried to dig herself out of the hole she felt she was in. 'But with respect, ma'am, you said yourself you've never seen anything like it before. I just thought you might want to try and get an idea of what the killer might be thinking.'

Phinn lifted a hand to silence O'Dowd before she could reply. 'What are you getting at, lass?' When he spoke his tone was businesslike without crossing the line into brusqueness or condescension.

Beth felt her cheeks colour as the entire focus of the room shifted to her. She gave a little swallow before opening her mouth. 'I've been wondering what the killer's reasoning is. He's put wings on a victim and fire in their mouth.' Beth hesitated as she summoned the courage to share what she was thinking. 'What do you think of when someone tells you about breathing fire and wings? Because my first thought was a dragon.'

O'Dowd's curled lip combined with Phinn's lengthy sigh pierced Beth's confidence. Defeated she slumped in her seat and looked at the wall.

This theory would probably now be used as a stick to beat her with. She knew how the police worked behind the scenes;

there were few officers who didn't glory in the mickey-taking of a colleague. She'd done it herself and had it done to her before. Perhaps it was a coping mechanism for the stress of the job, but the slightest wrong word or silly idea was pilloried for weeks or sometimes even months. All the same, Beth, like everyone else, never wanted to be the butt of others' jokes.

Her saviour was the one person in the room she least expected to have her back.

'Actually, I think she's onto something.' Thompson rubbed at his ear. 'Can you think of any other theory that ties together what our killer did to the victim?'

Phinn gave him a withering look. 'To mess with our heads? To throw us off the scent?'

'Fair points, but why would he want to mess with our heads? And if he wanted to throw us off the scent, why didn't he hide the body instead of setting it up on display?'

'You're giving me a theory, but you're not giving me a motive. We know the how and the where. What we need to discover is the who and the why. Get one and you'll get the other.' Phinn scratched at his turkey neck while chewing on the inside of his lip. 'So you think he's trying to make a dragon?'

'No, sir.' Beth was back on her feet as she spoke. Even to her, what she was thinking was outlandish, but there was no escaping what the facts were pointing to when she lined them up and considered them as a whole. 'I don't think he's trying to make *a* dragon. I think this is him just starting.'

'And what, pray tell, makes you think this?'

'The evidence, sir. The cuts to Angus's back were made with near-surgical precision. The wings were to hand and were ready to be attached. The killer had the accelerant with him. The post he was attached to. The cable ties that held Angus to the cross member nailed to the post. That all speaks of preplanning to me. He was organised; I don't believe for one second that killing his victim in that way was something the killer did on a momentary whim. I think it was his plan all along, and I think he'll do it again.'

Phinn scratched at his jaw. 'What you're saying makes sense, but why are you so sure he'll try again?'

'Think about it, sir. From the moment the killer poured the accelerant down Angus's throat and lit it, to the point where Angus died would only have been a few minutes at most. Possibly less than a minute. Our killer wanted to make a dragon. His dragon died. Maybe after only a couple of fiery breaths. I think our killer would have been disappointed to lose his dragon so quickly after all his planning. After all his anticipation, it would have been a massive anticlimax. He'll still want to have a dragon. Therefore he'll try again.'

Beth watched in trepidation as Phinn looked at Thompson then O'Dowd. Saw the two nods he got.

'Right, Zoe, run with that theory. I'll get you some extra bodies to interview the evacuees and former servicemen once you've identified them. I'll also let you have the budget for a criminal psychologist.' Phinn looked at Beth with a mixture of exasperation and respect. 'I don't know whether I hope you're right or wrong, but that's neither here nor there. What matters is catching the killer before he strikes again. Work whatever hours you need to, I'll sign off on your overtime. I want this guy caught and caught soon. Do you understand me?'

Phinn didn't wait for an answer, he just turned on his heel and marched out of the office.

Beth sank to her chair relieved at the way things had turned out. She knew exactly what Phinn meant: if she was right they had a heinous killer to catch before he killed again. Yet if she was wrong, they would waste a lot of precious time and resources on her theory.

She caught Thompson's eye. 'Thanks for backing me up.'

'I didn't back you up, Young Beth, I just happen to agree with your thinking.'

'Either way, thanks.'

She turned her attention to the brochure she'd collected from Arthuret Hall and flicked through its pages until she found the name she was looking for. Two minutes later she was speaking to the secretary of a private school.

CHAPTER TWENTY-TWO

The waitress who brought his Caesar salad over was a pretty girl. She had an easy-going manner and a ready smile, but she didn't interest him. The delectable Sarah Hardy was the one who dominated his thoughts.

Since meeting Sarah, he hadn't been able to find any joy in his hobby. None of the other women he'd seen since had measured up to her.

Just a couple of days ago, the waitress would have been admired for her girl-next-door looks and the well-filled blouse. Now she held the same attraction as a rotting carcass.

He knew it wasn't the waitress's fault and he recognised that she had a pretty face and shapely figure. It was all to do with him, and the fact he didn't fancy her. Yet despite not feeling drawn to her today, he knew that in the normal course of events, he'd want to make her one of his angels.

Instinct turned his head when he heard the clack of high heels on the wooden floor. He saw a woman in a smart two-piece suit striding across the room towards the bar. The leather briefcase under her arm bulged, and she greeted the barman by name.

He watched as the barman came round and joined the woman at a vacant table. From where he was sitting, he could see the shape of her nylon-clad legs.

All he felt was sadness, bereavement even. The sleek and supple Ms Hardy had stolen his hobby and ground it into the dirt with a well-shod heel. Her beauty and radiance outshone that of every other woman he'd ever met. For him it was a cursed blessing. He'd met a woman who could dominate his thoughts whether awake or asleep, yet at the same time, her incredible beauty had denied him the appreciation of others.

Other women couldn't be compared to her. Their looks were something he could no longer revel in. Where he'd once seen beauty he now saw pale imitations. Perfections were now marred by obvious flaws. Mismatched dimples, an over-padded backside or clothing that didn't encase the body like a second skin were now noticed. Each tiny imperfection was overblown in comparison against the sublime Sarah. He often thought of her in alliterative terms. Sublime Sarah, statuesque Sarah, supple Sarah, even super-sexy Sarah.

If Sarah Hardy was a depiction of Helen of Troy, other women were the crude drawings of parents done by primary school pupils.

It pained him that he'd lost his appreciation for others. Many times he'd pulled out her card and thought about calling to cancel the test drive he had booked for Wednesday.

Something always stayed his hand though. He wasn't sure he could endure not seeing her again, but by the same token, he knew seeing Sarah again would make other women seem even less desirable.

With his mind in a quandary, he picked up his fork and speared a crisp piece of lettuce. Despite it having a liberal coating of Caesar sauce, it felt dry and arid in his mouth.

Sarah Hardy was the one thing in the world that now gave him pleasure. He knew as he crunched on a crouton that he'd have to see her again. Have to make her his chief angel, regardless of how much of himself he'd invested into identifying his other angels.

CHAPTER TWENTY-THREE

Beth was running the names of the evacuees from Rossall School through the registry of births, deaths and marriages and adding their names to her lists of those who were still alive or were deceased. The names of those who were still alive went onto a spreadsheet she was compiling. It included their addresses and, where known, contact numbers.

She also ran the names of the living through the PNC – Police National Computer – to see if any of the children who'd been evacuated from the private school had grown up to live a life of crime. Even with Arthuret Hall's history of ownership by someone with alleged gangland connections, it was a stretch to imagine that the offspring of some gangster or other had been sent to Rossall prior to being indoctrinated into the family business.

While it might be too simplistic or coincidental, it was something she hoped would prove to be true. That way they'd hopefully be able to solve the case before anyone else was hurt. It would also mean that she'd be the one to bring forth the connection which solved the case, even if it wasn't her idea.

Her spreadsheet was also arranged by proximity so those who'd remained or returned to the area were at the top of the list. While her notes were filling up, she realised almost none of them were still in the local area. Most of the names had moved south towards London as the lure of the capital and its promised riches for the well-educated had proven irresistible. Their addresses ringed London like a halo of respectability.

She rose to stretch her limbs and made the universal gesture at Unthank to see if he wanted a cup of tea. He stuck his thumb up and let a smile cover his weary face as he held his phone to his ear.

To Beth, Unthank was one of the good guys. His descriptions of people never failed to amuse her. He could sum up people with a deft turn of phrase which encapsulated their looks or personality in a way she could only dream of.

Her smile faltered as she wondered, not for the first time, how he'd describe her. A shake of the head dislodged the dark thoughts that his description of her would centre around her scarred cheek. This was information she didn't need to know, as possession of it would do nothing but harm. Her confidence might not be fragile, but neither was it cast iron.

As she made her way back with their drinks, some of her tea slopped over the rim of her mug and onto her hand. She managed to bite down on the swear word that leapt to her lips before it came out. It wouldn't do for the person Unthank was calling to hear it. While she'd had full cooperation from the people she'd spoken to at Rossall School, Unthank was getting the runaround from a series of bureaucrats.

Beth placed a mug next to Unthank's elbow and nodded at his smiled thanks. As he was a DC, the same as she was, she'd tried chatting to him, but while he'd always been polite, he'd not mentioned anything personal other than his fiancée, Lana. He didn't even say if they'd been to the pictures, or for a meal or anything like that.

A part of Beth couldn't help but wonder if Lana even existed. Unlike Thompson, there was no photo frame on his desk and he'd never shown her a picture of the two of them on his phone. It might just be that he was very private, or it might be that he was hiding something. Either way, she supposed she'd find out in due course.

CHAPTER TWENTY-FOUR

No matter how Beth had tried convincing her friends, none of them seemed to believe her when she'd told them how much of her job was about painstaking research and reading statements, reports and interview logs. She was sure they imagined that she spent her days kicking down doors and slapping cuffs onto people as she told them they were 'nicked'.

For some officers the drudge of compiling evidence to support theories was a necessary evil, but if she was honest with herself, sitting in a nice warm office with a computer in front of her was a lot better than wrestling drunks in the pouring rain.

Like every other officer who'd ever walked a beat, she'd endured abuse that was aimed more at the uniform, and what it represented, than the individual wearing it. Beth was proud of the fact she'd always managed to maintain her composure in the face of insults, but she had enough self-awareness to know that she'd been very close to snapping on several occasions.

Her brain was focussed on the spreadsheet she was compiling as she added every bit of information she could gather. For her, this was a new kind of puzzle and she revelled in the challenge. As horrific as Angus Keane's death was, Beth knew it also presented her with an opportunity to establish her own credentials and prove to O'Dowd that she was worthy of a place in FMIT.

Regardless of how his death may end up benefitting her, Beth's primary instinct was to make sure that Suzy and her daughters would know who'd taken their husband and father from their lives. Whether it offered them a sense of closure or not, as a police officer, it was as much as she could do for them.

Beth had no connection to Angus other than the fact she was part of the team tasked with investigating his murder, yet that didn't stop her from getting mental pictures of his dying moments and imagining that she could hear the gargled screams as his throat and mouth burned, as the fire was drawn down his throat into his lungs. She could see that her thoughts were shared by her colleagues too. Each of them wore a haunted look, although with everything that was going on with Thompson's wife, maybe the sense of isolation on his face wasn't just caused by work.

How it must be for Suzy to imagine her husband's death was something Beth couldn't begin to comprehend. As a couple they would have laughed, joked and faced life's hardships together. Their relationship may well have been fractious at times, but the way they kept patching things up spoke of an inherent love that neither could deny for long periods.

Suzy had gone into shock when O'Dowd had told her the gorier details. She'd sat there with a blank expression and tears pulsing down her cheeks as she'd heard without listening. It was bad enough to witness someone receiving the worst news, but when the news had to be garnished with unpalatable honesty about the way their loved one had died, it made the moment even harder.

This was a part of her job that Beth wouldn't discuss with her friends. It had felt wrong that she'd been present at what must surely have been the worst moment of Suzy's life, to then share that experience chatting over a cuppa or a glass of wine would remove the intimacy she'd felt. Besides, her two closest friends worked in offices and they couldn't begin to understand the toll police-work could take. Rather than burden them with the darkness of her job, Beth took lightness from her friends.

She knew that her parents would always listen if she needed to talk something out, but so far she'd always been able to deal with things herself. Always at the back of her mind was the knowledge that her mother had episodes of depression, and she tried to take care not to give her mother any triggers. The worst bout of depression Beth ever saw her mother suffer had been in the weeks after the bottle had slammed into Beth's face. Her mother had tried to be strong, tried to support Beth, but she'd been able to see past the façade of everyday cheerfulness and see the effort it was costing her mother.

Beth could have talked to her father in confidence, but she knew he worried about her and she didn't want to add to his worries by opening up to him. When he'd spotted that she was preoccupied or a bit down he'd always made a polite enquiry, but he'd also always given her enough space to shrug off his concerns with a disclaiming phrase like, 'don't worry, it's nothing I can't handle'.

How O'Dowd felt about having to be the one to give voice to another person's nightmare was something she didn't want to think about, yet she knew that one day her turn would come, and it would be she who was staring into fearful eyes and beginning a sentence with, 'I'm so very sorry to have to inform you.'

When that day came she would have to face it with the same strength and tenderness O'Dowd had shown to Suzy. Much as Suzy may have needed a shoulder to cry on, she didn't need a weak copper fighting her corner. What she required was a detective who'd be described with terms like dogged, resolute and determined.

All victims and their families deserved such a detective and that's what Beth strived to be. For the victims, their families and for herself.

O'Dowd was all the things Beth believed a good detective should be. Beth planned to watch the DI closely so she could learn from her, osmose her techniques and bear witness to all the traits that made O'Dowd's tenure as the DI in charge of FMIT so successful.

She knew that O'Dowd would have faults and flaws like any other human, but for Beth, there were a lot of things to admire.

CHAPTER TWENTY-FIVE

The tray Sarah lifted from the bed bore a plate that still held most of the meal she'd put on it. Her nana's appetite had all but failed as she neared the end of her life. Once a vibrant woman, possessed with an indomitable strength of character and a wickedly inappropriate sense of humour, she was now bedridden.

Six months ago, Nana's doctor had told her that she had less than a year to live. Like the battler she was, Nana had taken the news without complaint and had resisted all offers of help until she became too infirm to care for herself. It was at this point Sarah and her mother had tried to insist Nana live with one of them. The old girl had refused though, and Sarah and her mum now alternated nights at Nana's house. Social services had carers who'd visit in the mornings and at lunchtimes, but Nana refused all their attempts to bathe her. That task was just one of the many which fell to Sarah and her mother.

Between the two of them, they now had three houses to keep, a full-time job each and lives of their own to live. But they didn't complain, and just tried to remember that Nana had enriched their lives with imparted wisdom, sage advice and a constant supply of home baking that threatened to make their waistlines bulge.

Sarah filled a bowl in the shower and, using a facecloth, washed her nana down. She chatted as she worked, but the old lady had fallen asleep a minute after refusing the sixth forkful Sarah had tried to feed her.

Once she'd straightened the covers and laid the remote control for the TV next to the elderly woman's right hand, Sarah went downstairs and filled the kettle. While it boiled she ate the tuna salad she'd made for herself.

The nurse who visited daily had intimated the end was approaching. On a detached level, Sarah knew that her grandmother didn't have long left; her cheeks were sunken and she was spending more time asleep than awake. Her brain may have told her this, but her heart wasn't ready to admit defeat, wasn't ready to accept the inevitable and prepare to say goodbye.

As a distraction she flicked through a fashion magazine and then used her mobile to check Facebook. Neither held her interest for long, so she bent her mind to the contents of her wardrobe. She'd had a root through it before coming to Nana's and had selected three outfits she could wear on Wednesday. It was important that she struck the right balance between professional and alluring. The guy she wanted to snare was the kind of guy who'd be used to a certain amount of female flattery; while she may get his attention with a flash of cleavage, that wasn't enough for her: she wasn't interested in having a one-night stand, what she wanted was longer term.

While the timing couldn't have been much worse, she couldn't pass up this opportunity. There weren't a lot of men in the Kendal area she considered to be a decent catch, and therefore she couldn't allow someone else to snare him first.

Her ex always used to say her legs and backside were her best features and with this in mind, the favourite of her three options was a tight skirt that showed off her legs. The problem was, the only shoes she had that worked with the burgundy skirt were four-inch heels that were likely to cripple her if she wore them for a full day.

With luck, tomorrow may be quiet enough for her to sneak off and buy a pair of shoes with a lower heel.

'Sarah.'

The lone word had her on her feet and dashing up the stairs in an instant. Nana's voice was hoarse and strained. Were it not for the baby monitor hidden beside the bed, Sarah would have never heard her calling her name.

CHAPTER TWENTY-SIX

O'Dowd powered down her computer and gave Beth a long hard stare. Returning it, Beth saw that there were bags developing beneath the DI's eyes and that her shoulders had a stoop to them which she'd never seen before.

'Everyone else has beggared off, yet you're still here. I'd have been gone by now if Phinn hadn't rambled on needlessly for hours about the need to find our killer and left me to catch up on my paperwork after *he'd* gone home.' She brushed a hand through her hair. 'Jeez, I can't believe he thinks we need motivating after seeing the victim.' O'Dowd shook her head. 'Right then, Beth, cards on the table, you're smart, there's no denying that, you also have initiative and you see things more experienced officers need to have pointed out to them. What I want to know is, what drives you?'

Beth didn't have to think about the answer. 'I want to right the wrongs, ma'am. Too often people get off with whatever crime they've committed. That's not right. Not right by the law and certainly not right for the victims expecting justice.' She pointed at her scarred cheek with the pen she was holding. 'I didn't get it, so I know exactly what it's like to have your life turned upside down through no fault of your own. How it feels to see the people who've wronged you receive no punishment whatsoever.'

'I thought that might be the case, but I wanted to make sure. Just promise me one thing, Beth.'

'Ma'am?'

'What happened to you was terrible, but while the desire to bring justice is a wonderful thing, it needs to be guided by an open mind. I don't want you setting your sights on the wrong person rather than admitting you've got no leads. There no place on FMIT for vigilantes.'

Beth stood, struggling to keep her tone respectful. 'I'm not some crazy vigilante. I believe that victims deserve justice. Nothing more, nothing less.'

'So our little tiger cub has claws.' O'Dowd's smile was disarming. 'I'm pleased to see it. Sit back down, Beth, and wipe that scowl off your face. You've just been tested, don't turn a pass into a fail.'

Beth sat and turned back to her screen.

O'Dowd called over, 'That list you mentioned earlier, have you finished it?'

The reason she was here so late was to finish working on the list of evacuees. 'Not yet, but I'll have it done in another hour or so.'

'Good lass. Do that and then bugger off home. We'll be going through it in the morning with a nit comb.'

'What are your thoughts, ma'am?'

O'Dowd rubbed her eyes before answering. 'My experience tells me that until we get something more concrete to pursue, we need to follow every lead we get, examine every last piece of data.'

Beth returned to the screen and typed in the name of the next evacuee. The result spat out by the computer made her add the boy's name to the deceased column. Then she started on the list of the teachers who'd travelled with the children to continue their education and the locals brought in to care for them. She gasped when she saw a name connected to the evacuees. Beth dashed to the corridor, but was too late. O'Dowd had left for the evening.

Her discovery would have to wait until morning.

CHAPTER TWENTY-SEVEN

Beth took a break to make herself a cup of tea and strode around the office while the kettle boiled. Her mind was awash with details of the evacuees but she knew she needed to shift her focus for a short period.

It wasn't that she was fatigued by the amount of information, it was more that she knew that her brain sometimes worked best if she wasn't thinking directly about the matter in hand. Instead she let her mind go back to what Unthank had unearthed while she and Thompson were at the mortuary.

He'd been given the task of tracing Angus's last days and had pinpointed the time of Angus's disappearance. Angus had moved to his mother's house on Saturday, and had failed to show up for work on Tuesday morning; he had been working on the extension he was building until five the previous day. Suzy had told Unthank he'd called his daughters that evening around six and had then gone to the pub as he always did on a Monday night. She'd asked him to come home and talk to her but he had refused and they'd exchanged a series of harsh words that culminated in him hanging up on her and switching off his phone.

The landlord of The Globe had confirmed Angus's presence. Monday was darts night and Angus was a key player in the darts team. He had supped a few pints, played his darts and was last seen heading towards Longtown's takeaway kebab house.

Unthank had traced him to the takeaway and he'd followed the route Angus would have taken to get to his mother's house.

The news hadn't been good.

Angus's mother lived in a house 200 metres beyond the town boundaries, a good twenty-minute walk from the kebab shop. The road was tree-lined; therefore it would be easy for someone to ambush Angus. The fact he'd a few pints on board would make the killer's task easier.

To Beth's way of thinking, it was a perfect storm. A tipsy, if not outright drunk Angus, alone on a deserted road, his mind preoccupied with the latest fight with Suzy. He'd be easy pickings. Unthank had covered the bases and got a team of officers doing door-to-doors along the route, but so far, their reports had yielded nothing.

The triangulation of Angus's mobile showed he'd left it in his mother's house when he'd gone to play his darts match. Suzy didn't have a spare key, and they'd had to wait for a locksmith to open the door so they could find Angus's phone. Digital Forensics had it now and once its secrets had been mined, they might have some more leads to follow.

Beth read over the notes she'd taken. Before she presented anything to O'Dowd and the others, she needed to make sure of her facts, be confident that she'd followed all the correct procedures and that she hadn't overlooked anything.

She'd tried calling O'Dowd, without success, as the implications of her discovery became clear. In the absence of O'Dowd, she'd tried speaking to a chief inspector who was on duty, only to be brushed off with a curt dismissal that her theory could wait until morning. She'd tried to argue her case, but he'd pointed at the door of his office while looking at the papers on his desk. As Beth had stomped her way back to the FMIT's office, she hadn't been able to argue with Unthank's description of the humourless chief inspector as a stand-up comedian who didn't know it was time to sit down.

Now with all her facts together she was certain of her theory. All of it made sense and whichever way she looked at it, she couldn't find a flaw.

Another idea struck her, but rather than wait for her computer to power up again, she decided to use her phone. The information she needed would be found on Google rather than any of the police systems or databases anyway.

Beth ran a series of searches on the effects of swallowing flammable liquids that were then ignited. She knew that Dr Hewson could give her the same information, but she wanted to do her own research, so that when his report came in she'd better understand it.

With a few extra scribbled pages added to her thick bundle of notes, Beth stood, pulled on her jacket and set off for home. A look at her watch told her she had to be back there in seven hours, but that didn't worry her. She was used to six hours' sleep a night and could manage for the best part of a week on four.

Beth knew that tonight she'd be lucky to get more than four hours the way her brain was firing. She'd experienced a buzz during other investigations, but none had energised her the way this case did. Despite the tiredness and the tedium of some of the tasks, she felt more alive than ever. Her pulse raced and there was an unfamiliar spring to her step. The anticipation of this feeling was just one of the reasons she'd applied to join FMIT.

Beth flicked on the TV and channel-hopped until she found repeats of a sitcom she'd seen a dozen times before. It was the televisual equivalent of a comfort blanket and required no mental effort from her as she watched the familiar characters go about their lives. A half hour later when she climbed into bed, her brain still wasn't ready to shut down.

While Angus Keane was in his mid-forties, it was still too early in the investigation for them to work on the assumption the killer would strike again and assign a type to his choice of victim. What she couldn't shake from her mind's eye was the mental snapshot of Angus's daughters. Their father had been taken from them and it was up to her and the others in FMIT to at least give them the closure of knowing the person who'd killed him was locked up in jail.

As well as shelves of puzzle books, the bookshelf she had in her bedroom was filled with books about serial killers. Some focussed on one particular killer while others looked at many. She had a fascination with serial killers and had read up on every one she could.

Other than Harold Shipman, all the British cases that she could think of which involved multiple murders had young women or children as their victims. From what she could remember from her training, and the manuals and books she'd read, she also knew that a high percentage of serial killers had a sexual element driving them. Whether it was a desire to have sex outside accepted societal norms, or just a desire to have someone beyond their reach, they'd capture their victims and then rape and kill them.

Beth knew it was a sad fact of life that too often women were blamed for their rapes or sexual assaults. A short skirt or a revealing top were used as excuses by the vermin who preyed on women. They'd say the girl or lady in question was too drunk to remember giving consent, that their clothes and flirtatious behaviour were giving men a come-on.

None of the excuses washed with Beth. For her, no meant no.

The men in her social circle all held the same view, which is why she'd kept in touch with them after leaving school. They were decent and saw a drunk woman as a drunk person, not as an object to be used for their gratification. Beth's male friends talked to her face and listened to her views, treating her as an equal.

Sadly though, she knew her male friends and family members weren't typical of all men. There were still those who held the genuine belief that women were inferior to men and should know their place. These unenlightened fools were the problem.

They were the vultures, the carrion who preyed on vulnerabilities and insecurities. They were the ones who controlled their wives or girlfriends, the ones who dominated supposed loved ones in the name of masculinity. To Beth they weren't men, they were prehistoric beasts who were still millennia away from discovering fire and the wheel.

She'd had her share of encounters, the same as every other woman on the planet. An unwelcome hand on her backside in a crowded place, the leering gazes delivered without discretion as one lecherous fool or another talked to her chest or legs rather than her face. Beth remembered her brief experience as a model for online stores and various amateur photographers. She could never know for certain, but she was sure she'd lost a number of modelling jobs by rejecting the overtures made to her by promoters and organisers.

Those were as bad as her experiences had got though.

It pained Beth that women had to always be conscious of their surroundings and worried how they were perceived by men. She believed that everyone had the right to feel safe, but sadly, that's not how things were.

As these thoughts went through her head, she hit on a realisation. When she was on a night out, she'd always get a taxi to take her home. What if Angus had done the same thing?

Yes he may have been snatched from the street, wherever he was working, or his mother's home, but that was unlikely to happen in a residential area. Plus, it was the best part of a mile from where he'd got the takeaway to his mother's house. Who would he trust? Two answers: someone he knew, or someone whose job it was to ferry people around. Namely, a taxi. It was the perfect cover for someone looking to abduct people. Angus's killer may have posed as a lost driver asking for directions, but she didn't think Angus would have got into a stranger's car.

She made a mental note to pass on the idea to Unthank and closed her eyes.

CHAPTER TWENTY-EIGHT

O'Dowd scowled around her yawn as she trundled into the office and dumped herself into her chair. Her eyes were red and there was a whiff of alcohol crawling out beneath her perfume.

'Right my little bunch of reprobates, today is the day we catch a killer.' A finger was pointed at Thompson. 'Have you learned anything new?'

'Not yet. Paul has come up with the theory that it may have been a taxi which picked Angus up.'

O'Dowd scrunched her nose in thought. 'Makes sense. He'd trust a taxi. Nice thinking, Paul.'

'Actually, ma'am, it was Beth's idea not mine.'

'You never told me it was Young Beth's idea.'

Beth felt her temper rise when she heard Thompson's sneered rebuke of Unthank the moment he realised it'd come from her. 'I just put myself in his place. Thought about whose car I'd get in if I was in his position.'

'You could be right.' O'Dowd turned to look at Thompson. 'Get onto the CCTV boys, get them to pay close attention to any taxis that left that area.'

'Already done, but I doubt we'll get much. There's only one camera in Longtown and it looks along the A7. We'll see if any taxis turned onto Moor Road, but that's all. I was going to get onto the taxi companies, but then I realised it would probably be a waste of time.'

Beth was about to ask why, when she realised the answer to her question. No driver working for a firm would take unsolicited pick-ups – only the black cabs in Carlisle did that – therefore the person who picked up Angus would more likely be working for themselves. There were a couple of dozen independents in Carlisle and probably only a couple of one-person operations in a place as small as Longtown. Once Unthank had spoken to them all, she'd get his notes and add them to her spreadsheet in case one of them had a connection to Angus.

O'Dowd fixed Thompson with a look. 'So what are you doing?'

'I've asked Paul to contact the council licencing office when they open at nine. Once we know the name of every independent registered taxi in the area, we'll run a trace on where their mobiles were. With luck one will be a match for Angus's movements and we'll have our murderer identified.'

O'Dowd jabbed her pen towards Unthank. 'Don't bother calling the council office. Get down there in person. Shout all you need to, and if you're not getting results, call me. I'm in the mood to shout at someone today.'

Thompson left the room with Unthank striding after him.

Beth wanted to speak, but was afraid of how O'Dowd would respond. The DI was slamming papers about and looked as if she was getting ready to explode. Until she knew the reason for O'Dowd's anger, Beth planned to tread with great care.

'Right then, Beth. Spill it. You're sitting there itching to say something. I just hope it's to do with the case.'

'Angus Keane's grandmother used to be a cook at Arthuret Hall. She worked there when they housed evacuees.'

O'Dowd's eyes lit up for the first time that morning. 'Is she still alive?'

'Yes. I've traced her to an old folks' home.' Beth averted her eyes from O'Dowd. 'I called Angus's wife when I learned of this connection. She doesn't know anything, but Angus's mother will be home tomorrow.'

'Tomorrow? Her son has been brutally murdered and she's not back until tomorrow? What the hell is wrong with some people?'

Beth picked her words with care.

'She's driving back. Apparently, she winters in Spain every year and drives so that she has a car and she can take her dogs with her.'

O'Dowd harrumphed as she collapsed into her seat.

'There's something else, ma'am. One of the evacuees, a George Bellingham, has done time for arson. Admittedly it was back in the seventies, but still…'

'He's got to be too old to be the killer; I mean, he's bound to be at least mid-seventies by now. Give him a quick look over in case he's put the killer up to it. What else do you know about him?'

'Not a lot.' Beth made a sheepish gesture. 'I didn't want to spend too much time looking at him until I had gone through the whole list. Since he came out of prison, he has worked for a firm called RGKMS Limited and he's listed as a director on their Companies House profile, but there's no website for the company on Google, and when I did a Street View on their registered address in Manchester, it's nothing more than an abandoned warehouse.'

'So, we've got the dinner lady's grandson turned into a dragon, and a man who likes to play with matches. Our arsonist knows Arthuret Hall and has a derelict building as his business address.' O'Dowd grimaced. 'That speaks of organised crime to me. Like the building it uses as an address, RGKMS Limited may be a shell.' She pointed at Beth's computer. 'What did the PNC say about him?'

'Just the arson.'

'What about HOLMES?'

The Home Office Large Major Enquiry System allowed all the police forces in the UK to simultaneously access information connected to large investigations, such as murder cases. Its database held case notes and details of all people connected with any particular case, and allowed officers to follow cases in real time.

'I didn't find anything. I've sent an email to his local force asking if he's on their radar.'

'Good. If you haven't heard anything by noon, follow it up with a call.' O'Dowd took a noisy slurp of the coffee she'd carried in with her. 'C'mon then, let's go and see Granny Keane. With luck she'll still have her wits about her.'

CHAPTER TWENTY-NINE

Pine View Residential Home for the Elderly was everything Beth expected it would be and nothing more. It carried the look of a former hotel; one side was backed against an industrial estate, while the front had a road, a stone wall, and a view of a strip of pine trees that was just thick enough to obscure the view of the fields beyond it.

Other than cars passing by, there was nothing for the residents to look at. The frontage was more car park than lawn and there was a narrow flowerbed containing not quite enough flowers to hide the weeds.

Beth stood to one side as O'Dowd pressed the bell and waited. A shadow appeared behind the door's frosted glass. When the door was eased open there was a rasping squeak as the hinges protested.

'Sorry. Visiting's at ten. No exceptions.'

O'Dowd's foot thumped against the closing door as she lifted her warrant card. 'Police. We're here to speak to Mavis Keane.'

The care worker pulled a face. 'You'd best come in then.'

As she stepped inside the old folks' home, Beth was struck by the banality of the place. It was held in a time warp. All the ladies wore floral dresses and the two men had slacks pulled up over their bellies. The air hung with the antiseptic smells of liniment and detergent with an undertone of fried bacon. A wall-mounted TV blared out the last remnants of a breakfast show presented by a smug man in a crisp suit and his put-upon co-host.

The care worker led them along a corridor. 'She's just down here.'

'Thanks.' Beth spoke before O'Dowd could unload on the care worker. 'What's her state of mind?'

A malicious smile spread across the care worker's face as she stopped and opened a door without knocking. 'See for yourself.' With the door swung wide, the care worker leaned a shoulder on the wall where she could oversee her charge.

As Beth followed the DI into the room she saw Mavis Keane wasn't going to be much use to their enquiries. The elderly lady lay on a surgical bed which had both guard rails lifted to prevent her from falling out. At the foot of the bed, she saw a red light indicating it was powered by electricity. The only reason she could think of for this was that the bed was a hospital-type which moved its base so as to prevent its occupant getting sores. Therefore Mavis Keane must be more or less immobile.

'Hello, Mrs Keane? Mavis?'

Beth marvelled at the way O'Dowd had the self-control to park her anger and use a soft tone. It was a skill she knew she'd have to master if she was to succeed as a detective. Various situations called for different tactics and her own emotions would always have to take second place to the needs of the investigation.

The woman's head turned to look at them. 'Are you doctors? HELP! There's doctors in here. I don't want them touching me.'

'We're police. We have a few questions to ask you. Do you think you can help us?'

Mavis shrank her head back as far as her frail body allowed, her eyes suspicious in a fearful face. 'You're not doctors?'

'No. We are police officers. We're here to ask you some questions about your grandson.'

'I haven't got a grandson. Nor a son. Who are you? Are you doctors? If you are doctors, my bunions are killing me. Can you take a look at them?'

While nobody had said as much, it was clear that Mavis hadn't been told about her grandson's death, or in her confused state the news hadn't registered. There were no family photos in the room and the old girl appeared to live in a world populated only by doctors. O'Dowd shot Beth a look full of exasperation.

Beth took the cue and stepped forward a half pace. Mavis had turned her head to face the far wall. Her white hair was so sparse Beth could see her scalp between the strands.

Perhaps a little role play might trigger something. 'Mavis, do you remember working up at Arthuret Hall with me?'

'As a doctor? You're a doctor, aren't you?' Mavis's voice went from confused to proud. 'I used to be a doctor.'

Beth painted a smile on her face and tried to layer it into her voice. 'No, silly, we worked in the kitchens there. You were cooking and I had to do the dishes. Surely you remember me?'

Mavis's face lit up. 'Joanie, is it really you, Joanie?'

'It is. Do you remember feeding all those kids? I certainly remember washing all their plates.'

'I didn't feed any kids.' Mavis's head rolled to face Beth and she fixed her with a proud stare. 'I was a doctor. You're not a doctor. You're probably not even a nurse.'

Beth felt O'Dowd's fingers give a gentle pull at her arm. When she turned to look at her boss she saw nothing but sadness and pity in her eyes. It was clear Mavis's mind had failed her, and now all her thoughts were about doctors. Had it not been for the handwritten nameplate on the door, Beth would have suspected the surly care worker had brought them to the wrong room out of spite.

As she walked back to the car, Beth pondered on the futile existence of Pine View's residents. There would be infrequent visits from relatives they no longer recognised, regimented days and carers who earned minimum wage washing them down with a haste and roughness borne of uncaring indifference.

Their days would blend into uniformity with the only highlights the addition of a new face. They'd also witness the decline of others, notice the empty chair or see a place at the table no longer set at meal times, and they'd wonder how long it would be before their space at the table became unoccupied.

Once they were in the car, O'Dowd pulled out the list of people they had to talk to. Each one had a connection with either Angus Keane or Arthuret Hall. The list had been compiled from conversations the Family Liaison Officer had had with Suzy and from things the Digital Forensics Unit had found on Angus's laptop. As they drove away from Pine View, Beth vowed to herself that, when her time came, she'd have to find a way to make sure she didn't end up in a place like that. It wasn't so much God's waiting room, as the outer circle of Dante's hell.

CHAPTER THIRTY

The man picked his way through the house. He didn't get many visitors as he'd crossed swords with the few members of his family that remained. His list of friends was non-existent, that's why he trawled for angels to admire. When he opened the door he was met with a pair of women he didn't know. The older one was holding out a wallet containing some kind of identification. She didn't warrant the time it took him to look past her and see her companion.

The younger of the two women was stunning, a rival for Sarah Hardy in every way. While her trouser suit hid the shape of her body, he could see from her posture that she was lithe and his imagination filled in the blanks for him.

'DI O'Dowd and DC Young.'

It was the older one who spoke. She confirmed his name and he nodded agreement. His first thought was that one of his angels had made a complaint against him. It wouldn't be the first time.

'How can I help you?'

'You did some work a few weeks ago with an Angus Keane. Can you confirm that you and he didn't part company on the best of terms?'

The older woman looked past him into the house. His manners told him that he should invite them in. He would have done so, but he didn't want the junior one to see the mess.

'Well, what have you got to say?' The DI's tone was full of aggression, making the man feel there was an unspoken accusation.

'Angus and I never did see eye to eye for very long. We worked together on and off for years. He'd get me in on jobs where he needed an extra pair of hands. Problem was, he was years younger than me and he expected me to put in the same hours he did, and work at his pace.' He shook his head in sadness. 'I'm afraid time has caught up with me and I'm not as fast, or as strong as I once was.'

'Is that why you fell out?'

DC Young's voice was soft and there was only a trace of a Cumbrian accent to it. He wished he'd put on better clothes, maybe a tie, certainly a clean shirt instead of the grubby T-shirt he wore. A part of him wanted to invite them into his home regardless of the mess. To have such a beautiful woman in his home would be a high he could savour for months.

'It was. Except, it wasn't so much of a falling out as a parting of ways.' He used a thumbnail to scratch his ear. 'I told him I was too old to work as hard as him and that in future he'd be better off getting someone who could. I shook his hand and wished him well.'

'Are you sure that's the way it happened?' DI O'Dowd's eyes were full of suspicion.

'Yes, I am. He may have told it differently, but that's how it happened. He's more of a private ranter than an arguer. He probably went home and told his wife I'd let him down. Can you tell me why you are asking these questions?'

The beautiful DC turned to face him. 'Angus Keane has been found dead and we have strong reason to believe he was murdered.'

'That's terrible.'

He felt one of his hands lifting to his mouth, but his mind was elsewhere. It was busy trying to work out if the shock he felt was his response to Angus's murder, or whether it was to do with the destruction of DC Young's left cheek.

To him, the idea that looks like hers were damaged was nothing less than sacrilege. That her scars looked as if they were the result of a brutal attack was an affront to his very being. It was all he could do to tear his gaze away from the scar and look downwards to let the desecration to her face tumble from his eyes.

He could feel his temper rising and was aware he must contain it. The police were here pursuing a suspect. Should he let his temper display itself he'd put his name at the top of their list. That would never do.

'Do you have any idea who Mr Keane may have fallen out with?'

The man pulled his attention back to the DI and focussed it on her question.

'Not really. He was a hard taskmaster, but otherwise he was a decent guy who got on with pretty much everyone. I know he had a few ups and downs with his wife.' He liked that line. It shifted blame away from him. 'They had something of a volatile relationship.'

'So we've heard.'

The DI's comment was laced with a substantial level of dryness. As far as he was concerned, she could never be an angel. She didn't have the looks or the personality. Sarah Hardy did. As did DC Young.

'Are you able to account for your movements over the last week?'

The man stiffened, this was a dangerous question. One he knew must be answered with care.

'I can.' He gave a smile he hoped would come across as self-deprecating. 'I live alone, so I'm afraid I've nobody to verify what I say, but I go out for lunch and dinner most days. I have receipts that show where I ate.'

He saw the dumpy DI exchange a look with the gorgeous DC. Caught the fractional shake of the head and realised he was being discounted as a suspect.

After watching them walk back to their car, he shuffled into the house and took a seat in his chair. He let his mind wander to the place where he kept his angels. There was a new one now. A special one who needed more care than the others.

DC Young was more than worthy of her status as an angel, even with her scarred cheek. To him the disfigurement only accentuated the beauty of the other side of her face. In his mind, the injury was fixable and would heal with love and adoration. She was an angel with a broken wing. Treated properly, she would once again fly.

He'd seen enough wounds in his time to recognise her scar was caused by an unconventional weapon such as a broken glass or bottle. As he lit a cigarette, he turned his mind to her psyche, and speculated how a young woman would have coped with such a dramatic change to her looks.

There was also her choice of career to consider: had she picked up the injury separating a bar fight, or had it been with her when she joined the police? Either way, she'd chosen to continue meeting several new people every day. To have them appraise her and see the result of what must have been an agonising injury. That spoke of bravery and he liked the idea of his angels possessing courage.

Another point to consider was her relationship with her boss. There was the natural deference of the subordinate, along with something more. He got a sense that despite being several inches taller than her boss DC Young looked up to her DI.

Their dynamic was an interesting one; the DI was grumpy and irascible. A trait he put down to having a younger, fitter and far more attractive woman alongside her. It would grate on any woman to have an angel beside them for comparison. They'd always come off second best, and he could tell that even twenty years ago, when she was in her prime, DI O'Dowd wouldn't have been comparable to her protégé.

That had to be a source of resentment, of bitterness at the genetic lottery favouring someone else more than her. Now there she was, her looks fading, grey hairs and crow's feet appearing as life's stresses took hold of her.

While the angel's eyes held a certain amount of sadness, they also showed intelligence, drive and a sense of purpose. He could tell she had ambitions, goals. The DI would recognise this too, feel threatened by it.

How long she tolerated the bright and beautiful creature at her heel before stomping on it was anyone's guess.

CHAPTER THIRTY-ONE

Beth and DI O'Dowd started their interviews by speaking to Arthuret Hall's gardener and the woman who manned the little shop and looked after the weddings.

The gardener had been seventy if he was a day and the arthritic way he'd moved put doubts into their minds as to his ability to overpower the younger and stronger Angus Keane. Beth couldn't help but think he was only still working at Arthuret Hall because he was knowledgeable about plants, rather than for his physical ability. There was also the chance that he was doing odd days for cash in hand.

When they'd spoken to the lady who dealt with the shop and the weddings, they'd instantly crossed her off their list. Ginny Anderson was a small woman who'd been gentle and unassuming. She'd cried the whole time they'd been speaking to her and had twittered about Arthuret Hall and the 'poor poor' victim more than she'd focussed on their questions.

Beth rapped her knuckles on the door of the next person on their list and waited for an answer. The door creaked open to reveal a man with a jaw decorated by sculpted stubble. 'What is it?'

The man had spoken a mere three words and Beth didn't like him. He was cocksure to the point of being arrogant. He wasn't interested in why they were knocking on his door and was treating them as if they were a nuisance.

'Are you Steve Jeffers?' O'Dowd flashed her badge at him.

'Yeah. What of it?'

'We'd like to ask you a few questions.' Beth liked the way O'Dowd had added an insistent edge to her tone. 'About a murder we're investigating.'

Jeffers folded his arms and rested a shoulder on the door frame. 'This ought to be good. C'mon then, let's hear what you've got to say.'

'Angus Keane was murdered at some point in the last week. According to his wife, you and he had words in a builders' merchant's yard.'

'I heard he was dead. Didn't know he'd been murdered.' Jeffers gave a shrug. 'That's a shame but it has nowt to do with me.' Another shrug. 'He and I had a disagreement. I tried to be civil, but he's a hothead and he turned a discussion into a slanging match when he started calling me names.'

Beth caught Jeffers's eye. 'What was the disagreement about?'

'He beat me to a few jobs.' Another shrug. 'It happens, but he was consistently getting jobs I'd priced for. When I made a couple of enquiries, I found his quotes were thousands of pounds cheaper than mine.'

'That must have annoyed you.'

'Like I said, it happens. When I saw him at Jewson's we had a bit of a craic as we always do and then I suggested to him that he might want to stop undercutting the rest of us. You have to work smart not hard in this business.'

'What did he say to that?' Beth could guess the answer, but she wanted to hear Jeffers's version.

'He said that I was too dear and that I should lower my prices. We argued back and forth for a while and then when he started calling me names I got in my van and left. If he won't listen to reason that's his problem, but there's no way I was going to stand there while he insulted me.'

'The jobs he undercut you on, did losing out on them harm your business?'

Jeffers gave a short laugh. 'Fuck no. They were good earners that I'd have liked to have picked up, but I won't be going bankrupt just because I didn't get them. I *do* work smart as well as hard.'

Beth tried a couple more questions, but it was clear to her that O'Dowd had lost interest. Jeffers might be the kind of rogue who overcharged his customers, but his motive for killing Angus was tenuous at best. People killed for love, for revenge and for money, but when the reason was money, it was generally for far greater sums than the few thousand Jeffers had missed out on due to Angus undercutting him.

Beth approached the reception desk a half step behind O'Dowd. The hotel they were in was a plush one overlooking Lake Windermere. The VisitEngland placard behind the counter showed four stars and Beth could see why. Everywhere she looked she saw clean lines and tasteful furnishings. The watercolours on the wall depicting Lakeland scenes looked to be originals rather than prints.

O'Dowd leaned on the counter and addressed the young receptionist. 'We're here to see Lawrence Eversham. Is he around?'

The over-presented receptionist flushed a little and glanced at a wall clock. 'I'm afraid he's in a meeting with our GM.'

'Interrupt him.' O'Dowd laid her warrant card on the counter. 'It's important.'

The receptionist hesitated, licked her lips and looked towards a door behind the reception. Beth didn't know if the girl was looking for help or hoping the door would open and Eversham would come striding out to solve her dilemma.

'Do I have to mention wasting police time to make you interrupt him?'

Beth kept her face neutral, but she was taken aback at the change to O'Dowd's personality. She understood the pressure the DI was under, but while O'Dowd might be brusque at times, in the short time she'd worked with her, Beth had never heard her be so rude to members of the public. She wondered if it was because every one of the potential suspects they'd spoken to this morning had turned out to either have alibis, or no discernible reason to kill Angus Keane. This would be their sixth call and they were still no further forward than before they started.

The gardener and shopkeeper at Arthuret Hall had been dismissed, as had the rival builder, Steve Jeffers. The man who'd worked with Angus hadn't panned out, and neither had the electrician who'd crossed swords with Angus over the late payment of an invoice. The electrician had admitted that he'd been at fault for the argument and that he'd planned to apologise to Angus the next time he'd seen him.

The receptionist lifted a phone and pressed a couple of buttons with a look of resentful defeat pushing to get past her thick layer of make-up. She spoke a few words and then adopted a pained expression.

'Mr Eversham will be with you in a minute or two. Can I get you any refreshments?'

'No thanks.'

Beth leaned against a wall and puzzled about the DI's agitation while O'Dowd paced back and forth across the reception floor.

After a couple of minutes a well-dressed man appeared. He wore the typical country-gentleman's uniform of corduroy trousers and Barbour shirt beneath a tweed jacket. All that was missing to complete the image of landed gentry, was a shotgun slung under an arm and a pair of Labradors at his heel.

'I'm Lawrence Eversham, how may I help you?' The welcoming smile he gave them was as suave as the rest of him, even if it was as false as the receptionist's nails. His eyes gave a cursory glance at their warrant cards.

Beth made sure she beat O'Dowd to the answer. 'Perhaps we could go somewhere private.'

Considering the way her boss was behaving today, there was every chance she'd start firing questions at Eversham in front of his receptionist. While catching someone off guard was never a bad thing, putting them in what they may consider to be a humiliating position wasn't always the best idea.

Eversham gave a nod and led them to a small office. Judging by the room's décor, it was used as a place to take complaining guests away from the reception counter, conduct private meetings with sales reps, and if the brochures and photo albums were anything to go by, sign couples up for the weddings of their dreams.

As soon as the door closed, O'Dowd rounded on Eversham. 'You hired Angus Keane to do some work for you, then argued with him about the agreed price. I've seen the emails you exchanged with him. You were angry in those emails. Some might say that a number of your comments were libellous.'

'I beg your pardon. You're here because I complained about a job running over budget?'

'No. We're here because the man you argued with was killed. Murdered actually.'

Beth saw Eversham's face blanch a couple of shades. 'I'm terribly sorry to hear that. What an awful thing to happen. His poor family.'

O'Dowd waited and looked at Eversham until he caught up. To Beth's mind it was a good tactic, not only could the DI monitor his reaction, she could react to whatever he said, as like a chess player, she was several moves ahead. Beth made a mental note of the way O'Dowd had sprung the trap.

Realisation dawned in his eyes. 'I'm guessing you're here because you think I had something to do with it. Am I right?'

O'Dowd nodded, letting silence be her friend and Eversham's enemy.

'I'm sorry, but you're mistaken. I may drive a hard bargain in my business dealings, but I am no killer.' Eversham spread his arms wide. 'Look around you, ladies. I'm the sole owner of this hotel and three others like it. Each has an annual occupancy rate in excess of 85 per cent. I also own a large country house, fifteen farms and around a hundred holiday homes. In short, I may pinch pennies from time to time with those I do business with, but a disagreement over a mere £1,300 is not going to leave me feeling murderous. It may be impolite, or even crass to say so, but I have millions in my bank account. Why would I risk everything because a bill went up by a measly £1,300?'

Beth saw that O'Dowd was floundering in the face of Eversham's logic, so she put forward a question of her own.

'What if the reason you killed him was more to do with principle than money? We've read all of the emails between you and the deceased. His remarks were a lot more vicious than yours. With your wealth, you're a powerful man. Perhaps you took issue with his choice of words, the names he called you and the tone of his emails. From what you say, your life is a privileged one. I'd also imagine that you took exception to one of the little people, an "oik" as I seem to remember you called him in one email, laying into you the way he did. A man of your status shouldn't have to stand for that. How dare he speak to you like that? Maybe that's why you killed him.'

Beth knew she was taking a chance by speaking to Eversham like that, but projecting the suspect's thought processes in this way was a recognised technique for tricking people into making an incriminating admission.

So far as Beth could tell, Eversham's laughter was genuine. It was filled with the kind of mirth that couldn't be faked.

When he addressed Beth he had to talk round his smile. 'My dear, you really should do your homework. Yes, my family was quite wealthy when I was growing up, but all they had was the house we lived in. My father died when I was six, so it was just me and my mother. All my businesses are ones I started myself or bought over. I've worked since I left school. Worked hours that would floor most people. Do you think I built all those businesses up without falling out with a few people? Without being called all manner of names?' He flapped a hand in a dismissive gesture. 'Of course not.' He cast an eye at O'Dowd. 'I'm guessing you're the superior officer here. You might want to have a word with your junior. Explain how the big bad world really works before she gets herself into trouble and drags you down with her. I mean, imagine if someone she wrongly accused of murder was to complain to the chief constable at the golf club, you know, the way rich and powerful men do.'

As Eversham dismantled her theory, Beth felt her face begin to flush and a dull throb fire up in her scarred cheek.

The glower on O'Dowd's face suggested that she was in for an industrial-strength bollocking as soon as they returned to the privacy of the pool car.

The first salvos from O'Dowd were interrupted by the ringing of her mobile. 'This isn't finished.' O'Dowd jabbed at her phone. 'O'Dowd. What is it, sir?'

Beth watched as the DI listened. If the sudden paleness of O'Dowd's face was anything to go by, it wasn't good news.

The silence dragged on as O'Dowd kept her mobile to her ear and her mouth shut. When she did finally speak it was a simple acknowledgement that they would attend at once.

'Shit, shit, shit.'

'What is it, ma'am?'

O'Dowd rocketed the pool car out of the hotel's car park. 'We've got another two victims.'

CHAPTER THIRTY-TWO

Beth sat waiting until O'Dowd finished ranting about the two new victims. The fact they'd been found in the cellar of an abandoned country house was indicator enough to suggest why they'd got the call.

Like her boss she'd recoiled at the idea of further victims, but also so soon. If either body had wings on their back, it probably meant they'd been killed by the same person who killed Angus Keane.

'I mean, what the hell is going on? First Angus Keane and now another two victims have been discovered in the cellar of *another* old house. The chief super said that one of the bodies had been in there a good while. Fuck's sake, Beth. What kind of fucking maniac are we after? I mean, killing people is bad enough, but what's with the hiding them in cellars? And fuck only knows if he's burned out their throats and stuck wings on their backs too.'

Beth had to brace her feet against the footwell as O'Dowd stood on the brakes after entering a corner faster than was safe. 'Easy, ma'am.'

As soon as the words left her mouth, she knew they were a mistake. The DI wasn't in the mood for censure of any kind, let alone criticism of her driving from a subordinate.

'I have driven at speed before, you know.' The reprimand was delivered in a snarled tone. 'Instead of worrying about my driving, your time would be better spent thinking about how two more innocent people have lost their lives. About how we've no decent leads to follow and about how we can find a way to catch the killer.'

Beth kept her mouth shut.

With little information to go on, Beth's imagination ran free and she pictured the victims set out as Angus Keane had been. Maybe they too had spent their last moments on earth confused and terrified, perhaps thinking of their loved ones.

While O'Dowd's anger was directed at the impossibility of the case and the horror of the murders, the fury Beth could feel growing in her belly was aimed squarely at the killer. He was the one who'd chosen these victims, decided how they'd die and then executed them. The killer had to be stopped. For the victims; for the bereaved families; and for whoever the killer might go after next.

When all was said and done, Beth understood O'Dowd's fury and drive to catch the killer. That her boss had vented was natural, but it had gone on too long and had been too intense. After five or ten minutes, Beth found herself wondering if there was a secondary reason for the DI's lengthy rant.

O'Dowd gave no consideration to the car's suspension as she barrelled along the dirt track that led towards Highstead Castle. Potholes, ruts and the few level areas were all treated as if they were billiard-table smooth.

They were in an area of the county Beth was unfamiliar with. She was aware it existed, but as it lay off the motorway roughly halfway between Carlisle and Penrith, she'd never had cause to go there before. A network of narrow roads linked the tiny villages and the farms to the larger arteries of the M6, A66 and B5305. This area was the heart of Cumbria's farming community. These rolling hills lay home to cattle, dairy and arable farms, with the better-known sheep farms dominating the Lakeland Fells to the south-west and the North Pennines in the east. Beth could see the peaks of Blencathra and Skiddaw; as always, they gave her a sense of belonging. The Lake District was in her blood and she adored its beauty and majesty.

O'Dowd parked behind the CSI van and they both exited the car as the engine pinged its protest at O'Dowd's rough treatment. They nodded at the crime scene manager who logged their names and needlessly pointed the way to go.

There was a cluster of CSI technicians standing by the door to the house. Off to one side, a uniformed officer was speaking to a man who had two pointers flanking him. Even from a distance, the dogs looked well-groomed and of excellent breeding stock.

The building was more of a manor house than a fortified castle with crenelated walls and a central tower. To Beth it looked Georgian in design, and she supposed that like so many old houses it had been rebuilt, renovated or extended many times since its foundations were first laid. The term 'castle' was a misnomer, but like so many of Cumbria's country houses, it had more than likely been built on the ruins of a castle which dated back to the days when the Border Reivers were an ever-present threat.

Highstead Castle retained an imposing frontage despite being nothing more than a shell. It sat on higher ground than the lawn Beth and O'Dowd were crossing and looked down on them. Like Arthuret Hall, there was a grass fringe running along its wallheads. Each window was an empty hole depicting the shambles of the interior. At the left-hand side a tubular scaffold had been erected. It reached the tops of the walls, but Beth couldn't see anyone working on the house.

O'Dowd caught the eye of one of the CSI team. 'What's the score?'

'It's a disaster zone.' He pointed into the house. 'Owner's dog wandered off. When he went looking for it, he found it in the cellar barking its head off. He went in. Found two bodies and came out and called us.' He shook his head in disgust. 'The other bloody dog went in with him.'

Beth knew he wasn't really blaming the house's owner or the dogs. More that he was frustrated his job had been made harder. Two dogs and a civilian had trampled over his crime scene. He was used to forensic sterility and avoiding contamination, which meant he'd have to sift through the evidence and work out what had been carried in by the dogs and their owner.

'What's the cellar like?'

'It's a cellar of a house that's falling down.' Again his head shook. 'It's not what you'd call the safest place. Looks like the ceiling could collapse at any moment.' He pointed at Dr Hewson who was loitering amidst a cloud of vape smoke. 'He's itching to get in, but until we can get the fire brigade to put some props in there, the site has been closed off.'

'Nobody is stopping me.' O'Dowd reached into the back of the CSI van and grabbed an oversuit. 'You coming, Beth?'

Beth was already reaching for an oversuit of her own.

The place may be a little unsafe, but the owner had got in and out unscathed, and so had whoever had left the bodies. The chances of a collapse when they were in there would surely be minimal.

CHAPTER THIRTY-THREE

Beth followed O'Dowd along the footpads laid by the CSI team as they made their way to the cellar. Either side of them, knee-high nettles brushed against their trousers looking for bare flesh to sting.

The nettles dwindled as they made their way into the house, which, despite its name, Beth couldn't think of as a castle without an encircling wall complete with crenelated battlements. In a far corner there was a tree stump whose top showed bright yellow, indicating the recent attentions of a chainsaw. Large areas of the floor were covered with debris that had fallen from the wall tops and every one of the walls featured the pink sandstone used to construct the house. Regular holes cut into the walls marked where floor joists had been positioned and there were empty blackened pockets which had once been fireplaces.

Unlike Arthuret Hall, Highstead Castle didn't carry so much as a hint of eeriness. It was tranquil, benign and seemingly innocent. But while the house couldn't assume guilt, there was no question that someone was responsible for the bodies that lay in its cellar.

The footpads led to a doorway in a wall where a staircase stretched down to blackness and then stopped. O'Dowd's torch flashed across the rubble and weed-strewn steps. 'Bloody cowards. When we leave here, remind me to let that bunch of CSI chickens know a pair of girls had more guts than them.'

Beth didn't answer. Instead she pointed her torch at the stairs and picked her way down carefully after the DI. Cobwebs lined the corners between wall and ceiling, and there were large patches where the plaster of the cellar's ceiling had fallen away to expose the timber laths. There was scurrying as rodents retreated from the invasion of their domain. The air contained mould and decay and hung with a stench that was dark and malevolent.

As Beth reached the wall that ran to her right at the bottom of the stairs, she realised that despite the fact she was breathing only through her mouth, the smell was pushing insistently up her nose. In the absence of VapoRub, she pulled a packet of mints from her pocket and stuffed one up each nostril.

O'Dowd's torch began a slow anticlockwise sweep of the cellar. When it got to ten o'clock it picked out a body. A naked man.

Further round it swept, nine, eight o'clock, more than once it picked out a pair of eyes or a long tail, and then at seven, it picked out another naked form. This time it was a woman.

Together the two police officers stood at the foot of the stairs – O'Dowd had insisted they go no further so as to minimise their contamination of evidence – and shone their torches over the woman's body.

What Beth saw would live with her forever. The lower parts of the woman's legs were eaten away to the point of being skeletal, her arms hung from the ties binding her to the wall and while they couldn't see her face to judge her age there was a firmness to her form that suggested youth.

When their torches played over her back, Beth's gasp beat O'Dowd's by the merest fraction of a second. A pair of colourful wings were fixed there. To Beth they looked to have belonged to a parrot or some other exotic bird. Like the ones on Angus Keane's back, the wings were folded neatly against the body. There were areas on the woman's shoulders and neck which showed where rodents had climbed up and, having found a perch, gorged upon her bare flesh.

Something at the edge of the torch's beam caught Beth's eye and made her redirect her aim.

'Ma'am, do you see what I see?'

'If you mean the scorched effect on the laths by her head, then yes, I see it. Let's have a look at the guy now.'

Beth's torch found him first. He was tied to hooks, which she guessed once held cuts of meat or game birds. His arms were spread wide and there was not a stitch of clothing on him apart from laceless boots on his feet.

It wasn't the most striking thing about him though. That was the pink flesh which remained unsullied by decay. A number of bite marks covered his body, but unlike the woman in the opposite corner, at no point could Beth see bone.

Her torch crept up his body, past his genitals and over his taut stomach and hairy chest until it showed his face. His mouth was a blackened pit, with burn-blistered lips that had contracted back to expose every tooth in his mouth.

O'Dowd's torch then traced the outline of his body and, just as Beth expected, the tip of a wing protruded from his back. This wing bore no vibrant colours, instead it was made up of speckled brown shades designed to camouflage its owner rather than attract a mate.

Holding her torch away from her body, Beth gave the cellar another scan. As much as she wanted to leave and breathe fresh air again, there was something nagging at the back of her mind and she knew it was connected with a detail she'd just seen in the cellar.

The foot of the walls gave her no clue, so she lifted her torch and traced round the edge of the ceiling. Nothing. She zig-zagged the beam across the floor and still found nothing. Exasperated, she eased the torch around the room at waist height. When the beam returned to its original twelve o'clock position, she found what she was looking for.

There was a door handle protruding from the wall on their right.

CHAPTER THIRTY-FOUR

Beth nudged O'Dowd, eliciting a shriek and a curse, as she drew the DI's attention to where her torch was shining on the ground beside the door. There was a quarter circle where the door had scuffed its way through the detritus on the floor of the cellar when swung open.

'I hope to God I'm wrong, ma'am, but something tells me there's more than just these two bodies down here.'

O'Dowd gave a hissed sigh as her answer.

Beth eased past the DI and, with her torch pointing down, picked her way to the door. It was half rotted in its frame. She cast a look at O'Dowd, who'd followed, for permission, and once she'd seen the curt nod, wound her fingers around the handle.

When she swung the door to open it, it came free in her hands and toppled towards her. O'Dowd's shoulder was the first thing it hit before pivoting towards Beth and thwacking rotten timber into her forehead.

'Careful!'

There was more than admonishment in the DI's voice. Fear and disgust added layers, as did excitement.

Beth understood the emotions. She felt them too. Her pulse was racing at the horrifying thrill of finding dead bodies in such a derelict environment. The idea of breathing your last in such a place terrified her, but it was counteracted by the charge of excitement that came from the knowledge she was exploring a killer's stomping ground. Tracing his footsteps and looking for clues which would help her catch him.

With the door leaning against a wall, she flashed her torch into the opening. The remnants of a partition crossed the room and disappeared into blackness.

She inched forward, sliding her feet so she didn't trip over anything. As they bumped against something, her torch picked out a skeletal hand ahead.

Beth felt hot breath on her neck as O'Dowd crowded into her back.

'C'mon, move forward so I can get a decent look.'

A push on her back caused Beth to stumble forward before she could lift her foot over whatever it had butted up against.

She staggered three paces before gravity won its battle with posture. As she fell, Beth tumbled into the base of the partition. She had just enough time to duck her head into her shoulders so her face wasn't the first point of contact. She dropped the torch as her hands reached out to break her fall.

Even over her pained yelp, she heard the splintering of timber, and felt the whoosh of air caused by sudden movement and the pitter-pattering that forewarned an avalanche. She tried to stand so she could make a run for it, but she was trapped beneath what she guessed was the partition.

Beth thrashed for a moment to no avail. As the splintering sounds increased in volume, she did her best to curl into a ball and wrapped her hands over her head.

A loud crack filled the air and there was a sudden thumping on her body as the ceiling fell in on her.

The air was knocked from her lungs, and as Beth gasped for oxygen she inhaled through her nose. The relief of getting a precious breath was tainted by the foulness of the room and its contents permeating the air.

Now she had to fight the gorge rising in her throat, as well as the oppressive weight pushing down on her body. There was no way she could allow herself to be sick while trapped.

Beth forced herself to swallow the bile so she could concentrate on breathing again. She couldn't die in here. Wouldn't die in here. She refused to accept the possibility that she would die in this rat-infested cellar. Too many others had and she wasn't prepared to join them.

Something crashed against her head and she felt everything go fuzzy.

CHAPTER THIRTY-FIVE

The man who used a false name sat in his favourite chair and sipped from the mug of coffee he'd made himself.

He needed time to reflect, to regroup his thoughts and plan for what lay ahead.

That the police had visited him wasn't the greatest surprise. He'd expected it to happen at some point in his life. Just not so soon.

His plans wouldn't change, there was no call for alarm, but there was a call for caution. Selecting Angus Keane for his project had been delightful, but he now realised it had brought him the wrong kind of attention. He'd wanted to make a statement, with Angus, he just wasn't ready to be recognised as the speaker.

Still, he reasoned, the police had been on a fishing trip. Casting their bait onto his waters to see if he'd bite.

Like that was going to happen; he was too smart to be caught by a couple of women. One of them may have risen a few ranks, but if her age was anything to go by, she'd peaked at detective inspector. That meant she wasn't clever enough to play the game. And if she couldn't get herself up the police ranks, there was no way she was going to have the intelligence to catch *him*.

The younger one may be a different case. Her eyes held traces of wisdom and worldliness that belied her tender years. If they came to him again, she was the one who would bear the most watching.

The man's fingers drummed on his knee as he thought of her. The disfiguring of her face made him interested. He knew her surname was Young but he didn't recall her full name. His mind went back to her flashing the wallet with her badge at him. He visualised the moment and let his subconscious pull up the details. He'd only had a brief second to look at it and hadn't paid much attention, but in a flash he recalled her Christian name.

He closed his eyes in rapture as he thought of how delicious it would be to involve a police officer in his project.

The more he thought about it, the more the idea grew on him. It would be dangerous, audacious and very relevant to his project, but most of all, more than anything else, if it went to plan and he got away with it, he'd demonstrate his superiority. Prove that he was the cleverest. The best. The bravest.

Too many people looked at him in ways he didn't like. They were jealous of him. His money, his success in business. He'd show them all just how inferior they were to him. The snide looks would stop then. So would the whispering that he knew went on behind his back.

That Carleton Hall was police headquarters added an extra layer of deliciousness to the idea. To take someone from the police's stronghold and transfer them to a grand house of *his* choosing, turn them into a tribute and display them would prove his worth.

What a message it would send.

More than anything else he'd done, or planned to do, using DC Young as part of his project would deliver the message of his superiority. He would show them all. Every last one of his doubters. They may not know of his role in it, but they would all know about his project. Each would marvel at the man who led the police on the merriest of dances. Wonder who it was.

In his own secretive way he'd achieve infamy, a modern-day Scarlet Pimpernel, although Jack the Ripper would be a more accurate allusion.

He'd broken cover with Angus Keane. Left the builder in a place where he was sure to be found. After that he'd retreated back to the shadows for his next kill. There was no telling when the victims at

Highstead would be found, but that didn't matter to him. So long as he knew they were there, the project could continue.

The venues where he housed his darlings were chosen with care. They made a statement, although he doubted that anyone was clever enough to understand it. He had the site for his next display already earmarked, and it, far more than Arthuret Hall, would announce his presence to the world.

No longer would he be the boy who cowered in a cellar where his dragon of a mother couldn't find him.

CHAPTER THIRTY-SIX

Consciousness returned to Beth in a series of incremental stages. Her entire body ached, and when she teased her eyes open, there was nothing but blackness. A heavy weight pressed down on her body making it hard for her to move and tough to breathe. There was a muffled shout as someone called her name. She tried to shout in reply, but her mouth didn't produce anything beyond a croak.

For a moment Beth struggled to identify where she was. Why she couldn't move and why someone was shouting for her. She just wanted to wriggle herself comfortable, find somewhere she wasn't crushed and didn't have jagged things sticking into her.

Some of the weight shifted from her legs.

Again the voice shouted for her. 'Beth? Are you okay? Please, Beth, answer me.'

The shouts were punctuated by crashing sounds as weights were lifted from her body and tossed away.

It sounded like O'Dowd's voice. Why would she be trying to wake her?

'Ma'am?'

'Beth? Oh thank God you're alive.'

Why wouldn't she be alive?

It was when Beth drew a breath through her nose that her memory came back. The stench of death was a reminder like no other. She gagged and swallowed three times before she got control of herself.

Her breathing stabilised itself in the exact moment confusion became fear. She was trapped in a cellar with three dead bodies. O'Dowd was there and although she could feel an incremental lightening of the weight pinning her to the floor, it wasn't happening anything like quick enough for Beth.

Around her was blackness, death and decay. She lay in filth and detritus among the droppings of mice, rats and other wild animals. Fear turned to panic. She thrashed, squirmed and wriggled to no avail. Thanks to O'Dowd's efforts, her legs had some room to move but there was no space for her torso or arms to travel more than an inch before they met resistance.

A hand grabbed her ankle. Squeezed. Not hard, but there was enough pressure to offer comfort and support.

'Keep still. I'll get you out.'

'Hurry. Please hurry.'

Another brief squeeze was followed by the sounds of more debris being lifted from her. Beth could feel a continual easing of the pressure on her body as O'Dowd doubled her exertions as she fought to free her. Unable to have any input with the rescue, Beth lay still and concentrated on taking steady breaths and keeping her eyes pressed shut.

Beth felt her legs come free, but she lay still in case she kicked her rescuer. There were grunts and curses flooding from O'Dowd until all of a sudden there was silence.

Some rubble was lifted from her head and she saw the flash of a torch beam against her eyelids. When it shifted she opened an eye and saw O'Dowd illuminating her own face.

The DI had blood running from a cut in her forehead and she was grubby, but there was relief in her eyes.

'Beth, there's a large beam that's trapping you. It's too big for me to lift by myself, which means I have two options.' Even before she paused her sentence, Beth could see the hesitation on O'Dowd's face. 'I can go and get help. Or I can try to pull you out.'

'Please, don't leave me. I don't want to be left alone, not in here.'

The words were spoken before Beth had given any thought to O'Dowd's suggestions. There was no way she wanted to be alone down here. Not when she was surrounded by death.

Besides, how long would it take O'Dowd to persuade some of the men to come and rescue her? They may well refuse on the grounds of their own safety. It was a right they had. She and O'Dowd had taken a risk and it had backfired on them. They had to get themselves out of this. Beth wasn't an arch feminist, but neither did she want to come across as the kind of helpless bimbo who was forever needing a man to rescue her.

'Please, ma'am. Don't leave me.'

'Okay.' O'Dowd lay down the torch so it was illuminating them. 'I'm going to try and drag you out. Wriggle your body when you feel me pull. You ready?'

'Yes.'

Beth held her body tense and got ready to follow O'Dowd's instructions.

'On three.' She felt two hands wrap themselves around her right ankle. 'One. Two. Three.'

On three, Beth drove her arms upwards to minimise her width and thrashed her body while trying not to wrench her foot from O'Dowd's grip.

She felt herself slide about six inches before coming to a halt. As well as the distance travelled, she'd managed to roll herself from her left side onto her back. There were rocks and other things pressing into her back, but they were minor discomforts that were more than tolerable if it meant she'd soon be free.

'Again.' This time, O'Dowd tucked each of Beth's ankles under her arms and gripped her calves.

Even with all the other aches and pains, she could feel the DI's fingernails digging into her soft flesh.

'Three.'

O'Dowd's screamed grunt echoed round the cellar as she dragged Beth free.

As she was pulled along the floor, Beth could feel her jacket and shirt rucking up and scooping earth and other substances from the floor as her paper oversuit was now in tatters. It didn't matter. Neither did the scrapes the rocks left on her back. O'Dowd stopped pulling and buckled over, hands on knees gasping for breath.

With only her head left beneath the beam, Beth eased first one arm to her side, then the other. She put both hands on the beam and pushed herself free.

When she clambered to her feet, O'Dowd enveloped her in a crushing hug. 'Thank God you're okay.'

Beth understood the older woman's relief. They'd catch merry hell from the brass when word of this got out. O'Dowd as the senior officer would get the worst of it, but Beth knew that wasn't the major reason for her relief. It was bad enough the DI had led her down here, but the knowledge she'd been the cause of the accident would have eaten at her had Beth suffered any significant injury. Yes, the DI could be a grumpy sod at times, but the more Beth was getting to know her boss, the more she was seeing that, as well as being an excellent detective, Zoe O'Dowd was a good woman with a decent heart.

When she was released, Beth leaned forward and untied her ponytail. Her fingers weren't exactly clean, but after dusting them on her thighs, she used them as a comb to brush out all the rubbish that had lodged itself in her hair.

O'Dowd lifted her torch and pointed it towards the door. 'C'mon, let's get out of here.'

'Wait. I'm not going through all that without getting a look at what we came for.' Beth put her hand on the torch and pointed it around the cellar.

'You stay right there, lady.'

Beth smiled in the darkness. O'Dowd's authoritative tone was underpinned with a parental concern.

The torch swept the cellar and when it reached the far side, it illuminated a section of the partition that had remained upright after the collapse of the ceiling. Bound to the partition was a skeletal frame with the tiny folded yellow wings of a canary attached to its shoulder blades.

There wasn't enough flesh on the bones to guess whether the victim was male or female. It was a moot point. All that mattered was that there was another victim. What flesh there was lay inside the skeleton's ribcage and looked to have rotted to the point where not even carrion feeders would eat it.

Beth completed her sweep of the cellar, fearful there would be a fourth victim, but to her relief, found no more bodies.

'Let's go.'

Beth took a handful of O'Dowd's jacket and trailed her, elephant-style, back towards the stairs.

CHAPTER THIRTY-SEVEN

When they emerged from the cellar, Beth drank huge breaths of the sweet, fresh air into her lungs. Beside her, O'Dowd was lighting a cigarette and dusting down her suit. Beth's glance at her own clothes told her they were beyond repair. There were myriad minor tears in the fabric of her suit and when she looked at her blouse she saw the bottom two buttons had been torn off.

The CSI team's manager, a short man with an intense manner, came running over. 'What the hell happened? I told you it wasn't safe in there.'

'I tripped and we went down in a heap.' Beth gave a dismissive gesture. 'Just my luck to land on top of a pile of timber which had nails sticking out.'

She heard a muttered, 'Bloody women', as the CSI manager turned away.

'Yeah well, sorry about that, but us *bloody women* have just done something you haven't had the guts to do. And we've found a third body.'

The CSI man didn't turn round at Beth's rebuke but that didn't matter to her. She'd spotted the stiffening of his shoulders, and that was enough. She hadn't meant to vent at him, but after the scare she'd just had, it wasn't a surprise that she'd spoken out the way she had. A bigger surprise was that it was her and not O'Dowd who'd delivered the admonishment.

'Thank you.'

O'Dowd's words were no louder than a whisper, but Beth heard the gratitude in the DI's voice. Time would tell whether she'd just played an ace, or if she'd folded on a good hand. Still, she reasoned to herself, it was the right thing to do. The cave-in was an accident and Beth wasn't the kind of person to hold a grudge.

A uniformed officer approached them. 'Ma'am. I've taken a statement from Mr Cooper, the house's owner.'

'What does he say?'

'Just that he returned from holiday yesterday. He picked up his dogs from his brother this morning and was walking them around the house when one of the dogs took off. He went after it and found the two bodies in the cellar. After that he came out and called us.'

Beth noticed that there was no mention of the third body. She nudged O'Dowd's elbow. 'Ma'am, we need to speak to him.'

The uniformed officer's report told them nothing they didn't already know, and Beth was sure that Cooper would have more information, provided he was asked the right questions.

A flash of irritation crossed O'Dowd's eyes before she reined it back. 'We do indeed.'

The uniformed officer took them across and made the introductions before sloping off.

'Mr Cooper, we've heard the gist of your statement, but there are a few details we'd like to clarify.' O'Dowd shifted her gaze to Beth.

It was obvious to Beth that O'Dowd was still reeling from the events in the cellar. She knew she should be too, but after a moment of panic when trapped, she now felt imbued with an icy coldness. Following the horror of coming to and not knowing where she was or why she couldn't move, this was normal, everyday stuff, and it kept her on an even keel. The pain and bruising would no doubt kick in soon, but for now, she had a job to do.

'You said you were on holiday, Mr Cooper. From what we saw, those bodies have been in there some time.' Beth was thinking of the skeletal frame with the canary wings and the woman whose back sported the parrot wings. 'How long were you away?'

Cooper ran a hand through his unruly mane of white hair. 'Call me Max. We were away for six months. It was our silver wedding anniversary and we went on a tour of the world to celebrate.' He gave a self-deprecating shrug. 'It was my wife's idea. I wanted to get on with the house. We did a deal, she wanted to go on holiday, so we did the holiday first, and now I'm going to rebuild this house.'

'You're a builder?'

'An architect.' Another shrug. 'I made some decent money on a few projects and I'm now semi-retired. Restoring Highstead Castle is going to be a real labour of love for me. I've always wanted to restore somewhere like this to its former glory.'

Everything he was saying made sense to Beth. Doing up a place as decrepit as Highstead Castle would cost a fortune, yet he seemed to have money. There would be few better people than an architect to evaluate the costs and work to the specified budget.

The six months Cooper had been away would explain why the bodies hadn't been found sooner. The body with the canary wings had been there for quite some time but in any case, left to their own devices, the rats and other creatures which inhabited the house would have soon stripped the body of its flesh.

The woman with the parrot wings had obviously been there for less time, but more than the man with brown wings.

Beth felt a lurch in her stomach as she realised that she was thinking of the victims by their wings rather than any other factor. She supposed it was because they didn't yet have names for them, but she knew there would have to be some other kind of assignation to identify their individuality.

That there were three new victims of what seemed undoubtedly the same killer meant the investigation had escalated rapidly. Beth tried looking at it with objectivity. There was a definite sequence. Canary Wings. Parrot Wings. Angus Keane and, finally, if her assumptions were right, Brown Wings. What she now wondered was whether there were more bodies at other derelict country houses they were yet to find.

She tossed a look at O'Dowd and didn't like what she was seeing. The DI was floundering. She was casting her eyes around watching what was happening, but Beth could tell none of it was sinking in. The irascible mood, the rash move of going into the cellar others deemed unsafe, and then the impatient push which sent Beth sprawling were all out of character for her. Beth didn't know if O'Dowd was cracking under the strain of the case, or if it was something else, but whatever was ailing the older woman, it had to be dealt with as they had a vicious, twisted killer to catch.

Beth didn't know where to start. Should it be the missing persons' files to see if she could identify any of the victims? Or should they locate all the derelict country houses in the county and have them searched to see just how many more contained dragon corpses? She thought checking the misper files would be the best use of her time, but it would be O'Dowd's call.

Forensics may get some clues from the man and the woman, but she didn't hold out a lot of hope. If the scene at Arthuret Hall was anything to go by, the killer seemed to be forensically aware and would have taken steps to eliminate the possibility of leaving trace evidence. The skeletal figure wouldn't offer many clues due to the fact it had decomposed so thoroughly, but the person would still need to be identified. Relatives for all would have to be told their loved one had been murdered. The hardest part of those conversations would be telling the grieving brother, sister, child or parent just *how* they had been found.

Two fire engines rumbled into view followed by a support truck. Both engines disgorged a team of firefighters. None wore flameproof clothing but they all had their helmets on.

As a matter of habit, Beth's eyes scoured the left sides of their necks looking for tattoos of kisses. It was something she never failed to do as she sought to find the man who'd deflected the bottle her way.

The support truck reversed as close as possible to the front door of the house and the firefighters got to work unloading it. Beth watched as they stacked up tubular supports of varying lengths beside the cellar door. Next to them a pile of adjustable props grew.

Once the truck was unloaded, the firefighters each attached a small lamp to their helmets and started to move towards the cellar. Like a team of ants, all knew their jobs and they worked with the minimum of fuss and direction. Two lifted a support and made for the door while another picked up two of the adjustable props. A minute later, three more replicated the task and then a third group followed. After a minute or two, a human chain was formed and they fed a support then two props into the cellar in regular succession until both piles were gone.

A generator was placed to one side of the cellar door and Beth saw a man carrying an extension cable and some portable lights down the stairs. One of the firefighters pulled the generator's starter cord, and there was a roar as it jumped into life. He bent over and fiddled with a lever until the generator settled into a quiet hum.

The firefighters all came out of the building and were approached by the CSI team, O'Dowd and Dr Hewson. When she looked at the firefighters she saw they all wore grim expressions. One or two cast a glance her way, but looked away again before eye contact was made.

Beth heard the crew manager say that it was now safe to go into the cellar, which started a row between Dr Hewson and the CSI manager as both vied for superiority, until O'Dowd stepped in and told Hewson to wait until the CSI manager had done his first sweep. He retreated to the edge of the lawn and stood beside Beth.

'I'm guessing from the state of your clothes you've been in there.'

His tone had lost all of the aggression he'd just shown. It only took Beth a fraction of a second to realise the pathologist had played O'Dowd and the CSI manager. Preserving the scene always took precedence over examining the bodies when there was no hope of preserving life. What O'Dowd had done was get himself access earlier in proceedings than he'd normally be afforded.

'You're not wrong.'

'What did you find?'

'Three bodies, though one was little more than a skeleton, all three with pairs of wings. Both the bodies showed signs of burning at the mouths.'

'I see.' Hewson lifted a bushy eyebrow. 'And what did Dowdy have to say about them?'

'Swear words mostly.'

'I can imagine.' He picked at something on the back of his hand then looked at her. 'You haven't mentioned the report I emailed you, so I'm presuming that you haven't read it yet.'

Beth's pulse quickened. 'No, we've been out of the office all day. What did it say?'

'A few things. The keys points are that Angus Keane died of heart failure that was brought on by the trauma of the burns he received. The insides of the mouth and the top of his trachea showed the greatest amount of fire damage, but there was also substantial burning to the lung tissue which indicates that our victim breathed the fire into his lungs.'

'What about his blood, did you find any evidence of drugs in there?'

'None. Not so much as a painkiller.'

While she didn't doubt Hewson's expertise, Beth couldn't believe that Angus had lain still while the squares were cut from his back. 'Surely he wouldn't have knowingly let someone carve lumps out of his back without trying to break free?'

'Absolutely not. But a lot of drugs don't show up in bloods. I'd guess that he was doped up with something for his compliance.

Rohypnol would make a lot of sense; it would make him compliant to the killer's commands and if enough is taken it acts as a painkiller. However, it doesn't leave a trace in the blood after twenty-four hours or the urine after seventy-two. Because we obviously missed both of those windows by a couple of days, I sent off a hair sample to the lab. It's the most conclusive test, although it can take a bit longer.'

'Not that this isn't enough, but was there anything else significant?'

'Just that the wings were attached with surgical glue, and that they showed a multitude of holes when I opened them to their full extension. If pressed I'd say they belonged to a crow that had been shot with a shotgun.'

Beth was trying to assimilate this knowledge and work out what she should be asking when O'Dowd called Hewson over.

With the opportunity for further questioning lost, Beth looked to O'Dowd for instruction. Not getting any, she turned on her heel and walked over to a uniformed sergeant who had just arrived along with two constables.

'There are a couple of houses and a farm over there.' Beth pointed to the sole access road to Highstead Castle as she addressed the sergeant. 'Can you get someone on with door-to-doors, please?'

The sergeant harrumphed and made Beth wonder if she would need to get O'Dowd to make the request official, when he passed on the instruction to the constables. With nothing left to achieve, Beth walked back over to O'Dowd. The DI held an unlit cigarette between trembling fingers.

'Ma'am, we need to talk.'

'Not now, Beth.'

O'Dowd stuffed the cigarette into her mouth and thumbed the wheel of her lighter. Once the cigarette was lit she pulled her phone out and wandered off towards the farm steading at the far side of Highstead Castle.

CHAPTER THIRTY-EIGHT

Beth gave up waiting for O'Dowd to return to the crime scene and went looking for her. Hewson and the CSI man had made a couple of barbed comments about her whereabouts. It had been a full half hour since she'd last spoken to the DI, and considering O'Dowd was the most senior officer on site, it was unthinkable that she wasn't at the centre of things.

She marched her way to the area where she'd seen O'Dowd walking towards the old farm steading. A tractor rumbled in the distance and there was the unmistakable smell of fresh manure in the air.

It was one thing nipping off somewhere to make a call, but not for this length of time.

Beth rounded a corner and found O'Dowd. The DI was sitting on a hay bale with her head in her hands and there was no mistaking the fact that she was crying. O'Dowd's shoulders heaved as sobs wracked her body and whimpers escaped her mouth.

Unsure what to do, Beth stood frozen to the spot. But a minute later, with O'Dowd still absorbed in her sorrow, Beth knew she had to act. She took the last five steps across to where the DI sat.

'Ma'am. Are you okay?' Beth laid a hand on O'Dowd's shoulder.

O'Dowd brushed the hand away, but she did at least turn her head to look at Beth.

'C'mon, ma'am. It can't be that bad. Whatever the problem is, I'm sure you'll find a way to deal with it.'

The DI didn't answer; she pulled her cigarettes from her pocket and fed one into her mouth. The glimpse Beth got of her boss's face showed red puffy eyes and tear-streaked cheeks.

Beth allowed O'Dowd a few drags on the cigarette before crouching down so she could look her in the eye. She knew the next few minutes may well define the rest of her police career, but this was a conversation that she had to have.

The victims needed a police team firing on all cylinders. A team led by someone with their eye on the ball and a complete focus on delivering their killer to the justice system. Beth knew O'Dowd was this person, but right now, she seemed to have fallen to pieces.

Summoning her courage, she opened her mouth. 'With the greatest of respect, ma'am, you need to pull yourself together. What happened in that cellar scared the crap out of me, but all's well that ends well. Yes, we could have been killed, but we weren't. Three people *were* killed in that cellar, and it's our job to find out who killed them and Angus Keane.'

O'Dowd's jaw trembled as she levered herself back to a standing position. Her eyes flitted over Beth's shoulder and blinked furiously. The cigarette dropped to the ground where it sent tendrils of smoke up O'Dowd's leg until she ground it out.

Beth waited, she'd said her piece and now it was a case of seeing how the DI reacted. She felt like it could go either way – O'Dowd could bollock her, but maybe she would snap out of her funk and tell her she was right.

What she didn't expect was for O'Dowd to crumble again. The DI's legs went unsteady as if she would fall and her mouth widened as she fought to not release the tears which had suddenly filled her eyes.

Beth grabbed O'Dowd's shoulders and guided her back to the bale of hay. She used her own body to shield the older woman from the view of anyone who passed their way. The only consolation she had was that they were out of sight of the house and all the people attending the crime scene.

At a loss as to what else to do, Beth patted the arms O'Dowd had wound round her waist. 'That's it, ma'am. Let it out. In five minutes you'll be right as rain and spitting orders at me the way you usually do.'

Stoicism turned into sobs again as O'Dowd sounded like her heart was breaking.

It took every one of Beth's prescribed five minutes for the tsunami of grief to wash over O'Dowd and ebb away. While she waited for it to pass, Beth rubbed O'Dowd's back and tried to offer her reassurances that everything would work out fine in the long run. That they'd survived the ordeal in the cellar and, bar a few cuts and bruises, hadn't been harmed.

When the tears subsided and O'Dowd released her grip, Beth took a half pace back and let the DI have a moment to collect herself.

'You're right, Beth. I should be in charge here, not crying like a baby or wandering about in a trance.' Another cigarette was plucked from a packet and stuffed into her mouth. 'It's just… just, there's stuff going on at home as well as this…' Her hand flapped in the general direction of Highstead Castle. 'The toughest case of my career. And shit, I thought you were a goner when that partition fell on you.'

Beth noticed the tremble had gone from O'Dowd's hands and that she'd straightened her posture from its tearful slump. 'If you want to tell me about it, it'll go no further. If you don't, that's fine so long as I get my boss back. There are four victims we have to fight for.'

'I know.' O'Dowd pulled a face then lifted her head and looked Beth in the eye. 'Tell me straight, do I look old enough to be a grandmother to you? Is that what I am now? An old woman with a hanky up the sleeve of her cardigan and knitting needles by her side? I'm not ready for the scrapheap yet. I've still got plenty of good years in me. I'm not old enough, am I?'

The questions caught Beth by surprise. Of all the things she'd been expecting, grandmotherdom wasn't one of them.

'Depends on the era, ma'am. Sixty years ago you'd be considered old to be having your first grandchild.' Beth made a helpless gesture. 'If someone saw you with a baby now though, they'd probably wonder if you were its granny or its mother.'

'That's what I thought.' O'Dowd ground her latest cigarette into the dirt of the farmyard and pulled out another. 'It's my daughter. She's pregnant. Seventeen years old and not a live cell in her pretty little head. Oh, and here's the best bit. She doesn't know who the father is because she was at a couple of parties where things got, to use her term, "hot and sweaty".' Smoke was blown from O'Dowd's mouth with an exasperated fury. 'That's my little girl for you; the kind of idiot who thinks getting knocked up after being so out of it that she wasn't sure who shagged her isn't going to be a problem. Jesus, it's all she can do to make beans on toast for herself. How in the name of God is she going to care for a baby?'

Beth got the whole picture in an instant. No wonder O'Dowd was so distracted. Her daughter's behaviour would impact on her and the rest of her family. If the daughter stayed with her and her husband, as Beth expected she would given O'Dowd's comments about her, there would be sleepless nights, babysitting duties and a whole host of extra work, not to mention that a large part of financing the child's upbringing would fall on its grandparents.

'She has no idea how hard being a parent can be. I had a husband to help me and I still found it a struggle at times. What am I going to do, Beth?'

There was no definitive answer to the question, so Beth answered it in the only way she could. 'You're going to cope. The Zoe O'Dowd who's my boss is someone who copes. I'm sure there will be tears and tantrums along the way. But you'll cope. Plus, if your daughter is anything at all like you, she'll put on her big-girl pants and rise to the occasion.' Beth took both of O'Dowd's hands in hers, taking care not to burn herself on the cigarette. 'I fully expect my DI to bore the arse off me with pictures and tales of the grandchild she loves. Yes, it's scary just now, and there will be a lot of scary moments to come, but there will be so many wonderfully special moments as well. One day, you'll look back and remember how you're feeling now and wonder what you were so worried about.'

O'Dowd wiped her face with the palms of both hands. 'That, Beth, is the best get over yourself speech I've ever heard. Thank you.' She pursed her lips together. 'You're an odd one, but in a good way.'

Beth smiled at O'Dowd, pleased with her praise and glad to see a semblance of the DI's usual personality coming back. 'Just find my grumpy-arsed boss, I kinda need her now. And so do four dead people.'

O'Dowd pushed herself off the hay bale and straightened her shoulders. 'She's back. Now let's go and see if our friendly pathologist has anything for us.'

Beth wasn't fooled by O'Dowd's sudden appearance of strength. But she admired her all the more for pulling herself together for the greater good of the team.

As she returned to the crime scene with O'Dowd, Beth couldn't help but remember the way she'd been at the start of the week. O'Dowd's confident can-do attitude had been infectious and had inspired her, yet she'd now seen another facet to her boss's personality. The worrier, the person who despaired and looked to others for answers she couldn't find herself.

Beth's next thought was that O'Dowd's confident manner was sometimes a front as she battled to hide her own insecurities. The realisation made Beth feel closer to O'Dowd as there were times she had to deal with her own feelings of unworthiness.

More than anything else though, Beth couldn't shake the memory of the life that had once grown in her sixteen-year-old belly.

CHAPTER THIRTY-NINE

The sparkle in Dr Hewson's eyes should have been at odds with the nature of his job and what he'd just examined, but Beth knew what caused it. Because as much as he might feel for the victims, he clearly couldn't help but also feel a thrill in trying to work out the cause of their deaths.

As he stripped off his oversuit, boots and gloves, he nodded at O'Dowd before she could speak. 'You want time and cause of death for all three. I get that. I'm going to tell you all I can for certain. The man was killed most recently. Judging from the number of bites on him, I'd say he's only been there a day, two at most. The woman, she's been there a couple of weeks, perhaps three at the most. As for the skeleton, I'd suggest that's been there at least three months. Cause of death can't be formally diagnosed until after the post-mortems, but based on what I've seen of the remains, I believe it'd be fair to work on the assumption that they all died the same way as Angus Keane. Both the man and the woman had scorching in their mouths.' He pulled a disgusted face. 'From what was left of the skeleton's internal organs, I may be able to match up what happened to them, but I think the wings fixed to the shoulders say enough. I'll be able to tell you more when I get them on my table.'

'What else did you find? Were there any distinguishing marks, something to help identify them? How old were they?' Beth led the questions to give O'Dowd time to get back to full strength.

Dr Hewson's smile was benevolent. 'You've trained this one well, Dowdy. She's proper sharp.'

'She's her own woman. And you should know I don't tolerate idiots on my team.' O'Dowd jerked her head. 'How about answering her question instead of trying to charm someone young enough to be your daughter?'

'Touché.' A smile caressed the doctor's lips. 'The man had the name "Dylan" tattooed onto his right forearm along with two dates connected by a hyphen. The dates were three years apart. I'd put the man in his thirties and the woman in her twenties, but I'm not prepared to guess at the skeleton's age yet.'

Beth jotted down the dates from the man's tattoo with a mixture of emotions. She felt for the unidentified man, the dates on his arm suggested that his son Dylan had died at an early age. However, it should make it easier to identify him.

'What about the skeleton? Can you tell us what sex it was at least?'

'Good question.' The doctor's eyes gave a twinkle. 'It has a woman's pelvis.'

'Is there anything else you can tell us? Anything we should have asked but haven't?'

'Not at the moment. I'll know more when I get them on my table, but for now, you've had all the facts I have and all the educated guesses I'm prepared to make.'

As the pathologist wandered in the direction of his car, Beth was thinking about the interchange between him and O'Dowd. Their mutual animosity almost seemed fake, as if it was for show rather than really felt. The more she thought about it, the more she realised that whatever their differences may be, their squabbling was underpinned with a professional respect for the other's skills.

CHAPTER FORTY

The TV hadn't been entertaining, the shows a mixture of the bland, the overacted and the downright brainless. The reality shows that dominated the schedules may well include the occasional stunner, but after a few minutes of admiring their beauty, he'd invariably find himself repulsed by their personality. Some were narcissists of the highest order, others were so competitive they trampled over others with nary a thought for the feelings of their competitors, and the rest, they were just bitches.

Even the soaps he'd once watched had turned every decent woman into screaming, mewling shrews. Their beautiful faces twisted into angry gargoyles by implausible storylines and bad direction.

Sometimes he'd get lucky and discover a decent series. Most of these were American-made, although there was the odd British one that delivered both good drama as well as angels for him to idolise.

As he lumbered from his chair and went about his bedtime routine, he thought about tomorrow. The test drive was something he was excited about in a way he'd not experienced for many months. He'd have time alone with the delectable Sarah Hardy; if he managed things the right way, he'd be able to enjoy her company for at least an hour. An involuntary shudder passed through him as he thought of her.

The route he'd take was etched into his mind. As the test drive was scheduled for eleven, he wondered if it was possible he could entice her to grab a spot of lunch with him. Oh, how good that would feel, to walk into somewhere with her by his side. The sensation would make him feel ten-feet tall.

The man could only imagine what it'd be like to be seen in the company of someone like Sarah. There would be jealous looks from men; he'd see the other, less-attractive women glance at her and pull a face of dismay at her obvious superiority in the beauty stakes. There would, of course, be whispered insults. It would be claimed that she was only with him for his money. Some would assume that he was her father or uncle.

Perhaps, if he could get her to take his arm, that would dispel a lot of the naysayers, put them in their place and keep them from making the wrong assumptions.

He'd have to choose the venue with care though. It couldn't be too swanky or he'd scare her, make her realise that buying her lunch was more than a friendly gesture. He'd also have to pick a busy place, one that was well known for its food; as much as he wanted to have her to himself, he also wanted to savour the admiring looks other men cast her way so he could revel in the envy shading their eyes.

As he turned on the bedside light he saw the trousers and shirt hanging on the wardrobe. He'd wear them with his old regimental tie. It carried less weight than it used to, but there was a time when it had earned him respect.

Like a child on Christmas Eve, he was going to bed earlier than usual so that tomorrow, and the joyous gratification the day would bring, would come sooner. He closed his eyes and pictured her: she was striding across the garage's showroom, all dimpled smile and bouncing curls, when out of the corner of his imagination he caught a movement. It was the two cops. The younger, taller one with the beauty-defiling scar was pictured in crisp, high definition, whereas the dumpy inspector was blurry, out of focus.

That they'd shown up in his thoughts about Sarah was telling. He supposed that O'Dowd was only there because he thought of her and DC Young as a pair. He had no objections to Young populating his thoughts, even if she was gatecrashing on Sarah. Had it not been for the scar on her cheek, she would have been every bit as beautiful as the car saleswoman.

His thoughts centred on the two angels as sleep came for him.

CHAPTER FORTY-ONE

Beth twisted each of the bath's taps and discarded her clothes. Only her underwear would go into the wash basket. The trouser suit and her blouse were ruined and, as such, only fit for the bin.

Her body had begun to stiffen as the various aches and pains she'd collected from the ordeal in the cellar manifested themselves. There was not a part of her that didn't hurt in one way or another. She had multiple scrapes and there were bruises starting to show in a variety of colours on her legs, arms and torso.

She poured a few slugs of antiseptic into the bathwater and added a generous slop of bubble bath. A shower would be quicker, but there was something about a bath that soothed aching muscles and tired limbs.

As much as her body was spent, Beth's mind was still on overdrive. So much had happened during the day that she'd barely had a chance to properly collate her thoughts. Three more victims; the drama of the collapse and the subsequent rescue by O'Dowd; the information learned early in the day; and not to mention O'Dowd's breakdown and revelation about her daughter.

The first thing she put her mind to were the victims. If Hewson was right, and she had no reason to doubt him, the first two victims had been women, followed by two men. The killer could be working to a pattern, or it could be pure chance. If it was coincidence, then what connected the victims? And if it was a pattern, and everything about this killer suggested there was a hidden agenda, then that suggested a woman would be the next victim, assuming, that was, that they'd found all the people he'd killed so far. The media were already putting a lot of pressure on them for Angus Keane and it was only a matter of time before they learned of the poor souls killed at Highstead Castle.

Another factor she had to consider was how the killer was getting his victims into the abandoned places while still alive. Nobody would have gone down to that cellar without protest. She supposed the killer may have used a gun or knife to force them, but wouldn't there have been a point when they refused to cooperate? Angus Keane was a builder, his body was lean and taut. Dylan's father was a muscular man who looked as though he either worked out, or had a job that kept him physically fit.

She couldn't get her head round either man acquiescing to the killer's instructions without putting up a fight. But neither had shown wounds consistent with an attack. There were no knife wounds other than the surgery required to fit the wings to their backs. Bullet wounds were also absent.

All this meant the killer had found a way to control his victims. Drugs were the obvious answer, with Hewson's suggestion of Rohypnol being a standout candidate. A pill dropped into a drink could render the person incapable of independent thought. They'd do as requested without question. That's why it was known to many as the date-rape drug. Once taken, the user lost the power of free will.

With luck, the drug could still be traceable in the urine of the male victim.

Next on her mental checklist was to find a connection between the two country houses where the murders took place. She'd floated it as a theory to O'Dowd and had been given instructions to compile a list of other derelict houses in the county, in case there were more victims hidden in other cellars. After popping into the office first thing in the morning, Beth planned to visit the library to do this research. Penrith had a library, but Carlisle's was far more likely to have comprehensive records.

Beth's memories of Penrith library were sketchy at best. She knew she'd been there a few times as a child, but other than the constant reminders to be quiet, she remembered nothing other than tall shelves stacked with books. What she did recall were the news items about cuts to the library system; Penrith was large enough to have avoided the accountant's axe this time round, but many of the smaller towns in the region had seen their libraries closed or cut back to minimal hours. She wasn't big on reading – apart from her puzzle magazines and the books she bought to keep on serial killers – but if the libraries were first, how long before cutbacks were made to other essential services?

She'd had a look online, but hadn't found what she'd needed. In among the listings which came back was a book on country houses in the north-west. It looked as if it would hold the information she needed. In the morning she could check to see if Penrith library held a copy. If they didn't, she was sure that Carlisle library would have a copy in their archives.

O'Dowd hadn't instructed her to do so, but she planned to extend her search to neighbouring counties as well. Dumfries and Galloway was only a few miles from Arthuret Hall, and she reasoned that the killer may not respect county boundaries the way bureaucracy did.

The fact that all three of the latest victims seemed to have been killed at different times, though all at Highstead Castle, made her wonder if the killer had a connection to the house. Max Cooper had told them he'd recently bought the place, therefore she needed to concentrate on the previous owners – families who knew the building and more than just its existence – who would know of the twin cellars, and of the building's isolation.

The killer would have an affinity to the house. Perhaps they'd see it as a special place, one worthy of being the scene of a murder. Could that account for the connection with the dragons? Some mythical link which the killer believed tied the beasts to certain locations? Even as she thought this, Beth recognised the idea as fanciful. Still, until they had a suspect to focus on, they had to consider all possibilities. While to Beth, mythology was nothing more than a collection of tall tales embellished through centuries of retelling, she knew many people believed in horoscopes, the occult and dozens of other things that defied logic, so there was no way she was going to discount any mythological connection without hard evidence.

Though none of this explained why Angus Keane had been left at Arthuret Hall. This was out of sync with the other killings in terms of location; therefore she reasoned that either Angus or Arthuret Hall was significant in some way.

Beth cast her mind back to the beginning of the day and re-ran the interviews with the potential suspects for the murder of Angus Keane. None had presented a strong reason or motive to kill the builder, and the meetings had all passed without incident. The only thing of note had been the man who'd given her the creeps in the way he'd stared at her scar. But even that hadn't been worth remarking on at the time.

His gazing *had* gone beyond a polite look, travelled past the point of interest and had set up base camp at obsession. The man's eyes hadn't held lust or longing, rather they'd suggested he was reconstructing her, transporting her back to the time before a scarred cheek dominated her looks.

Beth dismissed thoughts of the man on the basis that he had not seemed a likely suspect in other regards, and reasoned that if she suspected every person who looked at her strangely, she'd never solve a case.

She turned her mind to her discussion with O'Dowd at Highstead Castle. Of their four-strong team, it looked as if only herself and Paul Unthank were not dealing with personal problems.

Unthank's world centred on his job and spending time with his fiancée, whereas her life, well, that was about the job and the job alone. Besides, police work was hard on relationships. There were unrelenting shift patterns, the traumas of the job and a dozen other reasons why coppers struggled to maintain long relationships. If love came her way, so be it, but she wasn't interested in looking for it.

Her friends were forever trying to set her up with someone, but none of the guys they suggested appealed to her. She was confident that she'd find someone herself, but for the time being, she was in no hurry.

Another concern was how distracted her superiors were. O'Dowd had intimated to her that Thompson had turned down her offer of a transfer to another team where he'd be able to work less-intense hours, and the DI's situation was such that Beth didn't think today's lapse of focus would necessarily be a solitary event.

The severity of the case demanded that all the detectives be at the top of their respective games. Distractions caused by family issues, regardless of how upsetting they might be, couldn't be tolerated if they were to succeed in catching the killer. As it was, it looked as if Dylan's father had been murdered after they'd got the case, and it would be horrific if another life were to be lost because the team lacked direction. As much as she felt for both Thompson and O'Dowd, she knew they would need to put their personal problems aside before more people were killed. In the meantime, she resolved to do everything she could to solve the case, covering for her new colleagues if necessary.

CHAPTER FORTY-TWO

The shower pummelled his body with spikes of icy water but he didn't reach for the controls. He'd set the temperature to its lowest setting the way he always did when he was ready to rinse the suds from his body.

Cold was his friend. He much preferred it to heat. Too many times in his life, he'd suffered because of heat, and now he made sure that he never felt heat in the wrong way again.

Drinks and meals were allowed to cool until they were tepid before he consumed them. His home was always cool, and when the sun blazed from the sky, he'd slather himself with sunblock so his skin didn't burn.

His body was covered with scars, but he'd never been into battle. At least, not in a physical sense. The battles he fought were psychological. For too many years he'd been dominated by a vicious dragon and had endured all manner of punishments.

Every scar on his body told of a lost battle.

His combatant was the person who should have cared for him. Giving birth to him may have turned a wife into a parent, but it didn't mean it turned her into a good one. And after his father's death, his mother had grown more vicious with every passing week. Complaints became criticisms, which became punishments.

When he turned seven, the punishments were no longer delivered with an open hand. On the day of his eighth birthday, he was made to stand in silence while his mother stubbed out a cigarette on his chest. His crime – a missed full stop in a 'thank you' letter he'd written to an aunt for the football he'd received as a birthday gift.

As he aged, the punishments became worse. His mother would blow her cigarette smoke in his face at every opportunity and when she wasn't lashing him with her viperous tongue, she was stubbing out cigarettes on his body.

She was careful to concentrate on his torso, until his back and chest were a patchwork of scars both old and new. He'd been made to stand and endure the punishments in silence. His lips and inner cheeks became scarred from his attempts to not cry out or plead with her to stop. He'd learned the hard way that begging and pleading with his mother had no effect other than the hardening of her resolve. When he swore at her aged thirteen, she'd put out her cigarette on his tongue then made him wait until she smoked another so she could repeat the punishment.

Like any normal teenager, he'd developed an interest in sex, and when she caught him looking at a girl from the local village in a way she deemed unacceptable, three cigarettes had been extinguished on his scrotum.

When he'd managed to get himself free of her, she'd remained in his thoughts.

He never showed his scarred body to anyone. He didn't build any relationships with women as he couldn't bear the idea of them seeing the results of his punishments. Even if he insisted on keeping the lights off, caressing fingers would have found the scars.

He'd considered visiting a prostitute on several occasions, but had always found an excuse not to do so. He knew it was a form of cowardice, but he'd rather die a virgin than expose himself and see pity in a woman's eyes.

As he towelled himself off, he thought about the day ahead of him and all the things he must do. Some were more appealing than others, but that was the way of his life.

CHAPTER FORTY-THREE

Beth stood in front of the desk and explained to the librarian why she was there. She got a raised eyebrow and an instruction to give the librarian a few minutes until she found the necessary books.

The morning had gone well so far. O'Dowd was back to her irascible best and even Thompson had seemed focussed.

A check of the registry for births, deaths and marriages had identified the Dylan mentioned on the male victim's arm. Dylan Langley had died six weeks before his third birthday. He was survived by his mother Melanie, and father Nick, who had been reported missing yesterday morning when he hadn't come home on Monday night. O'Dowd had gone to deliver the death knock with an FLO. Before the DI left, she'd requisitioned a spare pair of hands to go through the missing persons' reports to look at possible identities for the two women. Anything that could narrow the search would give them a much-needed advantage.

The librarian returned with a stack of books, some she'd retrieved from the Jackson Library. She told Beth those books were rare and could not be removed from the premises, but the others could be withdrawn.

Beth found a table and started to scan through the first of the books. It was the tome she'd found online: *Benson's Guide to North West Country Houses*. As interesting as she found it, Beth was keenly aware time wasn't on her side, so she flicked her eyes across the descriptions looking for words like 'derelict' or 'abandoned'.

She wrote the names of the houses which met those criteria on a notepad, but after completing the book, had only a few stately homes on her list. Beth wasn't sure if this was a good or a bad thing. It would narrow down their search criteria, which was good, but it also meant that perhaps there were other places that hadn't made it into the book.

Plus, the book itself was old news, it was published more than twenty years ago, which meant there were two decades for houses to have fallen derelict to lost fortunes or the ravages of fire since then.

There were many other possibilities Beth was sure she was missing, but at the same time, the book was comprehensive and while some of the stately homes, manor houses and castles were familiar to her, the majority were ones she'd never heard of.

She bit down on a yawn and picked up the book she'd requested on Highstead Castle. It wasn't for lending, so she made copious notes about the castle's history and turned her attention back to the first book she'd consulted.

Beth didn't want to waste too much precious time on her research, so she used Google Maps to identify the locations of the names she'd discovered, and mapped out three possibilities which, like Highstead Castle and Arthuret Hall, were in the north-eastern part of Cumbria. Next she picked up a couple of books that listed Scottish country houses and searched for ones in the eastern areas of Dumfries and Galloway. She knew it was a long shot and may well prove to be time wasted, but she was trying to cover every eventuality she could think of.

What surprised her most was the number of grand houses in the county. She loved Cumbria and had thought she had a good handle on the area and its people, but the snippets of history she'd absorbed during her search had left her wanting to know more.

The houses dated back to Georgian, Jacobean, Tudor and Victorian times, although most of them had been rebuilt at some point in their history. Their owners included philanthropists, slave traders and a dozen other professions as the march of time deposed feudal landowners in favour of more peaceful owners.

Many of the houses, especially in the northern parts of the region, had been sacked by the reiving Scots. Beth knew from long-ago history lessons that, for a number of years in the seventeenth century, Carlisle Castle had been in Scottish hands.

As instructed by O'Dowd, she passed the locations and names of all the possible sites she'd found to Control so they could send officers to search them for bodies. Beth also passed on the details of the ones she'd found in Northumberland and Dumfries and Galloway, but she didn't expect they'd receive the same priority as the ones in Cumbria.

She gathered up her notes and filed them all into the laptop bag she used as a briefcase. A snap decision made her trot down the stairs from the library and go to the cookie stall. With several cookies in a bag, she felt prepared to face the remainder of the day, comfortable in the knowledge there would be an energising sugar boost at hand.

While she drove back down the M6 towards Penrith and Carleton Hall, Beth ran a new series of questions through her head. Most of them had her finding more questions than answers, but at least they would open up some other lines of enquiry.

CHAPTER FORTY-FOUR

When she looked up from her desk to scan the showroom for customers who may need her attention, Sarah Hardy saw a man who made her think today just couldn't get any worse. It had started off badly and it had now taken another turn south. The rot had set in when she'd missed her mouth while taking a drink of orange juice. The liquid had splashed not just her crisp white blouse but had also soaked her skirt making it stick to her thigh.

That had necessitated a last-minute outfit change. Instead of the tight burgundy skirt which clung to her hips, she now wore a flared one. While inches longer, this one had a habit of riding up when she wasn't paying attention. To exacerbate the problem, she'd put a fingernail through her last pair of tights and hadn't had time to replace them.

She could accept flashing a little extra thigh for a handsome man with money, but for the older guy who was ambling across the showroom, it was a different matter. He may think he was being discreet when he looked at her, but it was obvious where his gaze was landing.

The blouse was another mistake. Where the first one had been loose and billowy, this one was tight across her bust and she knew that it often gaped enough to show her bra when she put her shoulders back.

The man came nearer and nearer, and it was then she remembered that he was here for a test drive. She'd forgotten to put the appointment in her diary and now she'd have to take him out and spend at least half an hour in his unsettling company.

She looked around for a colleague to offload the man to, and to heck with the commission she'd lose, but she saw they were all busy. With nothing left to do but accept the situation, Sarah rose to her feet and applied a fake smile.

'Good morning. Are you here for your test drive?'

'I am indeed, my dear.'

Sarah knew the 'my dear' was a generational thing but it still rankled her. As did sweetheart, love and a thousand other terms of address which demeaned women.

'If you just give me five minutes, I'll get the car ready for you.'

As she walked across to speak to the Dealer Principal to find out which car to take, she could sense the customer's eyes caressing her bare legs. She almost hoped the right model wasn't available. As she'd neglected to log the test drive, there was every possibility of that being the case, but that wouldn't help her in the end. She'd either lose the sale, or worse, he'd come back another time. Her luck wasn't in today though.

As she walked across the forecourt with him, she took the precaution of positioning herself in a way that hid any possible gapes in her blouse from his prying eyes. Sarah led the man – she was at a loss as to his name, and didn't dare to mentally christen him with a nickname in case she called him Larry the Lech, or some other insult to his face – across to the car. She got him into the driver's seat and showed him the controls to adjust it to suit his preferred driving position.

When she slid into the passenger seat, she made sure that her skirt was tucked beneath her bottom and that there wasn't a hand lying in wait for her. With her seatbelt on, she told him to proceed in his own time.

A mile down the road she'd exhausted her small talk about the car. The man had listened to her spiel with only the odd word or nod as acknowledgement of what she was saying.

'This is a very beautiful car.'

It took all of Sarah's self-control not to shudder at the way he drew out the word 'beautiful'. His inflection made the concept of beauty appear seedy.

A junction appeared ahead of them, and when the man pulled to a halt he checked both ways several times before drawing out. Sarah knew it was so he could spend a few seconds looking her way.

They were on a straight piece of road now and he drove at a low speed with regular glances at the mirrors. When they pulled up behind a car waiting to turn across oncoming traffic, he looked around the car then dropped his gaze to her legs.

'There's plenty of room in here. I mean, you're quite tall and you appear to have more than enough room for those long legs of yours.'

'Yes, it's very spacious.'

Even as the words left her mouth, Sarah was sickened by what she was putting up with to make a sale, yet there was no way of changing the narrative.

Except there was.

At the first opportunity, she'd tell the lie and watch him pull back. She'd learned years ago that the best way to deal with unwelcome advances was to pretend to have a boyfriend.

They reached another junction and this time she turned her head and gave him a report on the oncoming traffic, or rather, the lack of it.

He pulled away after a sizeable delay, but at least she hadn't had to endure his gaze. Rather than wait for the opportunity to slip the lie into conversation, she decided to create it.

'This is a very nice car. My boyfriend has the same model. He loves it.'

'As well he should. It's a lovely car he can use to drive a lovely lady.' The man gave a contented smile. 'He's a very lucky man.'

Sarah wasn't sure if the man meant her fictitious boyfriend was lucky because of his car or girlfriend, but she suspected the latter and had to fight not to pull a face.

'He is.' She pointed at a sign indicating an approaching junction. 'If you take that road it'll bring us back towards the dealership.'

'You certainly know your way around. Feel free to say no, my dear, but how do you feel about stopping for a bite of lunch before we return?'

This was too much for Sarah to tolerate without laying down a marker. 'I'm sorry, but I have a very busy schedule today, and if my boss was to find out I was fraternising with a customer, I would get the sack. And I have to warn you, my boyfriend is a very jealous man.'

'Of course, my dear. I was only trying to be kind. I was feeling hungry and thought you might be too.'

The lack of rebuke in the man's voice combined with his polite, even tone made Sarah feel as though she'd been too harsh with her reply. Maybe the old guy was just lonely.

She'd have left her thoughts there had he not snuck a look at her legs when reaching down to fiddle with the controls for the air conditioning.

He drove her back to the showroom without further comment. When he pulled into the forecourt, she saw her boss chatting to one of the sales team.

Now was the hard part for her; after all his leers and sly looks, she had to turn her charm on full to see if she could close the deal. With her boss hovering around, she'd have to give her very best sales pitch; otherwise she'd find herself standing like a schoolchild in the headmaster's office, as he delivered another version of his infamous '101 ways to make a sale' lecture.

The car came to a halt and the man turned off the ignition.

'So, now you've had a chance to drive this wonderful car, what do you think? Could you see yourself driving one every day? Perhaps taking your lady friend for a nice drive?'

She'd picked her words with care. Used 'wonderful' instead of a word that could be used to describe looks, hinted that she thought he was attached as a way to remind him that she was.

'That is a capital idea. However, I do have appointments to test drive an Audi later today and a Mercedes tomorrow. Once I've tried them, I'll drop by and let you know my decision.'

The handshake he gave her went on a beat too long and his eyes met hers then slid down her body.

She bade him farewell and took a step backwards, as much to distance herself as dismiss him. Her plan was that she would watch him leave rather than offer him the chance to ogle her as she walked away.

A quick check of her watch told her she had half an hour to finish typing the email she'd been working on when he'd interrupted her, grab a bite of lunch and fix her make-up before the man she actually wanted to meet was due.

The experience with the older man had almost put her off the idea of letting the dashing younger man know she was interested in him. It was hard for her to feel attractive after being ogled so openly. She turned and strode to her desk. Perhaps seeing the man again would give her seductiveness the kick up the backside it needed.

CHAPTER FORTY-FIVE

Beth slumped back in her chair and nibbled on one of the cookies she'd bought earlier. Across the desk from her, O'Dowd was stuffing one into her mouth as if she hadn't eaten for a week.

They'd had reports back on some of the locations she'd found. So far none had turned up any more winged victims.

At Beth's suggestion, O'Dowd had asked Control to get in touch with every police station in Cumbria to see if any older officers knew of any country houses that weren't mentioned in the book. So far, no reports had come in, but it would depend on each station's workload and shift pattern, and how quickly the request would get to the people with the right local knowledge.

Beth picked up the notes she'd made on Highstead Castle with one hand, as she used a saliva-dampened finger to collect the crumbs from the paper bag she'd used as a plate when eating her cookie. The most interesting link between the houses, as far as she was concerned, was that they had both been ravaged by fire: Highstead in the fifties and Arthuret Hall some time later she understood, although the details she'd gathered on Arthuret Hall had failed to specify when the fire had taken place. Logic told her that it must have happened many years ago due to the fact there was so much vegetation evident in the house.

Still, she couldn't help wondering if the fact both buildings had fallen victim to fire was significant to their selection as murder sites for victims whose mouths were scorched like dragons. She explained the connection to O'Dowd who got onto Control and suggested that they amend her request to every station to also mention any country houses that had suffered fire damage.

'Ma'am, do you think it's worth getting someone to check the fire-brigade logs too?'

'Good call.' A finger pointed at her list. 'Those houses you've got there, how did they become derelict? Was there a fire at any of them?'

Beth was scanning her notes before O'Dowd had finished speaking. 'Just Brayton Manor House. Back at the end of the First World War. My notes say it's a caravan site now. Is it worth installing a surveillance team?'

'No, the link is too tenuous for that.' O'Dowd reached for her phone. 'I'll get someone to check it out on a regular basis instead.'

Beth nodded at O'Dowd and went back to her notes on Highstead Castle. Nothing she'd unearthed so far told her who owned Highstead before Max Cooper. Nor was there information on the farm beside it, or the two houses they'd parked beside yesterday. Perhaps the killer had grown up in one of those houses. The old building would be a magnet for an inquisitive child. Therefore he'd know it as well as anyone alive.

The Land Registry would have the information about Highstead and the farm; however she'd need to get the addresses for the houses to locate them through an online search of the Land Registry database.

She logged onto her computer and looked up the statements the officers had taken yesterday. Armed with the addresses, Beth ran the searches and listed the owners of each property right back to 1940. One of the houses had the same name as the farm, which told her the house came with the job and that she'd have to speak to the farmer to get a list of all those who'd lived there. The one saving grace was that the farm had remained in the same family for the whole of her search period.

She figured that her killer would be no more than sixty years old due to the physical aspect of his kills, but she wanted to make sure her bets were well and truly hedged.

Now there were multiple victims, the investigation had shifted and what had seemed like good ideas when looking into Angus Keane's death, now looked like a waste of time and resources when set against the bigger picture.

From across the desk she could hear O'Dowd's tone show gratitude as she got approval for something. The DI's good mood evaporated when the printer clacked into life as she made her second call. The office printer was nearing the end of its life and made a lot more noise than it should. As it whirred and clacked, O'Dowd pressed her free hand to her ear and scowled at the machine as if she could scare it into silence.

Beth collected the sheets of paper from the printer and looked at the names and dates. Working on the theory the killer would be a man aged between twenty and seventy, she used a highlighter to mark all those who fell into that category. The others may well be a possibility, but she thought it best to play the odds first. If O'Dowd disagreed, then so be it. Her thinking was that those whose ages fell within her chosen demographic were those who'd be physically strongest and the most confident of their ability to get away with the murders.

When the DI came off the phone she looked triumphant.

'I just spoke to the brigade manager for Cumbria. He's getting someone onto my request for information on fires at stately homes, country houses and any other large rural building that has gone up in flames in the last hundred years.'

'Excellent.' Beth went on to tell O'Dowd what she'd done regarding the houses flanking the track to Highstead Castle. She also mentioned that she'd traced George Bellingham to a hospital bed in Manchester Royal Infirmary. He'd been there for a fortnight and was receiving palliative care for leukaemia. His being the killer would have nicely tied up the case in a neat bundle, but there was no way it could have been him.

'Who's he again?'

'The gangster's son who got evacuated to Arthuret Hall.'

O'Dowd looked at her with assessment decorating her face. 'I'm bloody glad I retire in a few years. Otherwise I'd have to worry about you getting my job.'

As unexpected as the compliment was, it still brought an impromptu smile to Beth's lips and a flush to her face.

'I've been thinking, ma'am. Dr Hewson said the crow's wings that were on Angus Keane's back had a lot of holes in them, as if the crow had been brought down with a shotgun. Should we be looking at people who own a shotgun?'

'It's a good idea, but you're looking at hundreds of people, possibly thousands in Cumbria alone. Most farmers have a shotgun and there'll be a lot of shooting enthusiasts. And that's only the people who have a gun license. Someone who's killed four people might not worry about owning an unlicensed firearm. You're also working on the assumption that it was the killer who shot the crow. I've seen crop fields where the carcasses of crows have been tied to a fence as a warning to other crows not to eat the grain. What if the killer just helped himself to a crow a farmer had shot?'

'Sorry, ma'am. Just trying to think of everything.'

'Don't be sorry.' O'Dowd gave her an indulgent look that renewed Beth's blushing. 'Now then, Beth, while the colour is still in your cheeks, what other ideas are rattling around in that brain of yours?'

'None for the moment, ma'am. I'm still new to this and just spitting out whatever I can think of.'

'Keep spitting, you're doing a good job. Have you considered the wings at all?'

'I've given them a bit of thought, but if I'm honest, I've been concentrating on trying to identify the victims and find out if there could be any others in places we haven't looked. Why, what do you think?'

O'Dowd stuffed the last piece of cookie into her mouth and talked around it. 'I don't know what to think, that's my problem.' A pause to swallow. 'In chronological order of kills we've got a canary, a parrot, a crow and then what appears to be some kind of bird of prey. What does that tell you?'

'That the killer is escalating? That he's going for bigger birds as he tries to make the perfect dragon?'

'That's what I'm thinking. Problem is, we need to get an expert opinion on that. We need a specialist.'

'Where would you get a specialist on so many different birds?' Beth couldn't begin to think who'd know about canaries, parrots and birds of prey as well as crows.

'We may have to use a couple. A pet-shop owner should be able to help with the first two, then perhaps a handler at a bird-of-prey centre would be best for the oth—'

'A gamekeeper would, ma'am. They'd know about birds of prey. And I bet they'd know how to catch one.'

'Good call.'

'There's something else. Should we check if they can tell the sex of the birds from the wings? I'm not sure if it will be relevant or not, but I feel it's worth finding out if we can.'

'You're right.' A snap of the fingers. 'We'll need to get onto one at once.'

Beth reached for her keyboard. 'Leave it to me.'

CHAPTER FORTY-SIX

The name he gave to Sarah Hardy wasn't the one on his original driving license, but it was a match for the one in his wallet. When you were in his position, setting up a false identity or two was neither hard nor expensive.

On a secular level he could appreciate that Sarah was a very beautiful woman and had the kind of body others torture themselves in the gym to achieve. That didn't matter to him. His appreciation of her lay in a different direction:

Her beauty will dominate headlines; her picture will be broadcast everywhere and will eclipse the bold move he planned to make before turning her into a dragon.

The copper will garner a lot of attention when she's found. The damaged damsel with the wings on her back. A hunter who fell prey to a bigger predator. Yet because of the copper's disfigurement, the newsreels will focus on Sarah.

He brought his attention back to the moment. Sarah was talking to him in a way that was a step over the line of professional flirtation. Her clothes showed off her body and she angled herself in ways that displayed her figure.

When she'd climbed into the passenger seat, she'd made no effort to pull down her skirt. He noticed this only because that's how he stayed ahead of others, by noticing things. He didn't feel any attraction to her, but then, he didn't feel a physical attraction to anyone. He hadn't for years. To him, sex was little more than an abstract idea, a tool that could be used to manipulate other people. It used to be different for him, but became something he'd managed to eradicate from his thoughts.

To his mind, in this moment, Sarah is displaying herself like a wanton hussy. It's obvious she fancies him and that's just what he planned on. He'd picked up on the signs on Sunday when he'd entered the showroom looking for a new car. Spotted her appreciative glance at his watch. He'd dressed to impress her today, and he'd seen the way she'd run her eyes over him. There had been a mixture of lust and greed. He supposed she thought of him as a meal ticket, his obvious wealth a way for her to clamber up the social ladder and better herself.

Her spiel about the car was delivered in a soft, almost seductive tone. How much of her flirting was a professional desire to make the sale and how much was aimed at snaring a rich husband didn't matter. He liked the car and would have bought it even if the salesman was a fat bald man in his fifties, complete with halitosis and BO. That he'd found a delicious addition to his project was nothing more than an unexpected bonus.

He made a little joke about another driver and her laugh carried on that beat too long. She was trying hard to impress him. He could sense it in her every gesture and mannerism. When she leaned over and pointed out the controls for something or other, she brushed her palm across the knuckles of the hand he'd rested on the gearstick, her fingers trailing across the back of his hand in a way that was suggestive.

He flicked the indicator on and joined the M6. The car was a powerful one and he wanted to get it up to speed, see how it handled. See how Sarah coped. Would she get an adrenaline rush as the speedometer crept to twice the speed limit, or would she pin herself in the seat, terrified they'd crash?

Either way, the high-speed drive would leave her flushed and with heightened emotions.

Once he'd got past a couple of wagons, he planted his right foot to the floor. 'Let's see what this bad boy's made of.'

'Sure.'

He tossed a look at her. She was relaxed, calm. The speed didn't yet worry her.

The powerful car forged past a hundred. Still there was no concern or censure in her movements. When the speedo reached 130 she laughed and clapped her hands together.

'Remember, it's limited to 155 miles per hour.'

'Will it do it?'

'There's only one way to find out.'

From the corner of his eye he could see her shuffling her legs, pressing one thigh against the other.

Ahead of them a car pulled into the fast lane. They were closing on it at pace, so the man eased off the throttle and feathered the brake.

'We got to 153.' He smiled at her as he indicated to come off at the next junction. 'That's good enough for me. If I order one today, how soon will I get it?'

'Depending on the spec you want, it's eight to ten weeks.'

'I'll have the full spec thanks. If I'm buying the fur coat, I want it to come with a pair of knickers.'

His little joke had her both laughing and blushing just as he'd hoped it would. The reference to underwear was a deliberate one, designed to add to the sexual charge of the high-speed drive.

He noticed that she took the front of her blouse between her fingers and flapped it back and forth to cool herself down. He also paid attention to the fact that her fingers landed on a closed button and alighted from an open one. It was a subterfuge of hers. She'd made the professional sale, now her focus was on making the personal one. He didn't have to do anything beyond allowing her to ensnare him.

As they travelled back to the showroom her chatter ranged back and forth from details about the car to the forthcoming weekend. The opportunity to ask her out was being presented time and again, but he kept playing dumb as he enjoyed watching her try ever harder to get him to suggest a date.

It was when they pulled up in the forecourt outside the showroom that she made her boldest move yet. He was putting the handbrake on when she leaned across him, her blouse gaping open to give him a look at her cleavage. He didn't like how obvious she was, but he had brought it on himself with his playing hard to get. Still, he didn't bite. Teasing her was enjoyable.

*

An hour later he used his phone to transfer payment and signed the last of the paperwork for his new car.

She'd never admitted defeat and had manoeuvred herself around in ways that let him either see a lot of leg or the gap between the buttons of her too-tight blouse that showed off her patterned bra.

The way her eyes had widened when he'd transferred the money from one of his shell companies and paid for the car outright told him she'd underestimated his wealth.

'I know this may be a strange request, but are you free for dinner on Friday? I'd like to mark my new purchase with a celebratory dinner in the company of a gorgeous woman. And who better than the beautiful saleswoman who sold me the car?'

She gave a self-deprecating smile at his compliments. 'I'd love to. Thank you very much.'

He made the necessary arrangements about where and when to collect her and suggested they dine at Sharrow Bay. The luxury hotel had an excellent reputation for its food and was sure to wow her. It was important to him that she was relaxed in his company. It would make snatching her so much simpler.

CHAPTER FORTY-SEVEN

The man who greeted Beth and Unthank at the Lakeland Bird of Prey Centre looked every inch the expert they needed. From the olive green corduroys to the Barbour shirt and the tweed waistcoat he wore, the man exuded the air of one who was most at home out on the fells and the high moors. The only thing that looked odd about him was the combover flapping in the breeze.

The centre was just five miles south of Penrith and to Beth's mind it was the ideal place to start looking into the wings attached to the bodies.

'I'm DC Young, this is DC Unthank. Is there somewhere we can pick your brains about a case we're working on, Mr…?'

'Call me Eric.' An easy smile crossed Eric's lined and weathered face as he pointed at a door. 'We can talk through there if you like.'

Eric's voice was soft and his words were delivered in the drawl common to many East Cumbrians. As with many men of his generation, he suffixed every sentence with 'like eh?' and turned a statement into a half question.

The room Eric led them to was half storeroom, half cloakroom. Battered clothing hung on pegs screwed to a timber rail and there were bags of feed, heavy leather gloves and wellies on timber shelving that looked as if it may collapse at any moment.

Beth reached into her folder and pulled out a file. 'Have you heard about the bodies that have been found with wings attached to their backs?'

'Yeah, I saw it on the news, like eh?'

'I have some pictures of the wings. Could you take a look at them and help us identify the birds?' Beth paused before opening the file. 'Most of these pictures were taken when the wings were still attached to the victims' bodies. I'm afraid they're rather grisly.'

'Don't worry, I work with birds of prey. I have a strong stomach.'

Beth opened the file and passed Eric the four pictures she'd brought with her. Each was a close-up of the wings.

'Hmm. You've got a *Serinus canaria domestica*, which is your typical domestic canary; an Alexandrine parakeet or *Psittacula eupatria*; a *Corvus corax*, which is your common crow; and an *Accipiter nisus*.'

The way that Eric had used the birds' Latin names without so much as a pause for thought gave Beth reassurance that they'd come to the right place to get the info they needed.

'What's an *Accipiter nisus*?'

'Sorry, it's a sparrowhawk, like eh?'

'Okay.' Beth pointed at the pictures. 'Correct me if I'm wrong, but I'm guessing that the canary and parrot could have been bought at a pet shop.'

'Aye. There are breeders as well. A good Alexandrine will fetch a few hundred quid.'

Beth tried not to mirror Unthank's wince. With the first two birds available from many sources, tracing them would be next to impossible.

'The crow and the sparrowhawk.' Beth locked eyes with Eric and tried not to look at his ridiculous hairstyle. 'If I asked you to get me those birds, how would you do it?'

'I'd use a humane trap on a crow. They're like a cage which has bait in the middle and when the bird steps on a pressure pad, the open side closes.' Eric pulled a face. 'It's a slow process though and if you wanted a specific breed it could take weeks. Anyway, the crow's wings have been damaged by pellets. I'd say that it was shot down. That's the easy way to get a pair of crow wings.'

Unthank leaned forward. 'And the sparrowhawk, how would you suggest our killer got the sparrowhawk's wings?'

'If it was me, I'd buy a bird from a registered breeder, or,' Eric paused and rubbed at his jaw, 'I'd buy a stuffed one and cut its wings off.'

'Are you able to tell the sex of the birds from the wings?'

'Of course.' Eric's tone held affront at the thought he couldn't fulfil this request rather than ego that he could. 'The canary and sparrowhawk are female while the parrot is male. I can tell that from their plumage. There's no way of sexing a crow by its wings alone. I'd need to see the entire bird.'

Beth tried a few more questions without learning anything more. The fact there was no correlation between the sex of the birds in relation to the victims whose backs they were affixed left her thinking the birds had been chosen at random.

As they were walking back to the car, she could tell Unthank was about to pass one of his pronouncements on Eric.

'C'mon then, let's have it.'

'Have what?'

'Your description of Eric.'

'He's a nice guy with a comb-over that looks as if it was done with a garden rake.' Unthank gave a pretend bow before sliding behind the wheel of his car.

Beth tossed him a wry smile as she placed her folder on the back seat. 'All true, but it's not funny and I've heard you do much better.'

CHAPTER FORTY-EIGHT

Beth rejoined the motorway and, not for the first time, cursed the geographical challenges of policing Cumbria. She'd already been to Carlisle once today and while it was only twenty minutes up the M6, by the time she'd crossed town and made her way to Cumberland Infirmary, it would take at least three quarters of an hour.

Having the morgue and police headquarters so far apart was an inconvenience to say the least, but Penrith was a good location for the HQ and the town just wasn't large enough to have a hospital with a morgue and pathologist in situ. The only places in Cumbria which had such facilities were Carlisle, Workington and Kendal and she knew they were under threat from cutbacks.

As a part of FMIT, she understood that she had to get used to spending time driving from one location to another, it was just that she felt her time would have been better spent sifting through evidence, or compiling her data-laden spreadsheets, instead of repeating journeys between Carlisle and Penrith.

Policing never worked out that way though. Many times in her career, she'd been called to a disturbance at a domestic property. After attending and dealing with the situation and returning back to the station, with or without people who'd been arrested, a call would come in and she'd be on her way back to the same street to deal with an incident a few doors along from where she'd just attended.

It would have been a lot more practical for her if Dr Hewson had called this morning when she was still in Carlisle, but that wasn't the reality of her world. Coincidences didn't happen and now whenever she did encounter one, her training had taught her to question it.

And she was questioning something at the moment. The closer she got to the hospital, the more she found her interest piqued by Hewson's insistence that his report would be better delivered in person.

CHAPTER FORTY-NINE

Beth knocked on Dr Hewson's office door and waited for a response. She could hear a voice coming from inside the room but couldn't make out any words. There was the clatter of a telephone handset being dumped into its cradle and then Dr Hewson's door swung open and a head of curly hair appeared. 'Ah, it's you, the protégé. Come on in.'

Beth gave an awkward smile at Hewson's description. She didn't want to be anyone's *protégé*, she wanted to be her own person. At the same time, it was a flattering thought that an experienced DI like O'Dowd was mentoring her. On the other hand, perhaps the doctor wasn't being entirely flattering, given Beth knew his relationship with O'Dowd wasn't the friendliest. Nevertheless she decided to accept the comment as a compliment.

'Enough with the flattery. DI O'Dowd said you wanted to speak with one of us.'

'Not just speak, show.' He reached behind the door and produced a lab coat. 'Come with me.'

As she followed him to the lab, she tried to find out what he was going to show her, but Hewson deflected all of her questions with a polite, but infuriating, 'wait and see'.

He guided her to a bench and told her to wait a moment. Beth watched as he opened a refrigerated cabinet and pulled out a tray.

When he laid the tray on the bench, she saw there were four different versions of the sliced-open trachea she'd seen during Angus Keane's post-mortem. Each was positioned next to a label.

Going left to right they were: 'Woman 1', 'Woman 2', 'Angus Keane 3' and 'Man 4'.

'What am I looking at? Or should I say, for?'

'Patience, DC Protégé, patience.' Hewson pulled out another stainless-steel tray and laid it beside the first. It contained two longer versions of what looked to be tracheas. 'The ones in the first tray are the tracheas, the second tray holds Man 4's oesophagus and a sample one from a non-victim.'

'We've identified Man 4. His name was Nick Langley.'

The tattoo had been referenced as identification and while there was no doubt Man 4 was Nick Langley, his wife would still have to make a formal identification.

The sample labelled 'Woman 1' was half the length of the others and had pieces missing where animals had feasted. The other three were similar in size, but she didn't see a lot of differences until she took a deep breath and bent over for a closer inspection.

A part of Beth knew Hewson was testing her, and it was this knowledge that kept her leaning over the two trays until her back ached.

She looked at the facts. Woman 1 had a scorched trachea. Woman 2 only had scorching on the upper part of the trachea. Angus Keane's trachea showed worse burning than either of those two, while Nick Langley's trachea was even worse. In one or two places the fire had burned holes which allowed her to see the polished stainless steel of the trays beneath.

None of it made sense to her and she couldn't see what the doctor's point was. Rather than admit defeat, though, Beth kept looking at both trays until her mind interpreted what her eyes were seeing. Back and forth she gazed until she made a connection.

She straightened up and resisted the urge to massage her lower back. 'Correct me if I'm wrong here, but are you trying to tell me that the killer has been experimenting with the fire breathing for his dragons?'

As soon as she'd verbalised her theory, Beth felt stupid. Only a handful of people knew the dragon theory, and it was by no means something everyone agreed on.

Hewson's face was impassive. 'What makes you say that?'

His question was a double-edged sword. Either he was of the same thinking and wanted her thought processes explained, or he was mocking her and seeing just how long she'd keep digging herself deeper.

She didn't believe he was the type of person to mock her, so after a deep breath, she opened her mouth.

'The first woman's burns look to be lesser than those of the others. In fact each victim shows more fire damage to their trachea than the one before.' Beth looked at Hewson's face again but saw no indication of whether she was right or wrong. She'd come too far to stop now. 'He's trying different things to see which burns the best. Not only has he been using an accelerant, but it looks like he's been putting more of it into each of the victims. Am I right?'

A smile creased Dr Hewson's face. 'You would indeed be right. At least with most of your theory. Woman 1's death was not a pretty one. When I examined what was left of her lungs and stomach, I came to the conclusion that the accelerant in her stomach, which for the record was petrol, poisoned her. I hate to say it, but she would have had a slow agonising death until dehydration overwhelmed her.'

Beth reeled at the thought of the poor woman, abandoned to die in that foetid cellar. Her throat ruined by fire. Every breath filled with agony as the poison attacked her body. Not only would her death have been excruciating, but she'd have felt her strength fading. Try as she might, Beth couldn't help but hope the woman's injuries had caused her to pass out so she didn't experience either the pain or the horror of her last hours of life.

'What about the others?'

'My best guess is that the killer put too much petrol into Woman 2. Her lungs were saturated with the stuff and I'd say that she was technically drowning when he put his match to her. There would have been a huge puff of flame but it wouldn't have travelled far inside her. She'd have died instantly as the fire would have burned all the oxygen in her mouth and throat.' He leaned forward and assessed her with a careworn expression. 'Not a good way to go, but better than her predecessor's by a long way.'

Beth stepped away from the bench and put her back against a wall. The room was in danger of spinning as she contemplated the women's horrific deaths in the dingy cellar that had almost taken her own life.

The pathologist gave her a couple of minutes to pull herself together, then walked across and stood in front of her. 'You ready to continue?'

Beth nodded and let Hewson lead her back to the bench.

'Do you see this?' He used a pen to point to the pair of oesophagi. 'Man 4's, sorry, Nick Langley's, is charred away whereas the unburned one is in good order. This is wrong. The epiglottis wouldn't normally allow a fire to travel down an oesophagus. However, his was all but burned away. I'm not sure how, but it looks as if there was substantial burning that went on after he died.'

'How could that have happened?'

Hewson turned from putting the trays back into the chiller and stood in front of her. 'C'mon, DC Protégé, you can have a seat in my office while I tell you the rest of my findings and my suspicions.'

With a mental girding of her loins, Beth pushed herself off the wall and trailed behind the doctor as they walked back to his office.

It had been kind of Hewson to not comment on how she'd reacted. Instead of asking if she was okay, he'd recognised that she wasn't and had offered a distraction, a way out. There was little doubt in her mind that he'd seen many different reactions to his work over the years, but he'd managed hers with compassion and understanding. If asked, she'd have guessed that he'd have been the type to point her to the ever-present sick bucket, or worse, hand her a mop if she didn't make it to the bucket.

His actions proved to her that people should never be judged until there was enough information to make an accurate assessment of their character. She'd had him down as a grumpy and thoughtless man and had been proven wrong.

'Take a seat.' He pointed at the plastic chair to one side of his desk.

Beth sat down and glanced round the office. It was pretty much as she'd expected it to be. There was a whiteboard bearing names in different colours, detailing his schedule, a filing cabinet and a few shelves that were laden with medical textbooks.

A calendar hung on the wall beside his desk and its picture was of York Minster. There was the obligatory photo frame on the desk alongside the telephone and a computer screen.

Though it was tidy, the office displayed the signs of being well used.

'What else did you find?'

'After coming to the same conclusions you've just reached, I consulted with a colleague in Manchester. She's a specialist in burns, both pre- and post-mortem. I told her what I found and she agrees with our assessment. She's drawn up a database of burns received from various accelerants and has consented to give me the benefit of her expertise. I've taken cross-section photographs of each trachea and sent them to her. She will examine them and then give her considered opinion on each one. I don't know how much use it'll be for you, but it may just give you a clue, or better, some evidence you can use.'

'That's very thorough of you, doctor.'

'We have to be thorough. The dead deserve answers every bit as much as the living.'

'What you said before, about Nick Langley's epiglottis being scorched, have you any ideas on that?'

'One or two. Do you have any yourself?'

Beth had some ideas, but she didn't like them. If they were right, the implications for the victims were horrific. 'I may be wrong – part of me hopes I am – but it seems to me that he's learning as he goes. His first victim had the least burns, which suggests that he didn't use enough accelerant to get his desired effect. That he'd more or less drowned Woman 2 with the stuff backs up this theory.' Beth lifted her eyes from the floor to look at Hewson. 'Would I be right in saying that it was only a lack of oxygen which prevented the accelerant from exploding inside her?'

'You would. When I tested her organs, they were all showing signs of poisoning from the petrol. The two men – what are your thoughts regarding them?'

'Horrific deaths. Agony. Calculated. Experiments.'

Hewson's bushy eyebrows twitched as the words tumbled from Beth's mouth. 'Interesting that you used the words "calculated" and "experiments". Can you expand on your thinking?'

'Angus Keane had worse burns than Woman 2, so that suggests there was less accelerant used, but what was there seems to have burned better.' Beth leaned back in her seat and closed her eyes in thought. 'What if more accelerant was added after the first flames died out? You know, either poured or squirted into his mouth and then lit, would that cause the burning you found?'

Hewson rested his elbows on the desk and steepled his fingers beneath his chin. 'That's what I was thinking. I'd even suggest he could have been using something like one of those plastic spray bottles to deliver the petrol. I'd say he only stopped after his victim's heart gave out. For Man 4, on the other hand, the killer didn't stop; I'd say that he kept going long after the poor bugger died.' Hewson slid one of his desk drawers open, reached inside and pulled out an evidence bag. 'I found this block of wood jammed between his teeth. It would keep his mouth open so that more petrol could be sprayed or poured in. The trachea was so badly burned that there's no way our victim would have been able to breathe. He'd have died of suffocation due to a trachea that was either blistered or punctured.' Hewson closed his eyes for a few moments. 'Like the others, his death would have been inevitable and a release. However, I do think you're right about the killer experimenting. He's refining his methods to ensure the fire is breathed for longer.'

Beth tried not to revisit the cellar in her mind, did what she could not to picture Nick Langley repeatedly breathing fire. Not now that she knew the horrors that had taken place in there.

As a distraction from her thoughts, she fired more questions at Hewson. 'What else do you have to tell me? Can you make a more informed guess as to how long the bodies were in that cellar?'

'My initial impression was wrong. Woman 1 had been in there at least four months, but not more than eight. I'll need to check some reference books, but I should be able to narrow that window down for you. Woman 2 was around four weeks give or take a day or two. Nick Langley was very recent. I'd say he was in there no longer than twenty-four hours.'

'That ties in with what we've heard from his wife.'

'That still means you'll have to do two sets of dental records and DNA in the hope of getting a match. Dowdy won't be pleased about her budget.'

Beth ignored the jibe about O'Dowd's budget. Her mind was focussed on the various lengths of time the victims had been in the cellar. Now they had some hard facts to work with, they could focus their investigation into the victims' identities with more accuracy, and once they knew who the two women were, could start looking at links between the victims. Furnished with an idea as to when the two women had died, they could narrow down the number of potential victims by using the missing persons' reports.

'What else have you got for me?'

'That isn't enough?' Hewson raised an eyebrow, so Beth put a stern look on her face. 'Okay. Judging by her teeth, Woman 1 was in her fifties. There were no distinguishing marks on what was left of her and all of her joints were her own.'

Beth understood why Hewson commented about the woman's joints being her own. Hip and knee replacements all had serial numbers that could be used to identify the victims.

'What about Woman 2?'

'I'd say mid-twenties. No distinguishing marks. She was in good health and when I checked her internal organs, other than the damage wrought by the killer, I found them to be in good condition. Her muscle tone had obviously degraded after death, but from what was left, I'd say that she kept herself in shape, but I wouldn't say that she was obsessed with exercise.'

Hewson bent down and scratched at his ankle.

'What about the wings? Were they attached with surgical glue again?'

A nod.

'Where are they?'

'In evidence bags ready for you to take with you.'

Beth gave a polite grin. 'I should have known, shouldn't I?'

'You should indeed.' Hewson pointed at the bags. 'I had a wee look at the wings; I'd say the canary, parrot and crow were from birds that he'd killed for the purpose, but I'm no expert. However, the bird of prey's wings were different. They had a kind of lustre to them as if they'd been treated with something.'

'Do you mean a lacquer? The kind of thing a taxidermist might use?'

'I do and I don't. Taxidermists soak their charges in acetone to preserve them. The wings are being tested as we speak and I am confident the results will be positive.'

This fitted with what Beth had been thinking on the drive up from Penrith. Eric's suggestion that the easiest way to get the wings of a bird of prey was to use a stuffed bird made sense on every level.

'Did you get anything from their bloods?'

'Nothing from the women, but Nick Langley's blood shows traces of flunitrazepam.'

Beth cast her mind back to her training. 'That's Rohypnol, isn't it?'

'Indeed it is.'

'That explains how the killer got his victims to go down to the cellars. How he got them to stand still while he tied them up and attached the wings to their bodies.'

'It does.' The smile faded from Hewson's face. 'This case is affecting you. I can see it's already changed you a little. You got upset earlier and it was nothing to do with controlling your gag reflex. If you have a bottle of wine in your fridge, do yourself a favour when you get home, leave it there. Too many good coppers start with a glass of wine or a tin of beer, only to end up borderline alcoholics. Don't let that happen to you. Knock seven bells out of a punchbag, or go somewhere you can scream and shout at the injustices of life without anyone seeing or hearing you, but don't get into the habit of using alcohol to mask the trauma. Trust me.'

'Thanks for your concern, but don't worry about me.' Beth jabbed a finger at her left cheek. 'I didn't turn to drink when this happened, and I won't now.' She rose to her feet. 'If you'll let me have those wings for evidence, I'll leave you to carry on with your day.'

Even as she marched back to her car, Beth was feeling guilty for the way she'd snapped at Dr Hewson. She knew her overreaction was due to how close to the truth he'd come. The bottle of wine in her fridge would have been opened tonight. But after what he'd just said, there was no way she was having even one glass.

CHAPTER FIFTY

The man folded his glasses and placed them into the case on the passenger seat of his van. Since the test drive with Sarah he'd done nothing but curse himself.

He knew he'd come on too strong. That he'd let his eyes wander too often. That his clumsy attempts to share a joke with her had backfired. Most of all, he knew that he'd blown any chance of seeing her again after tomorrow's visit to inform her that he wouldn't be buying the car.

If he had the money he'd buy the car tomorrow. That way, he could go and see her every now and again. He'd have to make silly excuses like imaginary rattles, but every time the car needed a new tyre or was due for a service, he'd be able to go to the dealership and wait around until the work was done. For him, that would be perfect; he'd just take a seat and pretend to read his paper while she got on with her day. He'd be able to admire her flawless face and desirable figure as she strode back and forth.

The problem was, he didn't have the money. His army pension was decent, but if he bought the car, he'd have to change his lifestyle, eradicate the meals out, save money on petrol.

As beautiful as Sarah was, there was no way he was prepared to give up his search for angels. Especially for one who'd shunned him. Yes, she may have done it with a false smile and good manners, but he knew she wasn't happy to have him around her.

Painful as the experience may be, he needed to move on from her. She was an angel who'd got away and he had to let her go, give her the freedom to fly. After tomorrow he'd never see her again. That was the way it must be.

He clambered from his van and walked into the Hare and Hounds. Wednesday's were one of Tamara's working days and he needed a distraction from his thoughts about Sarah.

The bar was almost empty when he walked in. A couple of men were sitting in a corner. Judging by the slur of their voices and the glassiness of their eyes, the man reckoned that they'd been drinking since opening time.

Tamara put down her mobile and came over to him. Her voice full of welcome. He loved that she greeted him by name and asked if he wanted the usual.

She'd reverted back to skinny jeans rather than Saturday's skirt, but on the plus side her hair was tied in a ponytail, which showed off her graceful neck.

The man climbed onto a bar stool and prepared to spend an enjoyable couple of hours in the company of a beautiful young woman.

Tamara would be his salvation. She would erase Sarah from his mind and mend his breaking heart.

CHAPTER FIFTY-ONE

Beth returned to the office at Carleton Hall to find Thompson working alone. She recounted what she'd learned from Hewson and her own thoughts then settled down at her desk ready to update the files and fill out the necessary reports.

Thompson gave her a look. 'Sound like you've been busy, Young Beth.'

'I have, Old Frank.'

As soon as the words left her mouth, Beth regretted them. Hewson's comment about not using alcohol as a crutch still rankled her, and now she'd gone and given the irritating Thompson confirmation that he was getting under her skin.

'I did wonder how long it would take you to get sick of that.'

When Beth looked at Thompson she saw a genuine smile.

'I got sick of it at the age of eleven when I first heard it from a registration teacher. He thought he was funny. He wasn't, but a lot of adolescent boys thought he was.'

'Ouch. Did it follow you? How long did it last?'

'Until I started to develop. It's funny how boys stop taking the piss when you grow a pair of breasts.'

Beth looked away. She was ashamed of the vehemence to her tone. The memories of mocking boys turning into gawping teens still ate at her. Worse than that, she'd just overshared with the kind of prick who'd regurgitate her admission to anyone who'd listen.

'That sounds like a typical boy thing.' Thompson drummed his fingers on the desk. 'For what it's worth, you're a good-looking woman. It's no surprise teenage boys took an interest in you when you were growing up.' He pointed at his own face. 'Me, I had a face like a pizza and bugger all confidence. I married the one girl in the school who gave me the time of day, and now she can't remember who I am.'

Even though she knew about his wife's condition, Beth played dumb to protect O'Dowd. 'What do you mean?'

'She has early-onset Alzheimer's.' He turned away from Beth. 'She's forty-seven and no longer recognises me, or our daughters.'

Beth didn't know what to say, so in place of saying the wrong thing she kept silent.

'I took the girls to see her on Sunday. I agreed that it could be the last time they had to visit her. They hate going since she stopped remembering who they are.' Thompson turned to look at her. 'I am not sure you can ever see pain like a child saying goodbye to their mother for the last time.'

Beth shook her head and tried not to see the hurt in his eyes. 'No. I can't imagine how hard that must have been for you.'

'However hard you think it was, double it. I took each of my girls in by themselves, which meant I had to see it twice. My girls are hardly eating, they're grunting at me and they spend all their time holed up in their bedrooms with music blaring.'

'They're teenagers, aren't they? That's what they do. It's what I did. Give them space and time. Be there if they need you and don't expect them to understand something you can't.'

Thompson wiped a hand over his face. 'Shit, Beth. I'm sorry for dumping all this on you.'

'Don't be. I'd rather deal with this version of you than the DS Thompson who's been nipping my head all week. For the record, I don't know how you cope, but that's what you've got to do. Keep putting one foot in front of the other. The only advice I can offer you is to try and look after yourself too. Somehow you've got to give yourself a break. Go for a few pints with a mate, or take your girls to the pictures, just do something that puts a smile on your face for a couple of hours.'

'Thanks.' He gave her a sidelong look. 'I half-thought you were just a pretty face when I first met you. Then I saw the scar on your cheek, and I realised you were probably tougher than I'd realised – to be a copper with such an obvious target for abuse on your face. Then I saw you at work. You're bright, you cover all the normal bases and then you come up with some great ideas. I shouldn't have taken credit for your idea the other day though. That was wrong of me. You deserve better than that.'

'You were a bit of a dick that day.' Beth gave him a gentle smile. 'Now I know why, I will try to forgive you.'

Beth found herself wondering how many more pressures were going to show in the team's personal lives. In less than twenty-four hours she'd had both of her superiors opening their hearts to her. It was flattering that they trusted her, but also worrying that they had these distractions while investigating such brutal murders.

The fact her own temper had been frayed for her to snap at Thompson just hours after snapping at Hewson concerned her though. She'd endured enough abuse in the past to know the best defence was to ignore it and move on. Yet she'd still gone ahead and said her piece. Worse, she'd lashed out at a man she knew was in pain. She'd meant what she'd said to him though; she'd forgive him for his unnecessary snaps at her, but she sure as hell wasn't going to forget what he'd tried to do by stealing her idea and then embellishing it with his own sexist take. Beth vowed to herself that every time he crossed the line, she'd call him on it.

But it wasn't like her to get so wound up; she realised the stresses and horrors of the case were getting to her. With both Thompson and O'Dowd struggling with personal issues, as well as dealing with the horrors of the case, Beth knew there was more pressure than ever before on her if FMIT were going to succeed with this investigation.

It was bad enough that these heinous crimes were taking place, but the idea that the perpetrator of the killings may escape justice was something Beth couldn't accept. She vowed to herself that she'd keep pushing forward as much as she could, because whatever happened, she wasn't going to let any of the victims or their families down. Not when she had the memory of Angus Keane's daughters spurring her on.

CHAPTER FIFTY-TWO

The atmosphere in the office was subdued. O'Dowd and Thompson were cloistered over the DI's desk while Beth and Unthank were hard at work. Beth was going over the missing persons' list and Unthank was looking into Nick Langley's life.

O'Dowd had decreed that they were to leave a lot of the donkey work to the officers DCI Phinn had seconded to their investigation. The four members of FMIT would collate, examine and work to identify the killer and his two female victims.

Beth's eyes flicked back and forth between the screen and the printed notes she'd made about the two unidentified victims. It didn't take her long to find a possible match for Woman 2. Rachel Allen had set off to backpack around Europe four and a half weeks ago. Her parents had reported her missing a fortnight later when they'd heard nothing from her.

According to the report filed by the person who'd taken the parents' call, she'd set off from Carlisle train station and they'd never heard from her again. A perfunctory check had shown that Rachel had got on the train south only to get off again at Penrith station. The officer had gone so far as to run Rachel's passport through the various databases. She'd never left the country. A footnote gave the officer's thoughts; namely that they presumed Rachel had lied to her parents and run away from home.

To Beth's mind such thinking was lazy. There were other avenues that could have been pursued. Rachel Allen was an attractive young woman; therefore she was in the high-risk category when it came to possible abduction by rapists and murderers. On the other hand, there was no evidence to suggest that she hadn't just run away from home.

She put in a call to the train station at Penrith to see if they had any CCTV coverage from the day Rachel Allen stepped off the train. With luck, they may see if she met someone.

The person she spoke to was abrupt. When she asked about CCTV footage she got a curt laugh and was told that the camera hadn't worked for at least six months.

Beth dug further into the file opened on Rachel Allen. When she saw the picture, she felt a mixture of elation and sadness. The face looking back at her from the screen was a happier version of the one Dr Hewson had supplied of Woman 2. While it felt good to make the connection, there was now another family who'd have to be told of their bereavement.

'Ma'am, I've got an ID on Woman 2. She's Rachel Allen. Twenty-two years old, from Carlisle.'

O'Dowd looked up and gave her a nod. 'Good work. Have you an address for the next of kin?' The printer starting with its usual racket made O'Dowd turn her head. 'That it?' Beth nodded. 'Good. Unthank, what have you got on Nick Langley?'

'There's nothing of note in his life other than the neighbour we're getting picked up for fighting with him. His bank accounts are all normal and there's no indication that either he or his wife were playing away from home. He's a kitchen fitter and when I spoke to his boss, he was full of praise for both his workmanship and the way he kept customers happy.'

'What's the story with the fight?' This part was news to Beth and she wanted to know more about it.

'It was a dispute over the hedge at the back of his house. He and his wife were trying to grow it to give themselves some more privacy, when their neighbour started cutting a foot off the top of it. Nick had challenged him and the guy had just kept cutting away. Things got heated and blows were exchanged. A different neighbour dialled treble nine, but by the time someone got there, the fight had all but ended. The responding officers' reports suggested that Nick had got the better of his opponent. Both of them got a caution and life moved on.' Unthank shook his head. 'It happened last year, so it's more than likely a waste of time speaking to the guy.'

'Well, we're going to do it anyway.' O'Dowd lifted the sheet of paper from the printer and pointed it at Thompson. 'Go and do the knock. Take Unthank with you.'

'Ma'am.' There was reluctance as well as obedience in Thompson's voice.

It was tough on him to have to go and inform Rachel's parents of her likely death when he was so emotionally fragile, but Beth saw a certain logic to it. If Thompson was dealing with someone else's grief, he wouldn't be able to wallow in his own.

As for Rachel's next of kin, they wouldn't get the closure of saying goodbye. Along with the killer's work, Dr Hewson's post-mortem had left Rachel in a condition that no parent should see. The formal identification would have to be done from the pictures Dr Hewson had taken of her before starting the post-mortem.

'See if you can identify that other woman, Beth. Once the plods bring the neighbour in, we'll see what he has to say for himself.'

Before he left the office, Beth got Unthank to print off the details of the fight. If she was to sit in on an interview, she wanted the relevant knowledge in her head so she could make a contribution, or at the very least, not sit there looking as if she hadn't a clue what was going on. Although, she'd already heard enough to assume it was a typical domestic argument. When in uniformed response, she'd been called out to many a dispute between neighbours. Whether it was to do with a boundary wall or hedge, or the playing of loud music, there was always a source of irritation that saw neither party willing to compromise.

She turned back to the list of missing people, and scrolled down the database until she was looking at the names of those who'd been reported missing between four and eight months ago. This would be a lot harder than identifying Rachel Allen. Woman 1's eyes had been removed. Her face had been eaten away, and lacking any tattoos on the scraps of flesh the animals hadn't eaten, the best she could hope for was to narrow the list of possibilities to an acceptable number of women whose dental records would have to be checked.

First off she listed the missing women whose age was similar to Dr Hewson's estimate of Woman 1's. Next she looked at the length of time they'd been missing and eliminated those whose dates were after Woman 1 was estimated to have died.

Beth picked up her phone and dialled the first of four numbers. Her priority now was checking to see if any of the remaining four missing women had turned up. Many of the people reported missing would return home after a few weeks away. Some would have dropped out to cope with a life event; others would have returned to their spouse when they realised their lover wasn't all they dreamed of. When these scenarios happened, there were only a few who bothered to let the police know.

The person who picked up was a woman, so Beth asked her name. It matched the missing person, and she made a note in the database and gave the woman a short lecture about wasting police time.

She had the same result with the next call.

The third call she made put her into contact with a man whose voice wavered with grief when she explained why she was calling. His wife had been found a week after he'd reported her missing. Her car had left the road and plunged into a flooding river. It was only when the waters receded that her car was found. He'd never thought to cancel the missing persons' report because the police knew about his wife's death.

Beth cursed the fact that she'd dredged up painful memories for the man. She'd blame the officers who were involved in the recovery of the vehicle and informing the man his wife was dead, had she not been aware of the pressures on officers of every rank. As well as there being fewer officers, there seemed to be more paperwork than ever, more databases to update. It was inevitable that on occasions some things would get missed due to someone being overworked and overstressed.

The fourth and final call put her in touch with someone whose wife had returned home, stayed long enough to pack a bag, and had then flounced out the house and into her lover's car.

With all four options exhausted, Beth gave the database another scan in case she'd missed something. But nothing obvious presented itself.

She was about to extend her search by a month either side of Dr Hewson's guess when O'Dowd's phone rang.

The DI listened for a moment then hung up. Her mouth twisted into what could only be described as a determined pout as she pulled on her suit jacket and straightened the collar. 'Let's go ask a man some awkward questions.'

CHAPTER FIFTY-THREE

Beth laid the folder with her notes onto the table and listened as O'Dowd went through the formalities for the benefit of the tape.

'Mr Fielding, we are interviewing you under caution regarding the murder of Nick Langley and three others. Do you understand what we mean by that?'

Fielding glanced at his lawyer, an earnest man who carried the air of someone who'd seen every possible outcome of a police interview.

'Yes, I understand. How may I help you?'

Beth noticed how calm Fielding was. There were no trembles to his voice or his hands. The looks he cast them were assured and there was no stress on his face.

'Can you account for your whereabouts on Monday evening?'

'I was at home most of the time.'

'Can anyone verify you were there?'

'No.' Fielding tilted his head. 'I'm not married and I have no kids. Maybe one of my neighbours saw me putting something in the bin or noticed my lights on.'

'May I ask why you are asking my client about these murders?'

'Mr Langley had a brawl with your client last year. Apparently Mr Fielding took it upon himself to cut Mr Langley's hedge.' O'Dowd shifted her gaze from the solicitor to Fielding. 'Care to tell us why you were cutting another man's hedge?'

'I wasn't cutting another man's hedge. All I was doing was making sure that my garden got plenty of sunlight. Vegetables need light, you know. He wanted to grow the hedge to six feet high and I wanted it at four maximum. I cut it at five and he went off his head. Called me all kinds of names. That wasn't acceptable.'

'So you just went ahead and cut the hedge at the height you deemed was a fair compromise. Except Mr Langley didn't see it that way and the two of you came to blows.'

Fielding spread his hands wide. 'It was wrong of me, I know. I got beat up for it at the time. I shouldn't have done it, and I paid the price. But if you think I've waited a year to kill him, then you've got to be joking.'

'Excuse me for butting in.' Beth put a hand on O'Dowd's arm. 'I read the reports from the arresting officers. It would appear that Mr Langley did indeed win the fight you had. That upset you at the time. You made threats. Threats against his life to be specific. What do you have to say about that?'

Fielding lifted his right hand from the table and used his forefinger to point at Beth. 'Pardon me for saying so, but you look as if you've been in the wars yourself. I'd say that judging by the scar on your face, like me when I fought Langley, you got a silver medal. Do you remember feeling angry, wanting to hurt the person who done that to you? Did you at least want them to feel as scared as you were? I was angry at myself for getting into a fight. Disappointed that I lost it, and scared that I'd cross swords with him again and get another pasting. Because my emotions were running high, I said some stupid things that I didn't mean. When you got that scar, did you say anything you now regret, even though it was said in the heat of the moment?'

Fielding had a good point and Beth knew it. She had been angry and scared after the bottle had been thrust into her cheek. In the first few weeks after it happened she'd entertained many thoughts of vengeance and retribution. Yet she'd never wanted the perpetrator killed, just punished.

'Don't try to deflect this, Mr Fielding. You threatened to kill someone, and lo and behold, that person is murdered.' Beth glared at Fielding as she waited for his answer.

Fielding smoothed his moustache. 'Over a year later. I'm sure you've checked me out in your database. You'll have found that in my fifty-two years on this planet I have collected one speeding ticket, three parking tickets and one caution for the fight with Mr Langley.'

The lawyer leaned back in his chair. 'My client is innocent of the murder of Mr Langley. He is more than happy for you to check his whereabouts by triangulating his mobile phone signal.'

Beth looked at O'Dowd and saw uncertainty. A man Fielding's age wouldn't necessarily use his phone the way someone her age would. His might well get left in the house for days.

He had it with him now; she could see it wedged into his shirt pocket. It looked to be similar to the old Nokia her father had. He'd kept the same phone for years as all he wanted it for was making and taking calls.

'We'll take you up on that.' O'Dowd pressed on regardless of their confident smiles. 'Let's be clear though, it proves where the phone was, not Mr Fielding.'

'Of course.' The lawyer's smile was like an oil slick. 'Is there anything else, or is my client free to leave?'

Beth seized the opportunity before O'Dowd let Fielding leave. 'One thing. Do the names Angus Keane and Rachel Allen mean anything to you?'

Beth watched Fielding closely as she posed the question.

'I heard something about Angus Keane on the news. Wasn't he the guy whose body turned up with wings attached to his back?'

His eyes widened. 'If you're asking me about him as well as Langley and whatever the woman's name was, it means you think their deaths were connected. I'm sorry, but you're asking the wrong man. I didn't know any of them, and I'm sorry I ended up brawling with Mr Langley.'

O'Dowd wrapped up the interview, and they returned to the office.

CHAPTER FIFTY-FOUR

Sarah lifted the brush and ran it through her nana's hair. The old woman was unaware of her granddaughter's actions, but for as long as Sarah could remember, she'd never had a hair out of place. To not maintain that tradition now would be to let Nana down.

As she brushed the hair into its usual style she recounted her day to her grandmother. She told her of the different test drives, of the customer who came in complaining that the cruise control didn't actually steer the car, and how her boss had praised her for the way she'd managed to sell a top of the range car with every possible optional extra.

She even told her nana about the date she had arranged for Friday night. The old woman lay unmoving as she described every detail of her encounter with Kevin Ingersoll. Sarah chatted about the date and how she was looking forward to eating at Sharrow Bay. That would be a treat in itself. To dine there with a rich man who found her attractive would be even better.

The biggest issue for her was choosing the right outfit. Sharrow Bay was a classy place and, as such, she'd have to dress appropriately. While on the one hand she wanted Kevin to be attracted to her, she also wanted to create the right impression. What she had to achieve with her outfit was a mixture of sensual, alluring and respectable.

Sarah gave her wardrobe a mental rifling through and remembered a pale-green wool dress. She'd got it last year and had only worn it once. It was perfect. Mid-calf; it was appropriate for the venue and the way it clung to her legs as she walked would add a level of sensuality.

When she settled down with a cup of tea, she contrasted the two test drives she'd had today. The old man with his military tie had been a waste of time. He'd never tried to put the car through its paces and had spent more time leering at her than paying attention to the vehicle he was supposed to be interested in.

It hadn't taken her long to realise that his main interest was in her.

Her next thoughts were about Kevin and how he'd driven with flair and confidence. He'd been interested in the car and his questions had all been about the vehicle. He'd wanted to know about performance, the car's statistics and the range of extras.

When he'd taken the car up to 150 it had been all she could do not to squeal in pleasure. An ex-boyfriend had once got his clapped-out Golf up to 120, but that had been during an argument and had left her scared rather than exhilarated.

By comparison, Kevin had been his normal self and hadn't shown the slightest hint of fear or concern about the high speeds he'd reached. Nor had he shown exhilaration. He'd been flat, dispassionate to the point of being emotionless.

He had been indifferent to her charms at first and she'd had to become more brazen than she'd expected. She'd begun to think he wasn't attracted to her, when he'd sprung the invitation to dinner. Her agreement had been given at once and it was only when he'd left the showroom that she realised Friday was her night to be here with Nana.

Her mum had agreed a swap, although it meant Sarah would have to cancel her night out on Saturday. If things worked out with Kevin, missing a Saturday night in Kendal with the same faces telling the same stories was a tiny price to pay.

As she kicked off her shoes, Sarah caught the whiff of hypocrisy from her recollections of her day. She'd had two encounters with two very different men. Both had been polite and neither had touched her beyond a polite handshake. One man had paid attention to her body. His wandering eyes had creeped her out and made her feel like she was being ogled by a pervert, while the other had kept his eyes on her face and had shown indifference to her physique, even when she'd flashed a bit more leg.

It was counter-intuitive, because she knew she had a good figure and was used to the attention she got when she wore a short skirt or a low-cut top. She dressed for work in a way that attracted male attention, to help her make sales, while still looking smart and professional. Perhaps that's what was responsible for the way she felt about the older man, the fact that somewhere in her subconscious, she knew he was never going to buy a car and was only there to perv over her.

Her choice of outfit for Friday night was another indicator of her shifting boundaries. The wool dress was sexy in a non-revealing way. It would showcase her figure to perfection without revealing anything more than a few inches of ankle and calf. It would be suitable for dinner in a posh hotel, and yet she also wanted it to be a catalyst of desire.

There was no doubt in her mind that she wanted to sleep with Kevin, but she wanted him to have to work for it first, to prove that he wanted her for more than just a one-night stand. Then, and only then, would she let him make love to her.

CHAPTER FIFTY-FIVE

Beth went back to the list of missing persons and checked a month either side of her original parameters. The list yielded one possibility, but even they didn't seem like a cast-iron certainty.

When she called the number of the person who'd reported the lady missing, the call was answered by a sleepy voice. Beth explained who she was and why she was calling so late. The man at the other end of the line perked up a little. A minute later Beth thanked him for his candid appraisal of his wife and ended the call.

The woman had been located at her sister's house five days after he'd reported her missing. A week after that he came home from work to find most of his furniture and all her belongings had disappeared.

A quick check of their address yielded three treble nine calls from neighbours in the weeks before her disappearance. Each call had been made after the neighbours had heard a man shouting and a woman screaming.

Beth gave the woman a mental high-five. She'd escaped the clutches of a man who didn't value her, freed herself from a life of terror and had possessed the courage to make a new start.

While pleased for the woman, Beth knew that it meant she'd drawn another blank unless the victim had been in the cellar a lot longer than Dr Hewson had stated. It was easy to cast the blame for her failure to name the victim onto the pathologist, but Beth wasn't keen to believe he'd got it so wrong. Plus Max Cooper had only been away for six months, so it seemed unlikely that the body had been there before he'd gone on his world tour.

Hewson had covered his bases by not being specific and giving a wide parameter for the length of time the woman had been in the cellar. She'd extended the dates without success, which meant one of three things: the doctor was mistaken, the woman wasn't local to Cumbria, or she hadn't been missed by anyone.

If she'd been a tourist holidaying in the area, she'd have been missed when she hadn't returned home. But with Cumbria as her last known position, her disappearance would have been flagged on the searches Beth had run.

Beth's next thoughts were about who wouldn't be reported missing. Homeless people were always moving about and were prone to vanish for weeks at a time before popping up somewhere else. Nobody on the streets would miss her, and if they did, they often weren't the type to walk into a police station to discuss anything other than their personal conspiracy theories.

Even if she wasn't homeless, the woman could otherwise be the kind of recluse who lived alone and shunned contact with other people. Already in Beth's short career, she'd twice attended calls where a neighbour had been worried about an unusual smell. Upon breaking into the houses, they'd found decomposing bodies that had lain for at least a month. Without a body to create a smell, the neighbours had no reason to call the police about the pain in the backside who lived next door. They'd figure they'd just got lucky and had missed bumping into their crotchety neighbour.

Beth spent a few minutes looking at the missing persons' reports from neighbouring counties and drawing up a list of possibilities. It seemed less likely than being local to Cumbria, but there was no other course of action she could think of right now, other than waiting for a result from the woman's dental records.

By 10 p.m., she had a list of nine names which fit Hewson's timescale. They could be called in the morning though. Even with the urgency of the case, Beth knew she'd get far better responses if she didn't wake up people to ask if their loved ones had returned home.

There was nothing further to be found in the missing persons' reports. Or in the ones that had been filed about the people they'd spoken to when canvassing the area for witnesses.

Beth tried not to slam the office door behind her when she left, or to stomp her feet in frustration at her lack of progress as she walked to her car. She achieved the first.

The bottle of wine in her fridge called to her and she planned on having a large glass. To hell with Dr Hewson and his warning, she was a grown woman, and if she wanted a glass of wine, she'd damned well have one.

CHAPTER FIFTY-SIX

Beth couldn't help but notice the air of dejection when she entered the office. It was a physical thing which polluted the atmosphere. Both O'Dowd's and Thompson's faces wore harried, uninspiring frowns and there was no sign of the always-early Unthank.

'Morning.' Beth cast a look at Unthank's seat, noticed the lack of a jacket hanging from the back of it. 'Where's Paul?'

'He phoned in sick. Said he'd been up all night spewing.'

Beth winced at the grumble in O'Dowd's tone. Illness happened, and while Unthank wasn't to blame for his, it couldn't have happened at a worse time for them.

'Anything else happening?'

'Yeah. The DCI has invited me to join him for a press conference.'

From the way O'Dowd spoke, Beth could tell the invitation was one which couldn't be refused. She'd never had to take part in a press conference, but it was a box she'd be quite happy to leave unticked. With so few leads to pursue, one unidentified body, and no obvious link between the victims apart from how they died, there was next to no information to share with the press. And when the journalists sensed they were being fobbed off with stock responses, their questions would become sharper, more pertinent. DCI Phinn would probably want O'Dowd there as the sacrificial lamb should the press conference turn tricky.

'So we've got the missing persons to track down. What else do we have, ma'am?'

'Nothing. That's the bloody problem. We've got nothing. There's bugger all to go on, and in a few hours, I've got to sit next to DCI Phinn and tell journalists from national newspapers and the TV news as much. Jesus, we still haven't identified the fourth victim. What the hell am I supposed to say?'

'Actually, ma'am, I was thinking about that last night. I went through the misper reports and eliminated everyone from Cumbria who's a match for what we know about Woman 1. With that done, I looked at the matches in the misper files for Dumfries and Galloway and Northumberland, in case the first victim wasn't as local as the other three. I've got a list of nine people to call this morning.'

'Well done. If you can get me a name, at least I can tell those jackals we've identified all the victims.'

'I did have another thought.'

'What is it, Young Beth?' There was now kindness in Thompson's voice where there had once been mockery.

'Woman 1 was in her fifties, according to Dr Hewson. It's possible she was a little older. If she lived by herself and didn't have any family, there's a possibility her disappearance has gone unreported. She may also have been homeless. Again, nobody would miss her.'

O'Dowd skewered her with a glare. 'You started out so well there. Do you have any more ideas? Good or bad, I'm almost past caring.'

'I've been thinking about the wings, ma'am. Specifically the sparrowhawk's wings that were attached to Nick Langley. I think it might be worth trying to contact local taxidermists. One of them may have sold a stuffed bird to the killer.'

'You're redeeming yourself. Get on the phone and see what you can find out.'

An hour later, when Beth was finished speaking to the last of the relatives, she had all nine names crossed off her list. Most had returned home, although one had been found in the mangled wreckage of a car which had careered off the road.

Beth looked at Thompson; his head was buried in a sea of reports as he looked for that one detail which may give them the breakthrough they were desperate for. O'Dowd had tasked him with looking for people with grudges against Rachel Allen and Nick Langley.

O'Dowd had gone to speak with DCI Phinn in preparation for the press conference, which meant only the two of them were left in the office.

'Beth, I've got the psychologist's report here.' The printer rattled its way into action.

Thompson's eyes scanned the screen as Beth stood waiting by the printer.

The first sheet she read was nothing more than a condensing of facts. The second looked more promising until she realised it was mostly medical terminology and in plain English had very little to say. And as she read the third and fourth sheets, such was her rage that she was tempted to deliver a series of kicks to the printer.

'This is garbage. He's telling us nothing. He suspects the killer is a man aged between twenty-five and sixty. That he's well-funded and has a purpose "or project". He suggests in one breath that the man is a loner and in the next that he may have an accomplice. A fiver says the line about the killer possibly being from a broken home is a standard inclusion. He even goes on to say that our killer will most likely pursue his project until it's completed. Have you seen this line about the idea he worships his victims?' Beth threw the pages onto her desk and glared at them. 'I bet he got paid a fortune for writing that report. It's like those horoscopes that tell you it could be A or B, but to watch out for C. It's all just vague statements.'

Thompson fixed her with a hard stare. 'What did you expect, some kind of magical insight that would give us the killer's name and address? This is real life not the movies. Yes the report seems generic, but the psychologist only had our statements and a few pictures to go off. We know about the extra three victims, but he doesn't. Sure we can tell him about them and he can maybe give us a bit more, but don't expect him to give an opinion on deaths he doesn't know about. He's probably some fat bloke from Doncaster who's been handed a near-impossible task. Trust me, when you've seen how the human mind can work, or rather stop working, you'll recognise the hopelessness of trying to understand one that doesn't work like yours.'

'Sorry. I was just expecting more, that's all.'

'We're all expecting too much.' He picked up the pages she'd tossed down and straightened them. 'I'm going to let O'Dowd and Phinn see this. Have a fag or a coffee, do whatever it takes to calm down and then get back to it.'

CHAPTER FIFTY-SEVEN

With an anger that was unfamiliar to him, the man dragged his wheelie bin to the front of the house and along the narrow path. The chore was a regular one, yet today he resented it. Just as he resented the rain, and the news, and everything else he'd encountered since saying goodbye to Tamara yesterday.

The visit to see her hadn't worked as intended. Rather than cure himself of his obsession with the delectable Sarah Hardy by providing a new focus for his appreciation, he'd found himself contrasting and comparing again. Tamara's voice was harsh and guttural; Sarah's soft and mellifluous like a fine jazz track.

Where Sarah's skin was smooth and unblemished, up close he'd seen the layer of make-up Tamara had used to hide acne scars. Whatever measurement of beauty he used, the barmaid always came off second best.

After a while he'd given up trying to eradicate Sarah from his mind and accepted that he was fixated by her beauty, poise and the perfection of her figure.

That he was going to see her today should be a good thing. He ought to be looking forward to the encounter with a smile and excitement. Instead he was filled with an uneasy dread. Today would be the last time he'd have a legitimate excuse to see her. Future visits would guarantee his presence became unwanted. Of all the agonies in the world, none would compare to Sarah chasing him out of her life. That could never be allowed to happen. Such a turn of events would break his heart.

In a last-ditch attempt to conjure a further reason to see her, he counted his finances for the umpteenth time. It was no good; whichever way he tried to do the sums, he was always left with a shortfall that would see him unable to afford even one trip out per week.

As beautiful as she was, he was not yet so deep into her thrall that he'd imprison himself just to gain a few more tenuous reasons to spend time in her company.

A way that he could continue his appreciation of her came to him as he was entering the kitchen. It didn't sit easy with him and betrayed a lot of the principles he'd set out when he began to collect the angels he committed to memory, but it was a way that would still allow him to revel in her beauty, absorb the grace and sensuality she moved with and appreciate the gift he'd been given from the heavens.

Years ago, the army had spent many months and countless thousands of pounds training him for missions like the one he was going to undertake for Sarah. He might be a little out of practice, but he remembered everything that he'd been taught, and compared with the targets he'd engaged with then, Sarah was as helpless as the last biscuit at a kid's birthday party.

With his frustration ebbing away, he returned to his usual good mood and prepared to travel to Kendal. Where Sarah would be waiting for him.

CHAPTER FIFTY-EIGHT

The Range Rover purred along the road, its mighty engine coping with the various gradients with smooth efficiency. When the man who used a false name flicked the indicator, he saw a girl standing by the road with her thumb out. She was maybe eighteen and would probably be pretty if she smiled.

Whether it was the drizzling rain or some other factor that had spoiled her day didn't matter to him. She was alone in the middle of nowhere. Brown hair was matted to her head and there was a rucksack hanging off one shoulder.

He'd seen enough hikers in the Lake District to know the rucksack on her back was designed more for the odd night away than serious camping. Her clothes were wrong too. Instead of breathable waterproofs, she wore a pair of denim shorts with thick tights and a fleece that may keep the cold out but that, when it got wet, would become a sodden weight which sapped both energy and heat from her body.

It was unthinkable that she be left out here to suffer the cloying dampness. He had to come to her rescue, be the white knight.

He pulled over and lowered the passenger window. 'Where you going?'

'The nearest train station, please.' She gave a helpless shrug. 'I don't even know where it is?'

The girl's accent was more Liverpudlian than a plate of scouse and a season ticket for Anfield. Even in the face of his offer to help, there was a set to her jaw that spoke of more than the discomfort of a soaking. Her eyes looked as though she'd been crying, though not so much they'd become puffy.

'The nearest station is Oxenholme. It's just the other side of Kendal. I'm going that way if you want a lift.'

'That'd be boss.' The girl climbed in and rested her rucksack between her feet.

He pulled away and pointed the bonnet towards Kendal. 'How come you ended up standing out there in the middle of nowhere?'

'I picked up my boyfriend's phone. To read the text message he'd just got, like.' From the corner of his eye he saw her jaw stiffen. 'It was a message from his ex. Said she still loved him too. Like I was putting up with that. Nobody cheats on me, like.'

'Sounds like you're better off without him if he put you out in the middle of nowhere after you confronted him.'

'Like he got a say. I tossed his phone out the window, and when he stopped to get it, like, I did one.'

The girl's speech patterns weren't easy for him to follow and he despised the interspersion of 'likes' into her sentences, but there was little he could do about that. A knight didn't get to choose the damsel he saved. He just answered the distress call.

That the girl was sharing her break-up with him so soon after meeting him also felt wrong. He put it down to the rise of social media and the way some people couldn't live their lives without posting every detail for the world to see.

He didn't understand why people would share every aspect of their lives. Nobody knew anything about his private life. Everyone was kept at arm's length, even those who thought of him as a friend knew very little about him. It had earned him a lot of strange looks over the years, but he'd never cared for the opinions of others. They could think whatever they liked about him; as far as he was concerned, they were serfs speculating about their king.

'I take it you're going home then?'

'Too right. Gonna go right back home, get myself changed and then I'm gonna shag both his brothers. That'll, like, show him.'

The man who used a false name doubted the teen Romeo would be shown anything. So far as he could see, the damsel and her ex had the morals of rattlesnakes and the libidos of rabbits.

When he looked past her to check if he could pull out of a junction, he saw something that quickened his pulse.

Hanging round her neck was a thin chain with the letter 'C' hanging from it.

'What's your name?'

'Caitlin.' A piece of chewing gum was fed into her mouth.

There it was; the confirmation. He'd had to ask. The letter may have been for the errant lover or a deceased sibling. Yet it was there, freely given, the affirmation of her eligibility.

Change of plan.

The next part was simple. He took a drink from the bottle of water in the cup holder then lifted another water bottle from the door pocket. 'Do you want a drink?'

'Ta.'

The girl took a couple of healthy swigs from the bottle.

The man with the false name drove around the back roads until he saw Caitlin succumb to the effects of the Rohypnol he'd laced the spare bottle of water with.

She was no longer the damsel he'd deliver to the safety of Oxenholme Station. He had another destination in mind for her. He knew exactly where he'd leave her and the message it would send.

After leaving Angus Keane at Arthuret Hall he'd returned to Highstead Castle for Nick Langley. It didn't matter that the police had learned of the other site as quick as they had, what mattered was that they'd be unable to work out why he'd chosen to use Highstead again.

He'd returned for no other reason than to make them wonder. They'd be able to tell how long each body had been there, but not why he'd gone back. They'd waste their time looking for reasons and connections that didn't exist.

He smiled as he realised he was no longer the knight.

St George had become the dragon.

Or rather: the dragon maker.

CHAPTER FIFTY-NINE

Beth kept her back straight and her eyes forward as the chief super marched into the office flanked by DCI Phinn. O'Dowd had warned the team of the impending visit and had more or less assembled them in parade-ground fashion.

From what Beth could gather, the press conference had been a complete disaster, with both O'Dowd and Phinn coming in for criticism for their failure to apprehend the killer.

In typical tabloid style, the press had given the killer a moniker. The Dragon Master was the title they'd chosen, and they'd been both scathing and unrelenting in their attacks on the DCI and DI who'd been there to speak to them.

Like a general inspecting his troops, the chief super's back was ramrod straight as he stalked in front of them. He advanced along their line in crabbing movements, pausing at each face to peer into their eyes. When it was Beth's turn she felt herself fighting a tremble in her knees as the chief super's piercing gaze examined her. When he spoke his voice was calm and laden with the expectation that he'd be listened to without interruption.

'I don't recognise you. You must be the new lass.'

O'Dowd leaned forward. 'DC Young, sir. She only joined the team at the start of last week. Decent mind and good initiative.'

'Good initiative, you say. Is that a euphemism for maverick, DI O'Dowd?'

Beth saw the chief super shoot a glance at O'Dowd.

'Actually, sir, I just meant that she doesn't need to be *micro-managed*.'

When Beth saw the chief super's pupils contract, she knew O'Dowd was in trouble for that emphasis.

'"Micro-managed", you say.' The chief super moved himself along the line so he was in front of a defiant O'Dowd. 'Is that what you think I'm doing here, *micro-managing* you? Because if you think that's what I'm doing, it tells me that you are aware of your failure to identify a credible suspect. That you're grasping at straws. The way it looks to me, DI O'Dowd, is that you're floundering about without making progress. We have four dead bodies, and you've still to identify them all. Do you think that's an acceptable position to be in?'

Beth kept her face straight as she gave an inward wince. There was no way that O'Dowd could answer the chief super's question without dropping herself in the shit. Answer yes and she'd be admitting that she didn't care. To say no would invite the chief super to ask why she hadn't pushed harder to identify Woman 1.

'With respect, sir, it's not—'

'It's a yes-no answer, Inspector.'

O'Dowd bridled but kept her mouth shut as the chief super gave them all a dressing down for their collective failure to catch the man they were all now calling the 'Dragon Master'. Even DCI Phinn received a level of criticism, but the barbs he received were more to do with his failure to support and manage the FMIT rather than outright criticism of his lack of input into the investigation.

Beth couldn't help feel the dressing down was unnecessary. The team were pursuing every lead they could think of to catch the so-called Dragon Master, and both O'Dowd and Thompson were doing their best to put aside their personal issues so they could work the case.

As tempted as she was to speak up and defend the DI and DS, she knew it wasn't her place to share their personal problems, and there was every chance that instead of the chief super showing compassion, he'd stand them down; so rather than risk getting them into more trouble Beth kept her mouth shut and stood in silence as the chief super continued to press upon them the urgent need to catch the Dragon Master.

After the first twenty minutes, Beth had to fight every one of her independent notions. While the chief super's voice was never raised and he didn't once insult them on a personal level, he eviscerated each of them in turn while exhorting them all to work harder and smarter.

It was the most polite bollocking Beth had ever received, but also the most comprehensive. Another reason she didn't speak out in an attempt to mount a defence was that she trusted O'Dowd's instincts and experience in this situation. If the DI was keeping quiet, she must have been here before and, as such, knew that answering back would only make matters worse.

CHAPTER SIXTY

The man with the false name put his feet onto the low table and sipped at his drink. Today had gone far better than he'd expected it to. His act of charity had borne the sweetest of fruits for him. His generosity in offering to do a good deed had presented him with a gift.

Not just any gift, a missing link in his chain. He'd been trying to find a candidate but none had presented themselves. Then from nowhere, one had dropped into his lap.

He now had the next part of his project. All he had to do was offer her up and he could move on.

Caitlin was the gift. Not only was she the right fit, but the way she'd been standing alone at a deserted junction meant he'd been able to get her into his Range Rover without any witnesses.

To make things even sweeter, her break-up with her boyfriend, and the way she'd been speaking indicated that she was the kind of person who did what she wanted, when she wanted. Her boyfriend wouldn't know she was missing as she'd dumped him and stormed off. Her folks wouldn't be worried about her, because as far as they knew she was with the boyfriend. The impression he'd got of the young man from her comments suggested he wasn't likely to contact her parents to make sure she'd got safely home.

The evening news had been full of the investigation into his project. There had been footage of a press conference, where the dumpy copper who'd spoken to him had sat beside someone and failed to answer any questions without humming and hah-ing at every turn. The journalists didn't let the coppers deliver their statements, they just wanted news on the investigation into the murders.

Except they weren't murders, not in his mind. They were necessary sacrifices. An offering to earn appeasement and prove the worthiness of a son who'd never been loved by his mother. By recreating the dragon that Mother was, he could prove himself worthy of her love.

He knew that if she was alive and aware of what he was doing, she'd be furious. As always, she'd want to manifest her anger both physically and verbally as she puffed on cigarettes and used him as her ashtray. Regardless of the years that had passed since her death, he'd never forgotten the pleasure in her eyes as she ground the cigarettes into his skin.

He had two issues to deal with on his immediate horizon: the date he'd asked Sarah on and the missing link between Caitlin and Sarah.

The plans he had for Caitlin would send a message to the world in general and the dumpy detective in particular. He just wasn't sure the copper was smart enough to recognise what he'd be saying in his unspoken message.

The date was something he was dreading. He'd have to make small talk. Feign interest in her likes and dislikes.

He would, of course, be the perfect gentleman; he'd hold doors for her, stand when she came into the room, and make her feel every bit as special as she probably thought she was. To him she was only special because she'd be a part of his project. At least he could use the time spent with her to find out her routines. That way he could engineer a way to capture her. Like the hitchhiker, she'd get into his car without hesitation.

At the end of the night he'd drop her off at her home and leave her there. Any offers to go in for a coffee would be refused. Sarah appeared to be a sexual woman, if her clothes and behaviour towards him were any kind of indicators. The last thing he wanted to do was find himself in a position where he was expected to sleep with her.

Rather than go on a second date, he planned to capture her and keep her locked up until he was ready to use her for his project.

It was the link between Caitlin and Sarah that troubled him. He needed another darling. He contemplated the one person he'd met who would fit, but as delicious and fitting as it would be to use her, she could be the hardest of them all to capture. She would be more wary, have greater awareness and take more precautions than the average person. But still she was perfect. And she would be the most fitting tribute.

It would begin with surveillance. He'd recognise her routines, find a time when she was alone. Then he'd pounce.

A smile crossed his face. Perhaps he should double her up with Sarah. A pair of beautiful women together. He could sacrifice them at the same time in order to keep his project on track.

His eyes closed in pleasure as he thought of the impact their deaths would have. How they'd move his project so much closer to completion.

DC Young would be the perfect darling.

CHAPTER SIXTY-ONE

Beth tried to hide the yawn behind a hand, but there was no disguising the crack of her jaw as her mouth stretched wide. The fingers of her other hand curled and uncurled as she repeatedly made a fist. She wanted a target for the fist, something to aim her frustrations at. Not only were they failing to make any decent headway with the case, they now had the chief super on their back.

The first thing she did once the chief super and DCI Phinn left the office, was check her emails. In among the departmental-bullshit ones, were a couple of gold nuggets. Dr Hewson's friend, the burns specialist, had come back to him and given their verdict on the four victims' burns. And, more significantly, the dental records team had come back with an identification for Woman 1.

Fiona McGhie was confirmed as the first victim of the Dragon Master. There wasn't a lot of information on her, beyond learning she was fifty-nine and lived in a cottage overlooking Derwent Water. Beth knew her priority would be to get every detail about the woman's life that she could.

But before she did, she wanted to see what the burns specialist had to say.

The report confirmed Dr Hewson's theory that different amounts of accelerant had been used on each victim. It also upheld the idea that the two men had had extra accelerant added to them once the initial amount had burned away. This all made sense to Beth in a sick and twisted way.

The report was detailed to the point where she could picture each of the victims as their mouths were ignited. Fiona McGhie would have given a brief puff of flame before death; Rachel Allen had been overfilled, and when the flames travelling down her throat had died due to a lack of oxygen, the remaining petrol inside her had dissipated through her body.

Of the two men, Angus Keane's death would have been the quickest. The Dragon Master had lessened the amount of petrol he'd fed into Keane's stomach, but the specialist still predicted that, after a brief flash of flame, the petrol would have burned out. The next amount added had increased his pain to the point where he'd gone into cardiac arrest and died of a heart attack.

According to the specialist, Nick Langley's death would have been slower, the amounts added smaller and, because his mouth had been held open by the piece of wood jammed between his teeth, the Dragon Master had been able to continuously add petrol so that his dragon kept breathing fire. The only problem Beth could see with this was that once Nick was dead, the flames wouldn't have had the power of exhalation or screams behind them. Therefore the flames wouldn't have shot from his mouth, they'd have gusted out at best before heading upwards as flames always did.

Beth lifted her gaze away from the screen and looked across to O'Dowd. There was a determined set to her jaw and Beth suspected the DI was reading the same email and seeing the same mental images: terrified eyes straining in darkness, gagging, choking mouths trying to reject the foul substances forced into them and then the flash. Bright flames shooting from human mouths only to be replaced with gurgled screams.

Suddenly very keen to distract herself from the unpalatable images, Beth got on with running Fiona McGhie's name through the PNC. Nothing came back. No convictions, no charges. Not even any complaints.

Her next move was to run the woman's name through Google.

A little to her surprise she discovered Fiona was a painter. She evidently sold her work through her website, and the 'about her' only mentioned living with a beloved cat. Her paintings were mostly watercolour landscapes with the odd commissioned portrait. From what Beth could judge by looking at the quality of her work, plus the prices Fiona charged for originals and prints, she would be classed as a successful artist.

The landscapes were all Lakeland scenes; Beth recognised lakes Ullswater, Windermere and Coniston. Some of the paintings looked to have been created from a vantage point on the high fells and there was one she recognised as a recreation of Honister Pass due to its depiction of the craggy outcrops towering over a narrow, winding road.

While she wasn't a fan of watercolours, Beth could appreciate Fiona's skill in capturing the beauty and primitive savagery of the Lake District.

Beth looked for Fiona's next of kin in the General Registration Office database, and learned that she was an only child who'd never married. Both her parents were dead and there was no mention of any partner on the database. Beth could imagine the long winter nights Fiona spent alone. Without a life companion her existence would be a solitary one. Perhaps the odd word with a postman or the person she bought her painting supplies from, but like so many of the creative arts, painting could be a lonely task. While Fiona may lose herself in the moment when she had a brush in her hand, she had nobody to share triumphs with or provide support on the bad days that life dealt out.

A forlorn smile touched Beth's lips as she realised the contradiction to her thinking. She herself lived alone, and while she also spent her nights alone, she had a job that saw her interact with other people during the day. Fiona's was the kind of existence Beth dreaded. For a time after the bottle had been slammed into her face, Beth had wanted seclusion, to hide away and amuse herself with her own endeavours. Yet when she'd tried to cloister herself in her bedroom, she'd found the boredom stultifying. She'd needed company, interaction with other human beings and, most of all, a purpose. Friends and family had provided the interaction, and the police had provided her with all the purpose she needed.

'What do you make of it, Beth?'

O'Dowd's question was a loaded one.

The DI was now asking her opinion, canvassing her thoughts. While this gave Beth confidence, as she felt her contributions were valued, she was still wary of saying the wrong thing and changing O'Dowd's opinion of her.

The Dragon Master was a step ahead of them whatever they did. He left no apparent forensic traces; he flitted in and out of places without being seen. At Highstead Castle, none of the people who lived in the houses by the track had even heard a vehicle drive by. He'd not been detected at Arthuret Hall, and there seemed to be no connection between any of his victims, or the two locations.

'I don't know. If we're right on the dragon theory, there has to be some kind of reason as to why he's doing it. Whether he's got a *Game of Thrones* fixation or he sees himself as some kind of modern-day necromancer, I believe he's got a reason. Maybe when the psychologist has studied the other victims and their deaths, his next report will give you a better answer than I can regarding his motives.'

'Agreed. But what about the victims? Two women and then two men. What's the reasoning there?'

'I don't know, ma'am. Maybe they fit his pattern. Perhaps there's a personal connection. Or maybe they just happened to be around when he needed his next victim.'

'I take your point.' O'Dowd pursed her lips. 'But I think that he's selected them for a reason. Everything he's done in terms of staging the bodies and leaving no evidence tells me he's not being random in any way. Even his experiments with making them breathe fire speak of refinement, a willingness to adapt and learn. That's not slapdash, Beth, that's organised, planned even. I want you to use that sideways-thinking brain of yours to see if you can find a connection between our victims.'

'Yes, ma'am.'

So far as Beth could see, O'Dowd's theory about the victims somehow being connected was about the only thing they could investigate. The way the Dragon Master was experimenting with different amounts of accelerant may have given them some clues were it not for the fact that petrol was something that could be bought in a hundred and one places. Had he tried paraffin or a different combustible then it may have given them a lead to follow, but all the tissue Dr Hewson had tested had proven to have been petrol.

If they'd been able to get a full sample of the petrol, they may have been able to trace it to a specific batch made by the refinery and then trace where it had been sold in Cumbria. However, even if they had CCTV footage for every petrol station, until they had a suspect, they'd do nothing but waste time watching endless footage.

For all of the victims except Fiona, they had reams of reports and statements galore. By tomorrow, a team of officers would have gathered further information on Fiona McGhie's life. In the meantime, the best thing Beth could think to do was to create a simple spreadsheet which annotated all the key details they knew about each victim. It would aid her thought processes by giving her a central source where she could take an overview of each of their lives.

Even as she glanced at her watch, another yawn threatened to dislocate her jaw. She'd give it an hour and then go home. There was still half a bottle of wine in her fridge. It would help her deal with the day and slow her mind down to allow her to get some sleep. And after a few hours' sleep and her morning run, she'd be better able to assess the finer details of the spreadsheet and hopefully highlight a connection between four very different victims. It was like a crossword. If there was nothing obvious, maybe there would be something cryptic that linked them.

The problem was, with no clear clues, where should she start?

CHAPTER SIXTY-TWO

The day had been both torturous and glorifying for the man. He'd returned to the showroom and had spoken with the gorgeous Sarah for a paltry five minutes. She'd been disappointed he wasn't going to buy a car, but that hadn't worried him in the slightest. She'd looked like a model in the long skirt that flowed round her nylon clad legs and the way she'd tied her hair into a mussy ponytail had showcased that wonderfully graceful neck.

Yet when he'd bade her goodbye, he'd felt a sadness within his soul. Never again would he get to chat to her, hear that melodic giggle and appreciate her beauty close at hand. From now on, his appreciation of her would have to be from a distance.

As much as he wanted to have more reasons to see her, there could be no more visits to the showroom, no deliberate meetings on the street outside her house or anywhere else. They could not happen, because if he spooked her, she could take out an injunction or whatever it was called and then he'd never again be able to worship at the altar of his most beautiful angel.

Today's surveillance of Sarah had brought back a lot of memories. About being back in Kuwait with Olly during the first Gulf War. Olly had been one of the best snipers the British army possessed and he'd been Olly's spotter. Many were the hours they'd lain up together waiting for the chance to take a shot.

They'd had several successful missions until things had gone tits up. An Iraqi sniper had taken a shot at them. The shot missed Olly, who was the real threat, but it hadn't missed him. On the

27th of February 1991 – the date was etched into his mind as it was his thirty-fifth birthday – he'd been crouched behind Olly, gazing through his binoculars, when the round had smashed into his pelvis. They'd repaired the bone and, although he now required a stick to walk, he'd retained the use of both legs.

It was his genitals that he lost.

Now he had nothing but scar tissue and a catheter.

His wife had left him after two sexless years. Not only had his manhood been taken away from him, but with it, his sex drive had gone, never to return. Once upon a time he'd appreciated beautiful women because of the way they turned him on. Now it was all about how they carried themselves, the way they felt in their skin, the confidence they exuded and the effect they had on other men.

These were his angels, the desirable and the unobtainable.

He'd never been blessed with great looks and his own lack of confidence had seen him marry the second woman who'd let him see her naked. For him, his angels were everything; they were the ones who brightened his day whenever he thought about their beauty and sensuality. They were barmaids, waitresses, receptionists and a dozen other professions. He found them wherever he went, although he made sure that he frequented places where there was a good chance of finding angels to worship. They were the only thing that made him feel whole again.

CHAPTER SIXTY-THREE

Beth turned off the shower and reached for her phone. Its ringtone was the one she'd assigned to O'Dowd, which was the only reason she hadn't let it ring out.

She listened while the DI spoke and then hung up. All of the endorphins boosted by her early-morning run were dispelled by those few short sentences. Beth had expected another victim to turn up at some point if they didn't identify the killer. Just not so soon. It seemed the Dragon Master was further escalating his actions. There had been a line about how serial killers often did this in the psychologist's report.

Between O'Dowd's brief intel and demand for her presence, Beth had learned that the latest find was different from the others. Rather than being arranged in the cellar of a grand house, this victim had been positioned outside the front of one.

Unlike the previous locations, Beth knew this house well. Lonsdale Castle was a local landmark. There had once been a wildlife park attached to it, and since English Heritage had taken responsibility for the castle and its grounds, the gardens were being restored to their former glory. Lonsdale Castle was more than a crumbling old building, it was a tourist attraction.

Once she was out of the shower she googled the castle on her mobile. Like Highstead and Arthuret Hall, it had been kissed by fire; although, in Lonsdale's case, the fire had been contained to one wing, which had been rebuilt around the turn of the nineteenth century.

Another thing bothering her was the victim's identity. That another person had fallen prey to the Dragon Master sickened Beth. This girl had fallen into the clutches of an ingenious killer who had so far managed to evade all attempts to identify, let alone catch him. She was sure that the girl would have died in agony. Her young life taken by a monster trying to recreate a mythical beast.

As much as Beth wanted to go straight to the scene and investigate what clues may have been left there, O'Dowd had instructed her to go into the office and search the databases first. Perhaps their young victim had been reported missing by a frantic mother.

The image she had in her mind was that of Nick Langley's wife, pining for the safe return of her husband. The faces may change, but the situations were the same for those who had family who cared about them. Family and friends would call their mobiles with increasing levels of regularity as their worry increased. As the hours scrolled by, they'd try contacting friends, and then the police and hospitals.

Beth threw on some clothes and ran out to her car. The sooner she went through the latest misper reports, the quicker she'd be able to get down to Lonsdale Castle and see the crime scene for herself.

CHAPTER SIXTY-FOUR

Lonsdale Castle was full of loom and menace as the early morning sun streamed through the missing windows in its towering walls. Like both Arthuret Hall and Highstead Castle, it was a shell of a building. Unlike the other two, it had already benefitted from a hefty financial investment.

The main house was grand and imposing despite being little more than a collection of walls, but the surrounding areas were manicured. The grass at the front of the house was shorn like a bowling green and the stone walling at the front of the lawn was in good repair.

A CSI tent had been erected at the front of the house, and there was a knot of police vehicles at the foot of the ramp leading to the main door.

Beth joined O'Dowd and Thompson as they struggled their way out of their protective suits.

Thompson's face was grim and severe, but next to O'Dowd's, it looked as if he'd just won the lottery.

As she gazed over to the CSI tent, a squat man emerged and made his way across the footpads. He passed a greeting or two to the CSI team who were scouring the lawn.

Short of a few cigarette butts and a sweetie wrapper or two, Beth didn't expect them to find anything. Even what they did find wouldn't be of much use. This was a public area; the detritus could have been there a month or more and Beth was sure the Dragon Master was too clever to have left anything lying around.

'Get suited up, Beth. Go and have a look for yourself. Maybe you'll spot something we haven't.'

Beth did as O'Dowd ordered and made her way towards the CSI tent. Halfway there she met Dr Hewson.

'You going for your own look?'

Beth nodded. 'Is it bad?'

'No worse than the others, but…' He paused to pull a face. 'Look, decomposition is never good, but I'd sooner deal with a rotting, stinking corpse than the body of someone who doesn't look as if they're old enough to drink, let alone die like this.' He waved a hand towards the tent. 'Do what you must, DC Protégé, just make sure you catch this man soon. This can't go on.'

Beth kept her eyes on the footpads until she was at the tent. She pulled back the opening and stepped inside. In front of her was the body of a young woman. A rope had been tied around the two pillars of the house's portico and the woman's arms had been attached to it with a series of cable ties.

From her back sprouted a pair of wings. They were the largest Beth had seen thus far. They must have belonged to a buzzard or maybe even an eagle. Unlike the wings on the other victims, these weren't folded, they were spread as if the bird was gliding on a light breeze.

All of these details were unimportant. What really mattered was the girl. She was naked and her body was white and pale in front of Beth. The only marks on her skin were put there by a tattooist who obviously didn't care about the quality of the work, or spelling.

Her small breasts stood proud and both nipples were pierced. The girl's face was a mess, her mouth was blackened and the lips scorched. Even the tip of her nose showed signs of heat blistering. It told Beth that the Dragon Master had found a substance that burned longer, or had worked out the right amount of accelerant to insert into his victims.

As well as decreasing the time between his kills, the killer was also increasing the audacity of his murder sites. He'd gone from the cellar of a deserted house to a well-used venue in Arthuret Hall and was now using the front lawn of a busy tourist attraction. Every kill was an 'improvement' on the last one in terms of the prolonged fire breathing, and the wings affixed to the victims' backs were growing in size.

Beth looked at the girl's fingers and saw no sign of anything lodged under her nails. She supposed Dr Hewson would have claimed it, but so far as she was concerned, she still had to look.

Applying gloves over her own hands and then inspecting the girl's nails, Beth saw they were covered in chipped nail varnish and there was an innocence to the primary colours that told of someone in the transition from child to adult. She might have her nipples pierced and own a number of bad tattoos, but she still seemed childlike in a way. This more than anything else disturbed Beth and made the tent feel claustrophobic.

She didn't know why she did it, but Beth took another look at the girl's mouth. It was open in a charred scream. Something made Beth pull out her mobile and switch the torch app on.

When she shone it into the girl's mouth, she saw a tongue that resembled a piece of overcooked bacon. There in the middle of the tongue was the thing she'd half-seen but not registered before.

It was a tongue stud, but instead of being silver and shiny, it was twisted and grotesque. Whatever accelerant had been used on the girl, it had burned long enough and hot enough to distort the stud through her tongue. At the corner of her mouth, jammed between the girl's top and bottom molars, was a small block of wood similar to the one used on Nick Langley. Like that one it was blackened and charred.

This new-found horror was too much for Beth. She stepped outside the tent and took in a few deep breaths.

When she had control of herself, she looked around her. Other than the presence of the police, there seemed to be no change to the landscape. Birds flew overhead, sheep and cattle grazed in the fields, and there was a tractor chugging along a lane.

As she kept gazing, she noticed a tree-lined avenue stretching two miles into the distance. It led from the centre of the portico to the horizon.

The more she stared along the avenue, the more Beth came to understand the reason why the girl's body had not been placed in a cellar. The positioning of her body in the portico was symbolic. It represented the killer's emergence from the shadows. The girl wasn't just elevated to a position in the house, she was at the front gate, looking down the drive. She was master of all she surveyed, no longer was she someone to be kept hidden below stairs, she was front and centre, ready to greet visitors, deal with problems and control her domain.

Except that everything which applied to the girl was also relevant to the Dragon Master. She was his representative, his envoy. He was communicating to the police that he was in charge. Even the choice of murder scene, the deposit site, spoke of grandeur. Lonsdale Castle used to be one of the mightiest seats in Westmorland, as this part of the county was once known, and throughout history it had played host to kings and queens, supplied members of parliament and controlled vast swathes of the area.

There was almost a challenge in the Dragon Master's actions, as if he was goading the police, showing off his superior intelligence and worth. He had flirted with them by leaving his third victim where it could easily be found and had then retreated back to his haven for the fourth. Yet this fifth kill was the boldest of them all; to Beth it seemed that the Dragon Master wasn't killing his victims in random places but that he was choosing deposit sites with care.

In the same way that puzzles unfolded for her, as patterns emerging from the darkness, Beth could see clearly in that moment that the Dragon Master believed he had a right to kill. He was more than just a twisted killer, he thought he was better than everyone else, and that none of the inferior people he met could possibly understand the message a great man like him was sending. He'd emerged from the cellars and *he* was now master of all he surveyed. His wings were unfolded and he was ready to soar, to look down on others. The Dragon Master was rising from the depths of burned buildings like a phoenix from ashes to encompass all before him.

As she made her way back to O'Dowd to share this theory, it was all she could do not to run along the footpads.

The DI's mood hadn't improved and there was no sign of Thompson. Beth supposed he'd either been sent to look into something, or he'd invented a reason to get away from O'Dowd.

'Whatever you're looking so smug about better help me catch this killer.' The reprimand came with a mouthful of stale smoke and staler alcohol. When Beth took a closer look at the DI she saw bloodshot eyes and an increased level of emotion.

By the time she finished sharing her ideas with O'Dowd, Beth noticed a lessening of the antagonism, although there was no less distress in her eyes.

Then she got it. The picture became clearer as she put herself in the DI's brogues.

'Oh God, she reminded you of your daughter, didn't she?'

Beth led O'Dowd a few paces away from the various cars so they could talk without being overheard.

'You have no idea, Beth.' O'Dowd was fighting back tears. 'It's not just that poor lass. I've been up all night with my Neve.'

'Was she ill?' A realisation struck Beth with the force of a wrecking ball. 'Oh no. She didn't lose the baby, did she?'

'No.' O'Dowd's head dipped forward as she shook it. 'She didn't *lose* the baby, she had it aborted. Not only is my little girl silly enough to get herself pregnant, she's also silly enough to go off and have an abortion without discussing it with anyone.' As

O'Dowd paused to sniff, Beth saw a pair of heavy tears tumble to the ground. 'You were right the other day when you said we would cope. We were looking at ways to cope. But then my Neve stamps down on the situation with all her customary impulsiveness.' O'Dowd's head lifted so she could look at Beth. 'Yes, I know what you're thinking, that maybe in the long term, her having an abortion is the best solution for everyone, but I was brought up in a Catholic household. My faith may have lapsed, but I still believe in the sanctity of human life. And I think what she's done is wrong. Does that make me sound like a bad mother?'

'Of course not.'

On the one hand, Beth felt for O'Dowd, but she could readily imagine the DI berating her daughter about the pregnancy. Neve would have been terrified that she'd ruined her life. Her mother's rants would have reinforced that thinking, so she'd taken matters into her own hands and had the baby, and ergo the problem, removed.

The flip side of this was that O'Dowd was clearly anti-abortion. Therefore the DI now blamed herself for the termination because of the pressure she'd heaped onto her daughter.

It was a situation that would require time and a lot of understanding to resolve. Both mother and daughter had lost something with the abortion. It was vital that they didn't lose each other as well.

O'Dowd sniffed again and dabbed at her eyes. 'It's my fault. If I'd been more understanding about her getting pregnant she wouldn't have done it. She'd have kept the baby and in a few months I'd have been a grandmother. No.' Another shake of the head. 'I'd have been the best grandmother a child could ever hope for. And now, now it's all gone because I was too hard on her. Because I scared her half to death with tales of how tough it would be, how much her life would change. It's my fault; I as good as performed the abortion myself.'

'Bollocks. You did what any parent would do. She's a big girl and she made her own decisions. The first one was rolling the dice by having unprotected sex, the second was in deciding to take the action she did.' Beth fixed O'Dowd with a sympathetic but hard look. 'I'm sorry if this sounds harsh, but if she was anything like me at that age, she'd have ignored every word that came out of your mouth. Yes, it's shit that her decision has broken your heart. But it's her life and she has to make her own mistakes. Trust me. Having an abortion isn't something you ever get over. You look at the calendar and remember your due date. You never forget the date you went to the hospital for an operation to kill the embryo growing inside you. And to manage your guilt, that's how you always try and think of it, as an embryo, not as your child. You don't forget that you chose to have the life of your first child ended because you were terrified that you wouldn't cope, that you'd not be able to give a child everything it deserves from life.'

Beth had to turn away from O'Dowd so the older woman couldn't see the tears filling her eyes. It had been seven years since the day she'd visited the clinic, but she regularly found herself thinking about the child she'd never given birth to. On the anniversary of the clinic visit she would buy a bouquet of flowers and leave them on a random grave in Penrith's Beacon Edge Cemetery. It was a small gesture that she knew she did to salve her conscience.

'You had an abortion?'

'Yes, I did. Now, please, for your daughter's sake, take a walk over to where no one can hear you, phone your daughter and tell her that you love her. Believe me, you have no idea how much she needs to hear that from you.'

Amazingly, O'Dowd followed her instructions, while Beth turned away and took a few steps in the opposite direction to distance herself from the growing crowd of CSI technicians.

She hadn't meant to reveal her past to O'Dowd. It had all taken place years ago. She'd been a naive sixteen-year-old who'd believed that she wouldn't get pregnant just doing it the once without a condom.

She'd been wrong. As soon as her period was four weeks late, she knew she had a decision to make. At the time her modelling career was starting to take off, and she had only just begun putting money away for the time when she joined the police. She hadn't been ready to be a mother and at the time wasn't confident that she'd be able to become one. She'd chosen to have an abortion because she was convinced that she'd fail her baby in every possible way once it was born.

Even so, she often wondered what the child would have been like if she'd not made the choice she had.

Other than the people at the clinic, O'Dowd was the only other person who knew about it. She'd kept her pregnancy and abortion a secret through shame and selfishness. The whole thing had been traumatic enough, without her parents weighing in with their opinions. With her mother battling depression, there was no way she could throw an unplanned and unwanted pregnancy into their lives.

Before Beth returned to the crime scene she took a few minutes to compose herself. While thoughts of the abortion she'd had, and the latent feelings of guilt associated with it were never far away, O'Dowd's news had brought everything to the surface. The DI's reactions were the ones she'd known her parents would have had if she'd told them. Her mother never mentioned children to Beth, but she'd seen the way she'd shot envious looks when her neighbour had enthused about her grandchildren.

CHAPTER SIXTY-FIVE

The man stretched out his limbs and settled into the office chair. The building was abandoned; it was perfect for his purpose. It was far enough away from the car showroom that he couldn't be seen by the naked eye; it was also to the south which meant he didn't have to worry about the sun glinting off the lenses of his binoculars and betraying his position. As a precaution against being seen by anyone in the vicinity, he'd climbed up to the old textile mill's first floor and positioned the chair a good ten feet back from the window he was looking out of.

He focussed his binoculars and took a careful sweep of the car showroom until he picked out Sarah Hardy. After adjusting the zoom, he was able to appreciate her beauty once more. She'd dressed in a way that made her allure reach new heights. The dress she wore was a simple flowing summery one. It was tight across Sarah's upper torso and chest but below that it flared out. As she walked across the forecourt he could see it catch in the breeze and wrap itself around her graceful movements.

Everything about her suggested that she was happy about something. Her smile didn't fade, even when there was no one to smile to. She made constant checks of her watch and it was only then that her smile threatened to fade.

The man was pleased she was in a good mood. As beautiful as she was, the natural glow from her happiness made her even more desirable.

He didn't like where his guesses as to the cause of her happiness were taking him though. The obvious one was that she was looking forward to something. It may well be a holiday or something equally innocuous, but he didn't think so. She was too happy and she checked her watch too often.

In his mind there could be only one reason: she had a date.

This wasn't a problem for him. He wanted her to be happy, to enjoy life and experience the indescribable joy of feeling loved.

His concern was the man she would be joining on the date.

He wanted to question this man the way a father would grill a daughter's new boyfriend.

Would he place her on a pedestal? Promise never to hurt her? Support her? Most of all, would he treat her like the angel she was?

CHAPTER SIXTY-SIX

Beth dropped the wrapping from her lunch into the bin, shut out the chatter from Unthank and Thompson and focussed on her spreadsheet. She'd got all the basic details into the appropriate columns and was inputting the lesser-known facts. Nothing had leapt out at her so far, but she was sure that the key to the case would lie in those pages. All she had to do was get the details down and then cross reference them.

The job was a boring one, but that didn't bother her. She thrived on picking over mundane details. For her, it was crucial to learn as much about the victims as she could. Once she knew their likes and dislikes, she could gauge their temperaments and look for commonalities.

As the stream of data filled the screen, it became clear to Beth that while there were a number of possible overlaps between any two of the four identified victims, there was nothing to link all of them together.

'We've got an ID on our girl. She's Caitlin Russell, eighteen years old, from Liverpool. I've checked her out, she's had three arrests for common assault and two for possession of narcotics. Her family are well known to the local police. To quote the PC I spoke to "she's a right little charmer from a family full of them".' Thompson's voice was layered with sorrow, and Beth wondered if he was thinking of his own teenage daughters. 'Still, I don't suppose she deserved what happened to her.'

'What's her story?'

'We don't know yet. The officer I spoke to said that someone from their station is going round to speak to her family. They'll let us know what the score is.'

Beth added Caitlin's name to her spreadsheet and started inputting the details she knew about the Dragon Master's fifth victim, while she thought of the girl's parents receiving the terrible news that their daughter was dead.

Beth tried to work out why she might have been chosen as a victim. The first four victims were all Cumbrians. While there might be others as yet undiscovered, she couldn't include them in her thoughts; she could only go with known facts. Caitlin was from Liverpool, which meant she'd either moved to the area or was holidaying in the Lake District.

Aware that she could do nothing more than speculate until there were some hard facts to deal with, Beth concentrated her focus on the four people she knew something about. Fiona McGhie's file was still thin compared to the others, but it would fatten when the reports came in from the officers speaking to neighbours and people she'd had dealings with. And, with luck, the search team would find a client list for commissioned pieces that would have the name of someone closely associated with one of the other victims.

She reached for a pen and started to make notes of the known commonalities. Both men were staunch Carlisle United supporters. Both worked with their hands, as did Fiona McGhie. While there was a connection there, it was a stretch and Beth knew it. Yes they may all be skilled at what they did, but a secretary who could type 120 words a minute was just as skilled with their hands as a builder or an artist, it was just a different skill.

Rachel and Nick both lived in Carlisle, but Angus's house was in Longtown, whereas Fiona lived in the countryside.

The men were married, while the women were both single.

Beth picked up the phone and asked the guys at Digital Forensics to check the social media profiles of the four Cumbrian victims. She wanted to know if they were connected on any sites, if they liked similar pages or even frequented the same places.

The fact that Caitlin wasn't a local played on Beth's mind. It would be so much easier to get onto the Dragon Master's trail if they could watch the missing persons' list. His pattern had been two women, two men and now he'd targeted another woman. If he stuck to his pattern of two, then his next victim would also be a woman.

The idea that the killer was operating on a two-by-two basis flitted across her mind and produced the obvious biblical connection: could the Dragon Master be making pairs of mythical beasts? She pushed aside the idea. Whatever the killer's motives may be, unless the police knew for certain what they were, they were irrelevant to the investigation. Should they guess at the wrong idea, all that would be achieved was a waste of time and effort.

The more she researched the lives of the first four victims, the more Beth got the feeling that at some point in the investigation she'd seen or heard something which would prove significant in catching the killer. She knew the clue would be listed in her document, that it was a connection between the victims that didn't show itself directly in the columns or rows.

Even as she was feeding more data into the spreadsheet, her mind was poring over all the known and new facts.

That she'd overlooked a clue, or not made a connection, was a thought which haunted Beth. Caitlin may have died because of her failure to work out the connection between the first four victims. But then she rejected the idea before the tentacles of self-doubt could worm their way into her mind and suffocate her thought process.

As she returned her gaze to the list of commonalities, Beth twirled a pen around her fingers. Her phone beeped and when she checked the message, she saw it was O'Dowd requesting that she get herself to Penrith's station at once.

CHAPTER SIXTY-SEVEN

Beth dumped the heap of reports onto her desk. The summons from O'Dowd had been for assistance with interviewing several people the DI had hauled in because of the various beefs they'd had with either Fiona McGhie or Rachel Allen.

While Carleton Hall may be the official HQ for the Cumbria Constabulary, it had neither cells nor interview suites, so any interviews the team conducted had to be done at Penrith's station.

None of the men and women she'd interviewed with O'Dowd had presented themselves as anything other than innocent. What had been interesting though, were the extra details she'd picked up about each of the victims' lives.

Fiona McGhie may have been a talented artist, but she was an acerbic woman whose tongue was famed for its sharpness. The arguments she'd had had all been minor ones that had been escalated by the viciousness of her response about trivial matters.

From everything Beth had heard about her, it was little wonder the artist had cloistered herself away. She had no friends outside the art world and even then, the people she associated with described themselves as acquaintances rather than friends. They spoke of her talent with a brush, not her likeability as a person.

Rachel Allen, on the other hand, was gregarious and outgoing. She had a wide circle of friends and only a few people had anything negative to say about her. A co-worker had described her as a tease. He'd shared a kiss with her after a leaving party, but she'd not let things progress and had blanked him the next day.

Rachel's friends had told of similar experiences with other suitors. By all accounts, Rachel had often dressed to impress – one of her friends went so far as to use the term 'fuck-me dresses' – but had rarely hooked up with any of the men she attracted.

As Beth and O'Dowd had dug deeper into Rachel's life, they sketched a picture of a confident young woman who always loved to be the centre of attention. On more than one occasion, Rachel had fallen out with a particular girlfriend over her flirting with the girl's boyfriend. Rumours had circulated that she'd slept with the guy, but both Rachel and the man in question had apparently denied anything had happened.

One of Rachel's ex-boyfriends had described her as a wannabe princess who'd expected him to wait on her like a slave. He'd broken up with her when she'd refused to do anything for herself other than buy clothes and beauty treatments.

Neither Beth nor O'Dowd had picked up any signs from anyone they'd spoken to that they had a serious grudge against Rachel, or that they'd kill her let alone embark on a killing spree. Even the girl whose boyfriend had allegedly slept with Rachel had admitted she'd used the flirting as an excuse to dump the guy, rather than having any real belief he'd cheated on her.

With so many possibilities exhausted, there was nothing to do but keep going over all the statements until she found the elusive connection between the victims.

Beth checked her emails and found another update from the Digital Forensics Unit, plus an email from the Merseyside police.

Caitlin's life was laid bare for her. The girl had been in and out of trouble since she left primary school. Her family were well known to the police as small-time drug dealers who also dabbled in stolen goods and whatever else they could lay their hands on. Two of her brothers were currently residing at Her Majesty's pleasure, as were an uncle and a cousin.

According to her parents, she'd left the house on Wednesday after a row with her mother and had gone to stay with her boyfriend. The notes on the boyfriend's family showed them to be almost as troublesome as Caitlin's.

Like Suzy Keane, Caitlin's family had swiftly moved on from grief to anger. They'd threatened to complain to every paper in the land should their precious daughter's killer not be caught. Her father had even requested that the Merseyside police turn the killer over to him so he could deliver a biblical revenge.

It was a normal response to sudden violent death. Beth knew that despite any family tensions or petty squabbles, the Russells would miss and mourn Caitlin. Grief was a raw and visceral thing, and the first instinct was always to lash out, to try and achieve the transference of pain.

Caitlin's boyfriend was the obvious next step in her investigation. The Merseyside police had done their bit and had gone round to his house, but he'd left with Caitlin an hour after she'd arrived. His mother had said they were going to the Lakes, but she didn't know why, or had deigned not to say, as she perhaps had felt that the truth would be incriminating.

Whatever the reason, they had to find her boyfriend. Beth felt it was unlikely he was mixed up in Caitlin's death, but he still needed to be interviewed as he would have been the last person to see her.

A worse thought entered Beth's mind. Maybe he too had been killed. His body displayed with a pair of wings emerging from his back after the killer had snatched the couple in a weird two-for-one deal.

As she read on, she was pleased to note that a trace had been issued for both his mobile phone and his number plate – finding him shouldn't be too hard.

She moved on to the second email.

The various social media profiles of each of the known victims were telling if not informative.

Angus Keane had used Facebook as a place to advertise his business. He had a page where he uploaded photos of completed work and his header picture was little more than a billboard for his building work. He didn't engage with anyone other than those who messaged his page or commented on the pictures of the completed projects that he posted.

Beth remembered her training and tried to get a measure of the man from his posts. The spelling and grammar were good; even the timings of his posts suggested a consideration for others. He'd go online once a day between eight and nine at night and post his messages. Beth could imagine him reading his girls their bedtime stories, tucking them in and then heading downstairs to do what needed to be done online before settling down to watch some TV with his wife.

Nick Langley had used Facebook to discuss football, politics and generally complain about the state of the country. His posts were full of misspellings and littered with mild xenophobia, but other than references to Carlisle United or generic local places like the cinema, there were no obvious connections with any of the other three Cumbrian victims.

Rachel Allen's social media was what Beth expected from a single twenty-something. She was on Facebook and Instagram. Her Instagram posts were connected to her Facebook account and there were countless selfies of her in her mirror at home and on nights out. Looking through the pictures, Beth could understand the friend's comment about Rachel's dress sense. Almost every picture of Rachel showed her in clothes that accentuated her figure or downright flaunted it. Each one was a prime example of a person screaming, 'hey, look at me'.

Beth knew one or two people who dressed the way Rachel did. Behind all the front and the noise, they were insecure and she pitied them for thinking they had to dress provocatively just to get attention. There was nothing wrong with wearing an outfit that made you look and feel good, but for Beth, there had to be a balance. If the pictures of Rachel were anything to go by, she'd never heard the old rule about showing either legs or cleavage, but never both.

Facebook comments and emojis to friends' posts, check-ins at every place she'd been, and countless tags in the pictures of others – her profile was typical of her age group: whinges about work; excitement for forthcoming events and a plethora of shared memes.

As with many people her age, Rachel hadn't yet settled on a particular career path. She was listed as having one job after another, the longest lasting just over a year. She worked as a secretary or admin assistant and had been employed at a variety of different locations around Cumbria.

Beth supposed she had been trying out various things until she found a job she loved. When that had failed, she'd decided to go travelling.

Fiona McGhie's Facebook was little more than an advertising hoarding, in the same way Angus Keane had used his account. It listed nothing bar her latest works and provided links to various blog posts. Her Twitter account told a different story. It was here that she expressed her opinions on all manner of topics in caustic 280-character soundbites. No target was immune from her scorn, although Beth noticed she had the good sense not to criticise her customers.

When Beth checked out the blog attached to Fiona's website, she found a collection of posts which commented on the issues facing independent artists mixed in with posts on Fiona's inspirations and some of the artistic techniques that she used.

While the blog might have been of interest to some of her customers and fellow artists, Beth found it had an undercurrent of unspoken rage. The post on her blog about the supplier who'd failed to deliver on time had been a vitriol-fuelled hatchet job that bordered on the libellous.

Beth finished her reading and pushed her chair back so she could stand and stretch her limbs. After everything she'd learned about the minutiae of the victims' lives, she now felt closer to them, understood them more.

CHAPTER SIXTY-EIGHT

Sarah slid her feet into three-inch heels and walked across the room to check herself in the mirror one last time. She applied a final layer of lip gloss and inserted another kirby grip into her hair. All day she'd agonised over whether to wear her hair up or down and in the end she'd decided on up. That way she could also leave her neck exposed for any kisses that may come its way.

For what seemed like the thousandth time that day, she looked at her watch. Kevin was due in ten minutes and she wanted to be ready when he arrived. Not that she wanted to be too keen and be waiting at the door, but she prided herself on her good manners and she didn't know whether he'd be early, bang on time or fashionably late.

The last thing she did before going down the stairs was to dab a little perfume behind her ears and stuff her mobile into the clutch bag alongside the lip gloss and the one or two other pieces of make-up she always carried for emergencies. Her credit card was there too, along with a couple of twenties.

She didn't expect that she'd need any money tonight, but if he suggested they stop off somewhere for a drink on the way back, the least she could do was offer to pay for it.

Sarah had planned on switching her mobile to silent and leaving it in her bag all evening, but her mother had called to say that Nana had taken a bad turn earlier in the day. It would be rude to take a call during dinner, but she planned to forewarn Kevin of the situation. If he was as decent as he purported to be, he'd accept the intrusion with polite grace.

Should it prove to be an issue for him, then she'd know from the start that he wasn't the right man for her. Family was everything, and if he couldn't accept that she may get a call summoning her to her nana's deathbed, he wasn't the kind of man she wanted in her life.

As she looked out of the window to anticipate his arrival, Sarah felt an unfamiliar flutter of nerves. She was used to going on dates and wasn't sure why she was nervous until she admitted to herself how badly she wanted tonight to be perfect.

There was already a spark, obviously, but she wanted to know he was kind and respectful. She also suspected, like lots of men she met, that he might be dating other women. So she knew she had to stand out – be the kind of girl he'd take out again and again.

Another factor to consider would be their disparate backgrounds; she would have to find common ground and shared interests.

The main thing was, she had to leave him wanting more.

As she gazed out of the window, a gleaming Range Rover pulled up outside her door. She liked how he climbed out and walked up her path to knock on the door instead of just beeping the horn. He wore a designer suit, and an open-neck shirt without a tie and there was a suaveness about him that made her nerves give way to a far more primal feeling of desire.

CHAPTER SIXTY-NINE

Five names in succession on the notepad. Each of them a victim, yet all of them were speaking to Beth. Their voices almost became one as they mocked her for her failure to solve the case. Loudest of all were the vicious tongues of the cultured, but acerbic Fiona McGhie and the half-educated, coarse scouse accent of Caitlin Russell. Rachel Allen was full of accusations about Beth letting her down, while the two men implored Beth to give their families the closure of justice.

Beth re-ordered the names on her list in several ways to try and find a pattern.

Old to young didn't make any sense as the oldest victim was the first and the youngest the last. Reversing the list didn't work as the middle three victims' ages were out of sync with the order of their deaths.

Rather than list them horizontally, Beth tried listing them vertically, and added their jobs and careers alongside:

Angus Keane – Builder
Nick Langley – Builder
Rachel Allen – Secretary
Fiona McGhie – Artist
Caitlin Russell – Unknown / Unemployed ???

As soon as she'd written the five names, she realised her mistake. It had been habit that had made her write them that way, as it was the order in which she thought of them: that's how they'd been introduced to her. She re-wrote the order of the list from the victims' discovery to the chronology of their murders:

Fiona McGhie – Artist
Rachel Allen – Secretary
Angus Keane – Builder
Nick Langley – Builder
Caitlin Russell – Unknown / Unemployed ???

No matter how she stared at the names, they didn't speak to her in a way she could understand the connections between them.

With nothing obvious coming to her, she decided to grab a drink and give her brain a chance to reboot itself.

'D'you want a cuppa, Paul?'

Unthank was the only one in the office. Thompson was off speaking to Fiona McGhie's neighbours again, and O'Dowd was in conference with the DCI, ACC and the press officer. It was a meeting Beth was delighted not to attend.

'Please.'

As she waited on the kettle boiling, she considered Unthank's reason for being off yesterday. She'd not seen him leave the office even once today, which suggested he'd been cured of the sickness he'd suffered from.

Except it must not have been a miracle cure. He'd picked at a sandwich for lunch, but that didn't explain the lapses of concentration he'd shown today. He was normally a solid worker, focussed on the task at hand. For him to be daydreaming indicated that he was undergoing something more than a bout of food poisoning.

When she'd asked how he was this morning, he'd looked away from her and given a mumbled reply. She could only think of one reason he was being evasive. He'd been dumped and couldn't face work yesterday. He'd tried to get through today, but his mind had kept returning to his ex. It explained everything.

Rather than confront him with what may be a wrong idea, Beth decided to do a little fishing to find out if she was right. He'd either tell her or he wouldn't, but she wouldn't pry or badger him for an answer.

'Are you seeing Lana when you finish? Or has she got the bug you had yesterday?'

Unthank's head turned away from her. When he spoke, his muttered answer was heavy with raw emotion.

'Not tonight.'

She had her confirmation and decided to leave the conversation where it was.

It would have remained that way, had Unthank not looked so distraught.

After letting him have a minute to himself she walked over and rested a hand on his elbow.

When he lifted his head she found herself looking at a broken man.

'You've worked it out, haven't you?'

'That you and Lana have split?' Beth gave a little shrug. 'I guessed, that's all. It's none of my business, so you don't have to tell me anything you don't want to.'

Unthank's lip wobbled as he shook his head. 'She said that she doesn't love me any more. That I suffocate her. She's moving back to her parents. It's the only reason I'm in today. I couldn't bear to watch her walk out of my life.'

'I don't know what to say beyond the clichés and platitudes you don't want to hear. Yes, time will heal your broken heart. Yes, you should get back in the saddle as soon as possible, and yes, you will be okay in the end, but the next few days are going to be shit and there's not a lot anyone can do to take the pain away for you. Shit as it is, having your heart broken is something that happens to pretty much everyone at some point in their life. I guess it's just your turn.'

A wan smile pulled its way onto Unthank's face as a fat tear rolled down his cheek.

'Thanks.'

'Don't mention it.' Beth nodded towards the door. 'Maybe go to the toilet and wash your face before anyone else comes in though, yeah?'

As she flopped back onto her seat, her eyes were drawn to the list of names.

She saw it before her backside connected with the chair's thin padding. In her revised listing, the initials of the Christian names of the victims was an acrostic that spelled out the word 'FRANC':

Fiona McGhie – Artist
Rachel Allen – Secretary
Angus Keane – Builder
Nick Langley – Builder
Caitlin Russell – Unknown / Unemployed ???

CHAPTER SEVENTY

The lad sitting across the table from Beth and Thompson was cocksure. Even without having read his record, Beth would have been able to tell he'd seen the inside of an interview room before.

Thompson went through the routine of naming everyone present and stating the reason for the interview.

Billy Sullivan was nineteen years old and still had a rash of acne. Everything about him spoke of an unshakeable self-confidence. The tilt of his head, the set of his jaw and the challenge in his eyes showed he was more than comfortable. He wouldn't be easy to get talking; it would take all their cunning to get the truth from him.

Rather than go straight in with news of Caitlin's death, Thompson had suggested they ease into the interview, as he wanted to get Billy used to talking to them before he brought up the subject of murder.

Beth knew that if Billy clammed up from the off, it would be a red flag, but if he went along with their questions and didn't try to be clever or obstructive, depending on his answers they'd be able to eliminate him from their enquiries or charge him for Caitlin's murder.

Thompson opened the questioning. 'Do you know why you're here, Billy?'

'Something to do with Caitlin. The mad bitch, like totally flipped. I was like, what the fuck, at the way she went off on one.'

'She flipped, did she? Why was that?'

'She found a text she shouldn't have.' Billy gave a man-of-the-world shrug. 'Man, I'm too young to, like, get tied down to some madwoman. Gonna play me the field and hope for a crop failure.' Billy gave a forced laugh and twisted his head to see who was laughing with him.

His laugh halted when he was met with three stony faces. The duty solicitor made sure he could see her rolling eyes.

'So what happened when she flipped out?'

'The mad cow launched my phone out the car window. When I stopped to get it back she got out the car and, like, stormed off. My phone was in, like, a thousand pieces, so I let her go. Plenty more where she came from.'

'You're from Liverpool, aren't you? Why were you in the Lakes?'

For the first time, Beth detected a touch of fear in Billy.

'We just come away for a couple of nights. You know, dirty weekend in the week?'

'Try again, Billy.' Beth could detect the deliberate cynicism in Thompson's voice. 'We've seen your record, and Caitlin's. We don't for one minute think you were in the Lakes on holiday. You were up to something. I'll be honest, I don't know what it was and I don't really care. I have more important things to worry about and, right now, I'm trying to find out who murdered Caitlin and left her with a pair of wings sprouting from her back.'

'She's dead? Shit, that's sooo not cool.' A hand with dirty fingernails swept across his face. 'How did she die and what's that shit about wings?'

'She had a pair of wings surgically attached to her back, and she died after someone poured a flammable substance down her throat and then lit it.'

The room fell silent as Billy processed the news of Caitlin's murder. Billy looked shocked and his trembling fingers and tear-filled eyes destroyed any illusion of his toughness.

Beth was the one who broke the silence. 'What are you thinking, Billy? If I was to guess, I'd say you're wondering why Caitlin was killed, why we're speaking to you and whether we think you killed her.'

'You ain't no fool, lady. But before you start asking questions, I didn't kill her. Way she was freaking out, I was glad the bitch pissed off when I stopped the car. Didn't want her dead, just away from me, and she went away. Job was a good'un s'far as I was concerned.'

'Where did this happen?'

'Some place in the sticks. Was going from Kendal to Windermere, like. She wanted me to take the back roads so she could see more animals. She loved seeing sheep and cows.' A shake of the head indicated Billy's incomprehension at someone wanting to see animals. 'I only want to see them on my plate.'

Beth tapped on the table's Formica top before she spoke. 'Seriously, Billy. We need to know where you last saw her. If you can't be more specific, then we'll start thinking you're being deliberately vague because you're lying to us. When we think people are lying to us, we wonder why. In your case it doesn't take a lot of wondering to get from an argument where she dumped you and smashed your mobile, to you being so mad with her that you killed her, and made it look like she was murdered by the person who's been killing other people the same way.'

'What other people?'

Beth realised that Billy was probably the type of person who'd only watch the news to see if his own crimes had been reported. He hadn't heard of the Dragon Master's killings, and if her impression of him was anything to go by, he sure as hell wasn't smart enough to be the Dragon Master himself.

Thompson's hand slapped down on the table making them all jump. 'Cut the nonsense, Billy, we know what you're at. DC Young has it right. You're a copycat; you killed her and copied details of the other killings in the way she was left, didn't you?'

'I didn't copycat nothing. Caitlin dumped me and fucked off. End of. If you're dumb enough to think I'd risk jail for that bitch, you ain't got no hope of catching no killer.'

Beth and Thompson probed at Billy for another half hour before admitting defeat and releasing him.

Billy Sullivan didn't possess the intellect to have committed the murders. He was small-time and always would be. His braggart nature and failure to understand anything beyond his own desires would prevent any organised criminals hiring him.

He'd seemed like a good lead but his story had panned out. They hadn't told him, but the trace they'd run on Caitlin's mobile had shown where and when he claimed they'd parted company. His car had been picked up by an ANPR camera at the edge of Windermere soon after Caitlin had got out of it, so there was little likelihood he'd stayed around or gone back for her.

The trace on Caitlin's phone had shown her waiting at a junction for a while and then she'd moved towards Kendal before her phone signal dropped away. That meant her phone had been smashed, as the triangulation signals on all mobiles work even if there's no battery power or a battery in the phone.

With the interview a waste of time, Beth and Thompson headed for the car park as soon as they'd written up their reports.

As she trudged towards her car, Beth felt her dejection in the slump of her shoulders and the heaviness of her feet. Tomorrow promised to be another long day and if it was anything like today, it would involve a lot of dead ends and futile interviews that brought them no closer to catching the Dragon Master.

The demoralising effect of such days was bad enough for Beth to endure, but what really burned at her was that she, and the rest of the team, were no closer to finding a killer who showed every sign of planning to kill again.

CHAPTER SEVENTY-ONE

The noise coming from the lips of the man who used a false name would only be called a tuneful whistle by the most charitable of people. Tonight had gone far better than he could have hoped for. The date with Sarah Hardy had been more enjoyable than expected, as she'd talked and listened with equal interest. The food had been delicious and the service impeccable.

The only slight concerns were the two surprised looks she'd given him. He knew those looks all too well, and he'd spent years trying not to show the side of his nature that elicited them. He'd glossed over them by professing to be nervous and she'd smiled and confessed to her own nerves.

For him though, the best part had been looking at Sarah and imagining what she'd look like when she became part of his project. Of all the tributes he'd offered up, she would be the most beautiful. The grace and poise she moved with was second to none and he couldn't help but be reminded of graceful birds in flight.

Her body would be a perfect muse for his project. When he added the wings to her back she would be the closest match he'd made yet.

The conversation he'd shared with her had been meaningless in a lot of ways, but he'd inserted a few topics in the name of research. Now he knew where he could snatch her and remain undetected. How he could bring her under his control.

Once he'd done that, he'd be ready to prepare her as an offering.

She'd mentioned the Dragon Master killings to him, and even though he'd been aware the topic may arise, it had been surreal to discuss his crimes with a virtual stranger over dinner. Sarah had speculated about the way Caitlin had been displayed, and he'd struggled not to look smug when she'd mentioned the press theories about the Dragon Master and his kills. All the theories were off base, which had only proven his smartness to him.

The news that the police had discovered the three dragons he'd created at Highstead Castle didn't worry him as he had no plans to use the castle a fourth time. They would have found them at some point and he felt it was for the best that the police and the press knew of all his kills. It wouldn't take them long to establish the order of his victims, but he doubted that they'd be able to work out the finer, more nuanced details of his reasons for making dragons.

That Sarah had an ill grandmother she was worried about had been a godsend. It meant she hadn't invited him in for coffee. He'd even bade her goodbye with the line, 'I hope your nana is okay, you should call her.' When she'd smiled and said she would, it felt obvious to him that it'd be the first thing she would do once she was in the house – to call and see how the old girl was. It would establish that she'd returned home from the date, thereby proving his innocence. Should the police come a calling again, he'd be in the clear.

With each new tribute, he was getting closer to appeasing the torment of his childhood. The hours he'd spent hiding from his mother. She'd called him a devil. But she'd been the fiery hell-beast. She'd soared above him and filled him with terror.

While she had actually breathed smoke rather than fire on him, every word that poured from her mouth had burned his soul with viciously expressed criticism. Choosing Fiona McGhie as his first tribute had been so perfect. He'd bought a few of her paintings over the years and had never forgotten the mouthful of abuse he'd received after asking for a discount when he'd bought six pictures in one day. She'd been every bit as critical of him as his dragon of a mother. Her words cut deep searing wounds into his flesh, and she'd waved a cigarette around exactly the same way his mother had. As soon as her diatribe had started, he'd known what he would do to her.

Tonight, not only had Sarah played right into his hands during the date, he'd also managed to get a lock on the copper without too much hassle. Electoral records were so giving, and they were just the first step. They called themselves detectives but they weren't the only ones who could find out stuff.

With the copper's home located, he needed to learn what the neighbourhood was like. Google Maps would show a certain amount, but they didn't give the full story.

The copper was involved in the investigation into his project, which meant she'd be working long hours, often with colleagues ever-present. He knew if he wanted her alone, she'd probably have to be snatched from her home in the middle of the night.

He picked up the keys to his car and strode to the door. Reconnaissance was an important part of a successful operation and he refused to be thwarted at this stage.

CHAPTER SEVENTY-TWO

The office hung with the smell of air freshener when Beth switched on her PC. As she'd entered the room, the cleaners were finishing off their lackadaisical efforts.

All night she'd thought about the acrostic she'd noticed. O'Dowd and Thompson had listened with interest when she'd told them of her theory, but neither had shown a great deal of enthusiasm about the idea. Thompson had even gone so far as to warn her not to get swept up by coincidences. He was probably right. It wasn't even really a word. And this wasn't a crossword, it was a murder investigation.

Still, sleep had been a fleeting beast which had shown its face only for short occasions as both her conscious thoughts and her subconscious tried to find the meaning of the acrostic. Assuming no one was complaining about Swiss currency, she had to make the assumption that the word 'FRANC' was incomplete. But France, Francis or franchise made no more sense in showing the connection between the victims or as a way of identifying the murderer.

Any connections with the country of France didn't seem very apt. As for the names, maybe they could belong to the Dragon Master or someone the killer revered. A check of the electoral register would give her a list of all the matches within Cumbria. The names could then be cross referenced against the PNC to offer up the most probable suspects.

'Franchise' might have seemed like a better option, perhaps. But outside of organised crime, there were few connections between murder and business, unless there was an as yet undiscovered financial link between all the victims.

Try as she might, she couldn't make any further headway without more information.

Rather than do nothing, she reached for her keyboard and typed an email to Control and every police station in the county, requesting that if anyone was reported missing and their name began with a vowel or an 's', she was to be informed at once, regardless of how little time they'd actually been missing.

Before she sent the email she checked the missing persons' report. She was pleased to find there were no new reports; therefore if she was right, nobody was in immediate danger.

When the others trooped in they each had a look of defeat on their faces. The horrific nature of the investigation was taking its toll on them and Beth had seen the haunted look her own eyes had developed when putting on her make-up.

She brought them all up to speed on what she'd done, then went back to her spreadsheet to add all the information she'd gathered on Caitlin.

O'Dowd clapped her hands.

'Right then, listen up. Boys, I want you to find out more about our victims, speak to anyone who knew them and get me as complete a picture of their lives as is humanly possible. Beth, you stay here and keep plugging away with your spreadsheet. Find me a connection between those victims. One way or another, we've got to predict where the Dragon Master will strike next and then make sure we're there waiting with a bear trap.'

As the office emptied, Beth felt both isolated and empowered. She'd been left with an onerous task that may just break the case open. If she succeeded, no more lives would be lost. The guys had got to leave the office and conduct interviews, whereas she was left here to collate the information they fed her. She couldn't work out if she'd been handed the rubbish job because she was new, or because she was trusted to spot something in the new information the others gathered.

She checked her computer and found that Dr Hewson had sent through his report from Caitlin's post-mortem. Wading through the medical terminology, she learned that the girl's trachea had been scorched every bit as much Nick Langley's.

When the report moved onto the internal organs, it stated that the oesophagus had next to no damage compared to the lungs which had suffered third-degree burns.

Dr Hewson's notes suggested that he thought the killer had changed from petrol to a gas, and that Caitlin had inhaled large amounts of the burning gas into her lungs, which had caused the extensive burning. Like Nick Langley, traces of Rohypnol had been found in her blood.

CHAPTER SEVENTY-THREE

When Sarah came to she found that she was bound to the metal frame of a bed. Whichever way she tried pulling and twisting, all that happened was the chafing of her skin from the rough nylon ropes. Her head thumped as if she'd had a night on vodka shots, and her mouth was furry and dry. She was also struggling to get her brain to work. She remembered the date with Kevin – that had been fantastic – and getting home afterwards.

How she'd got from home to here was a blank.

She cast her eyes around and found she was in a windowless room illuminated by a bare bulb in an old-fashioned fitting. A single door gave access to the room. The walls were scratched and marked, and when she looked at the scratches a little closer, she saw they were crude attempts to draw various beasts. The biggest one was a great winged creature. Above them pictures of derelict country houses were taped to the wall. She recognised the houses but couldn't say why she knew them.

When she looked down her body she saw that she was wearing a thin nightgown with spaghetti straps. It wasn't one of her own. It was cheap and drab, but that wasn't her greatest concern.

She gave a wriggle on the bed and felt none of the support or friction offered by underwear. Whoever had brought her here must have stripped her and then re-dressed her in the shapeless nightgown.

She opened her mouth to scream and then closed it again. That she hadn't been gagged told her that her abductor wasn't worried about her shouting or screaming. Therefore it was probably futile.

Sarah's first thought was that she might have been raped, but she felt no pains. That fact didn't mean it hadn't happened yet though, and didn't mean it wouldn't. Screaming might bring help, but it may also bring the person who'd kidnapped her. If he was waiting for her to wake up so he had a live victim, screaming would only inform him that she was ready to be raped.

Sarah knew that rape was about control and power as much as sex. That rapists got off on seeing the terror in their victim's eyes, that they enjoyed the struggle and the subsequent conquest.

Sarah turned her attention to her bonds. One by one she tried to free her limbs, first one hand and then the other. When she tried pulling her feet free, the only thing she achieved was a tightening of her bindings.

Each of the ropes securing her to the bed was tight enough to keep her spreadeagled, with only an inch or so of movement. No matter how she tried manoeuvring herself, she couldn't get room to allow her fingers to pick at the knots. When she tried to crane her neck over so she could chew through the ropes she couldn't get her mouth within a foot of them.

With escape impossible, Sarah went back to examining her surroundings. At the far wall there was a workbench. The area wasn't well lit, but when she peered at the workbench she saw a few stuffed birds.

The longer she stared at the birds, the more she thought they didn't look right. That they were missing something.

As soon as Sarah realised the birds were missing their wings, she began to shake. Her limbs thrashed as she tried to free herself by wrenching and riving at her bonds.

All she achieved was a further chafing of her skin where she was tied to the bed.

Sarah went limp and let the tears come. She knew she was going to die; she'd seen the news, heard how the Dragon Master was killing his victims, and how they were displayed in remote ruins; she'd even discussed it with Kevin on their date. And now she was in his clutches.

As she tried to work out how she'd ended up here, her memory began returning and she started to piece together the rest of her morning.

She'd got up early, as was her Saturday-morning routine, and after a call to her mother to see how Nana was, she'd gone out for her weekly run around the back roads surrounding Kendal.

At the halfway point, she'd heard a purring engine and saw the familiar shape of Kevin's Range Rover. He'd pulled up beside her and flashed that knee-weakening smile of his. 'When you told me last night that you run this route, I thought I'd surprise you with some refreshments.'

He'd offered her a bottle of lemon-flavoured water. She'd taken the water and chugged some of it back, grateful for his considerate thought even as she worried about her appearance. As pleased as she'd been to see him, she hadn't wanted him seeing her with messy hair and a perspiration-streaked face.

Her recollection got vague from that point, although she was sure she remembered walking round to the passenger side of his Range Rover.

What had happened from then on was a mystery. She must have been abducted at some point after she'd bade goodbye to Kevin: it was the only explanation she could think of.

As the tears of self-pity and terror rolled down her cheeks, she thought of her nana, alone and frail, waiting to die. Sarah's thoughts then turned to her mother, and how she would have to deal with the grief of losing not just a parent, but also a child.

CHAPTER SEVENTY-FOUR

Thompson strode into the office with Unthank trailing in his wake. Both men looked weary but determined.

Unthank perched himself on the end of her desk. 'I went back to see Eric and his comb-over. Showed him a picture of the wings. He says they're from a buzzard.'

Beth closed her eyes and digested this news. Not only was the Dragon Master escalating in every sense of the word, he must also be coming to the natural end of his killing cycle, as there were fewer birds she could think of with larger wingspans than a buzzard. Off the top of her head she got albatross, condor and golden eagle, but she couldn't think of any others.

She made a note to try and find out where stuffed birds could be bought. If she could find someone who'd recently bought a sparrowhawk, buzzard and larger birds as well, she'd have the Dragon Master.

Beth's attention returned to the notepad on her desk. A Google search had given her a list of twenty-three names beginning with FRANC. From there she'd identified thirty-nine people in the county called Francis, Frances, Francesca or Franco and a baby called Franciszka. Nine of them were either under sixteen or over seventy, which left thirty names: sixteen men and fourteen women.

Of the sixteen men, fifteen were unknown to the police and the sixteenth was only known to them because of his habit of making complaints about his neighbours. None of the fourteen women had a police record, but regardless, O'Dowd had insisted that all thirty were contacted by their local CID teams for preliminary questioning. It was a long shot at best, but with no stronger leads to follow, they had to chase down the ones they had. If it turned out to be another dead end, at least it would be the other teams' time that was wasted.

Because they had a definite time frame for Caitlin's murder at Lonsdale Castle, they'd be able to quickly establish whether or not the thirty people whose names fit the acrostic had alibis.

With the search for the killer now ranging countywide, Beth felt more like a coordinator than an investigator. O'Dowd had been in and out of the office as she liaised with the press office and DCI Phinn. Another press conference was scheduled for early afternoon and O'Dowd was to front the briefing once again. To say that the DI was crotchety was an understatement. She'd barked orders, railed against the impossibility of the investigation and exhorted them all to get her the results she needed.

Unthank answered his phone and passed the receiver to Beth. As she listened to the desk sergeant from Kendal, Beth scratched the few scant details they had onto her pad.

A young woman had been reported missing by her mother. Her name was Sarah.

Beth almost dismissed the call, but then she remembered that francs were a unit of currency. Surely that wasn't what this would be about? Nothing in the investigation seemed to connect currency to a killer displaying such personal, violent motives.

But she would still run the call about the missing woman past O'Dowd to see what the DI thought. With the number of victims spiralling, any missing person was at risk.

CHAPTER SEVENTY-FIVE

As Beth walked into the showroom, she had a growing sense of unease. She'd met with the missing girl's mother and hadn't liked what she'd heard.

Sarah Hardy had called her mother around seven in the morning to enquire after her dying grandmother. She'd then gone for a jog but hadn't shown up at the grandmother's house as she'd promised. When her mother had called her to say that her grandmother had taken another turn for the worse she hadn't got an answer.

That Sarah hadn't answered her phone was unthinkable as she knew how little time the grandmother had left. This was the point her mother had laboured and Beth had believed her.

This detail, coupled with the fact that Sarah was universally described as a sensible girl who'd landed herself a decent job, led Beth to fear for her safety. People would often be uncontactable, but Sarah had been fully aware of an impending family tragedy. It didn't make sense that she didn't have her phone with her, or that she hadn't been checking it every few minutes.

She introduced herself to a salesman with too much gel in his hair and a smarmy attitude. When his stare moved from her scar to her eyes, she asked him who Sarah was closest to at work.

'That'd be Veronica.' He pointed at a woman sitting behind a desk. 'Is Sarah okay?'

Rather than fob the guy off with a lie or a half-truth, Beth left him to wonder and strode over to Veronica's desk, where she laid her warrant card in front of the woman and took a seat.

'I need to ask you a few questions about one of your colleagues.'

'Why? What's up?'

'Sarah Hardy's mother can't reach her, so I'm trying to find out where she might be. Do you know anything?'

'No.' The shaking of Veronica's head made her severe bob swing back and forth. 'She's off this weekend, and as far as I know, she was going to spend some time with her nana. From what Sarah's told me, the old girl hasn't got long left.'

'That's why it's strange her mother can't get in touch with her. Do you know if she had a boyfriend? Her mother said she was out on a date last night, but it was a first date and all she knew was that Sarah had had a wonderful time and the guy was a perfect gentleman.'

'Lucky Sarah.'

Beth caught the flash of resentment. She'd seen a picture of Sarah and had noted how good-looking the missing woman was. Veronica wore a thick layer of make-up and she carried at least a couple more stones than her doctor might advise.

While Sarah and Veronica might be friends, Veronica was perhaps aware of more male eyes being drawn to her younger, better-looking and slimmer colleague. That Sarah hadn't told Veronica about the date also said a lot. Either it was someone she wasn't too keen on, which wasn't the impression she got from her mother, or she'd not told Veronica about the guy so as to not rub her colleague's nose in her good fortune.

She pursued the line of questioning. 'Why do you say that?'

'She deserves to meet someone. Besides, she hardly ever goes out these days because of her nana. The nearest she gets to romance is flirting with customers to make the sale. It's about time she found someone to make her feel special.'

This wasn't the answer Beth was expecting, but it told her more than the words themselves. Maybe Veronica wasn't jealous of her colleague's genetic advantage? Perhaps she just pitied Sarah's lonely existence and wanted her to be happy.

'You said that she'd flirt with customers. Do you think that any of them took it the wrong way and expected more?'

Veronica pulled a face and twiddled a paperclip between her fingers. 'Not that I know of. It's something you soon learn; you can flirt a little, but not too much. If you go too far and the guy's wife or girlfriend is around, there's no way you're going to make the sale. Her flirting was subtle, understated. Tell you what though, Sarah was complaining about a guy who was in a few times this week.'

'Really?' Beth felt her pulse quicken. 'What was the score with him?'

'He was this old guy. A tyre kicker of the highest order, if you know what I mean.' Beth nodded to indicate that she knew a tyre kicker was a customer who'd go through the whole sales rigmarole despite having little intention to buy. 'He creeped Sarah out. She told me he seemed far more interested in her than the car. Said he'd spent far more time looking at her than at the car.'

'Do you know if he was looking at her face or was he perving over her body?'

'Both. He'd take sneaky looks when he thought she wouldn't notice, but instead of being like most guys and stopping when he'd been caught out, he kept right on doing it.'

Beth had received her share of male attention in the past and knew exactly what Veronica was talking about. It was an instinctive thing. If a woman wore something revealing, a lot of men wouldn't just glance her way, they'd allow their eyes to linger for a second or two longer. But almost all women knew instinctively that there was an invisible line between what was a lingering look and something creepier.

'I don't suppose you know his name and where he lives?'

'I don't. But I can find out.' Veronica moved to another desk and rooted in the drawer until her hand pulled out some paperwork. She rifled through it until she found what she was looking for. 'Here we are. He's called Harry Quirke.'

'Harry Quirke?'

Beth turned and ran out of the showroom. Harry Quirke was one of the people they'd interviewed about Angus Keane's death. That his name had come up regarding Sarah's disappearance had to be way more than a coincidence. It wasn't like he was called Dave Smith or another common name; he had to be the same Harry Quirke.

Beth even remembered the way he'd looked at her too. It wasn't just that he was paying attention to her, it was the way he'd swept his eyes over her face and body as though he was committing her to memory.

Whether or not Harry Quirke was the Dragon Master, Beth feared for Sarah if she was in his clutches.

CHAPTER SEVENTY-SIX

The keys jangled in the hand of the man who used a false name. His other hand held a bottle of water he'd laced with Rohypnol and a powerful sedative.

When he got through the door he descended the stairs towards the cellar where he'd spent so much of his childhood hiding from his mother. He opened the door at the bottom of the stairs and looked towards the bed.

Sarah's face was full of relief when she saw him. 'Kevin? Oh thank God you're here. Quick, untie me. How did you know where to find me?'

He didn't speak. Instead he unscrewed the top from the water bottle and put it to her lips. She drained the bottle in several gulps.

'Please, Kevin. Untie me now.'

'I'm not Kevin. Not really. Kevin is just a name I use when dealing with my darling tributes. My real name is different, but some people have decided to call me the Dragon Master. I like that. It's fitting.'

'Kevin, stop dicking around and untie me. Please.'

'I've told you, Sarah. I'm the Dragon Master. How do you think I knew you were here?'

'I don't know.'

'When I met you earlier, you took a drink of water I'd laced with Rohypnol. I talked to you until it took effect and then you did exactly what I told you to do.'

'You mean I just walked down here myself?'

'Exactly. You stripped off when I told you to, put that gown on when I told you to and, best of all, you lay down and let me tie you to the bed. You were giggling as I tied the knots.'

'You bastard.'

'Sticks and stones, Sarah, sticks and stones.'

Sarah's eyes widened with realisation and horror. 'The water you just gave me. That was drugged too, wasn't it?'

'You could say that. I couldn't possibly comment.' He could feel the smile on his lips and hear it in his voice. In spite of himself, he was enjoying talking to her. The fear in her eyes was a wonderful thing to behold.

Sarah's voice held incredulity and terror in equal measure. 'Why are you doing this to me? You're not really the Dragon Master, are you?'

'I'm doing it to you because your name fits. That's the only reason you've been chosen as a tribute. You will be given the honour of being kissed by fire. Your breath will flame bright and you'll earn your place in history.'

'No, Kevin, or whatever you're called. No. This is wrong. Please don't do this to me. We went on a date last night. Remember it? It was lovely. You don't have to do this. I can be so much more than that to you. Let me join you, help you.'

'Do be quiet, Sarah. I know you're grasping at the proverbial straws, but you need to shush, to save your strength for your moment of glory. You're going to become a darling tribute to a fearsome dragon who spurned my love so often I grew to hate her.'

Sarah flinched as he caressed her chin.

'There's nothing you can do or say that will change my mind. Your fate is sealed.'

When he looked at Sarah's face there was no response other than a blank look as she fell victim to the drugs he'd put into the water bottle.

He untied her limbs one by one and told her to turn over.

She lay still as he refastened her bindings.

When he'd got what he needed from the workbench, her eyes were closed as the powerful sedative did what it was supposed to do.

He laid the plastic squares on her exposed shoulder blades and reached for a scalpel. The more he could do to prepare her for tonight's offering, the better, as tonight would be spectacular, but risky.

It hadn't been easy for him to learn how to perform this part of the process, but he'd managed to hone his skills by watching online tutorials and harnessing every scrap of his patience.

That he was removing skin and only a very thin layer of muscle made the actual operation simpler. At most he was cutting through a half inch of muscle before the tip of his scalpel scraped against the tribute's shoulder blade. He always was careful and precise with his movements, so making exact cuts wasn't something he found hard.

With the tributes drugged and compliant, their flesh was loose and malleable; it was now a matter of pride to him that the squares were as perfect as they could be.

Once the boundaries had been marked out with scalpel cuts, he'd swap the scalpel for a paring knife and remove the portion of flesh before running a bead of surgical glue along each edge of the cut to reduce the bleeding.

A pair of wings had already been removed from two of the stuffed birds he'd bought online – not from a taxidermist as there were licensing issues, but from auction sites – he'd learned from Caitlin's tribute that surgical glue took longer to set than he was comfortable with when affixing larger wings to his tributes. He'd spent fifteen nerve-wracking minutes at Lonsdale Castle holding each of the buzzard's wings until the surgical glue had set enough to support them.

Rather than take that risk again, he planned to use superglue on Sarah and her companion, as she had a pair of mighty wings awaiting her.

He believed his ability to adapt and evolve put him above all others. His project was growing wings of its own as he refined his methods. Petrol had been discarded in favour of gas, but he hadn't stopped there. With Caitlin he'd tried a new method of fire-making which had worked better than expected. With a slight refinement, the new technique would take his dragons' fire breathing to a whole new level. Getting the flames right had caused him the most trouble, but he was confident he could now deliver both a flammable substance and oxygen into the mouths and gullets of his tributes. The can of lighter fluid he'd used on Caitlin had been good, but his new idea was so much better.

He knew that if he could continue to refine his methods, he'd create a dragon far more fearsome than his mother had ever been, and that if he truly wanted to pay tribute to the woman who'd given birth to him, he'd find a way to show her that he could make something even mightier. Creating a copy of his mother was never his aim, what he wanted to do was create dragons he could have power and control over.

That two of his dragons had been male was of no consequence to him. They'd fitted the pattern and, as such, he'd selected them.

He lifted his paring knife and again bent over Sarah's back. The more preparation he could do beforehand, the less time he would be at risk. After all, there was another tribute to be made first.

He'd attach the wings in situ, but for now, he'd done all he could to prepare Sarah.

CHAPTER SEVENTY-SEVEN

The Drover's Rest was a regular haunt of his. Not only did the large country pub have an excellent menu, but the owner was a woman who insisted all her female staff wore skirts.

While a fair percentage of the staff were barely more than schoolgirls working their first job – and therefore out of bounds for his admiration – there was a pair of head waitresses who were pretty and could be considered as angels. They were who he was here to see.

He needed to savour the delights of sexuality and beauty. He'd not been able to watch Sarah today. She hadn't been at work and although he'd watched her house for most of the day, he'd seen no sign of her. He could only assume that she'd either left early, or spent the day at home.

Whichever it was, he'd missed her and he needed his fix of beauty.

One of the head waitresses came his way. She was a mid-twenties brunette who had long shapely legs and the kind of smile that could melt an iceberg in seconds.

'Hello, Harry. I haven't seen you here for a while.'

'I know. I meant to get back here sooner, but you know how life gets in the way of plans.'

'I do indeed.' A short tinkling laugh broke her sentence. 'Would you like a menu?'

Harry took the offered menu and made some extra small talk. When the waitress left, he watched the way her backside oscillated as she walked away from him.

The early evening passed in an appreciation of good food, nylon clad legs and pretty faces.

By the time he had paid his bill and pressed a generous tip into the head waitress's hand, his belly was full and his heart was empty.

The two head waitresses were each more beautiful than the average woman, but even combined, they were no match for Sarah, the most beautiful of all the angels.

A pair of police officers walked into the bar as he was leaving but he paid them no heed. He'd done no wrong and the half shandy he'd washed his meal down with wasn't likely to get him arrested for drink-driving.

But before he got to the door, the taller, bearded PC stepped in front of him and blocked his way.

'Mr Quirke. I'd appreciate it if you'd come with me.'

Harry's military training told him everything he needed to know. PC Beard was poised for action. His hands hung loosely at his sides ready to act and he'd shifted his weight to the balls of his feet in case he had to move in a hurry.

'Of course.' A thought struck him. 'Is it my sister? Is she okay?'

'As far as I know, she's fine. This is to do with another matter. You'll find out more when we get you to the station.'

PC Beard was courteous but uninformative, as he escorted Harry towards the police car and guided him into the back seat.

As they hurtled through the countryside, Harry sat in the back and tried to work out why he'd been lifted. He'd done no wrong that he knew of and he'd not witnessed any crime.

Again, his army training kicked in and he relaxed into the seat. As a sniper's spotter, he'd become accustomed to great periods of boredom followed by a few moments of frantic action.

CHAPTER SEVENTY-EIGHT

Beth could feel the rage emanating from O'Dowd as she took a seat beside her. Harry Quirke was sitting across the table from them and he carried the calm air of someone who was intrigued at the goings on.

They hadn't yet arrested him, but Beth knew it was a possible outcome of the interview. Like every other lead in this case, the link was tenuous and they had no evidence to back up their suspicions, but with no better leads to pursue, they had to follow those they had.

When O'Dowd went through the formalities Quirke's expression never changed. He just sat there with his fingers interlocked over his belly. To all intents and purposes, it was the behaviour of an innocent man.

His posture made her doubt herself and wonder if she'd got it wrong. If that was the case, not only had she wasted a large portion of a day when she should have been apprehending the Dragon Master, she'd put herself in O'Dowd's sights. The only thing that restored her faith in her theory was that Sarah's phone had been traced to the middle of nowhere and she still hadn't been found.

From what Thompson had told her, she understood that today's press conference had made the previous one seem like a summer picnic beside a babbling brook.

O'Dowd placed her hands on the table. 'Right then. Mr Quirke, do you know a Sarah Hardy?'

'I do, yes. I almost bought a car from her. Sadly when I checked my finances, I found I couldn't stretch my budget quite far enough.'

'What did you think of her?'

'I thought she was a very pleasant and good-looking young woman.'

'Good-looking you say.' O'Dowd was on the statement at once. 'Are you saying you fancied her?'

'I presume that if you're asking me questions about her, you'll already know that she is a strikingly beautiful woman. I cannot deny that I appreciate her beauty, but I wouldn't say that I fancy her. She is less than half my age and I felt no greater attraction to her than I do towards the lovely DC sitting beside you. She too is a gorgeous specimen despite the ugly scar on her cheek.'

'I'll beg your pardon, Mr Quirke, not to speak about one of my team like that.'

Quirke raised his hands from the table. 'If I've caused any offence, I apologise. All I was trying to do was pay her a compliment. She has enough beauty about her to compensate for the scar.'

'MR QUIRKE!'

As O'Dowd was staring Quirke down, Beth was digging into the psyche fuelling his words. Yes the guy creeped her out with his lingering assessments of her and the way he was talking about her scar. That he was having a conversation about a part of her that she didn't discuss was both surreal and invasive.

Yet at the same time, he wasn't showing any signs of lust and his voice was calm. It was as if he was discussing a painting or some other work of art rather than a human being.

Beth laid a hand on O'Dowd's arm. While she appreciated the DI coming to her defence, she didn't need protecting, and she wasn't offended by Quirke's words. She also wanted to play good cop to O'Dowd's bad cop.

'Mr Quirke, if you don't mind me saying so, you don't look to be a young man. What do you do with your days?'

'I'm retired. I was invalided out of the army a good few years ago.'

'You didn't answer my question. What do you do with your days?'

Quirke gave a helpless gesture. 'I potter about in my garden and I read.'

'What else do you do?' Beth put a smile on her face as she spoke. 'You were at The Drover's Rest tonight. Do you eat out often?'

'As I told you the other day, I eat out most lunch and dinner times. I live alone and I'm a rotten cook. To stave off the boredom, I dine out. There isn't a crime in that, is there?'

'That very much depends on how you behave. When DI O'Dowd was asking you about Sarah Hardy you seemed a fraction less relaxed. A colleague of hers told us that you "creeped Sarah out" with your behaviour. That she believed you wasted her time just so you could ogle her. You've also commented on my looks. I find that strange.' Beth turned to face O'Dowd. 'Boss, you've interviewed a lot more people than I have, let's face it, we're often called an ugly so and so, but how many times have you known suspects to positively comment on a police officer's looks?'

O'Dowd looked straight at Quirke. 'Never.'

Before he could speak, Beth pounced on the cue. 'That's what I thought. Correct me if I'm wrong, Mr Quirke, but I think you're a half step away from being a full-blown stalker. You have commented on Sarah Hardy's looks more than her personality. I want to know your movements today. Where you've been and who you've spoken to, because I'm now wondering if you've moved on from stalking to abduction and murder.'

'Why? Has something happened to Sarah?'

'That's what we want you to tell us.'

Quirke looked at both O'Dowd and Beth before putting his head in his hands. When he lifted his head, Beth saw the first traces of fear. She was tempted to add further pressure, but, as O'Dowd was silent, she followed her lead.

After the uncomfortable silence had dragged on for a full five minutes, Quirke opened his mouth to speak. 'You've brought me in here and you're asking me about Sarah Hardy, therefore something has happened to her and you think I'm involved, but you don't have any evidence that proves my guilt.' He waved a dismissive hand. 'The reason you don't have any evidence is that there isn't any. I've done nothing wrong. However, I found Miss Hardy to be a very pleasant young lady and I'm keen to help. What do you want to know?'

'She's disappeared. We want to know where she is and we think you can answer that question. In fact we think you're the only person who can tell us where she is.'

'I don't know where she is.' Quirke hesitated as if weighing up how much to say. A look of fear crossed his face before he spoke again. 'But I might have an idea who does.'

'Who?' Beth and O'Dowd asked the question at the same time.

Again Quirke lifted his hands in a surrender gesture. 'Please don't think ill of me. I'm only telling you this because I want to help Sarah.'

Beth planted her hands on the table and leaned over to address Quirke. 'Mr Quirke, we're investigating multiple murders and we think Miss Hardy might be the next to fall into the killer's hands. Right now, it's looking very much like you're the person who's abducted Miss Hardy, that you're the killer the press has called the Dragon Master. Don't make the mistake of thinking that just because you've not been arrested yet that it can't happen at any moment.'

Quirke squirmed in his seat and looked to O'Dowd for support. When he got none his mouth flapped a couple of times before he started gabbling a defence. 'Please, you don't understand. I'm not the Dragon Master. I'm not. You don't understand.'

'Then explain it to us.' Beth eased herself back into the plastic chair.

'When I got invalided out of the army, it was because I took a bullet. To my groin. I lost everything, and by everything I mean *everything*. Including my sexual desire. What I now have is an appreciation of beauty. I see beautiful women and I become captivated by them. I feel no desire for them. I just have a need to worship them. When I saw Sarah, I was entranced. After not being able to afford the car, I started watching her at work. Last night I followed her home. At seven o'clock she was picked up by a man. He was driving a big Range Rover. It might be innocent, but at the same time, he may know more about her whereabouts than me.'

'Did you get the licence plate of the Range Rover?'

Beth was amazed that she'd managed to keep the contempt she felt for Quirke from her voice. He was admitting that he was a stalker as if it was something as trivial as admitting he was a man, or that he lived in Carlisle. It would be O'Dowd's call, but she knew if it was her decision, she wouldn't just throw the book at him, she'd empty every shelf in the library.

When he scribbled the licence number down on her notepad, she went through to the main desk and fed it into the DVLA database. The car was registered to a Kevin Ingersoll. Ingersoll's address was in an area that she didn't know, so she googled it. There was nothing in the area but a solitary cottage. By the look of the cottage on Street View, it didn't sit with the image of someone who drove a Range Rover. She knew that some people would prefer to have a flash car than a nice home, but rather than jump to conclusions, she ran a few more searches for Ingersoll. All came back blank. It was as if the man was totally off the grid.

Instinct told her she'd missed a link. She just couldn't work out what.

Whatever the thing was, Beth knew it could be crucial.

At this moment in time, though, the priority had to be bringing in Kevin Ingersoll. Whoever he was.

CHAPTER SEVENTY-NINE

Beth sloshed some more wine into her glass and gave a dozen silent curses. Along with O'Dowd and the rest of the team, she'd run Ingersoll's name through every database and program they had.

The only hit they'd registered was when they'd checked the General Register Office and fed in his date of birth. According to their records, Kevin Ingersoll had died at the age of six.

This suggested that the Kevin Ingersoll they were looking for was an alias created from a gravestone that matched the imposter's age. People who created aliases almost only ever did so for nefarious reasons. Every member of the team agreed on this, a theory added to when Thompson and Unthank had visited his cottage, and they'd found it deserted.

When morning came around, they could get in touch with banks and other services, but until then, their investigation had ground to a halt.

They'd also press harder at Harry Quirke. O'Dowd formally charged him with stalking and harassment and had kept him in the cells at Penrith station overnight. As much as Ingersoll seemed to be a more promising candidate, the DI wasn't taking any chances.

Everyone's frustrations had boiled over and they'd ended up in a four-way shouting match until all of them saw the futility of arguing among themselves, calmed down and took themselves home.

Beth got up to go to the toilet and tottered as she went up the stairs. She was drunker than she'd planned, but she wasn't ready to stop drinking yet. Regardless of what Dr Hewson might think, alcohol wasn't her crutch. Today had ended in the worst way. They'd been so close to making a serious breakthrough, and then their investigation had once again ground to a shuddering halt.

When Beth got back downstairs she picked up the remote control and flicked through the channels without finding anything that grabbed her interest. Reality TV bored her and the dramas she usually watched were too heavy after the day she'd had.

Instead of the TV, she picked up a magazine and read non-stories about celebrities she didn't know, until the bottle of wine was empty and her eyelids were heavier than her mother's suet pudding.

Despite her best attempts to remove the case from her mind, it was still there when she ascended the stairs. Even with her vision slightly blurry from wine and exhaustion, she could still recount the details of her spreadsheet.

As she clambered into bed, Beth was mentally going through the list of places Rachel had worked when she hit on the connection. Rachel had worked for six months at a sister hotel to the one where they'd spoken to Lawrence Eversham; a hotel he must have at least partly owned. She could remember the Lake Windermere hotel's reception, see the overly made-up receptionist and the painting on the wall: a watercolour of the Lake District.

If the painting was a Fiona McGhie, then it connected Lawrence Eversham to three of the five victims. As always seemed to be the way with this case, there was no solid evidence to follow, just suspicions and coincidences.

Beth picked up her phone and looked at the screen as she battled indecision. She knew she was more than a little tipsy and she didn't want to call O'Dowd late at night to offer a drunken theory that may well be a waste of time.

On the other hand, if Eversham was the killer, the sooner they caught him the better.

CHAPTER EIGHTY

The man who used the name Kevin Ingersoll crept round to the back of the house. Just like the previous night, everything was dark. The moon was hidden behind a cloud, which added an extra layer to the blackness.

For a policewoman, her security wasn't up to much. With just his basic understanding of how to pick a lock, he'd got the door open in less than a minute. When doing his reconnaissance the previous night, he'd peered through the windows and spotted no signs of a dog. Neither was there a cat flap in any of the doors, so he was fairly confident there were no pets that would attack him or alert his target.

The house was illuminated by a light in the stairwell. A quick check of the lounge told him that his target hadn't fallen asleep on the couch. He saw the empty wine bottle on the coffee table and grinned. If she'd been drinking, his job would be easier.

As he made his way through the hallway, he was alert for signs of a male occupant, but he saw no men's shoes left beside a chair. Nor any men's coats on the hooks by the door.

When he got to the stairs he made sure he kept his feet to the sides to minimise the risk of creaks. He also took large steps to miss out every other stair tread.

At the top of the stairs he found three doors.

Two were ajar and the third was closed. A peek through the open doors showed him a bathroom and a spare bedroom.

He grasped the handle of the third door and, with slow movements, pressed it down and teased the door open. The hinges didn't creak in the slightest.

Even as he was opening the door, he was taking care not to let any light spill onto the target's face lest it wake her, though he was now close enough to manage the situation should his target wake and try shouting for help.

Four steps got him from the doorway to the bed.

She was on her back with an arm flung across the bed onto the empty pillow.

From his backpack he pulled out the first two items he'd need.

He looked down at her and took three deep breaths then bent over to apply a wide strip of duct tape across her mouth. Even before her eyes levered themselves open, he'd snapped one ring of a handcuff onto her wrist and was flipping her onto her back while reaching for her other arm.

She thrashed and tried to shout, but he'd expected that. It was natural, anyone would do the same, so he let her have a minute to realise the futility of her situation.

When she settled down, he lifted the shotgun he'd laid at his feet and aimed it at her.

'Hello, Elisabeth. Now listen up and do exactly as I say. I don't want to pull the trigger, but I won't hesitate if you leave me no choice.'

CHAPTER EIGHTY-ONE

Beth didn't bother struggling against the handcuffs that had been put on her. She knew from her training that doing so was a waste of time and effort.

She'd been terrified when she'd woken up and found herself staring down the twin barrels of a shotgun. Behind the shotgun was a masked man. Despite being groggy from a lack of sleep and the bottle of wine she'd torpedoed before bed, her brain flicked from idle to full power in an instant.

There was no doubt in her mind that she'd been captured by the Dragon Master. If his capture of Caitlin was anything to go by, she would die in the next few hours. Twenty-four at the most. That was a certainty unless she could do something about it. Nobody else would come to save her. She was in this alone and if she was to survive, she had to rely on her own wits and cunning.

As soon as the Dragon Master had picked a small hole in the tape covering her mouth she'd known what was coming. As she expected, he'd produced a bottle of water and put its sports cap into the hole in the tape.

He'd squeezed it until the water filled her mouth.

She'd done everything she could not to swallow the liquid as she was convinced it would contain a date-rape drug or a tranquiliser. In spite of her best efforts, some of the water had trickled down her throat.

As soon as she'd been pushed into the boot of the car, she'd wriggled until her nose was pressed against the rough material of the boot lining and let the water dribble back out of the hole in the tape.

Now she was doing all she could to fight the effects of whatever he'd laced the water with. The only hope she had of saving herself was to resist the drug and seize the right moment to escape her captor. She'd have to act as though she was drugged. She'd have to be compliant, keep her face neutral until the right opportunity came her way. Then it would be a case of fighting back or fleeing. There was no way of knowing which until the moment arose.

Now she was in the boot, she was able to feel the edge of the tape starting to curl. As tempting as it was to rub her face back and forth on the boot lining to remove the tape, she decided to suffer the discomfort rather than give the Dragon Master any reason to doubt that she'd fallen under the influence of the drug.

She tried to count time in her head, but it was a forlorn hope as she had no idea how long she'd been in here and it was too late to start counting minutes.

As much as she could, she tried to remain calm. It would be so easy to go to pieces and fall apart with the terror of what she knew was coming. Even the tape over her mouth would delay him pouring his accelerant down her throat for the moment it took him to tear it off.

To combat the despair and fear, Beth turned her mind to the man's voice. She'd heard it before, she just couldn't remember where.

The Dragon Master's voice was cultured. He didn't use slang and he spoke with the quiet tones of someone whose social circle included lords rather than laymen. He'd also called her Elisabeth rather than Beth. Elisabeth might be the name on her birth certificate, but she'd always been Beth. The only other place she was Elisabeth was on her warrant card.

FRANCE

She cast her mind back over the people she'd flashed her warrant card to over the last week. One by one she went through them until she happened on a voice that matched her captor's. Now Beth knew for certain that Lawrence Eversham was the Dragon Master. She cast her mind back to the previous evening and remembered how she'd made the connection. She cursed herself for being indecisive, but most of all, she berated herself for falling asleep before she'd screwed up the courage to call O'Dowd. She knew it was a mistake that may cost her her life.

The only part she couldn't work out was where Sarah Hardy fit in to the picture. The best she could think of was that Sarah wasn't actually a potential victim, although that Kevin Ingersoll was Lawrence made a lot of sense. Unless, of course, Sarah was to be his next victim:

FRANCES

Something about the car changed. The quiet hum of the engine disappeared, but they were still moving. The car tilted as if they were going uphill, but the increased noise of a straining engine was missing.

Beth struggled with the problem for a minute and then made the connection. The car was a hybrid with both petrol and electric power systems. Lawrence would be able to switch between petrol and electric at will. When using only electrical power, the car would be silent apart from the noise created by its tyres.

This explained how Lawrence had managed to drive down to Highstead Castle without any of the people who lived alongside the track hearing his car. In a low gear and with the lights off, his car would have been a silent ghost travelling onwards to deliver its grisly burden.

As the car jolted over a pothole, Beth had a terrifying epiphany. If the car was on electric now, it meant Lawrence wanted stealth. Which indicated the journey was about to end.

Behind the tape, Beth gritted her teeth and tried to contain the adrenaline that was flooding her body with a fight or flight instinct.

She would only get one chance to escape. One chance to save herself.

Whatever happened, she must recognise the moment when it came and take it.

CHAPTER EIGHTY-TWO

The car pulled to a halt and Beth heard the ratchet of a handbrake being applied. She was cold and stiff, but as much as she could be, she was ready to seize her chance.

When the boot lid was opened she was confronted by a figure dressed all in black. There was a shotgun over his arm and curiosity in his eyes. She knew the question he wanted the answer to and kept her face blank.

His face was uncovered now, but she didn't look at it. Didn't want him to see a spark of recognition in case he forced more of the drug-laced water into her mouth.

He seemed to buy that she was drugged. His gloved hands grasped her pyjama-clad legs and fed her feet out of the boot. Next he took hold of her torso and lifted her onto her feet. The grass beneath her toes was cold, but Beth kept her face in one position and forced herself not to shift from foot to foot.

When Beth moved her head to one side she saw the shape of another human.

Her heart plummeted into her stomach. It would be all she could do to escape Lawrence. If he had an accomplice, she was doomed.

Two killers made a lot of sense. Setting up the deposit scenes would be easier, as would snatching the victims. She had to get a look at this other person. See if she recognised them on the slim chance that she got out of this alive.

Before she could turn her head, Lawrence spun her round and freed her right arm from the handcuffs. As she turned, Beth got a glimpse of a female head and red hair. Even as she was wondering if the woman was Lawrence's accomplice, she heard the rasp of the handcuffs fastening again.

Beth turned her head and looked at the woman. Sarah Hardy's face was blank, registering neither fear nor happiness.

That was the look she had to achieve; the state of indifferent acceptance. Memories of her modelling days helped. When on photoshoots she'd had to arrange her face in various ways for hours on end. It was a form of acting, and while she'd never been likely to win an Oscar, she'd learned ways to manipulate her expression and hold it for as long as was necessary.

The confirmation that Kevin Ingersoll was an alias used by Lawrence didn't matter. Nor did the fact that she'd found Sarah alive and well. Sarah being here meant that Beth couldn't escape, even if they weren't handcuffed together. It was one thing to flee a killer to save your own life. To do so leaving someone still in the killer's clutches was wrong on every possible level.

As a police officer, Beth knew that it was her job to save Sarah. There was no way she could live with herself if she ran off and left the girl behind. That she was tethered to Sarah would only complicate things further. The redhead was fully in thrall to the drugs Lawrence had fed her, and she'd be slow to react and may even refuse to come along. Fleeing Lawrence would be tricky enough without having to drag an unwilling Sarah behind her.

Lawrence pulled two bags from the back seat of the car and slung a backpack over one shoulder. The shotgun was fed into the boot and the car locked up. With the shotgun out of harm's way, Beth considered making a run for it. Had Sarah not been so drugged she may have acted upon the idea.

Beth gave the surrounding area a quick scan. There was a huge old building with grills over the windows to one side and there was a smattering of trees topping a grassy bank. Streetlights peeked between the leaves of the trees and there were the sounds of occasional passing vehicles. Off in the distance Beth could hear the whoop of an ambulance siren. It took her a moment, but she recognised where they were. A place she used to picnic with her parents when she was a child, no less. Workington Hall.

Like the other murder sites, Workington Hall had fallen into disrepair and then ruin after a long and illustrious history. From her research into historic houses, Beth knew that it was once known as Curwen Castle; the building had started its life as a timber peel tower before morphing into a stone tower which in turn became a small castle by the fifteenth century.

Mary Queen of Scots had been received at the castle with full honours, only for the next day to see her hustled off to Carlisle Castle, where she was held for a short time before being transported to London, where her long years of captivity followed.

Workington Hall had fallen empty in 1929, only for the War Office to commission the building as a billet for troops during the Second World War. A significant fire had gutted large areas of the building and the troops had moved out.

Unlike the other grand houses used by the Dragon Master, Workington Hall was located in a built-up area. Namely the town of Workington.

Lawrence told them to each take a bag.

The one Beth picked up was three feet long and light. If she had to guess what was in it, she'd say a pair of wings.

Lawrence took Sarah's arm and led them towards the rear of the castle. Along the back wall there was a doorway with a metal grill bolted to the wall to prevent entry. It was darker here and while Beth could still see the odd streetlight, there was far less chance of anyone seeing them.

Beth stood motionless as Lawrence shucked off his own backpack and rummaged in it for a moment. When his hands emerged they were holding what appeared to be a small blowtorch. He lit it and fiddled with a pair of knobs at the base of the handle until its hissing flame turned ice blue.

When he held it to the brackets securing the grill, they glowed red then yellow as the metal melted away under the fierce heat. Beth used the five minutes it took him to cut through all four brackets to try and assess Sarah's state of mind.

It seemed as if Sarah was fully in the grip of the drug. There was no spark in her eyes, and when she gave a tug on Sarah's arm, the woman looked down to the handcuffs rather than at Beth. Due to Sarah's lack of comprehension of what was about to happen, Beth realised that she'd have to try to disable Lawrence, rather than flee him.

She was tempted to slam a fist against Lawrence's temple but knew that she'd be lucky to knock him out with just one punch. If she failed, she'd then have to fight a desperate and angry man with only the use of one hand. It was a fight she'd lose and she'd pay for her mistake with her life.

With the grill out of the way, Lawrence told Sarah to go inside. Like an obedient child, Sarah did as she was told, the handcuff on her right arm pulling Beth along with her. Even in the dark areas of the castle, there was enough ambient moonlight for Beth to see the two squares of missing flesh on Sarah's back. The fact Sarah was wearing a slip with narrow straps made Beth wonder if Sarah had been taken in her sleep the way she had and forced to make the call to her mother at gunpoint.

As Beth followed Sarah, she felt sharp pebbles pricking the soles of her feet, but that wasn't her greatest worry. What was really beginning to concern her was that she was feeling less and less like resisting. She knew it was the drug doing its job, having seeped into her bloodstream via her saliva glands, but she also knew that she had to fight it, had to recognise where her free will began and ended. She mustn't let the drug take control of her.

Everything must be questioned and if it didn't seem in her best interests, she must act to prevent the drug taking control so she could save Sarah and herself.

CHAPTER EIGHTY-THREE

Lawrence had to fight the urge to whistle in glee as he orchestrated his next tribute. Everything had gone far better than he'd dared hope. Snatching Elisabeth had been easy. The look in her eyes when she'd focussed on the shotgun had ensured her compliance.

If he was honest with himself, he knew that selecting her had been a dangerous gamble that may well have backfired on him. But now that she was in his clutches, the risk seemed minimal. Like Sarah, she was obeying his commands without question.

He directed Sarah to a room near the back of the castle and told her to halt.

Workington Castle was the perfect place for this twin tribute and this room was the perfect arena. Large enough for him to work, and yet, not so large that the flames would fail to illuminate the room when he made his tributes.

With the girls standing in the far corner, he strung a nylon rope across the room and tied each end to a metal spike protruding from the wall.

His next move was to bring the girls forward. 'Hold onto the rope.'

Sarah did as she was bidden at once, but he did notice that Elisabeth was a fraction slower. He put her slowness down to the wine she'd been drinking. She stank of stale alcohol, even with the tape covering her mouth.

He pulled a cable tie from his pocket, wrapped it over the handcuff and fed the end through the eyelet until it formed a circle a half inch in diameter. He secured Sarah's left hand and Elisabeth's right by looping a cable tie round their wrists and then using another to affix them to the rope.

With the girls secured he placed the oxyacetylene kit in front of their feet, pulled a pair of medical scissors from his bag and stepped behind them.

His first two cuts severed the thin straps of Sarah's nightgown, and it fell to the ground with a fluttering whisper.

Lawrence's next move was to slice through Elisabeth's pyjama top.

With their shoulders exposed, he stepped in front of them and retrieved from his backpack his scalpel and one of the plastic squares he used to measure his cuts.

'You two girls are so lucky. You're going to be the most beautiful tributes to the greatest dragon of them all. You will be immortal; your names will go down in the pantheon of history.'

He reached forward and, in one sudden tear, ripped the tape from Elisabeth's mouth. She gave a little gasp at the pain, but when he looked at her, there was still that dumb expression of non-comprehension.

His hand cupped her jaw and his thumb lay on her scarred cheek. 'You're quite possibly the most audacious, the most risky and the most rewarding of all my tributes. Your offering will attract a greater attention than I could have ever imagined.'

As he stroked the scar on her cheek, Lawrence saw a change in Elisabeth's eyes.

CHAPTER EIGHTY-FOUR

Beth regained control of her senses to find a hand on her face and a thumb caressing her scar. Her lips and cheeks stung and it was all she could do not to scrunch them around to ease her discomfort. Lawrence Eversham was in front of her and he was talking, but she couldn't focus on what he was saying.

She went to move her arm only to find it was attached to the rope stretched across the room.

The realisation of her predicament snapped Beth into full awareness. The drug must have affected her just enough that she'd allowed Eversham to secure her to the rope. Had she not regained her senses at this moment, she'd have fallen victim to him.

Her greatest fear was that she'd missed her chance due to the influence of the drug. That she was about to die in agony. Whatever the consequences, she had to act soon. Eversham was within reach and, judging by the rapturous, almost religious zeal in his eyes, he was close to being as far away from reality as Sarah.

This had to be her last chance.

Her only chance.

With no other means to attack him than her legs, she kept her eyes on his and swung her right leg forward, bending it at the knee and driving it upwards into his groin.

Beth didn't wait to take satisfaction in the oofed grunt that came from Eversham. She gripped the rope with both hands and used it to support her upper body as she leapt upwards and planted her feet onto Eversham's shoulders when he bent double to massage his injured groin.

The rope then gave her something to push against as she straightened her legs and drove Eversham towards the far wall.

His feet couldn't move fast enough and he fell backwards. A dull thud sounded when his head struck stone.

Beth looked at Eversham and saw that, despite the blow, he was still conscious, if stunned. He was lifting a hand to his head and groaning, which meant she only had seconds before he was back on his feet. A minute at most.

She crabbed sideways, hauling Sarah after her. Instructions spilled from her mouth, but Sarah was slow to follow them and sluggish with her movements.

When her fingers grasped the knot Eversham had tied to secure the rope, they fumbled and twisted without gaining the right kind of purchase. She could feel them slipping and, while she wanted to look at what she was doing, she daren't take her eyes from Eversham.

He swore and rested a hand on the ground as he tried to lever himself upright. Aware that time was running out, Beth gripped a part of the knot as tight as she could and pulled with all the strength she possessed.

The knot loosened.

Not enough to come free, but it was closer to unravelling.

Beth hooked two fingers into the hole she'd made and pulled.

The knot came apart and she felt a slackening of the rope securing her and Sarah.

By now Eversham was rising to his feet. All the genteel bonhomie had gone from his face as he shook his head and glared at her.

Not wanting to give him any kind of advantage, Beth charged forward while yelling at Sarah to come with her. The plan was to barge into him and crash his head into the wall for a second time.

It wasn't the most sophisticated plan, but it was the best she could come up with. Eversham was too big and powerful for her to stand a chance of taking him one-on-one. Perhaps if she had her baton and a clear head she could do it, but not when manacled to a drugged-up civilian she had to protect.

Four paces from Eversham, Sarah tripped and staggered as she began to fall. The handcuffs connecting them dragged down Beth as well. Instead of ramming an elbow at Eversham's head, as she planned, she thumped her shoulder into his gut.

He doubled over as they crashed to the ground, but there was no crunch of his head striking the stone wall for a second time. Even as Beth was trying to free herself, he was raining blows onto her back and shoulders. Each impact felt as if it was delivered by a heavy hammer. She could feel her limbs deadening from his onslaught and, despite her determination to save herself and Sarah, Beth couldn't help but worry how long she would be able to endure this beating. Beth tried to jab at him with her free hand, but she couldn't put half the force into her blows that Eversham was putting into his.

She felt the rope still in her fingers, got to her knees and thrust herself forward, ignoring his blows; a new plan fresh in her mind.

Her forehead collided with his chin rather than the nose she was aiming for. It didn't matter, she gained enough time to quickly wrap the loose end of the rope twice round his throat.

His punches were now bouncing off her head and face, but she ducked her chin forward until it pressed on her chest and hauled on the two ends of the rope.

After what seemed like forever to Beth, the power of his punches began to subside. She could feel her lips had split and her eyes were starting to puff out from the blows he'd landed. Her nose felt broken, but she didn't care.

She was winning.

Once all the power had gone from his body, Beth loosened her grip on the ropes and aimed a slap at his face.

He didn't respond, so she checked for a pulse. It was faint, but present.

Beth pulled herself to her feet and untied the other end of the rope. Once she'd got it free, she used it to bind Eversham's hands behind his back and then hog-tie him.

When she turned to Sarah, there was still that blank look in her eyes. Despite the battle Beth had just endured with Eversham, nothing was registering with Sarah yet.

'Shit. You're naked, Sarah.'

'Am I?'

Beth couldn't believe that she'd only just noticed Sarah's nudity. A look at her own body revealed she was topless.

She figured Eversham must have been preparing them when she was out of it. Since coming to, she'd been so wrapped up in making her escape that she'd paid no attention to any of the peripheral details.

Her pyjama top lay on the ground, but when she picked it up, she saw that it could never be worn again. To at least cover her breasts, she tied a few of the bigger pieces together to form a rudimentary boob tube. Next she pulled the nightgown onto Sarah and tied the straps off above her shoulders.

When she saw where Eversham had placed the oxyacetylene kit, her knees threatened to buckle. It was the perfect tool to dispense both gas and oxygen into someone's mouth and throat. That Eversham had swapped the nozzle he'd used to cut through the grill for one which had two open-ended pipes just confirmed her theory.

The last thing she did before going to get help was to check Eversham was breathing and that he couldn't free himself.

Together with Sarah, Beth walked out of the castle and padded down the hill towards the house at the entrance to Workington Castle. The rough, stony tarmac would have stung her feet were her mind not reeling from her body's reaction to how close to death she'd come. What had happened in the cellar at Highstead Castle was nothing compared to what she'd endured tonight.

Her imagination put a foul taste in her mouth as she fought against the horrors it conjured about what had almost become her fate. She forced herself to keep walking, to not worry that she was half dressed and to believe that, despite everything, she was safe. All that mattered now was getting help for Sarah and a pair of handcuffs onto Eversham.

CHAPTER EIGHTY-FIVE

Beth had to fight not to show her emotions as she faced off against Eversham and his solicitor. She wasn't going to give him the satisfaction of seeing either fear or loathing in her expression. The best way she could hurt him was to make what he'd done to her seem inconsequential.

A man with Lawrence Eversham's wealth didn't accept a duty solicitor. He had enough pull to get a senior partner out of their bed on a Sunday morning.

His brief was a Ms Jones from some high-powered firm with several offices and more partners than an oversexed rabbit.

Beth understood that everyone was entitled to legal representation, but she couldn't understand why someone as prim-seeming as Ms Jones would try to defend crimes as heinous as Eversham's.

O'Dowd was with her, and the DI's defeated attitude had been replaced with a triumphant zeal. It was she who opened the questioning.

'Mr Eversham. I have to tell you, you're in a lot of trouble. We've taken statements from both Sarah Hardy and DC Young about what happened last night. Miss Hardy told us how you kept her in a cellar which had images of dragons scratched into the walls. How you admitted to her that you are the Dragon Master. Our officers have found a cellar at your house which is exactly as she described. If they find so much as one of her hairs there, it will be irrefutable proof you abducted her. Your solicitor, Ms Jones, may well try to create reasons why she was in your cellar, but in light of last night's events, I don't think that a jury will believe a word you say. I should also say that above the dragons scratched in the cellar wall you had pictures of Arthuret Hall, Highstead Castle and Lonsdale Castle. Our search teams found guide books for Arthuret Hall and Lonsdale Castle, as well as papers and correspondence with the planning department and estate agents, which show that in the last five years you have tried to buy both Highstead Castle and Arthuret Hall. As far as evidence is concerned, you can't even begin to comprehend just how much we have on you.'

Eversham opened his mouth to speak, but Ms Jones's hand shot out and tapped his arm.

'My client naturally refutes all of your allegations. He is a pillar of the community who has been falsely accused by an overzealous junior officer and a woman who was infatuated by him. Once you start looking at the case with the objectivity your position dictates, you'll be making a formal apology to Mr Eversham.'

'Please, Ms Jones, spare us all the pointless rhetoric. Your client is guilty.' O'Dowd gestured at Beth. 'You only have to look at the injuries to DC Young's face to see that your client is a violent man, not to mention the wounds on Miss Hardy's shoulders.'

'My client states that he was trying to protect himself from your officer's heavy-handed and brutal arrest. I think that unless you can present some evidence to back up your spurious claims, you're going to have to release my client without charge.'

'What evidence would you like? The account of a police officer who witnessed the entire thing? The physical evidence that was found at Workington Castle? How about the wings we found in one of the bags your client made PC Young carry, would they do? Or perhaps the stuffed birds with missing wings that we found in your client's cellar. Shall we call that as evidence? If you look at Mr Eversham, you'll see he's wearing the kind of overalls racing drivers wear; they're flame retardant. We also found a flame-retardant hood and gloves in his backpack. He had a scalpel with him and a square of plastic that's the exact same size as the wounds on Miss Hardy's shoulder blades. It's also the same size as the squares cut into five other victims. He was literally caught in the act.'

In that moment, Beth could tell that Eversham had lied to Ms Jones. The expression on her face didn't give much away, but there were enough flickers of doubt and surprise to inform Beth that everything O'Dowd was throwing at her was information she hadn't heard before.

'What else do you have?'

'I think I'll let DC Young answer this one.' O'Dowd managed to keep the smile off her face, although she couldn't prevent it from creeping into her voice. 'In your own time, Beth.'

Beth leaned back in her chair and took up a relaxed posture. More than anything else, she wanted Eversham to see the lack of fear in her, to recognise that he was no longer in control: she was. It may have been petty, but she didn't care about that. She just wanted him to know that he held no power over her.

Rather than speak to the solicitor, Beth kept her focus on Eversham.

'Did you notice how DI O'Dowd used my name then? She called me Beth, but you called me Elisabeth. Names are important to you, aren't they?' She didn't wait for his answer. 'Names are very important to you. You chose your victims based on their names. Fiona, Rachel, Angus, Nick, Caitlin, Beth and Sarah. Except to you, Beth was Elisabeth. I'll admit that's the name on my warrant card. The thing is, you needed a victim whose name began with the letter 'E'. Enter me. I bet you felt oh-so-clever taking an investigating officer for one of your victims. Whatever, that doesn't concern me. You tried, you failed. End of. I'll bet your mother would be bothered though. You didn't get to finish what you were doing. At first I thought you were spelling out the name 'Frances' until I looked into your family. Your mother's name was Francesca. She was half-Italian, wasn't she? Italian women are famed for being passionate, aren't they? And, dare I say it, fiery?'

Beth knew that her comment about Francesca Eversham being a fiery Italian was nothing more than a cultural stereotype, but she was trying to goad him into making a mistake as it was obvious to her that Eversham had serious issues with his mother.

'This is preposterous. I insist you stick to the facts.'

'Facts. Names. Dragons. Obsessed.' Beth ignored the surprised looks at her outburst and pushed on with coherent sentences. 'I *am* sticking to the facts, Ms Jones. We know that Mr Eversham bought paintings from Fiona McGhie, that he used to employ Rachel Allen in one of his hotels, that he hired Angus Keane for some building work and had a kitchen fitted by Nick Langley. We believe he came across Caitlin Russell on a back road by chance after she'd fallen out with her boyfriend. We have found clothing in Mr Eversham's cellar that Sarah Hardy has identified as hers. He met Miss Hardy when buying a car; he met me when I was investigating the murder of Angus Keane. Another point to consider is that your client has the name 'Francesca' spelled out on his back, in what the police doctor said appeared to be cigarette burns. The doctor found this when your client was being examined for his own well-being. The doctor also said that it looked as though the burn scarring happened a long time ago.'

Beth slid a photograph across the table. 'This is a picture of the dragon scratched into the wall of Mr Eversham's cellar. Miss Hardy has already identified it as the same one she saw while imprisoned. The thing is, that's not the only dragon we found in the house. It would appear that your client has quite the fixation with dragons. My fellow officers have found dozens of books about them. Apparently Mr Eversham has pictures and ornamental statues of dragons in every room. Are those enough facts for you?'

Even behind the sculpted make-up, Beth could see the colour drain from Ms Jones's cheeks. 'It's not a crime to be interested in a mythical creature.'

Beth skewered the solicitor with a glare. 'Ms Jones, you can take the boredom out of your voice. You're not fooling anyone. Your client is guilty and everyone in this room knows it. I've just explained his connections to a seemingly random selection of victims. We have all the evidence we need to lock your client up for a very long time. In fact, we've now got so much, we'd probably only need to present half of it to ensure a conviction.'

She pulled another picture from the file. 'This picture is rather interesting too. It's Francesca Eversham's death certificate.'

The expression on Ms Jones's face suggested she was beginning to realise what a monster she was representing. Beth could see revulsion and horror in the solicitor's eyes as Eversham's crimes were laid out before her.

'It's framed, which is rather unusual. What's more, it wasn't just framed, it was displayed. Not in an office or study, but in the main living room of Mr Eversham's house, which, in case you aren't aware, is a massive country pile called Kirklinton House. Yes, that's right, he displayed his mother's death certificate front and centre above the fireplace. Personally, I think a picture or a portrait would be more appropriate, but hey, if he wants to celebrate his mother's death, that's his business.'

O'Dowd put a hand on Beth's arm. 'Excuse me for interrupting, but you're talking about Mrs Eversham's death when you should be talking about her murder.'

'I thought we'd been over that, ma'am. The Italian police who dragged her body out of the lake couldn't get enough evidence for a conviction. They had to take her son's word for it that she'd fallen out of their pleasure boat and drowned. Personally, I think he killed her. Snuffed out her fire in the lake. You read those reports; you saw that nobody liked her. That everyone hated the tongue-lashings she dished out. Even her own father admitted that she was a difficult woman who made her son's life hell.'

Eversham slammed his hands onto the table and rose to his feet. 'Can you leave my mother out of this, please?'

'Sit. Down.'

Beth pointed at Eversham's seat and glared at him until he sat down again.

'No, we can't leave your mother out of this. We believe you killed her because she was a horrible mother and that then you regretted it. You were obsessed with dragons, possibly because you thought of your mother as one, and then your guilt for killing her warped your mind. When you were "preparing" me and Sarah, you talked about offerings and tributes. Were you making dragons to replace your mother dragon? The initials of your victims' names were spelling out your mother's name. You made your dragons in the cellars of country houses, because you hid from your dragon of a mother in the cellar of *your* country house. That was until you killed Caitlin Russell and left her attached to the portico of Lonsdale Castle. For the record, the message you were sending with her was neither clever nor subtle. We all worked out that her positioning was you emerging into view and surveying all before you as you prepared to soar away and look down on us.' Beth was using the insult to needle Eversham's superiority complex. 'Despite everything, you couldn't replace your mother, could you? Tell me, Lawrence, were you making dragons because you loved her, or because you hated her?'

Something clicked inside Beth's head when she remembered what they'd learned about the artist's personality.

'Did Fiona McGhie remind you of your mother? Did she turn her venom on you? That's what started all this, wasn't it? Fiona was like Francesca: an older woman who thought nothing of telling you what she thought of you. Fiona became Francesca and you couldn't let that happen. Could you?'

Eversham was back on his feet in a flash. 'She was my mother. I loved her, but she hated me. Blamed me for everything. She *was* a dragon, but she was still my *mother*.' Tears formed in his eyes as his hands flapped as if swatting a fly. '*Nothing* I ever did was good enough for her. Nothing. Not one bloody award, achievement or exam that I passed at school made her proud of me. *Nothing*.' His tone went from distressed to vehement in a heartbeat. 'I showed her. I showed the bitch. I made my dragons. They were better than her. You and Sarah would have been the most darling dragons ever. I showed her. I did it; I fucking well showed her.'

Eversham slumped back into his chair and stared at the ceiling.

'Do you admit that you killed Fiona, Rachel, Angus, Nick and Caitlin? That you were going to kill me and Sarah?'

The nod Eversham gave was picked up by all three women. O'Dowd smiled, Ms Jones sighed and Beth turned her head to the recording device.

'For the benefit of the tape, Mr Lawrence Eversham has just nodded in answer to my last question.'

'I'd like some time to speak with my client alone now,' said the lawyer.

Beth and O'Dowd left the room and assembled in the corridor.

'You've done brilliantly, Beth. Now get yourself off home. I'll get Thompson to sit in with me for the next session.'

Two hours later, Beth climbed out of a soothing bath and dressed herself in a pair of jeans and a flouncy top. She'd felt a bit weird at first, alone in the house where she'd been abducted, but she'd double-checked every door and window lock and, to reassure herself, kept her pepper spray and collapsible baton within reach at all times.

When she'd dried her hair, she lifted a scrunchie that matched the teal of her top and made sure that every strand of her hair was pulled into a ponytail.

The face staring back at her from the mirror had a swollen nose, the beginnings of a black eye and cuts to both her top and bottom lips. The one part of her face that had escaped being swollen or scraped by Lawrence Eversham's fists was the scar on her left cheek.

This was the point in her getting-ready routine where she'd reach for the foundation and concealer. Not to hide her scar, nothing but a mask could do that, but to lessen its visual impact by dulling the sheen of the scar tissue and smoothing out the rougher edges.

Both items were left untouched as she gazed at herself momentarily and turned to pull on a pair of knee-length boots.

When she strode with a spring in her step into the King's Arms ten minutes later, she spotted her friends and went to join them with the sense that a killer was behind bars.

But even so, in this happy moment, her eyes were always scanning the crowd. She was looking for someone. And she wouldn't stop. Not until she saw the man with kisses tattooed onto the side of his neck, and brought him to justice too.

A LETTER FROM GRAHAM

I want to say a huge thank you for choosing to read *Death in the Lakes*. If you did enjoy it, and want to keep up-to-date with all my latest releases, just sign up at the following link. Your email address will never be shared and you can unsubscribe at any time.

www.bookouture.com/graham-smith

I've always had a fascination with derelict buildings, and for me grand country houses that have fallen into disrepair are the top trumps. For years now I've wanted to use some in my stories and with *Death in the Lakes*, I finally had an idea that would allow a little self-indulgence.

Of the four places used by Lawrence for his tributes, all are real locations, although I changed the names of three to Lonsdale Castle, Arthuret Hall and Highstead Castle as an authorial embellishment. The given histories of each location are accurate to their original names, and I do hope my descriptions of each site truly reflects their magnificent beauty. Workington Castle is as described and has perhaps the richest history of the four.

As a writer I was excited to embark to spend time with Beth as I feel she's a fascinating character who allows me to explore certain traits and thinking from a female perspective, an area where I've had infinite support and guidance from my wonderful editor, Isobel Akenhead.

It was also refreshing to write about a character in the early stages of their career, and I know that Beth's determination to see justice served will drive both character and author to new heights.

I hope that as a reader, you'll join me for more adventures with Beth Young as this is only the beginning…

I hope you loved *Death in the Lakes* and if you did I would be very grateful if you could write a review. I'd love to hear what you think, and it makes such a difference helping new readers to discover one of my books for the first time.

I love hearing from my readers – you can get in touch on my Facebook page, through Twitter, Goodreads or my website.

Thanks,
Graham

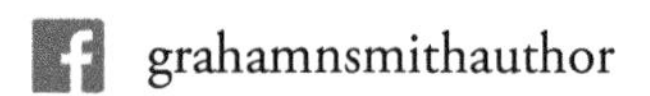
grahamnsmithauthor

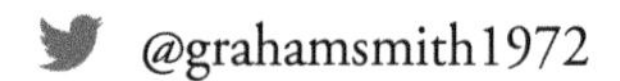
@grahamsmith1972

www.grahamsmithauthor.com

ACKNOWLEDGEMENTS

Apologies if I go all Oscar acceptance speech here. While writing a book can be a solitary thing to do, there are a lot of people who help and support in myriad ways.

First thanks go, as always, to my family and friends for their continued support of me and my writing.

Next up is Isobel Akenhead, who, as my editor, has shown incredible belief in me and has massively improved not just this book but my writing in general with her insightful observations and perceptive suggestions. Before embarking on writing this story I had a lengthy conversation with Peta Nightingale where I outlined my idea and every snippet of advice she gave me that day shaped the foundations of the story which became *Death in the Lakes*. Being honest, there isn't one member of the Bookouture team, from publishers to authors, who hasn't supported me, but two in particular deserve a mention. With their publicity and marketing skills, Kim and Noelle work wonders on a daily basis and their hard work is probably the reason that you, the reader, are reading this now.

Dr 'Becca' Higgs showed great patience in answering my often gruesome questions about how the various accelerants would ignite when added to the human body, and she kept me from making a lot of stupid errors. Any medical mistakes are purely down to me embellishing the story.

My team of beta readers are the first to read my manuscripts and their advice and notes have improved my stories and helped me polish manuscripts before submitting them. They're all stars who shine wisdom onto words.

The whole crime-writing community is a hugely supportive network and none more so than the Crime and Publishment gang. Each and every one of them has cajoled, listened and offered advice to me and their peers with a selflessness that belies a true generosity of spirit. The blogging community also deserve a special mention for their tireless work enthusing about my writing and that of a thousand other authors.

Last, but by no means least, I'd like to thank my readers; without you, I'm nothing more than a stenographer for the voices in my head.

Milton Keynes UK
Ingram Content Group UK Ltd.
UKHW021436090224
437562UK00010B/915